FREEDOM

FREEDOM

STORIES CELEBRATING

THE UNIVERSAL DECLARATION OF

HUMAN RIGHTS

AMNESTY INTERNATIONAL

BROADWAY PAPERBACKS · NEW YORK

Published in the United States by Broadway Paperbacks, an imprint of the Crown Publishing Group, a division of Random House, Inc., New York.
www.crownpublishing.com

Broadway Paperbacks and its logo, a letter B bisected on the diagonal, are trademarks of Random House, Inc.

Originally published in Great Britain by Mainstream Publishing Company (Edinburgh) Ltd., Edinburgh, in 2009.

"March of the Dinosaurs" by Liana Badr first published in 2007 by Saqi Books (Lebanon)
"Comrade Vadillo" by Héctor Aguilar Camín first published in 1991 by Ediciones Cal y Arena (Mexico) in *Historias conversadas*
"Gray Wolf (A Folk Tale)" by Alan Garner first published in 1998 in the UK by Scholastic Publishers
"Asylum" from *Jump And Other Stories* by Nadine Gordimer. Copyright © 1991 by Felix Licensing, B.V. Reprinted by permission of Farrar, Straus and Giroux LLC
"Mr. President . . ." by Juan Goytisolo first published as the sections *Espejo de demócratas* (pp. 41–2), *Aviso para malpensados* (pp. 49–50) and *El uno y único* (pp. 129–31) comprised within the novel *El exiliado de aquí y de allá* by Galaxia Gutenberg/Círculo de Lectores (2008) to be published in English by The Dalkey Archive Press
"Busy Lines" by Patricia Grace first published in 2006 by Penguin Books New Zealand in the anthology *Small Holes in the Silence*
"Tetanus" by Joyce Carol Oates first published in *TriQuarterly* in Fall–Winter 2008
"The Scream" by Rohinton Mistry first published in 2008 by McLelland and Stewart (Canada)

Library of Congress Cataloging-in-Publication Data
Freedom : stories by the world's most accomplished writers on the Declaration of Human Rights / Amnesty International. — 1st ed.
    p.   cm.
Summary: "Inspired by the Universal Declaration of Human Rights (UDHR), which starts memorably with Article 1: We are all born free and equal, Freedom is an enthralling anthology of short stories"—Provided by the publisher.
1. Human rights—Fiction.   2. Short stories.   3. Fiction—21st century.   4. United Nations. General Assembly. Universal Declaration of Human Rights.   I. Amnesty International.
PN6120.95.H784 F74
808.83'108355—dc22
2010010573

ISBN 978-0-307-58883-8
eISBN 978-0-307-58884-5
Printed in the United States of America

10 9 8 7 6 5 4 3
First U.S. Edition

CONTENTS

FOREWORD *Archbishop Desmond Tutu* vii

FOREWORD *Vered Cohen-Barzilay* x

INTRODUCTION *Larry Cox* xiii

Patricia Grace BUSY LINES 1

A. L. Kennedy THE EFFECTS OF GOOD GOVERNMENT
ON THE CITY 7

James Meek THE KIND OF NEIGHBOR YOU USED TO HAVE 18

Marina Lewycka BUSINESS PHILOSOPHY 37

Mohammed Naseehu Ali THE LONG RIDE BACK HOME 42

Gabriella Ambrosio STICKO 55

Joyce Carol Oates TETANUS 63

Walter Mosley THE TRIAL 81

David Mitchell CHARACTER DEVELOPMENT 107

Ariel Dorfman INNOCENT PASSAGE 117

Amit Chaudhuri ANIRUDDHA: THE LATEST INSTALLMENT 146

Petina Gappah AN INCIDENT AT LUNCHTIME 153

Milton Hatoum TORN 165

Ali Smith THE GO-BETWEEN 172

David Constantine ASYLUM 178

Jon Fosse HOMECOMING 190

Kate Atkinson   THE WAR ON WOMEN   *195*

Banana Yoshimoto   A SPECIAL BOY   *212*

Alexis Wright   BE CAREFUL ABOUT PLAYING WITH
THE PATH OF LEAST RESISTANCE   *217*

Helen Dunmore   WHERE I KEEP MY FAITH   *229*

Héctor Aguilar Camín   COMRADE VADILLO   *235*

Paulo Coelho   IN THE PRISON OF REPOSE   *261*

Mahmoud Saeed   WARRIORS OF THE SKY   *274*

Richard Griffiths   THE OBVIOUS CANDIDATE   *289*

Juan Goytisolo   MR. PRESIDENT . . .   *299*

Yann Martel   THE MOON ABOVE HIS HEAD   *303*

Chimamanda Ngozi Adichie   SOLA   *310*

Nadine Gordimer   AMNESTY   *315*

Xiaolu Guo   AN INTERNET BABY   *324*

Alice Pung   THE SHED   *330*

Ishmael Beah   ABC ANTIDOTE   *340*

Alan Garner   GRAY WOLF, PRINCE JACK, AND THE FIREBIRD   *351*

Liana Badr   MARCH OF THE DINOSAURS   *362*

Rohinton Mistry   THE SCREAM   *371*

Olja Knezevic   THE CLASSROOM   *383*

Epilogue: Henning Mankell   SOFIA   *396*

The Universal Declaration of Human Rights   *399*

CONTRIBUTORS   *405*

Foreword

ARCHBISHOP DESMOND TUTU

Storytelling is as old as the hills. It is the ancient and powerful way we humans have always used to communicate. Throughout our lives we tell stories and we listen to them, and when we do this we are building bridges. Our stories are carried on our breath into the minds and hearts of others.

Stories interpret the world around us, nature, stars, the movement of the sea, life itself. They explore the past, connect to the present, imagine the future. They have carried our histories, cultures, traditions, spirituality and morality through the ages.

And stories entertain and amuse, provoke and inspire. Through them we see into the world we live in, the people we are, the people we can be, and we understand that we are human. In many parts of Africa, we have an untranslatable word for "humanness"—*ubuntu*. At the heart of this concept, this philosophy, in all its versions, is this message: a person is a person because of other people.

The best of imagined stories always carry the ring of human truth and reality, while real-life stories convey the joy of love and achievement or tell painful truths of the agony of inhumanity. They touch the heart and stimulate the imagination, as the stories in this wonderful collection show. At the Truth and Reconciliation Commission in South Africa, I witnessed many remarkable people telling their own stories with dignity amidst their anguish and trauma. These stories are the stuff of history, they light up or dim the eyes of both teller and listener.

This book *Freedom* is a collection of stories that celebrate the

Universal Declaration of Human Rights. It is now sixty years since the United Nations adopted the Declaration, a remarkable achievement in itself, being the first international proclamation of the inherent dignity and equal rights of all people. It arose, like a fresh dawning sun, out of the terrible shadows of the Second World War. It is the foundation stone of all international human rights law and still holds enormous ethical value for all of us, wherever in the world we happen to live.

It is a huge tragedy that the Declaration's enlightened aspirations, the upholding of individual freedom, social protection, economic opportunity and duty to community, remain unfulfilled for so many people today. But the fact that so many people today know about it, know that these rights belong to us all, and stand up for our rights, is an enduring sign of hope that humanity will prevail.

Why are our human rights so crucial? It is because they have grown out of humankind's great instinct for what is right. We are all born free, as the Declaration says. We are made for goodness and for justice; we are not created for greedy, selfish and cruel behavior, nor to be enslaved to the whims of others. Dictators and those who keep them in power prefer to ignore that this is a moral universe and that right and wrong matter. The proof of the inherent morality of the universe is that we are all appalled when we encounter abuses—when, for example, we see long lines of refugees fleeing from atrocities. And we all know true goodness, true compassion, when we encounter it, because it shines out, often in the most humble of surroundings.

It always takes my breath away to see people sacrifice their comfort and even risk their lives to help others where they perceive a hurt or an injustice. It happens—and more often than you may think—because we are not single entities operating in a vacuum. No, we are all connected to one another, and our behavior, whether good or bad, reverberates across society and down the generations. This is *ubuntu,* again, and it is the essence of being human. If we dehumanise others, we dehumanise ourselves.

And what have art and literature to do with human rights?

They are all bound up with this wonderful talent we humans have: to empathize with others. If, by reading any one of the stories in this anthology, we are enabled to step, for one moment, into another person's shoes, to get right under their skin, then that is already a great achievement. Through empathy we overcome prejudice, develop tolerance and ultimately understand love. Stories can bring understanding, healing, reconciliation and unity. Our own feeling for their inner truth, our capacity to empathize with others, brings us closer to God.

If you are reading this book, there is a good chance that you have at least some of the advantages of freedom—you have been educated and are able to read, you can afford to buy this book or live in a country where public lending libraries exist, and, finally, you are *permitted* to read this book, which is doubtless banned in many countries of the world. No part of the world is free of injustice. All of us, everywhere, have a responsibility to try to make things better.

This is truly a great book of Amnesty's. To harness the God-given creative talents of these wonderful writers and connect them with each Article of the Universal Declaration of Human Rights is an inspiration. We are made for the sublime and for freedom: it is my hope that these stories will help us to achieve it. For these writers to contribute their remarkable gifts to the cause of human rights is a sign that injustice will not have the last word.

March 2009

Foreword

THE TREMENDOUS POWER OF LITERATURE

A very famous Israeli poem written by Shmuel Hasfari, called "The Children of Winter 1973," describes the process by which the children who were conceived during the 1973 Yom Kippur War become disillusioned with the promises of the old generation of a peaceful future with no wars. One line in the poem says: "You promised to do everything for us, to turn an enemy into a loved one"; it remained the echoing unfulfilled promise for the following generations.

This poem became the pledge taken by one of Israel's most loved prime ministers, Yitzhak Rabin, who was assassinated by an Israeli citizen fourteen years ago. Rabin, who maintained for most of his public life the image of a handsome, brave and much admired soldier, decided to abandon the path of hate and dedicated his later years to keeping the promise "to turn an enemy into a loved one." He used Hasfari's poem as a source of inspiration, and in times of great grief allowed its words to fill him with the patience, strength and hope necessary to shed the heavy armor of a warrior and wear the uniform of peace.

I am a child of the winter of '73 and, like many of my friends, was conceived during the war. Life has this strange habit of continuing to create life, even in a reality of death and hate. And war has this strange habit of invading the very essence, the DNA, of the conceived children of this land and creating yet another generation of warriors, laying upon them the heavy burden of continuing the conflict and the hate. So by the time we enter this world, we are already filled with anger. Our reality, packed with wars, fears and traumatic events, just triggers these feelings and turns them into a real burning hate, ensuring that no generation will be able "to turn an enemy into a loved one" and war or conflict will continue forever.

War is not predestined; it is created by human beings. Even if we are full of anger, we can choose to control it and to fight ourselves in order to change the way we feel. Following this reasoning, I decided five years ago to abandon my way as a "warrior" and to follow the tremendous power of literature, allowing it to take me into another reality. My journey began with my involvement with an Italian novel by the name of *Prima di lasciarsi* (*Before We Say Goodbye*), whose author, Gabriella Ambrosio, is featured in this anthology with the story "Sticko." The novel is based on a true story and describes the last hours in the life of a seventeen-year-old Palestinian girl from the Dheisheh refugee camp who committed a suicide bombing attack at a supermarket in Kiryat Yovel, Jerusalem, in 2002, and her victim, a young Israeli girl of the same age from Jerusalem. But this surprising novel is much more than a story about two young girls who come from either side of the conflict and, ironically, also have a striking physical resemblance to each other. It offers readers an opportunity to wear a uniform of peace and to see every human in human eyes, to make even an enemy into a loved one.

The novel opened my warrior's eyes, as I believe the poem did Rabin's. It nurtured my depressed feelings of compassion and hope, and allowed me to shed my heavy armor and to wear the uniform of a human rights defender. It wasn't easy. My angry core—the warrior inside of me, mixed with the post trauma I had suffered as a result of my work as a TV news reporter, covering dozens of suicide bombings—had strongly welded the warrior's shield onto my body and I was refusing to let it go. In order to walk along this new path, I had to adopt a point of view that would allow me to stop being scared and to judge my reality better, a point of view that was based on my personal judgment and a wider perspective of knowledge given to me by all kinds of sources, including Amnesty International's wonderful research from all over the world, Arab novels and poems, and much more. Unfortunately, these sources are still outside of Israeli mainstream conversation, therefore beyond most warrior's eyes.

Once I started walking down the path of human rights, I began to feel sorrow for all the years I had walked around with my infected DNA and had seen reality through an eye full of anger. I could no longer see humans as my enemies and I learned to cherish them more, and in this way to cherish myself more. Because of this, my warrior shield was slowly pushed away from my body, leaving me with a feeling of great relief and love that I had not felt properly before. I was able to develop for the first time a strong love for life, for humanity and for the tremendous power of literature.

Literature can be as powerful as life itself. It can be like our prophecy. It can inspire us to change our world and give us the comfort, hope, passion and strength that we need in order to fight to create a better future for us, as well as all humanity. We just need to keep on reading and to allow the tremendous power of literature to enter our hearts and lead us to our own path.

Vered Cohen-Barzilay,
Director of Communications and Publications,
Amnesty International Israel

INTRODUCTION

The authors of these stories are outstanding writers who come from many corners of the world. They have very different experiences of life, but they have one great thing in common: they are all inspired by human rights.

Our human rights are incalculably precious. They represent what each of us—man, woman, or child—needs to live with freedom and dignity and to contribute to the common good. The denial of human rights—and the instigation of pain and repression—is not only cruel and unjust. It dehumanizes both victim and perpetrator.

Fifty years ago, a British barrister named Peter Benenson had the brilliant, crazy idea that ordinary people did not have to be helpless witnesses to such suffering. After reading about two Portuguese students who were jailed for raising their glasses in a toast to freedom, he penned a newspaper appeal calling for the release of anyone imprisoned for political or religious beliefs. Benenson's radical proposition—that coordinated public pressure could shame tyrannical regimes into releasing "prisoners of conscience"—sparked the grassroots human rights movement known today as Amnesty International.

Amnesty International is celebrating its fiftieth birthday by advancing its vision of a world in which all people enjoy all the rights set forth in the Universal Declaration of Human Rights, which was adopted in 1948 to prevent the recurrence of the atrocities of World War II. Over the past fifty years, Amnesty

International has expanded its mission to focus on thematic advocacy that defines the human rights agenda, such as campaigns to end violence against women, the death penalty, and human rights abuses that are the cause or consequence of poverty. Yet the driving principle at the core of all of our work is the protection of the dignity of individuals.

The pen has always been a potent symbol for Amnesty International, an organization that has used the written word to defend human rights for half a century. Yet in many countries, authorities have responded to certain words with harassment, persecution, imprisonment, or even death. "Everyone has the right to freedom of opinion and expression," as Article 19 of the Universal Declaration of Human Rights famously states. Yet the people Amnesty International defends are, more often than not, in peril for publicly voicing their views about political, social, economic, or environmental oppression.

The courageous writer is the canary in the coal mine. The power of words is immense, and because of this, writers are among the first to be persecuted when governments become tyrannical. To the oppressors, literature is in fact a dangerous proposition, because it enables people to identify with others, no matter how different they appear on the surface, and to imagine alternative worlds. Literature transforms our understanding and our dreams. Literature instigates change.

Amnesty International is delighted to mark its fiftieth birthday with the publication of the first American edition of *Freedom,* a remarkable collection that will be read for many years to come. The Universal Declaration of Human Rights is a milestone in the evolution of humanity, and this collection brings alive the magnitude of this achievement.

To all the great writers who have contributed their stories, we thank you.

Larry Cox,
Executive Director,
Amnesty International USA

THE DECLARATION

When all else fails (and that's reliable)
What stays is how we keep this in our view:
A dream of freedom; peace turned bountiful;
The terms of hope continually made new.

Andrew Motion

All Are Born Free and Equal

Patricia Grace
BUSY LINES

Waking in the early morning, waiting for daylight, there was just one star visible through an eye-sized gap where the curtains did not quite meet. The peephole was at the top of the window where the first set of curtain hooks on either side fitted into the glides on the runners, leaving a triangular eye of black glass. Out in the dark one star had found that eye and put its own wink there.

It could be her husband looking in—fifteen years since he'd gone off to be a star—and if so he would notice most of the furniture had gone. Piece by piece she had given away the big bed, the bedside cabinets, the tallboy and dressing table. It could be him. One small bed and a set of drawers were enough for her.

Others had followed her husband to stardom. Off they'd gone, one after the other, as though he had left an irresistible tinkling trail for them, a plotted path out to that midnight-blue, crackling, spinning, fluorescent full bowl from where they all eyed down.

She listened this morning, as she waited for daylight under one star observation, for sea sounds, but there were none. There was no movement at all out there, the water being stretched to its edges, she thought, like a whole, black, drum-tight skin. She was certain there were fish in the weed and among the rocks but knew they would not cause a ripple on this still morning. There would be no one coming at daylight—as there had not been anyone for months now, or was it years?—row, row in an aluminium dinghy to disturb and entice them, to snatch them and fry them.

If her husband spied about, finding other gaps in curtains in other parts of the house that he could eye through, he would take note of mostly empty rooms now, though she had kept the sofa and a chair. He would see that she had kept the appliances, knew she liked appliances. Appliances gave their lives to you, worked hard for you for as long as they lived. But even after they died— no more hum, glow, heat, suck, blow—they could still restore something, as though in giving up their lives they returned something of your own life to you.

For example, sweeping was good. After plugging in the vacuum cleaner one morning and stepping on the button to hear a silence which no thump in the heart of it could cure, she said goodbye to it and took up a broom. A broom was light and easy. It had no roar. It was a dancing partner with a gentle voice taking her from room to room, finding every grain of sand that had made its way in. She would pause to take the mats outside and flap them at the sea, having a good look while she was out there, to find out what the water and the seagulls were up to, then continue with her sweeping. With a broom you could dawdle away half a morning and before you knew it, it was time to sit down with a cup of tea and a ginger-nut biscuit. A ginger-nut biscuit took a bit of time, was no easy swallow, and it was the same with double-decker cabin bread. She could gnaw away for some time on one of those, sitting in her chair by the window with the heater going in cold weather, or out on her step on warm days wondering what there was to think about or if anything was going to happen.

Sometimes in the mornings when she was talking to her broom or starting the washing machine, she would hear a scrape and shuffle on her doorstep, so she would wait-wait, become part of silence while listening for a tap on the door, a voice out there calling. After a while she would realize she was mistaken about what she'd heard, but just to be sure she would go and open the door, look out and have a few words to say to the air out there. If it wasn't too cold she'd leave the door open for the rest of the day.

The heater fizzled out one winter, which meant she had to scrape out her chimney so that she could light her fire. From then on it was necessary to go out along the beach with a backpack to collect firewood in the afternoons, making selections from among logs and sticks and branches that the rough seas had piled. It took time finding the right-sized pieces, but each selection gave satisfaction—which is something she explained to the wind, holding each piece up for it to see.

In summer she went out collecting wood too, stacking it for when it was needed, remembering that all of this walking and finding and carrying and stacking was work given to her by an old heater which had given up the ghost. She appreciated it. The winter driftwood often needed drying out on the hearth.

Sometimes on the way up from the beach with her backpack she would hear the telephone ringing but could never think who might be phoning her. She would hurry up to the house, leaving the backpack on the step, opening the door only to find that the ringing had stopped, or perhaps had never been. It was difficult to tell.

She had to boil water in a pot now that she had burned out the jug element, and since the toaster had stopped working she had to make toast on a wire rack over the stove coil, or sometimes over scratched-up embers in the grate, but she was rewarded with richer tastes and flavors.

Anyway, even though she was fond of appliances she knew it was all stuff. Over the years you became crusty with stuff, and even though she wouldn't want to outlive all mod cons a good scrape down did no harm. A starry eye would see that she still had television and the electric stove, and that best of all, the old washing machine hadn't given up. Because of having a stamped-on, skew-whiff spine and hands like broken-legged crabs, she was pleased not to have to rub and scrub at a tub.

Most of the gear from the shed had gone, but any one of them looking down from out there, her husband, or any one of those following bunch of nuisances gone to stardom, winking, spinning, sparking, dancing out in the big forever, could see, even without eyeholes in curtains, that she had kept the dinghy and all of the fishing gear.

Sometimes she thought she could hear chitter-chatter and the dinghy being pulled down to the water, sliding through sand and tumbling over stones. But on looking out would see that it was tipped over against the fence just where she had left it last time she'd tried moving it. What help were any of them when it came to getting it out on the water and spending a few hours?

Today was going to be one of those quiet and windless days with the sea silvery and calm, the kind of day when she would sit outside for an hour or two without moving, hardly breathing, as though waiting for some wild, clawed thing—like wind or lightning or dark or cold to set her in motion.

Gray light was fading the curtain-eye now, but she noticed a final wink, and at the same time thought she heard a voice telling her to get out and have another go.

So after her morning cup of tea, instead of taking up her broom, she went out and tipped the boat onto its foot, put her claws into its nose and tugged. It began to slide. Either I am receiving assistance, she told the air, or broken appliances have made my arms and legs strong.

Once at the top of the beach the dinghy began to glide down the slope, floating on air it seemed, as though being borne along by a row each side of hefty pall-bearers.

At the water's edge she tumbled herself into the boat, took up an oar and punted with it through to the far side of the channel, where she hooked the anchor up on a rock, allowing the dinghy to drift out until the anchor rope tightened.

The fish were hungry, snatching at bait as soon as her line touched the bottom. Looking down into the water, she could see them swarming, but because the hooks she was using were blunt and rusty and much too large, the fish were difficult to catch. It didn't matter. She didn't mind sitting there feeding them and spending a few hours. There were things to talk to them about as well.

The tide had turned before she pulled a fish into the boat,

pressing her broken-leg fingers in behind the gills and twisting the hook out of its pursed mouth. After that she rolled up her line. One was enough. But she sat for a time dropping the remainder of the bait into the water piece by piece while continuing to have her say.

When the bait was gone, a pull on the anchor rope dragged the dinghy into the channel. The tide moved the boat through and one push with the oar nosed it up on to the beach, where she tipped herself out onto the sand. Taking the anchor and letting the rope out behind her, she fixed the claws of it into the bared roots of a pohutukawa tree at the top of the beach. She decided that she would let the tide bring the boat up and when it did, she told the sun-beaten air, she would return and wind the anchor rope round the tree to keep the boat high and dry until it was noticed and taken away by someone who wanted it.

On the way up to the house she could hear the phone ringing but didn't hurry even though there was much to tell, but after putting her line away and still hearing the sound of the telephone, she hurried up to the door. As soon as she opened it the house became as silent as when she had first woken in the early morning, as silent as it was every day unless disturbed by wind or rain or appliances.

She took a knife and her fish down into the undergrowth at the back of the house, sitting down on a tree stump close to the lemon tree where the sun burned and stirred among the stalks and beards and tangles, and where the insects creaked and rattled.

Flies descended as she pointed the knife onto the pale belly of the fish. They zoomed onto her head, her neck, her hands. Onto her mouth. She spat and blew. The knife kept slipping from her screwball hand.

A prick into flesh at last, an opening, and with dark blood oozing she was able to hook her hooked forefinger in and draw out the fish's stomach. Flies were mad. She shook them off the fish and off her hands, shooing them and flinging the stomach pieces to the base of the lemon tree. After resting for a moment, she slid herself down onto the grass, placing the fish on the stump and doing her best to anchor it by its tail while she began scraping.

The scales flew. They twinkled in the drumming sun, and all the time, scratching and scaling, dropping the knife and picking it up again, beating at flies, she was listening along the track to the house and through the open door for the phone to ring because there was plenty to tell.

After a while she thought she might as well talk to flies. There were no phone lines where they'd all got themselves off to anyway.

The tide was in by the time she finished, so she returned to the beach to secure the boat. The rope was soaked and heavy and she became wet and a little dizzy as she went round and round the tree, winding it. It took a long time, and by the time she finished the day was bleeding away. The track to her house seemed to have stretched out and lengthened itself, so she found a good stick to help her along, stopping every so often to jab it into the ground in front of her so that she could lean and rest.

Once inside she removed her wet clothing, cleaned and scaled herself, and although she hadn't eaten all day decided she would leave the fish in the fridge and go to bed.

In the dark of early morning she opened her eyes to find that the stars had entered her room. There were pinpricks of them all around, one on the end of her bed, others dotted over the walls and ceiling. They winked like scales caught flying in sunlight. They flickered and hummed and began to move, swapping from one spot to another as in a game of Corners.

Soon they freed themselves from walls and ceilings and began to swarm and spin and dance in all the spaces of the room, alighting on the bed, on her face, her hands, her hair, resting on her eyes.

Universality of Rights

A. L. Kennedy

THE EFFECTS OF GOOD
GOVERNMENT ON THE CITY

Eventually he's going to say it: "You don't love me anymore." You can see it in him—a panicky, bleaty light about his eyes— and a couple of times he's actually started the sentence.

"You don—"

You don't let him finish, but not because he's wrong. You can't actually remember if he's wrong—this information has been mis-placed. It is true that you didn't think of him particularly while you were away. Then again, you thought of no one particularly while you were away. Your situation did not encourage thought.

"You don—"

You don't mean him any harm. You wonder if you should tell him, for example, *Stay on known safe areas. Avoid verges.* This is good and accurately retained information, but may not be appli-cable from his point of view.

He is making you tense and perhaps attempting to precipitate a confrontation.

"You don—"

You don't have clarity. It is unclear—no, it is *uninteresting* whether you love him—and your main aim at the moment should simply be to prevent the argument and the ending.

You can't break up with him here.

Not in Blackpool.

You don't want to break up with anyone in Blackpool.

You don't want to be in Blackpool and commit an act you may

at some later date recall. Not anyone, not anything, not at any time, not in Blackpool.

That should be the rule. Your rule.

Not in Blackpool.

Not in fucking Blackpool.

So hard to keep other details steady in your mind, but you're glad you can be sure that if Blackpool has touched a thing then it will stick. This is a macabre consideration but you still find it pleasantly amusing to picture yourself in your death's hour, your own death's moment, and with your inner eye drowning in a view from Blackpool Tower. You will maybe taste the memory of sterilized milk and cheap, overstewed tea, and also be aware of his face—the hurt in a face. And they'll watch you—whatever observers are there—and they'll possibly assume you are frowning at the inrush of angels, at heaven's glare, but it'll be Blackpool you're seeing and you'll want to laugh, but not be able.

This is good, excellent—so much to hate in Blackpool, such a focus. *Focus is essential for operational efficiency.*

The beach here doesn't even smell of beach—it's got that particular reek of small houses where they fry too much. You're right by it, a real sea with the wrong smell and this pretend shoreline, and you're on the sand and walking beside the cold of these huge concrete tidal defenses—giant steps like something left over from the Reichstag, something bloody vicious, something you'd fabricate to stop a car bomb, an assault.

Is that what they're expecting? Violence? A landing? Amphibious craft and enemies swarming in toward Louis Tussaud's, the Chamber of Horrors, the Mirror Maze.

There's a man up there with a high-pressure hose, wiping the algae and the seaweed off the steps. It'll take him days. And when he moves on he doesn't leave them really clean. Rubbish job, so why bother doing it well? Or maybe that's his best effort, right there—doing everything he can with what he's got, maximum input and no one should criticize. The observer can never tell.

Not that you're observing, you're flat-out staring at him—no reason to do it, but equally none to stop—and you're stuck in be-

tween the concrete and the poisoned wave tops on this dead flat
sand and the Central Pier's behind you and the South Pier's up
ahead. Hemmed in, as you might say. The South Pier being the
Scum Pier, apparently, and the North considered more sophisticated about its slots and twopenny falls and kiddies' rides and
variety shows involving people you thought were long gone,
boxed up years ago and nailed underground to stop them singing,
or dancing, or doing tricks, or cranking out gags to please the
boys on leave, or all of the above.

*Quite probably all of the above. Some of these people are highly
versatile—annoying the arse off you in multiple ways.*

*Vince Hill's here. My dad likes him. Vince Hill "singing and an-
swering questions"—bet he never thought he'd end up doing that.*

Questions.

About what?

What did you used to do when you were alive?

The whole of your childhood's television is still here, repeating—
hard to be sure which side of the equation is the one in Hell: the
waxworked entertainers or yourself.

But you would notice, wouldn't you? If you were in Hell.

The Central Pier is said to be, just as it ought, somewhere in
the middle when it comes to the style and tenor of its diversions.

Trust Blackpool never to miss the obvious.

And the boyfriend, too.

He's looking at you—easy to tell without having to check, because his attention is tangibly leaking, scampering, running down
the side of your face. Fair enough, your boyfriend's supposed to
pay attention, but his payment feels like a trickle of something
bad, feels like he's pissing on you.

It is offensive to be pissed on, a provocation in many cultures.

He does, of course, want you to be happy here and to accept
the blousy, big-grinning town in the proper spirit. He'd like you
to join in—this is absolutely the capital of joining in and being of
an age when fake plates of bacon and egg made from peppermint
rock should prove hilarious, or tasty, maybe even miraculous.

When you were little here it was all miraculous.

Recalling your childhood unleashes your capacity for wonder, appreciation of kindness and belief. There is a concomitant increase in your potential depths of helplessness and fear.

Half the shops are selling cocks made of rock now. Or sticks with rude words written through them. This isn't a kid's place anymore. It's all lap dancers and cider and sick lights squirming down in the rain and losing control with your mates as the night extends and tunnels through to somewhere inappropriate, somewhere in your head, your own personal brain.

"Are you tired?" He has to ask something, so he picks a weak question, one you won't block.

"No, I'm not."

"Are you sure? You look tired."

This is unsurprising because you do not sleep and, for the last three days, he has been with you and found that out. It is easy to imagine that your wakefulness disturbs him.

"You've got these big shadows under your eyes."

Lack of sleep cannot be underestimated as a modifier of behavior, personality, truth.

Easier to imagine your sleep has soaked out and caught him in the skull, oozed into his pillow from the mattress and then up, filled him with your dreams. It is Wednesday—he looks at you differently today—not the way he did on Monday or Tuesday.

"Are you listening?"

You offer him, "What?" Because you want to delay him, give him the opportunity to change direction.

"I said you seem tired . . ." He puts an unmistakable ache into his following, trailing silence while he scrambles about for other words, ones that you'll like. "I thought this would be nice for you. A holiday . . . To get away . . ." He keeps putting you in charge of conversations, choices, directions. You would rather he did not. You would rather be without authority.

Still, you'd wanted to leave the village, the cottage, he's right about that. As soon as you were back there you'd noticed the spiders and they'd worried you. Everyone said the weather had been wet for the whole of the summer and autumn—floods in the lower villages and warm, unremitting rain, damp plaster in your old bedroom's ceiling.

Not your old bedroom—your bedroom. No one else's.

For some reason these conditions had bred spiders, fat-bodied and numerous, an infestation your father had failed to mention in his letters. They hung in the corners of doorways and from lampposts, traffic signs, window frames, in the darkness of hedges and shrubs. They bobbed and fidgeted, a sense of unnatural weight about them. Your dad didn't seem to notice—almost gave the impression he had somehow encouraged them, let them colonize the fading raspberry canes and the beans, the shed, the chicken coop. For some reason, the chickens didn't eat them— perhaps this breed were venomous to some degree.

And he let them go into your bedroom. You killed four. Killed them for making it different when it should have stayed the same.

So you'd cut short your visit, left a bag to show you'd be back, indicate affection, and off to Blackpool with the boyfriend.

Stupid word—he isn't a boy and isn't a friend.

You are currently facing each other—no idea how that happened—and he is very visible, but you realize that if you reach out you won't touch him, he'll be farther than the moon, although this is not his intention.

"Do you want to go? Will we pack up and . . . There are other places . . ."

In the distance beyond him there are three dark shapes, thin men standing and angled perfectly into the breeze, the slack little gusts of dirty washing and stale fat.

They stick on your skin, the oily scents, because of the oil that you have on yourself, the greasiness of being human.

First time you go into the Castle, that's what you notice—the human stink. Made you gag. Nowhere else like it—not in a tent, not in the broil of a Saracen, not in the scared wet heat that you leave on your clothes.

You bring it out with you when you leave, the stink, and it doesn't go and you know each other by it—the ones who are your kind— know them in the dark.

It is sometimes very dark.

Your boyfriend is confused. This is your fault, because for a while you liked Blackpool, it was a buzz. You have misled him: first it was fine and this afternoon it's not. Up at the swaying top of the Tower and holding hands while you stood on that little square of plastic, the one that lets you peer down at the streets between your feet—that was okay. And rattling each other at the dodgems, the two of you by yourselves, chasing round and round alone, because the season's over, empty—that electric tang when you swallowed, those spiky little flowers of noise—two adults trying to laugh and yell and be surprising to themselves—that was okay, a bit shit but okay. And having an Olde Time photo taken together—you wearing a dress that didn't fit well, because you're lean, you're in shape, you're not an average customer—that wasn't so bad. The boyfriend keeping a copy for when you've left again—straight back, you're good at that, and sepia, an aspidistra on a table—and you will throw your copy away, because in Cloppa Castle it will not make sense. After that, though, you were discontented and anxious for cotton candy because that has a good smell, that's always been a good smell. You ate that until your teeth hurt so that it could be a part of you, a place you'll dip into later, but it did not cure you. And so you went back to the ballroom and watched the old, old couples creeping and sliding about to the jaunty organ medley—*Pack Up Your Troubles*—and this did not help you.

Pairs and pairs of people.

Pressure may be usefully applied or threatened against relatives and partners.

Same angles bent in their spines—and here they are dancing, wrapping each other around and high heads and big smiles and if you get to their age you still won't know the steps. You don't believe in dancing. It makes the body visible and is an invitation. It is reckless.

Ended in a club last night. No dancing. Not the music for it. Blue light darting about in rods and slices, a bit of smoke—skinny, big-

lipped guy on the karaoke singing "Nellie the Elephant"—sweating and screaming it.

You nearly laughed at that as well. Nasty crowd in the place. Nothing in the look of them, in the demeanor, that you could like. But you nearly laughed anyway, because "Nellie the Elephant" all the way through, that gives you your chest compressions and then the two breaths and then again. It helps you to do what you should.

FFD and pressure—Dressing soaked—HemCon—HemCon—Bleeding not controlled—FFD and direct pressure.

You have training for injury.

You have training for when their hearts stop.

And somebody doesn't want them to.

An observer.

He would like to see your eyes—everyone always wants that, point of contact, proof of humanity—but you've got on your new Inks—no sun, but the glasses anyway because you think better in their dark.

Sometimes very dark.

He has seen you, thinks he understands you naked.

Standard Operating Procedure—the utility of nakedness—necessary—you did ask—necessary—make them sing "Nellie the Elephant."

When you observe strangers in the usual world they seem cautious, bundled, prudish. They should be skin and singing—SOP.

You take off your glasses, show willing, show something, the color of your thought, a shade that he won't recognize, won't understand. SOP.

And you're nearer to the standing men by this time—except they're cormorants: obviously three birds and not three men. Completely unforgivable you'd get this wrong. They don't like you being so close and fit themselves into the air, long heads and lizard necks pointing into the whitewashy sky.

Nice to hop up like that—leave.

You smile for them and he misunderstands and smiles back and you stroll him in under the pier—repetitions of metal, verticals, diagonals, bad repairs—slush of surf to your right and mer-

cury pools seething in the hollows and at the pillars' feet. The rust
is so established it has bloomed into purples, oranges, greens—
wide flaking bruises that look infectious, predatory.

*Anything could happen under here—it has the taste of that. You
swallow that taste.*

This is not a good place and you should leave it.

And your skin doesn't want to, it tugs.

But still you go.

You lead him up to the pier entrance, wear your glasses again,
smile again as you step in and onto the boards.

Some of the wood is soft-rotted, unreliable underfoot, which is
amusing although you couldn't explain why.

In Cloppa Castle it is slidey underfoot.

*In Cloppa Castle there are hoses, funnels, baths, there is an endless-
ness of waters.*

*You have special notebooks you can write on when it's wet. Could
write on them underwater. You don't have to be underwater.*

*The notes may not be important. You once believed they were, but
now have no opinion. If they do not matter then you are someone else,
have become someone whose actions are of a different meaning. You
cannot do this, are not able.*

On the pier there is a dart game: throwing darts into playing
cards to win a prize of this or that useless sort. The cards are pin-
holed, they seem to have taken hits, which encourages, is intended
to draw you, and the stallman, boothman, whoever, gives you a
patter which makes it clear that he knows you are military, has
noticed it on you although you are not wearing combats because
this gets you stared at in the street—come home and be hated by
strangers in the street—hated by the women in the village who are
gathering shampoo and shaving things for returning men, but who
hate you nonetheless, who stink with their loathing. The man does
not hate you: he only lies to you in ways that mean he can steal
from you with a rigged game. He gives you a bit of a chat and a
consolation offer of playing cards—made in China—you'll take
them with you.

Handy for passing the time.

Games.

You play a lot of games.

A childish place, the Castle—even its name—they took it from this '70s show on the box—Cloppa Castle—puppets and a theme song that warned you'd be staying a while.

You didn't believe the Castle, couldn't.

First day.

All of them naked and singing the theme song—sounding scared when you started to want it, sounding angry, sounding angry when you'd changed your mind and needed them to be scared—and possibly this effect only in your attention, a reflection of your inner state.

Necessary evil.

Everyone's a victim.

No doubt about that.

You get an education in that.

Injured parties on every side.

No question.

You will go to the Pleasure Beach next.

Isn't a beach. Won't be a pleasure.

"Is it still the same? Still the same stuff?" He wants you to talk, unburden. "The job?"

"Yeah the same."

"Searching?"

"Search the women sometimes. Yes. First aid. Mainly admin with the other Dorisses." No reason to tell him.

Known only unto God.

What they say—isn't it? About the buried, the mystery flesh, the too far gone.

"Admin?"

"Admin."

At the Pleasure Beach you will be not able to meet your already dead mother and your already dead Nan and your grown-younger father and they will not tour you about in another time, a farther than the moon and boxed underground time when there were miracles.

Miracles of peppermint.

Silly.

Grown out of them.

Grown into the Castle.

White tiles inside the Castle—a flat white with squares on it, like squared paper, the type you'd use for math. When you picture it like that, whatever happens becomes calmer, quiet, no matter what you see.

Easy to hose down.

After the necessary evil.

Ask them questions, though, and the fuckers have nothing to say and they should say—stands to reason, if they'd actually fucking make an effort to help you then it would stop.

Or not.

It has a purpose.

A not clear purpose.

But faith in the purpose, that exists—belief.

There is belief.

If there was none, that would be

That would be

You remember being in a playground, school playground, and you were skipping this day—ridiculous—skipping—one and then another, then another—and in the end it's complete, there's nobody doing anything else—you are yourselves overcome by yourselves—and you're bounding, covering ground—slowly all of you are covering the ground and widening the circle until you skirt each wall and the footfalls are loud—they bounce off the concrete—and there's no talking, shouting, laughing, only the impacts and this movement you have—dizzy with it—roaring with it—each of you in this together and it's what you have to do, it's wonderful—it has no sense, it only is, it only is most wonderful.

"You have to pay to get in now." His body is sad, the will in it is deforming and soon he'll do something regrettable, undignified.

Seen it before.

"Where?"

"The Pleasure Beach—you pay to get in and then some of the things are free and other stuff you pay again."

You would like to hold his hand, suggesting compassion, but fingers are a difficulty. You cannot stand them anymore—how they are delicate, clever, talkative, ruined at a glance, in a breath.

Explained very early—information which serves you well—like the proper bulling of your boots—that real guardsman shine, cavalry shine, important and mind out for cracks—but more important, most important, is that you have the one mouth and two ears and so you listen and shut up, you listen and shut up and then you are right, you are all right. Then nothing is your fault.

You walk and are contained in lack of fault.

There is just something you haven't learned yet.

Something observers cannot see.

Missing.

You are missing.

Partly missing.

But you'll be all right.

Soon.

Back to normal in no time.

You're sure you mainly need to be out of Blackpool.

Once you're out of Blackpool you'll be fine.

Life, Liberty, and Security of Person

James Meek

THE KIND OF NEIGHBOR YOU
USED TO HAVE

Once Zac was through the door, it closed behind him and he heard it being locked. The bolts shot deep into the metal. There was no light. Zac shut and opened his eyes. It made no difference. He saw the faint graininess of total darkness. There was no sound after the bolts had gone in. Although he had been stripped of everything but his underpants, he couldn't feel a temperature: there was a perfect equilibrium between hot and cold. There was only a faint smell of lard and chicken skin, like at the butcher's counter.

"Hello?" said Zac. He could tell from the sound of his voice that the space was a small room with predominantly hard, bare surfaces. He began to shuffle forward, holding his hands out in front of him and sweeping them from side to side. The floor under the soles of his feet was unyielding and slightly abrasive, like fine sandpaper. It made a scraping sound as he shuffled over it. After a short distance his toes hit something. He almost tripped over it. Light blazed around him and he squeezed his eyes shut. When he opened them, and looked down, he saw he had collided with an object covered in a rough gray blanket. Feet in new white training shoes stuck out at one end. The shape under the blanket, about five and a half feet long, tapering at the shoe end and with a bulge in the middle, suggested a human body. Zac said "Hello" twice more to the form under the blanket, then "Hey!" more loudly. He pressed his toe slowly into the side of the shape. It yielded hardly at all. He knelt down next to the head of the person under the blanket, if it was a person, and reached to lift the blanket's edge. Before touching it he stopped and studied the shape. There was no sign of breathing. The smell was coming from under the blanket. Zac got up quickly, turned round, went to the door he had just come through and banged on it with his fists, shouting at whoever was on the other side to let him out, that there was a dead guy in here with him. Nobody came. He stopped and looked around.

The room was about the size of the smallest bedroom in his flat, where his youngest son slept. The walls and floor were made of the same hard, abrasive material, colored light gray, and the door, made of dark metal, fitted perfectly flush with the wall. Running two-thirds of the way down one wall was a solid concrete block, cast with curved edges and corners. There was a thick rubber strip, long enough for a man to lie down on, bolted to its upper surface. The body in the blanket lay between the door and this bed. Close to the door, in one corner, the floor erupted smoothly into a kind of blister, about two feet high, with a dark hole in the middle. When Zac looked into the hole, which was about six inches wide, he couldn't see or hear anything, but detected a smell of drains. There was another similar blister at the other end of the room, with a dimple at the top, and a smaller hole in the center of the dimple. When Zac looked into this hole, a thin stream of tepid water splashed down from an opening in the ceiling and hit him on the back of the head. The water stopped. By experimenting, Zac found there was an invisible beam triggering the fall of water into the hole. If the beam was interrupted, the water ran for ten seconds, then wouldn't come on again for another minute.

The ceiling was higher than the room was long, although it was hard to tell, since when Zac tried to look at the ceiling he was dazzled by the lights. The walls, floor and door were smooth and blank. Zac couldn't find a join between the concrete bed, the toilet and washing blisters, and the floor, as if the whole bottom part of the room had been cast in a single block.

The one exception to the blankness of the walls was a shutter opposite the door, a metal screen about the size of a letterbox with a bump at one side. Zac put his fingertips on the bump, hesitated for a while, and pushed the shutter to one side. It was stiff, and after he put pressure on it for a few moments it opened with a sudden screech. Behind the shutter was a dark strip of a transparent material and, inside it, illuminated figures. Zac read the number 175,327,853. The last digit changed to 4, then 5, then 6. Zac watched it count off, the number adding one every second.

Looking more closely, Zac saw that the edges of the display were clogged with a dark encrustation. It was as if the display had been wiped clean, yet the dirt that fouled it had simply been pushed out of reach of the cloth and was now clogging the grooves for the shutter. Zac leaned forward and sniffed. It smelled of shit. He slammed the shutter shut and rubbed his hands clean under the fountain. He sat on the bed with his head bowed and his hands hanging down between his knees. Every once in a while he glanced at the shape in the blanket. He closed his eyes and put his head back. "Help me, God," he said.

The lights went out.

He lay down on the rubber strip, which was smoother than the floor but not much softer, and hoped to fall asleep and dream. He did not. Every so often he got up and felt his way to the counter behind the shutter. After the numbers had advanced to 175,332,101—about an hour and a half, Zac reckoned—the bolts in the door slid back and closed again and a voice said, "Hello?" The lights came on. Zac stood up and saw his neighbor from the flats, Mo, looking at him. Mo was wearing a pink polo shirt, blue jeans and trainers.

"All right," said Mo.

"What are you doing here?" asked Zac.

"I don't know," said Mo. "They asked me to come in."

"Asked you?" said Zac. "What, like 'Would you like to be locked up today?'"

"What are you here for?" said Mo. He glanced down at the shape in the blanket.

"I don't know," said Zac. "But they didn't ask me anything. They didn't tell me anything. They just came into the house, dragged me out from the kitchen table, punched me in the side of the head, shoved my wife and kids out the way, threw me in a van and brought me here."

"I know," said Mo. "I saw it. I was looking through the, you know, spyhole."

"The spyhole?"

"Yeah, you know, the little hole in the front door, where you can see what's going on outside without opening the door. You look through it."

"Why not just open the door?"

"Well, you never know what's out there, do you? So I heard this racket, this rumpus on the landing, and I looked through the spyhole, and I saw these big guys, you know, dragging you along the floor, and punching you in the head, and your wife and kids shouting. It looked nasty. I thought you were being beaten up."

"I was being beaten up!"

"I thought you were maybe, you know, being kidnapped."

"I have been kidnapped!"

"Oh, terrible, I thought, Zac's being kidnapped. I went over to the other side of the house, looked down in the street, you know, and I saw them pushing you into a white van, and I took a note of the number before it drove away. I didn't know what to do. My wife and kids are at her parents. I was on my own. I was thinking somebody should call the police."

Zac laughed.

"And then I thought Zac's wife will probably call the police. But I thought, well, I should go over there. So I went over and knocked on the door a few times, but nobody answered." The two men looked at each other without speaking for a moment. Zac looked down at the floor.

"What's under the blanket?" said Mo.

"Why don't you look?" said Zac.

"Anyway, so I just decided to call the police myself." Mo put his hands in his pockets. "If I'd known they were police arresting you, of course I wouldn't have called the police."

"Why not?" said Zac.

Mo frowned. "Well, that wouldn't make sense, would it?" He laughed. "I mean, you can't call the police and report the police to the police, can you?" He scratched his head. "What I mean is, when I saw you being dragged out of your house and being roughed up, you know, by heavy-looking guys in civvies, I thought it was a bunch of thugs, criminals, bully boys. I didn't realize they were policemen. Obviously if I'd known, I wouldn't have touched it, you know. The law's the law."

"What law's that?"

"Well, whatever law you've, you know, broken."

"What law have I broken?"

"Well, you know."

"I wish you'd stop telling me I know. I don't know. As far as I know I haven't broken any law."

"You must have, otherwise what would they have arrested you for?" Mo pointed at him, cocked his head and raised his eyebrows. "Eh?"

Zac put his face in his hands and rubbed it.

"There's a bit of a stink in here," said Mo. "What's that under the blanket?"

"Why don't you look?"

Mo edged round the shape under the blanket and walked up to the bed. He stood over Zac, as if waiting to be asked to sit down. Zac, who was sitting in the middle of the bed, looked up at him. After a moment Mo asked if it was OK to sit on the nearest blister.

"I don't have any objection," said Zac.

Mo sat on the blister, his bottom fitting nicely into the dimple on top. A stream of water fell from the ceiling and splashed off his bald head. Zac laughed and Mo jumped up and brushed the water off.

"You knew that was going to happen!" he said angrily to Zac.

"It happened before," said Zac carefully. "But I didn't know it was going to happen again."

"Why can't you behave with a bit of common-or-garden decency?" said Mo. "Why couldn't you have told me about the water?"

"I needed something to laugh at," said Zac.

"And why won't you tell me what's under the blanket?"

"I keep telling you to look for yourself. I think you're scared."

"I'm not scared," said Mo. "Come on, budge up." Zac moved to one side and Mo sat down next to him on the bed.

"That's better," said Mo. "This isn't so bad."

A woman's scream, lasting, penetrating and agonized, rang through the room. They could tell it came from some distance away in the building, but not the direction. Mo and Zac sat in silence. The woman screamed again, with less strength this time, as if she were pleading for something to end.

"You never did tell me what you were doing here," said Zac.

"You're right!" said Mo, slapping his hands on his knees. "When I called the police, they asked me if I could come in to, you know, talk about it. I said I had to go to work, you know, and they said not to worry, they'd sort it out. So I came round, and they took me into a room, and there were two of them, you know, and they said the men I saw arresting you were policemen. And I told them that the last thing I wanted was to, you know, get in the way of the police doing their job, and I was sorry, it was a misunderstanding, you know, and I didn't want to take up any more of their time. So I was about to leave, you know, and go to work, and they asked me to stay for a bit."

"'Asked,'" said Zac. "They were polite with you."

"They were nice people. Very patient. They gave me a cup of tea and they put out a plate of cookies, although I didn't have one."

"Why not? Why didn't you have a cookie?"

"They were wafers. I don't like wafers."

"Oh well, if they were wafers."

"Did you get cookies?"

"No."

"But you got tea."

"No, I got a kick in the head."

"Yeah, anyway, what they wanted to know was, why I'd called them, why I'd been concerned about what I'd seen, how I knew you. So I told them the truth, you know, I said he's my neighbor, he's lived across from me about two years, he's quiet and polite, always says hello, keeps himself to himself."

"I don't keep myself to myself."

"Well, I'd say you do."

"No, I keep *my self* from *your self*. It's not the same. Just because I don't go to the pub."

"No, it's not that . . ."

"Did you say I was a loner?"

"No, I said you kept yourself to yourself."

"You might as well have said I'm a loner."

"I know you've got a wife and kids."

"Yeah. How can I keep myself to myself when I'm living with a wife and three small children in a three-room flat?"

"It's not a bad thing to say."

"It is a bad thing to say! 'He kept himself to himself' is what neighbors always say about people who—" Zac stopped, sniffed, looked down at the floor and began fidgeting with his big toe.

"People who what?" said Mo.

"People who've been arrested. People who are accused of things," muttered Zac.

"Well, I don't know what you've been accused of," said Mo.

"I haven't been accused of anything!"

"Ah, well, you haven't been *accused* of anything yet," said Mo. "But you will be, otherwise why would the police go to all this trouble? Now'—he frowned thoughtfully and pressed his

hands together—"it may be that you know you've done something wrong, you know, and you're hoping they don't know
what it is. Or maybe you've done something wrong without
knowing it."

"I haven't!" said Zac. "I haven't broken any laws, I've paid
my taxes, I've bought all the licenses, I haven't hurt anyone or
stolen anything, I haven't bribed anyone, I haven't downloaded
anything I shouldn't have. Believe me, I've been trying to think
what it is they think I might have done wrong."

"There you go," said Mo. "It's good that you're starting to
think about it. I'm sure you'll come up with something."

"I don't want to come up with something!"

"Nobody said it would be easy," said Mo. He looked timidly
at Zac. "You know."

"Stop saying 'you know'! I don't know. This isn't the way it's
supposed to work."

"That's not for you to say, is it? What does your lawyer
think?"

Zac laughed. "They haven't let me see a lawyer. They haven't
let me see or talk to anyone since I was arrested."

"They will," said Mo. "They'll, what is it, charge you." He
looked pleased to have come up with the word "charged."

"What if they don't?"

"They'll charge you, and they'll put you on trial."

"What if they don't?"

"Well, they'll let you go."

"But what if they don't? What if they just decided to arrest
me, don't want me to know why, don't ever tell me, don't ever
charge me, don't ever put me on trial, don't ever let me go and
just leave me here to rot?"

Both men looked at the shape under the blanket.

"That couldn't happen, though, could it," said Mo. "Not
here."

"Why not?"

Mo thought for a while, plucking his lower lip. "The media!"
he said. "They'd report on it."

"All those kinds of papers and news shows closed down 'cause they weren't making money."

"There are still some left. I think there are. They'd report on it."

"Not if nobody told them about it."

"Somebody would, you know, tip them off."

"Somebody like you? You didn't call the newspapers when you saw them taking me, did you? You called the police. And as soon as you found out it was them, you were ready to let it drop."

"Because it's the police. They must know what they're doing."

"How do you know?"

"Stop asking so many questions. You can't go around questioning all the time."

"Why not? That's what they do."

"Stop that right now!" shouted Mo. "Just calm down." His voice cracked.

"Is it hot for you?" said Zac.

"No."

"It's just that you're sweating a little."

Mo wiped his forehead with the back of his hand and stood up. "I suppose if you were gone for a while and we didn't hear anything, I might contact somebody."

"How?"

"What do you mean, 'how'?"

"How are you going to contact anybody if you're locked in here with me?"

Mo stared at Zac. He started to speak, glanced at the door, then laughed and smacked Zac gently on the shoulder. "You had me there, for a moment," he said.

"Seriously," said Zac.

"I'm not under arrest!" said Mo. "I just popped in to see you."

"Oh, you're popping in!"

"Yeah, I'm, you know, popping in."

"Popping in to my high-security prison cell."

"You can't call it a cell. It hasn't got any bars."

"That's because it hasn't got any fucking windows!"

"They just said, 'Do us a favor, go in and talk to your friend.'"

"How do you get out when you're finished?"

"Through the door."

"Have you got a key?"

"Zac, I'm not under arrest."

"So how do you get out?"

"Look at you. You look, you know, ridiculous. They took everything off you. They didn't leave you anything except your underpants. Whereas, whereas, I've still got my clothes and my shoes. That's what shows we're in different situations, you and me."

"The guy under the blanket," said Zac.

"What guy?"

"The guy you're too afraid to look at. He's got shoes on."

Mo looked at the shape under the blanket. He walked over to it and scanned it from feet to head, if it was a head. He walked round it so that he was on the side closest to the door, put his hands on his hips, and looked the shape up and down again. He squatted down on his haunches and looked more closely. He sniffed and grimaced. He stood up and prodded the side of the shape very gently with his shoe.

"OK," he said. He went to the door and knocked on it. It was evidently very thick. His knuckles made almost no sound. Mo knocked again, harder, and pulled his hand away, shaking in pain. His face was changing color. First it became bright red, then white. With his other hand, he struck the door hard with the side of his fist. The door neither yielded nor shook.

"Hey!" shouted Mo. He struck the metal of the door with what would have been a bang, but the door didn't bang. "Hey! I've finished in here!" He banged harder, with both fists, then with his feet, as his shouting got louder. "Hey! Open the fucking door! Hey!" He stopped, out of breath, then launched into another round of hammering and kicking against the impervious metal.

"Hey! He's not telling me anything! Hey!" His last "hey," after the token "h," was nothing more than a scream, rising to a higher-pitched shriek, then falling back, and ending in a gurgle. He twisted his body round and slumped so that he was sitting on the floor with his back against the door.

Zac came and stood over him.

"Telling you anything about what?" he said.

"Eh?" said Mo. His eyes were moist and his voice was faint.

"You said, 'He's not telling me anything.' Who are you talking to?"

"Nobody," said Mo. "I mean, you know, the men who asked me to come and see you. I want to go now."

"Oh, you want to go, do you?" said Zac, squatting down with his forearms on his knees and looking Mo in the eyes. Mo looked away. "You know what? I want to go too."

"You can't," said Mo, still not looking at him.

"Why not?"

"'Cause you're arrested."

"And you're not."

"No."

"Why aren't they letting you out, then?"

"Just gone away for a minute, I suppose. Gone to the toilet maybe."

"They're not going to let you out."

"Yes, they are."

"When? When I tell you something?"

"Do you know something?" said Mo, looking at him, his voice suddenly stronger.

"What is it they want to know?"

"They didn't tell me."

"Try again."

"Honest, they didn't tell me."

"I think you're lying, Mo. They told you what they think I've done. What is it?"

"They didn't! I don't know!"

"You're a fucking liar!"

"I'm not!"

"You are." Zac stood up and put his hands on his hips. "You're a nasty, sneaking liar, watching me through your fucking spyhole."

"I tried to help you!"

"You're in trouble, Mo. Whatever they told you they think I've done, they think you're in it too. And if I don't tell you what I've done, they'll never let either of us out. And since I haven't done anything, we're fucked."

"You're hard to follow," said Mo in a small voice. "They'll be along in a minute to let me out."

"You don't get it, do you?" said Zac. "You've always done what you were told. You've always been the big guys' friend. You thought there were two kinds of people, the big guys' friends and the big guys' enemies, and as soon as you found out I was the big guys' enemy, you were ready to dump me."

"It's not true."

"The big guys don't have any friends."

"Don't know what you're talking about."

"Tell me what they told you. Tell me what they think I've done."

"Didn't tell me anything."

"Do you think you're clever, pretending to be stupid?"

"I don't—"

"Shut up!" Zac's voice had been getting louder and louder: now it was a yell that made Mo flinch. Zac rolled his shoulders and began to walk up and down.

"So. I'll ask you again," he said. "What is it they think I've done? Come on."

Mo didn't speak.

"Come on, now. Don't be afraid."

Mo said slowly, in a low voice, enunciating each word: "They didn't tell me what they think you've done."

"You slimy little ponce," said Zac. He pointed to the blanket. "Do you know what's under there? If you weren't such a fucking coward, you'd know. There's a dead man under there."

Mo hugged his knees and hid his face behind them.

"He's dead. And you know why I'm sharing a cell with a dead man? 'Cause I killed him, that's why. I killed him an hour ago when he came in here, *in his clothes*, telling me he'd been asked to come and talk to me. I took these hands, and I put them round his fat throat, and I squeezed and squeezed until his eyes popped and his face turned blue and he choked and went limp. I was a good man when they brought me in here, but I'm an evil man now, evil, Mo, evil—ever met an evil man before? And I strangled him because he wouldn't tell me what they think I've done."

Mo's back was shaking convulsively.

"Do you think I won't kill you 'cause you're a nice guy? I will," said Zac. "Do you think anyone's going to help you? They didn't help him. I'm stronger than you. I'll beat you down and choke the life out of your fat carcass unless you tell me now what they think I've done."

"I don't know!" sobbed Mo, lifting his face and showing eyes blinded by tears. "I don't know anything! I'm just an ordinary man, I'm not clever, I'm not rich, I'm not good-looking, I don't know what's going on in the world, I don't read much, I don't speak foreign languages, I don't know about science or business. How am I supposed to know who's right and who's wrong? All I want is to do my job and have a place to live and bring up my kids and watch TV and have a drink and a holiday and a barbecue now and then. What's wrong with that? Why shouldn't I believe the police know what they're doing? You've got to trust somebody. I can't be a, you know, go on protests. It's too hard. It's too complicated. I'm too tired. I'd make too many mistakes. It's not fair. Please don't hurt me, Zac, please. I've got a wife and kids. I tried to help you."

Zac drew in a deep breath and let it out. He stepped over to Mo and put out his hand. Nervously, blinking with tears, Mo took it, and Zac pulled him to his feet. He embraced Mo, patting him on the back, and after a while Mo put his arms around him. They stood swaying in silence for a time.

Zac stood back and held Mo's shoulders and looked at him. "I didn't kill anyone," he said. "I couldn't do that. I haven't got it in me. I was saying that to frighten you. I don't know what's under the blanket either. I'm just as scared as you are. And it's true, you did try to help. You did a terrible job, but at least you tried. Most people, if they saw their neighbor being dragged away and put in a van, they wouldn't do anything. If there wasn't anything in the papers about it, they'd just think: I wonder what he did to get himself dragged away like that. It's confidence, isn't it? When they've got more confidence that they're allowed just to drag people away and lock them up than you've got confidence that they're not allowed to. I don't know, Mo. Where do they get the confidence from? Who let them have it? Where does our confidence go? How did we lose it?"

Mo went over to the bed. He moved slowly, like an old, tired man. Zac watched him.

"So do you often watch me through your periscope?" said Zac.

"Spyhole!" said Mo.

"Spyhole, I mean, spyhole." Zac tried to put his hands in his pockets, then remembered he didn't have any pockets. "So you've got no idea what happened to my wife . . ."

"No."

". . . and kids . . . ?"

"No."

"No." Zac nodded slowly, folded his arms, and began to walk up and down.

"Or mine," said Mo.

"Come on, Mo, don't talk like that," said Zac.

The woman screamed, a long scream with so many changes of pitch and volume that it seemed to tell an unhappy story, with an unhappy beginning and an unhappy end. Mo put his hands over his ears and bent forward.

"They're going to kill us," he said. "They're going to do terrible things to us."

"Listen, Mo," said Zac, going over to him, sitting down

next to him and putting one hand on his shoulder, "you can't give up."

"Why not?" said Mo.

"We can't let them think they've beaten it all out of us."

Mo looked up and narrowed his eyes. "We haven't got a lot going for us, have we?"

"In the first place, there are two of us, and two people can watch each other's backs, and raise each other's spirits. What if it was just you here by yourself?"

"I might get a bit of peace," said Mo.

"Is that all you want?"

"If they put a telly in, it wouldn't be so bad. What's behind that shutter?"

"It's not a TV."

The woman screamed again, and Mo covered his ears. "I can't stand that noise," he said. "What are they doing to her? Why do they have to do that?"

Zac punched Mo in the shoulder, not as hard as he could have, but not gently. "Come on," he said.

"What? What did you do that for?"

"To wake you up. Make you angry instead of frightened. So you won't start thinking about TV and a nice little nap when the screaming stops."

"I'm going to have a look behind that shutter," said Mo, getting up. Zac pushed him back.

"Listen," he said. "If we can hear that woman screaming, what does it mean?"

"It means we're next," said Mo, and shrank into the fetal position on the bed.

Zac punched and dragged him out of it. "It means she can hear us," he said. "We should tell her not to give up."

"What for?"

Zac slapped Mo across the face. "Sorry. Because we're human. We still have will. She'll know she's not alone. And if somebody stronger than you is giving you a going over, the best way to get back at them is to find somebody else who's getting a going over, and help them out."

Mo thought for a moment. "I suppose," he said.

"You see?"

"Maybe."

"Come on. Help me out." Zac cupped his hands around his mouth and yelled, "DON'T GIVE UP!" He nudged Mo and nodded encouragingly. Mo put his hands to his mouth, but when Zac shouted "DON'T GIVE UP!" a second time, Mo didn't join in.

"Maybe she'd be better giving up," said Mo.

"Eh?"

"Maybe she should tell them what they want to know."

"What if she doesn't know what they want to know? What if she's like us? We don't know why we're here. But what if they don't know either, and they want to make us tell them anyway?"

Mo cupped his hands around his mouth, and they both shouted with all the force in their lungs: "DON'T GIVE UP!"

The door opened. Without hesitating Mo ran toward it, jumped over the shape in the blanket and rushed through. He heard it closing behind him and he ran on down the corridor until he came across the two policemen who had escorted him in.

"All right, Mo," said the older of the two policemen. He wore a shirt and tie.

"All right," said Mo, breathing hard and smiling and blinking.

"You look a bit shaken up," said the older one.

"I am a bit," said Mo.

"You didn't think we were going to leave you in there, did you?"

"Heh," said Mo, unable to form words. He glanced over his shoulder, to see if anybody had followed behind him, but the corridor was empty, and the door he had come through was shut fast.

"Come on then, I'll see you out," said the elder policeman. He and Mo left the younger, uniformed one and began climbing the many flights of stairs to the surface. As they climbed, natural light started to replace the glare of fluorescent bulbs.

"Thanks for helping us out," said the policeman.

"I didn't do anything," said Mo. "I just did what you asked me to do. I just went in to talk to him. But he didn't tell me anything. He kept saying he didn't know anything, hadn't done anything wrong, didn't know why he'd been arrested."

"It's a strange thing," said the policeman, "but they all say that."

"Do they?" said Mo.

"You don't imagine we'd arrest people just because we felt like it, do you? At random? Mo, the forms, the forms! You wouldn't believe it. Here are your things."

They reached the top and a policewoman handed Mo his phone, his keys, his wallet and his watch in a plastic tray. Mo kept turning to see the street outside through the vast plate glass windows that covered the front of the police station. The sound of the traffic and the sight of the sky made a torrent of joy pour through his heart such as he hadn't experienced since he was a boy. The policeman was telling him that his wife had called and they'd told her he'd be home soon.

"Now you know what kind of man your neighbor is," said the policeman. He paused, as if waiting for Mo to speak, then went on. "He abused you, he humiliated you, he beat you, he even tried to use his pillow and blanket and clothes to pretend he was sharing a cell with a corpse. He's devious, I'll give him that." The policeman laughed, looked down and shook his head. "We keep telling them this old place needs thicker walls, but they say they don't have the funds for it. So when old Sara starts screaming . . . poor love, she shouldn't be on the streets, really, but it's just nightmares, and you can't cure nightmares, can you? She's safer in than out. But Zac had you going, didn't he? Dangerous chap. You really have helped us out, just by getting to know for yourself what kind of a man you used to have as a neighbor. So thanks for coming in." He smiled and held out his hand. Mo shook it.

"Is it all right for me to go now?" said Mo.

"Of course. Unless you have any more questions. Think carefully before you answer. Take your time."

"I just wondered—"

"Think carefully!"

"—if Zac—"

"Who?"

"No," said Mo. "I don't have any questions."

"Excellent," said the policeman. "Bye!" He watched Mo walk out of the police station and smiled when Mo lifted his face and squinted up at the sun.

Zac was alone in the cell. The temperature dropped, he began to shiver, and he took the blanket off the floor. Underneath the blanket was the corpse of a man wearing white training shoes and a tight-fitting garment of coarse white cotton which covered the body like the shroud of an Egyptian mummy. As well as arms, legs and body it covered the hands, neck and head, including the face. Spread across the shroud were blooms of what looked like dried blood. There was one stiff brown patch across the stomach, one across the left shoulder, a small one where the mouth would be and one over each eye.

Zac realized he was pressing his jaw between his hands so hard that it hurt. The door opened and three men rushed in, wielding short clubs. They were dressed in one-piece black suits covering their bodies, heads and faces, yet they must have been able to see out of them, because when they beat Zac, they were very accurate. They beat him unconscious.

A few hours later Zac woke up in the fluorescent light. He was lying on the floor. He ached from a number of bruises on his head, ribs, back and ankles. His nose was partly blocked by dried blood, which ran out of one nostril and diagonally over his cheek.

Now it was very cold and he didn't care that the blanket had been put back over the corpse. He pulled it off. As he wrapped it round his shivering body he saw that the corpse was gone. The shoes had been placed in such a way as to make it look as if it was still there, but in its place was a rough hunk of foam, a folded piece of white cloth and a large loaf of bread. Zac fell on the bread and ate two thirds of it. He felt nauseous. He picked up the cloth. It was a close-fitting cotton garment, covering the arms, legs and body, like long johns, but with curious ruffs at the wrists, neck and ankles. He took off his underpants, washed himself, jumped up and down to get dry, and put the garment on. He put on the shoes. He put the lump of foam down at one end of the bed, lay down with his head resting on it, and drew the blanket over himself.

"This isn't so bad," he said, imitating Mo's voice, and laughed. Laughing made his ribs hurt and he drew his breath in and swore. He lay there for a while, then got up and went to the shutter. He opened it. The numbers read 7,530, then 7,531, then 7,532.

Zac screamed. He stopped, drew breath, and screamed again.

From very far away, or through many thicknesses of steel and concrete, he heard a woman's voice shouting. She was making a great effort to be heard, but Zac could only make out the vowels. It could have been "Don't give up"; it could have been "Soak it up." It could have been "No, it's shut." After a while other distant, muffled voices joined in, until Zac felt that he was at the heart of a honeycomb of cells stretching many floors below, many floors above and along multiple corridors on his level. He wasn't sure whether they were telling him not to give up, or how it might help him if they were, but he wanted to believe that they were encouraging him, and it made it easier for him, when he lay down again, to sleep, and to be ready, when he woke up, for the slow increase in the numbers.

ARTICLE 4

No One Shall Be Held in Slavery

Marina Lewycka
BUSINESS PHILOSOPHY

Look at it from my point of view—it's not easy trying to make an honest living in these parts, but my business philosophy is to give my customers what they want. And what they want is girls. Nice, willing, pretty girlies.

Let's get one thing straight right at the beginning, because there's been a lot of misinformation floating around. No one goes out to hurt the girlies deliberately. I mean a punter doesn't want to screw a girlie with a black eye does he? So it has to be something serious to warrant a beating. Most girlies you don't have a problem with. They see what the game is and they just get on with it. I'm not saying they always like it, but they do what they have to do, they give the customers what they want. A happy customer is a paying customer, I say. So no one roughs up the girlies unless they ask for it. But sadly, it does happen.

You always get one, don't you? My one was called Katya, and she decided she didn't like my business philosophy. Said they'd told her she was going to be a waitress. Silly bint. Does she think there's a shortage of waitresses in the Balkans? So she decided she wanted to run back to Mummy. Looking back on it I probably should have let her go, but you can always be clever in hindsight can't you? I'd paid good money for her and she was a pretty dolly and I reckoned that once she'd quieted down a bit she'd be a good earner. Anyway, Mitar's son Branko said he'd sort her out for me. He's a big buttocky lad with a heart of gold and a potato dumpling for a brain, and he says, I'll fix her up for you uncle, and I should have said no there and then but my head was sore and my big toe was putting on a show, some people think gout's a big joke but I tell you, when your toe's as red as a beetroot and aching like a rotten tooth, it takes your mind off the job, so I said, all right, son, just make sure we can get her back to work in a couple of weeks.

Like I said, no one sets out to hurt the girlies deliberately, but Branko's a big lad and I sometimes think he doesn't know his own strength, so she ended up with a couple of fractured ribs and a few broken bones in her feet, nothing that wouldn't mend with a bit of rest. The bruises in her mouth and cigarette burns on her cunt I can't condone. Maybe he'd had a few drinks. Anyway, we had to keep her off work for nearly a month, put her on a mattress down in the cellar, chained her up of course, and Mitar had to keep swabbing her down with disinfectant. I tell you, he was not well pleased.

Probably I should have left her even longer, probably I put her back to work too soon, but you see she had regulars, this girl, and they were clamoring for her, like I said, she's a pretty dolly and high-spirited, and some of the punters like a bit of a struggle before they get down to it, helps get the old donkey-tizzle up, and these punters of hers, they were some of the big names around town, judges, politicians, police, so you have to keep them happy.

"Right," I says, "off your arse and on your back."

"I can't sit down on my arse," she says. "That big kiddo you set on me ripped me up inside."

Well no one wants a girlie that's gone mushy inside. Lucky for us one of our best customers is a surgeon—Doktor Sex, we call him—cheery soul, great sense of humor, stitched her up nice and tight, but that was another week off work, and then she starts whining that the handcuffs are making her sore. You can't win, can you?

So we take the handcuffs off her, and we reckon with Branko standing outside the door she won't be trying anything silly, but Branko's taken a shine to one of the other girlies, a little rosy-cheeked cherry pie from Kiev, and when one of the punters doesn't show up, in he sneaks for a bit of free wiggle. Well this Katya, she must have known what was going on, because she was out of the door quick as a wink, and splitting down the road like a runaway pig. As soon as he realized, Branko was after her, with his trousers round his ankles, and the Ukrainian tart yelling at him to leave her alone, then strike me dead, she gets her knickers on and legs it too, so we lose two of them in one night.

Well, the police brought the Ukrainian back, but the other one, Katya, she's cunning, she doesn't go to the police. She ends up in this women's refuge that some wanking do-gooders set up in town, and starts squealing about sex trafficking. The bitch that runs it is one of those hairy anti-sex lesbian communist religious sour-pants whores, you know the type I mean—can't get a man for herself so wants to spoil it for everybody else. Anyway she feeds Katya up on some human rights cow tripe, no one shall be held in slavery or servitude and other such piffle, and marches her off to the police, and because the lesbian sour-pants is backing her, the police have to pretend to be doing something for a change so they start asking questions. To be fair, the police did their best. Told her to shut up and promised they'd take her back home to her mummy if she behaved herself. But the lesbian dog has got hold of the bone and won't let go so then she marches the girl off to the papers and they start naming names. If you know anything about our business you'll know that no one likes to have their private bedroom activities dragged through the papers, and their neighbors and mothers-in-law asking awkward questions. *Is it true what I'm hearing, Zoran? You been a naughty boy, Luka? Been sticking your finger in the wrong honey pot, Janko? If you do that again, Mama'll have to chop it off.* I tell you the mothers-in-law are worse than the police around here.

Now it's starting to look bad for me. These big-name customers I told you about, they're all smiles and dollars when times are normal but as soon as things get a bit disorganized they want to find someone to pin the blame on so they start fingering me, and then even those that should know better begin to turn on each other, if only they'd all stick together it would be fine, but they're piss-pants scared by now and someone's got to take the bullets. Needless to say none of this is doing my gout any good. Both big toes swollen up like pumpkins. Avoid stress says Doktor Sex, like I said he's got a great sense of humor. The worst of it is, the city's crawling with foreigners, United Nations boys, international lawyers, advisers, peacemakers, every type of wanker you can imagine—don't get me wrong, some of them are our best customers but that's strictly nighttime—and the lesbian bitch gets her hairy legs out and starts kicking up and they all start singing like a bunch of choirboys and to cut a long story short it comes to trial. What a farce. Cost me a gold pig in bribes to get it stopped.

Mitar and Branko contributed—they can afford to now they've started shipping into Western Europe. Mitar says the men over there can't get enough of our girlies. I could have ratted on them, picked up a reward, but I'm not a squealer. Mitar says the return's better than drugs, or you can combine the two, stuff the girlies up and off they go waddling through customs with their fannies full of powder. That's what I call a good business philosophy. In fact I might look into it myself once this lot blows over. The beauty of it is, the penalties are lower than for drugs and if they catch you it's the girlies that get sent back; now he's waiting for Kosovo to get its independence, then our boys'll have a safe route right up through Albania. That's the funny thing, Serbs, Croats, Montenegrans, Kosovans, Bosnians, to read the papers, you'd think we're all at war all the time, but this business brings us together, and the more foreigners we get over here the better the business, so you could say that in our own quiet way we're the real peacemakers in this part of the world. Not many people appreciate that.

So after a while things get back to normal, and Katya goes back to Mummy and the lesbian goes off to brag about her wonderful women's refuge—what a load of donkey doo—and our punters breathe a sigh of relief and the girlies get their knickers off, and even my toes settle down. And then strike me dead, another bunch of wankers start poking their noses in. What happened to the trial? Why was it dropped? What about all the Big Names that were named—how come no one got punished? Questions questions. And when there aren't any answers, they start calling for the case to be reopened. Amnesty International, they call them. Amnesty. What a joke. I'm the one that needs bloody amnesty around here.

No One Shall Be Held in Slavery

Mohammed Naseehu Ali
THE LONG RIDE BACK HOME

Before their departure from Bolgatanga's lorry station Abure had told his son, Sando, that they would be on the road for only two days. But the journey was now in its third day and, from hushed conversations Sando overheard between the driver's mate and other disgruntled passengers, they still had at least another day of travel before they reached Kumasi, the big city down south.

The MAN diesel-headed lorry was packed with sheep, yams, goats, guinea fowl, cows, bags of millet, bales of hand-woven *fugu* fabric and about two dozen humans. The lorry's long rectangular trailer, divided in two sections, contained the beasts in one, while the food, human and merchandise cargos were held in the other. With little room below, about half of the passengers had to perch on the food cargo, their heads extending beyond the lorry's wooden frame, in danger of being tossed to the ground anytime the driver dodged a pothole.

The lorry traveled at donkey-trot pace. To make matters worse, the driver stopped at every village along the Bolgatanga-Kumasi highway, to either offload or replenish his human and animal cargos. Sometimes the driver would disappear for hours, visiting a relative, or a mistress, as some of the passengers insinuated. Some of the passengers would roam about the town or village to buy food. Others would bring down their animals, so they could graze in roadside bushes and also to defecate before they loaded them back onto the vehicle. There were three other boys and a girl in the lorry who were about Sando's age, and Sando had hoped he and they would perhaps form a friendship and play together; but all the kids acted as if they had sworn a vow of silence.

Between his chest and his raised knee Sando clutched a rubber bag that contained his only belongings: two worn-out *obroni-wawu* T-shirts, a sleep cloth, a pair of hole-in-the-knee khaki trousers, a straw hat and a cache of creative, handmade playthings that included his favorite and most valuable possession— the catapult he used for hunting small rodents and birds. The catapult, a gift from his maternal grandfather when Sando turned nine, was testament to the old man's confidence in Sando's hunting ability. Sando's marksmanship, the accuracy with which he nailed grasscutters, was so superb the grandfather nicknamed Sando "the shooting wonder of the savannah." Many times during the trip, Sando fingered the contents one by one, to make sure the catapult was exactly where he had put it when he had packed up the bag.

The air in the lorry was laden with the putrid smell of cow dung; the odor of unwashed human bodies; the acrid, sustained stench of oozes from open, untreated cutlass wounds the passengers had suffered back on their village farms; and finally, the odious and murderous reek of hunger. As if that wasn't enough agony, there was the incessant high-pitched quack of the caged guinea fowls, which continued throughout the journey. Shortly after the lorry had left the station, a bitter, sour, nauseating taste rose from the linings of Sando's colicky intestines. It made its way up his throat and then to his tongue, where it lodged throughout the journey.

Barely two years before this, Abure had taken Alaraba, Sando's older sister by three years, to Kumasi, where she worked in the household of one of the city's richest men. At least that was Abure's claim. Abure had also told Sando and his mother that the rich man Alaraba worked for had been so impressed by her diligence that he had enrolled her in a night school, to learn how to read and write. Whether this was true or not, Sando had no means of knowing, as both he and his mother had not heard from Alaraba herself since she was taken away.

Sando was one of thirteen children Abure had sired among five women. Like his father, Sando was short and wiry, though where the boy was as perky and nimble as a gazelle, the father was as slow as a tortoise, and when in conversation blinked slowly, like one who had seen a witch in broad daylight. Sando, as if to make up for not inheriting his father's blinking-eye syndrome, stammered when he spoke.

Sando's father had never married any of his children's mothers. The tradition of his Frafra people, a largely animist population with few Christians and Muslims among them, demanded from a potential suitor a dowry of four hefty cows and a lump sum of money before one was given a wife. A perpetual lazybones to begin with, Abure certainly didn't have the means to afford even a cow's leg, let alone four cows. He, like many men in the Frafra north, relied on the alternative, concubine arrangement, which conveniently suited Abure's amorphous lifestyle. He came to the women, impregnated them and left. But as soon as the children reached the age of ten or eleven, Abure returned and snatched them from their mothers. He took them down south, to work as house servants. With the monthly wages Abure collected for the children's labor, he purchased mosquito coils and bicycle spare parts, which he sold up north for much larger profits. With such a neat arrangement, Abure couldn't have asked for more from the god of his ancestors, to whom he now and then offered libations for lifting him out of the perpetual destitution in the north.

Five days after Sando and his father had set off from Bolgatanga, the lorry crawled into a parking slot at the infamous Kumasi Kejetia lorry station. As Sando and his father meandered their way through the city's humongous central market, where they delivered Abure's guinea fowls to his customers, the young boy fantasized about living in one of the multi-story buildings he had seen from the lorry's top when they drove into the city. *A real concrete-and-block house, with real aluminium roofing sheets and glass windows and real doors and a mattress for me to sleep on.*

Sando imagined his first three days in this sequence: Day One—take a bath, eat and sleep; Day Two—visit his sister; Day Three—go with his father to find a placement for him at the local elementary school, a promise Abure had made to the boy and his mother. What both mother and son didn't know was that Abure had months ago made a promise to a Kumasi Muslim man named Abdul that he would get him a good worker-boy next time he traveled up north.

"*Babu shakka,*" Abure had sworn. "In Allah's name, I will bring you a very, very obedient and hardworking boy. And this one is my very own son."

Like most men on Zongo Street, Abdul had multiple wives. Though Islamic shariah allows Muslim men to take up to four wives, Abdul, cognizant of his limited means, had married just three. With as many as a dozen and a half children from his three wives, and with no real vocation—other than being a *dillali* for pawned goods' transactions on the street—Abdul himself was desperate for a house helper who could serve the dual purpose of servant and income generator in one. Moreover, Abdul's second wife, Asanata, had been nagging him for a servant to help with the family's increasing chores.

"Thank you, thank you, thank you!" Abdul beamed when Abure appeared at his door mouth with Sando. "This must be the son you promised me, *ko?*"

"*Babu shakka,*" answered Abure in the affirmative. He inhaled his perpetual smoke pipe as deeply as if his very life depended on it.

"He looks like you, *ko?*" said Abdul.

"*Babu shakka.* And I promise you he will work well for you and your wife and your family."

After a period of sustained bargaining for Sando's services, the two men agreed on seventy cedis per month, and Abure demanded that Abdul pay the first three months up front. The haggling was carried out in Hausa, a tongue in which the father spoke only adulterated pidgin, and of which Sando understood just a handful of words. Abure looked at his son and grinned, exposing his tobacco-stained teeth. Though confused, Sando bowed his head, unwittingly acquiescing to the deal between the men. In less than five hours of Sando's arrival in Kumasi, the transaction of leasing him into bondage had been concluded. Sando was further confused, saddened even; the whole transaction reminded him of another that had transpired just an hour ago in the market, in which his father and his customers had haggled for the price of his guinea fowl.

Perhaps Abure had sensed that Sando was no fool after all, and that the son may have understood what was unraveling. He drew Sando aside and whispered to him: "You will start school in a few months, boy, when school reopens. But first you have to work to raise the money for the fees, you hear me so?" Sando did what was expected of an obedient son and nodded, though by now he had begun to develop a deep mistrust of his father. Abure left a few minutes later, promising he would take Sando to see his sister next time he returned to the city.

Barely seconds after Abure had left the vizier's house, Asanata, Abdul's second wife, handed Sando a sleeping mat, and guided him to one of the two rooms off the *zaure*—a long and narrow passageway that led to the house's open courtyard. Aside from being used for storage, the zaure room assigned to Sando also served as the mess hall for boys in the compound. It was there they took naps in the afternoon, played games and took refuge at night when they ran afoul of their parents.

Sando looked apprehensively around the darkly lit room in fear. He untied the rubber bag and pulled out his catapult. He did a thorough inspection of the contraption, then slid it in the front pocket of his khaki trousers. He tied the bag, which later became his pillow, and placed it next to the mat. As Sando sat still on the floor, he heard Asanata screaming, "Sando! Hey,

Sando! Saaandooo!" Sando answered, "A-A-Anti," and dashed out of the room into the courtyard, responding to the call for what was the first of a million errands he would run for the Abduls and other families in the compound.

The vizier's house was a rectangular behemoth, with more than thirty rooms, three open kitchens and half a dozen chicken coops. Not counting the Abduls, the house contained eleven other nuclear families and a total of eighty-three inhabitants. And very soon Sando's name was on everybody's lips. "Go buy me this, Sando." "Go and wash my clothes, Sando." "Here, Sando, take these shoes and polish them." "Sando, go climb the tree and fetch us some mangoes." He was ordered left and right by the old and the young alike. "Sando, you bastard, didn't you hear me call you?" the rascals would bark. Poor Sando would dash toward his commander with a "So-so-so-sorry, Papa" or "So-so-so-sorry, Anti." As his father had instructed, Sando called every female "Anti" and every male "Papa," no matter their age.

Sando's day started as early as the first cockcrow. His immediate set of tasks included sweeping Asanata's verandah, filling up the hundred-gallon drum in front of her quarters with water he fetched from the public tap outside the house, washing and sanitizing the sheep's pen and finally feeding the animals their breakfast of salted plantain peel and water. Then it was time for Sando to start a charcoal fire and boil bathwater for Asanata and her three children before he set off to buy *koko da kose* for the family's breakfast. No porridge and beancake for Sando; he was given the hardened surplus *tuo* from the previous night. And on the many occasions that Asanata didn't have any suppie for him, she would casually say, "There is no food for you this morning." To this, Sando would nod and bow his head.

Mid-morning Sando washed the family's dirty linens, polished their dusty shoes and ironed their wrinkled garments. By the time he was done with these chores, around one o'clock, Asanata had already bottled her *biyan-tankwa* for Sando to take to the market square, where he hawked the ginger brew until sun-

down. This business brought in a decent income to Asanata—
enough to buy ingredients for the family's supper and to pay
Sando's monthly wage.

Sando's only free time came after *lissha,* when the families had
completed the final obligatory Muslim worship and had gathered
in little clusters in front of their verandahs to eat supper. Sando
and the other worker-boys and worker-girls in the compound ate
only after their masters and mistresses had finished eating. Sando
accepted whatever portion was given to him with gratitude and
retreated to the zaure, where he ate in silence. The food was
never enough for him, so he topped it up with lots of water, and
also with the crumbs he sometimes got from other families—
their way of compensating him for the many errands he ran for
them.

Sando worked all day and every day, and was unofficially allowed
only two free days in a year: the day of the Feast of Ramadan and
the day of the Feast of Sacrifice, the two major Muslim holidays.
And only on those days was Sando left in relative peace. He
would sit in the zaure room as the streetfolk began the festival of
eating, dancing and gift giving that marked the end of the month-
long Ramadan fasting; he would also do the same during the
Feast of Sacrifice, when the city's Muslim residents slaughtered
thousands of cattle, sheep and goats to mark the end of the pilgrimage to Mecca. When would his own eternal fast and sacrifice
end, Sando wondered during those festive days, as music and
laughter poured in through the window.

Sando was lying in the zaure room on the day of his third Feast
of Sacrifice at the vizier's house when three boys barged in and
quickly locked the door behind them.

"Bend down," said Asim, the oldest of the gang.

"Wha-wha-wha . . . what now?" asked Sando. He was ac-
customed to all sorts of pranks and bullying from the compound
boys, especially when he returned late from their errands. But
Sando didn't remember running afoul of any of the boys lately. He
asked again, "Wha-wha-wha . . . what have I done now?"

"I said bend down," came Asim's menacing response, followed by a knuckle to Sando's head.

Confused, Sando laughed, but still refused to do Asim's bidding.

"Haba-haba . . . haba, wha-wha-wha . . . what have I done thi-thi-thi . . . this time, hah, hah?" asked Sando, trying to laugh his way out of his predicament.

"I said bend down!" Asim said, and slapped Sando on the head again. He instructed the other boys to hold Sando's arms, and before the poor worker-boy knew what was happening, the boys had pulled his half-torn pants down to his knees. Sando put up a struggle and managed to free himself from their grip.

"Wha-wha-wha . . . what is all-all, all this now? I don't like this!" sputtered Sando. The boys suddenly burst into laughter. But it took Sando a few seconds to realize that they were mocking his *koteboto,* which was an object of derision and even contempt on Zongo Street. "He is koteboto! He is koteboto!" they hissed and giggled. Sando quickly covered his nakedness with his open palms.

"Now turn!" Asim said angrily, as if the discovery of Sando's uncircumcised penis had further incensed his ire. He grabbed Sando's arm, then twisted it violently. Sando succumbed and lay on his belly. With his nose touching the floor, Sando blew dust into the air, only to inhale it again.

Asim quickly climbed on top of the servant boy, his erection blindly seeking the mouth of Sando's anus. Sando tried to move his body sideways, to thwart Asim's efforts, but he was overwhelmed by the other boys' grip on his arms and legs. Powerless, Sando gave up and could only imagine himself a lamb being sacrificed to Allah. A violent pain shot through Sando's body as Asim forced his way through. Sando screamed wildly, but nobody outside heard his cry. A commotion much more important to the compound of the vizier's house was taking place: a cow being led to the slaughter pit had somehow managed to set itself free. The beast ran amok, knocking down everything and everyone in its path, while the hysterical housefolk ran helter-skelter

for their lives. The compound was filled with the moos and bleat-
ing of the other soon-to-be-sacrificed animals which—in their
exclamations—appeared to be encouraging the aberrant cow to
elude its pursuers. Though Asim and his cohorts were oblivious
to what exactly was taking place outside, the loud noises certainly
encouraged them to carry on.

"Haba-haba, please. Wha-wha . . . what have I done? I be-be-
beg you, now," Sando pleaded, as the pain exploded. Asim continued, gasping with each stroke, while the two boys—amidst
suppressed laughter—hissed, "*I-mishi! I-mishi!*", urging him to
give Sando some more.

Personally, Sando had hardly thought about sex. He would
sit and listen quietly whenever the boys in the compound chatted about their adolescent fantasies and boasted about the
number of girls they had bedded. In his present agony he wondered if women, when penetrated by men, suffered the same
pain he was experiencing. Sando had heard that Kokobiro, the
transvestite chop bar owner on Yalwa Street, slept with men at
night, and Sando had often wondered how that could be possible. *How could anybody enjoy this ordeal? Why are they doing this
to me?* Though his body convulsed in shock, Sando feared he
might put himself in greater danger if he shouted for help. Master would likely take the boys' word over mine, he thought.
And, besides, wasn't a servant to obey? Always. He thought of
his father's whip and of the distant possibility of school.

After a couple of minutes or so, Asim pulled away from
Sando's rear. He was all sweaty and appeared to be gasping for
breath. Calm had also been restored outside in the compound.
The defiant cow had been apprehended, but not before it had
dragged its chasers all the way to Zerikyi Road and had trium-
phantly knocked over the tables and food trays of many vendors
and hawkers along its way. The captors flogged the crazy cow as
they dragged it back to the house in blind retaliation for the pain
it had put them through. The two dozen or so cattle, goats and
sheep slated for sacrifice had all been silenced by the *fawa*'s blade.
The zaure and the large porch outside were smeared with blood,

as young adults carried the animals into the courtyard, where they were skinned and hung out to dry in the sun.

With little noise coming from outside, the boys realized it was time to leave, lest they be caught should Sando decide to scream again. They sneaked out of the room, leaving him curled up on the dusty straw mat. Sweat poured from every pore. His breathing, short and irregular, prevented him from crying. He made an attempt to get up, but his backside hurt so badly he slumped back onto the floor. A sharp, burning sensation around his anus was followed by an oozing down his thighs. He rubbed his fingers on his skin and lifted his hands to the light. What Sando saw was a mixture of blood and a watery, milky fluid, which dripped from him the way water escapes a faulty tap. With a rag he found on the floor, Sando wiped off the mess, and with his backside still on the floor, he slowly managed to put on his pants.

The following day was the festival's "meat distributing day," when the dried meat of the sacrificed animals was shared among family members and friends and poor folk in the community. Sando was given a few pieces of beef and the innards of a goat, which he spent hours cleaning to get rid of the feces hidden in the animal's intestines. Later that day, as Sando joyfully made himself a pot of stew with his share, Asim and the two boys approached him.

"Let me tell you," said Asim, "if you dare open your mouth about what we did, the whole street will know about your kote-boto." Sando swore he would not say a word to anybody.

But the boys, assured that Sando would keep his word, raped him several more times, taking turns at each encounter. They stopped only when Asim, who was sixteen, got his first girlfriend. At one point, Sando considered waylaying his assailants near the football park and attacking them with his catapult. But he backed out in the end, afraid that his most-prized possession on earth might be confiscated if he used it in that manner.

In the eighth year of Sando's exile in Kumasi, a group of military officers toppled the country's government. The revolt that ensued after the coup d'état was very popular among the nation's poor, who chanted: "LET THE BLOOD FLOW!"—the blood of the small elite class that had oppressed the nation's majority since Ghana's independence from Britain in 1957. Sando, nineteen at the time, took advantage of the four-month-long chaotic, "freedom for the masses" euphoria that swept the nation. He fled the vizier's house.

Sando relocated to the Asawasi market, to the east of the city. There he found work as *kayaye* and also as errand boy for the rich cola-nut merchants. Very soon Sando was making four times more than his father had made on his behalf. But freedom, as they say, has its perils. Before long, Sando fell into bad company at the market, where he slept in big storage rooms with other migrant workers, in whose midst existed many miscreants. Soon Sando took to drinking *pito,* a favorite among his fellow northerners. This locally produced brandy heralded an ecstatic, if delusional, period for "the worker-boy from the vizier's house," as he was sometimes called. Sando truly felt that the revolution that followed the coup d'état, for better or for worse, and for all the killings and public floggings of citizens, was waged to free people like him, to give them back their lives—to restore their collective dignity.

Yet for all of Sando's newly acquired autonomy, sex eluded him to his grave. Apart from what the boys at the vizier's house did to him, Sando never managed to sleep with a woman—not even the prostitutes on whom he wasted some of his hard-earned income. He came very close to fulfilling this desire, once, when Suraju, Zongo Street's notorious swindler and drunkard, connected him with a woman at Efie Nkwanta, the old whorehouse on Bompata Road. But the girl fled the room naked on seeing Sando's koteboto, considered an ill omen by the city's prostitutes.

When Sando turned twenty-one, he developed a peculiar, if mysterious, disease. It started with a few boils on his left thigh, but within ten days of the appearance of the first boil, Sando was like a giant boil himself—the affliction by then covered his buttocks, legs and upper body. His face, body and legs swelled up as if being pumped daily with a toxic liquid. The boils would break open, releasing an ooze that attracted flies to his body.

Tormented by this unknown malady, and with no place in the city to call home, Sando headed for the only refuge he knew—the vizier's house. After their initial anger and the curses shot at him for running away from them, Abdul and Asanata, fearful of the karmic implications of turning away a human in dire need of help, had a change of heart. They pleaded with other folks in the compound to allow Sando the usage of the zaure room. The housefolks emptied the room of the bags of maize and *konkonti* they had in storage. Soon afterward they and their children avoided the room altogether.

A decade after his arrival in Kumasi, Sando had yet to set eyes on his sister. And as for Abure, the last time Sando had seen him was when his father trekked to the Asawasi market not long after Sando's escape from the vizier's house. His father tried then to persuade Sando to come with him back to Zuarungu, promising to make him partner in a farm he had started. Sando had flatly refused the offer and had boldly reminded his father of his many deceptions. Powerless against a now grown Sando, Abure had departed in shame. Sando had drunk himself into a stupor that night, a celebration of the fact that for the first time in his life he had mustered enough strength and courage to say no.

A decade after his arrival in Kumasi, Sando had lost all but one of the original possessions contained in the little rubber bag he had carried into the city: the catapult. It remained the only surviving link between Sando and his mother and his two sisters and his grandfather and his village. Though Sando never used the catapult in Kumasi, it imbued him with the hope that he would one day return home to Zuarungu—to the savannah and its exotic birds; to the lizards he and his childhood friends had chased and shot with their catapults; to the nocturnal calls of the black cricket, which at dusk emerges from its hiding place under the logs and burrows to sing and celebrate its mere survival for yet another night. It was in such a dreamlike state that Sando's hopes dissipated into the reality of his death as he slept one night in the zaure room. In his final seconds, Sando believed he was embarking on a journey, a rather long one, back to Zuarungu. And unlike the rickety, smelly lorry that had a decade earlier brought him to the city, *he*, this time, traveled in luxury, held aloft by white-feathered angels, who sang the songs of his childhood as they accompanied him, *the shooting wonder of the savannah*, on his long ride back home.

Freedom from Torture

Gabriella Ambrosio
STICKO

I am a Stick, I am the most advanced stage in the evolution of humankind. I remain motionless, still, exactly the same as everything else, spread somewhere in some way. I am here, but no one sees. I sit in front of the television in my flower-patterned cretonne armchair. I too am flower-patterned cretonne. I am watching a program in which they sell armchairs, one model is called Letizia, the other Gaia. Gaia has an extending footrest so you can stretch your legs out; if you want it you don't have to move either, Armchairs and Armchairs will send the Armchairs and Armchairs consultant to your home, call him right now at this number. I might even feel obliged to dial the number, but I can't: a Stick must keep still until nightfall, he mustn't move, otherwise they'll discover him.

Today she came, she took me by the arm, snap out of it Sticko she said, you can't go on like this. And she shook my arm really hard, she's been a bit on edge recently, but I've learned what to do, I left my arm in her hand. Anyway I know it'll grow again, it's happened before. She dropped the arm on the floor, let out a yell and went away. You have to understand her. Before this evolutionary stage I was twenty, and we used to make love every day.

But then she came back, and we began to talk things over seriously.

Allow me to remind you, I tell her, quoting an old book, that the struggle for existence can modify the structure of a young individual compared to that of his parents. As we know, natural selection accumulates variations in character or instinct, each of which is advantageous to the individual in his new living conditions.

I got her there. I feel that I got her there. Natural science and biology were my subjects, when I was a young man of twenty. Sticko, she says really brightening up, and there's no reason for that, you could go back to your studies!

I pretend to be thinking seriously about it, but then, choosing my words with care: although natural selection, I object, acts through every individual solely for his good, our ignorance doesn't enable us to judge which details and differences are necessary for the use and the disuse of the parts and sometimes variations accumulate in the wake of other, often entirely unpredictable ones. She holds her head between her hands and says nothing for a bit, then she goes into the kitchen to make me something to eat. My antennae are quivering, and I can't let them do that. I keep them as still as I can. After that, she didn't come back the next day, or even the day after, and the rubbish piled up in the kitchen.

At night the wind comes up and I move. I move very slowly, darker than the night itself, I go out of the house, I take two sidling steps, I roam the streets of my neighborhood. I follow the low breathing of the shadows, I slip along, I flutter in the air. I still like my city at night, and sometimes I even catch a glimpse of the sea.

I come across few people. Those who had to dash out because the dog was desperate, pajamas already slipping out from under their trousers, maybe they made it wait while they sucked the television down to the last drop and now they're being dragged along like the load behind a juggernaut in a skid. Those who are coming and going from a place or a person, and know why they're doing it, and carry traces of it, in their eyes and on their clothes. Those like me, who are never going to or coming from anywhere.

The city is calm, and if I ever walk again or not it doesn't notice. No one sees me. I let the wind drag me along every night.

This morning she has some very important news for me. We
had both been waiting for it for some time and mainly I was
waiting for it even though it doesn't seem like that. Sticko, she
says to me, it's horrible, I'm sorry. I don't know how it's possible.
They've acquitted all of them. I mean, no: some were convicted,
but not to serve time. And the real culprits? Nothing. The real
culprits were guilty of nothing, and so the careers they've
made since then have been consecrated too. I was hanging from
the ceiling when she arrived, but when she said this I threw
myself down and remained motionless until she despaired and
went away.

Then I moved slowly into the kitchen. I had to do something.
The kitchen is yellow and out of caution I also tinge myself yellow. It's the evolution of the species, I've told you that. The behavior best suited to the twenty-first century, counting only those
that came after Christ. A man gets to twenty and he learns to
disappear.

My legs have become frail but my jaws are robust. I chew
slowly on what she has left me in the kitchen.

Then I wait for it to get dark. And I feel the breeze coming up
from the street.

But tonight the city isn't as calm as the other nights. My antennae
quiver strongly with fear. I don't know what's going on but I
sense it, from behind me or in front or to one side or above or
below someone is coming. And then I see him. I freeze, I become
colorless like the wall and I flatten myself against it. He passes
close by and doesn't see me, I am wall. He almost touches me but
I'm good, I don't move a muscle and I don't make a murmur. A
whiff of tiger balm mixed with fresh, pungent sweat in his measured gait, he has this well-groomed sort of face, a steady gaze, a
firm tone, composed, you've always known at least one person
like this, you could trust him and that's what I did, he said strip

off and then turn round, and bend over, it was the examination, I had already stopped talking but I was thinking now he'll get a good look at what they did to me, and there I was naked with my back to him and bent over forward and I was cold and everything ached but I stayed nice and still as he had told me to and all the people around were looking silently at, I believe, the bruises the hematomas the blows the injuries when I feel the one who had brought me here resting his truncheon back there and he says you can see he likes the truncheon and they all burst out laughing then I wet myself with that truncheon resting back there and the piss running down onto the floor that has them dying with laughter, him too, with that strong smell of freshly rubbed-on balm mixed with fresh pungent sweat, fit, enrolled, and ready for the pokey he says now, but he was the doctor for crying out loud, I was in the presence of a doctor, and this had been his examination. I smell rancid, or maybe I've wet myself again and I'm cold again because he's no longer there but I can't move from here, I remain motionless for at least one hour, two, or I don't know how many hours more, no one sees me, I am wall. Only after a long, long time a new wind finally springs up, then without hurting myself I detach and let myself return. My house is at number 27 Via Ognissanti, the wind knows this. Right, here I am, I go up the stairs. And I am the door, I am the armchair. I am once more flower-patterned cretonne.

I saw him, I tell her as soon as she arrives this morning, he's here, he's come to live round here.

He who, she asks me and I point at the window, wait I say, last night he went into that building, wait and sooner or later you'll see him go in or come out, wave to his wife and children leaning out the window, adjust his scarf around his neck, get into his car turn the key and go to his place of work, he who, she asks me, the doctor, then she pales, shit, are you sure. I'm sure I tell her, even though it's not true.

Sticko, I've followed all the hearings at the trial, I've talked with the lawyers, I've read the documents, none of them lives here, it can't be him.

You know, that day I only went out to the cash machine, I only went out to the cash machine, I start to say, even though now this has nothing to do with it, but repeating it always helps me to calm down at least a little.

Enough, Sticko, she tells me, you're losing your mind and I can't take it anymore.

Look out the window, I tell her, I can't.

Enough, Sticko, she says, you're going mad, and you're making me go mad too. We can't go on this way, it won't work. I've thought things over, I've thought them over well: listen to what I think. There's the supermarket at the station that's open at nights too, you can do a bit of shopping there when you go out, throw the rubbish out by yourself, and you can pay the bills through the Internet, after all you don't need anything else and, well, what I want to say is that you have to start putting a little willpower into things, you can't always count on me. The more rope I give you the stranger you get. I still love you, Sticko, but you have to get out of this on your own, she says, you have to get out of this on your own I yell, and I don't know if you remember Sergeant Hartman.

She jumps back opens her eyes wide stretches out her hands and shaking her head says in a really low voice almost whispering don't be afraid I'm telling you for your own good you'll make it. You'll make it you'll make it you'll make it you'll make it you'll make it I repeat and I can't stop anymore.

Stop it I'm going crazy, she shrieks with tears in her eyes and her fingers all numb.

Stop it, I yell, you've got to stop it.

Now I'm sure she won't come back again.

The day after we had that ugly fight lots of spines grew on my legs, and spines on my arms, and now I'm covered with spines all over. But she's right, I can make it.

Now every night I get the bag of rubbish and I take it down

myself, without even opening the door anymore, if the wind gets up I waft lightly down from the window holding my rubbish tight.

I do the shopping, then I come back and cook for myself. It's not going so badly.

There's only one problem. Since she told me they had acquitted them all, they've all come to live round here. And every night I see a different one. So without a murmur I stay exactly where I am, I shrink as much as possible, I become pavement I become pole I become trunk and leaves, they pass close by and I am no one, and they don't change pace, and they carry on going where they wish to go.

Tonight there is a murmuring and a shuffling in the streets that rises up and comes in my window and spreads through the house, it slips into the cupboards and under the bed and puts its head inside the oven and I want to go out, tonight I must go out and I go out, here I am down on the street and here's what's going on, the neighborhood street party. There has been a procession, they all followed the priest, with their songs and their prayers, and then they didn't break ranks, the procession continues all the same behind the cotton candy, the families respond to the call, one behind the other, dragging along the kids, lovers, moving forward in twos and fours, the herds of friends swaying as they move off, bellowing, arm in arm, and the merry-go-rounds, still turning, and the stands, all lit up, with nougat, and carobs, and nuts. Words blaring from the loudspeakers.

And I know them all, because there, there they are: it's them.

They have the same smooth packaging, the same expression devoid of sense and devoid of blame.

The same as the pleasant taste of that day, that jollity of who goes there, that euphoria of nothingness, beside her husband the woman, the woman who as they were taking my photo winked and suggested now you have to smile though and I did, I had only gone out to the cash machine and I had no intention of contradicting them, so in the mug shot I'm grinning like an idiot even though at that point I had three broken ribs and a wound on my head. Behind her, surrounded by his children, a visibly satisfied man, well-fed, sated, full, now he explodes, the one who had ordered me to walk on all fours and to bark and I did that for as long as he wanted and after that he commented seriously: you're certainly a lad with no dignity. And after him that other one, chatting about this and that with an acquaintance, but he's craning his neck, looking round and to the sides all the time, paying more attention to some indefinite other thing than to the conversation, I know him too, he's the officer who when it was all over asked me to put my signature under a statement and I didn't want to because my eyes were full of blood and I couldn't manage to read and in any case in that moment I wouldn't have understood anything of what was written above, then he grabbed a pair of scissors from the desk and slowly began to cut the hem of the hood of my sweatshirt, and then my hair, selecting one lock after another, very small ones at first, and then bigger ones, rolling them up and carefully pulling them firmly upwards and snip, and I was already thinking I was going to wet myself again when he repeated sign and I signed.

They all move forward in the street party forcing me more and more into a corner, they are a crowd and an army with no banners, a swollen mass, a sweaty stinking flock, when a dog notices my presence and starts sniffing at my trousers then I throw myself to the ground, I wrap my arms around my head, I go stiff as a corpse. But a little boy, the only one who was chatting with the dog, now a little boy notices me too, he bends over, brings his face a few inches away from mine, dad, dad, he says, look what Blitz has found. Now they're all around me, not moving, their eyes peeled and: look, says dad to all the children, to those of the others too, this is really a stick insect, look how funny he is, he's not moving because he's scared of us, he doesn't know what to do, he doesn't want to be noticed, look, he's even taken on the color of the road, he thinks that this way we won't notice him any more, heh heh but here he is kids, ha ha.

And now the kids are sniffing at me with more attention than the dog and then all the parents around, and the others too, they all form a crowd, because they've nothing better to do, fuck, that day I only went out to the cash machine I tell you again but also the others, the others were completely unprepared for what was to be for them and had to be, and where the fuck are we living, if these are the people who live next to us, chat to us every day and tell us about the children's schoolwork and the holidays at the seaside, and Sundays spent with their old mothers and the good lunch they had together, and throng the streets and the squares, and every time they meet us they hug us and kiss us on both cheeks, and so they become us, and we become them, and we are them, how can we defend ourselves anymore, I thought, then I swelled up and I began to squirt shit all over the place, and to vomit on them, as long as I had stuff left inside.

Translated by Alastair McEwen

Joyce Carol Oates
TETANUS

Diaz, César. Like an upright bat, quivering wings folded over to hide its wizened face, the boy was sitting hunched over the table beneath glaring fluorescent lights, shaved head bowed, rocking back and forth and humming frantically to himself. Arresting officers had banged him a little, torn his filthy T-shirt at the collar, bloodied his nose and upper lip. His eyes, wetly glassy, frightened and furtive, lurched in their sockets. He was breathing hard, panting. He'd been crying. He'd sweated through his filthy T-shirt that was several sizes too large for his scrawny body. He was talking to himself now, whispering and laughing. Why was he laughing? Something seemed to be funny. Spittle shone at the boy's red-fleshy lips and the nostrils of his broad stubby nose were edged with bloody mucus. He took no notice of the door to the windowless room opening, a brief conversation between two individuals, adults, male, Caucasian, figures of authority of no more apparent interest to him than the tabletop before him. He was eleven years old, he'd been taken into Trenton police custody on a complaint by his mother for threatening her and his younger brother with a fork.

"César? Hello. My name is . . ."

Zwilich spoke with practiced warmth, calm. Pulling out a chair at the counseling table, at his usual place: back to the door. Outside were Mercer County guards. Mercer County Family Services shared cramped quarters with the Mercer County Department of Parole and Probation and was adjacent to the Mercer

County Youth Detention Center, which was an aggressively ugly three-story building made of a stony gray material that looked as if it had been pissed on, over a period of many years, in jagged, whimsical streaks. You came away thinking that these walls were covered in graffiti though they were not.

Early evening, a Friday in late June. Parole and Probation had shut for the weekend but Family Services was open for business, and busy.

One of those days that, beginning early, swerve and rumble forward through the hours with the numbing, slightly jeering repetition of an endless stream of freight cars. Even as Zwilich's life was falling into pieces he was speaking in his friendly seeming and upbeat voice to Diaz, César, whose latest arrest sheet lay before him on the table, beside a folder stamped *Mercer County Family Services: Confidential*.

"... and I'm here just to ask you a few questions, César. You've been in counseling with Family Services before, I think. This time we need to clear up some problems before you can go home. Can you hear me?"

The bat-like boy sneered, smirked. You had to think that he was very frightened yet his manner was hostile, insolent. He was rocking from side to side, gripping his scraped elbows. He was muttering to himself and laughing, and Zwilich, an adult male in his mid-thirties, old enough to be César Diaz's father and wishing to project a fatherly or old-brotherly manner, wishing to convey to César Diaz that he sympathized with him, he respected him, he was on his side and not on the side of the enemy, had no doubt that, if he could hear the obscene words the boy was muttering, a hot flush would color Zwilich's cheeks above his patch of whiskers and his heart would kick in revulsion for the boy but luckily Zwilich couldn't hear.

He would tell Sofia, it's been one of those days.

Which? Which days?

A day of temptation. Terrible temptations.

And did you succumb?

Goddamn, he was not going to succumb. He'd had a few drinks

at a late lunch to buoy his spirits, and the prospect of a few drinks this evening, alone or with another, somewhere improvised, filled him now with a gassy sort of elation, like a partly deflated balloon someone has decided, out of whimsy or pity, to inflate.

Zwilich spoke. Kindly, with patience. Such evil in him, his secret little cesspool glittering deep inside the well of his soul, it was a task, a sacred task, to keep the lid *on*. Yet the boy resisted. Staring stubborn and unyielding at a bloody smear on the table before him, where he'd wiped the edge of his hand after having wiped a skein of bloody mucus from his nose. Zwilich was thinking that César Diaz, exposed in pitiless fluorescent lighting, might have been drawn, with finicky, maniacal exactitude, by Dürer or Goya. No mere photograph could capture his essence. His forehead was low and furrowed in an adult expression of anguish indistinguishable from rage. His bony boy's head had been shaved as if to expose its vulnerability, breakable layers of skull bone upon which a scalp, reddened with rashes and bumps, seemed to have fitted tight as the skin of a drum. A very ugly head, an aborigine head, crudely sculpted in stone and unearthed from the soil of centuries. The arresting officers had pegged César Diaz as possibly gang affiliated but Zwilich thought that wasn't likely, the kid was too young and too scrawny, no gang would want him for a few years. The shaved head was more likely Mrs. Diaz's precaution against lice.

Zwilich suppressed a shudder. Itchy-scurrying sensation at the nape of his neck, his jaws beneath the whiskers. He'd caught lice from clients, in early years. But not for years.

According to César Diaz's mother, he'd been sniffing glue with other boys earlier that day and coming home he'd caused a "ruckus" in their building, he'd been "violent"—"uncontrollable"—"threatening." Glue sniffing! It was an epidemic among boys César's age, in certain Trenton neighborhoods. If Zwilich hadn't been assured that César had been examined by a doctor, passed back into police custody and delivered to Family Services for evaluation, he'd have thought the boy was still high, or deranged. Sniffing airplane glue was the cheapest, crudest high, scored by serious junkies (meth, heroin) for causing the quickest brain damage. The boy's bloodshot eyes shone with an unnatural intensity as if about to explode and a powerful odor of unwashed flesh, sweat, grime, misery, wafted into Zwilich's nostrils.

It would be traumatic for César to be kept overnight in detention but there, at least, he'd be made to take a shower. A real shower. As a slow-motion dream sequence Zwilich could imagine the bat-boy cringing beneath hot rushing water, layers of filth gradually washing off his skinny body, in swirls at the drain beneath the boy's bare feet. The darkish-Hispanic pallor emerging, a startling beauty, out of encrusted dirt.

He felt a pang of tenderness for the boy. As if he'd glimpsed the boy naked and vulnerable and begging for love.

"César? Will you look at me? Your mother has said . . ."

Now César looked up sharply. "Mama? She here?"

"Not just yet, César. Your mother is very upset with you, and worried about you, she's hoping that we can—"

"Mama comin' to take me home? Where's she?"

The bloodshot eyes were widened, excited. The bony shoulders twitched like broken wings.

"Your mother might—possibly—be coming to take you home tonight. Or it might be better for you to stay overnight at the—"

"Mama here! M*ama*! Goddamn fuck M*ama*!"

"César, hey: calm down. Sit still. If the guards hear you and come in, our interview is over."

Zwilich frequently saw young offenders, as they were called, not only handcuffed but their cuffs chained to waist shackles; not infrequently, since adolescents were the most desperate of all offenders, their ankles were shackled, too. Trooping in and out of the detention center next door, kids in neon-orange jumpsuits, cuffed and shackled, and it was an unnatural and obscene vision that passed over by degrees into being a familiar vision, one that induced a sensation of extreme fatigue in the observer like, simply, wanting to give up: die.

As if reading Zwilich's wayward thoughts César bared his yellow teeth in a taunting smile. "Hey man? You be cool? I goin' home, Mama come? Mama sorry now?"

"Maybe. We'll see."

"Mama sorry. Yes."

The boy spoke with such vehemence, Zwilich didn't doubt, yes Mama was very sorry.

The wan stale odor of sorrow blown through air vents in the old State Street building. Some smells, in first-floor men's lavatories, feculent, sulfurous, a prefiguring of the farthest-from-daylight pit of Hell.

Six years on the staff at Family Services, Zwilich would have been promoted to supervisor by now except for budget cuts through festering New Jersey, and departmental resentments. Inevitably he'd provoked resentment, being overqualified for his job and inclined, beneath his courteous manner, to exasperated patience, irony. Most days he wore black jeans and a white cotton dress shirt and sometimes a necktie, sometimes a lead-colored leather necktie. He wore expensive silver-threaded Nikes, in cool weather a black bomber jacket to align himself not with his colleagues, still less his superiors, but his clients. His bristly sand-colored whiskers were trimmed into a goatee, his still-thick hair, receding at his temples, was trimmed in a crew cut that gave him, in these uncertain years approaching forty, an air of youthful vitality and waywardness that, at times, Zwilich still felt. He hadn't quit his job as Sofia had quit hers, in disgust, dismay. He had plans, still. Environmental law, a PhD in social psychology. He wasn't old. He wasn't broken. Maybe inclined to sarcasm, can't be helped. He didn't want to think that, without a clear future, a vision of some sort of happiness, the present becomes unendurable in a very short time.

He asked César: How'd he like some pizza? A Coke? And César shrugged okay cautiously as if suspecting a trick, it's a world in which, if you're eleven years old, some older guy, or could be a girl, holds out a pizza slice for you, a can of Coke, and, when you reach for it, slaps your hand away, laughs in your face.

Zwilich made a quick call on his cell phone, the pizzeria across the street where sometimes he ordered takeout. Poor kid was probably starving. The least Zwilich could do, feed him.

It was Zwilich's task to interview the detained juvenile and make a recommendation to his supervisor, who in the flurry of late Friday, and in his trust in Zwilich's judgment, would no more than glance at the report and pass it on: whether to release César Diaz into an adult relative's custody or keep him overnight, or longer, in the juvenile detention facility. Zwilich disapproved of keeping kids as young as César Diaz even overnight in detention where the oldest boys were sixteen. Inmates were segregated according to age and size but still, a boy like César would be abused.

Probably, something like that had already happened to César. Not once but many times.

On Monday, a Family Court judge would rule on César's case. Probation and outpatient therapy was most likely unless, if Family Services recommended it, incarceration in a juvenile facility. A kid's life in Zwilich's hands, like dice to be tossed. A wild thought came to him: take César Diaz home.

A call to Sofia to come back, see what I've done.

Except Sofia wasn't answering his phone messages to her. Where was she staying, with whom, in Trenton or possibly in Philadelphia, Zwilich had suspicions, but no clear knowledge.

. . . *love you but frankly I'm afraid of you, terrified of going under with you, drowning*.

He'd been shocked: Drown? With him?

As if Zwilich was a depressed man, was that it? Sofia was fearful of contagion?

He'd hated her, in that moment. He'd wanted to slap her beautiful selfish face.

If they'd had a child. By now, children. When two adults cohabiting fail to have children, they remain perpetual children themselves.

"Well, César. See you've been busy."

Zwilich whistled through his teeth looking through the boy's file. He'd been taken into police custody five times, twice within the past three months. Vandalism, petty thefts, disturbances at school and at home, glue sniffing. A previous caseworker had noted that one of the vandalism episodes included "desecration of a cemetery" and another the torture of a stray dog. It was noted that an older neighborhood boy had tied a rope around César's neck and yanked him around causing him to faint, when he'd been nine; another time, César had fashioned a noose and stuck his own head into it; yet another time, more recently, he'd forced a noose over his six-year-old brother's head. He'd been picked up with two older boys for stealing from a 7-Eleven store and not long afterward he'd been arrested for vandalism in the rear lot of the 7-Eleven store. He'd been several times suspended from school. Following these incidents he'd been assessed by Family Services psychologists and counselors and given sentences of "supervised probation" with required therapy from Family Court judges who hadn't wanted to incarcerate so young a child. But Zwilich thought, the next judge isn't going to look too kindly on all this.

The prosecutor for the case had told Zwilich that he intended to ask the judge to incarcerate the boy in juvenile detention for thirty days minimum. César Diaz required psychiatric observation as well as treatment for the glue sniffing and it was "high time" for the boy to learn that the law is serious. Sour, prim as a TV scold, Zwilich's colleagues said how're kids going to respect the law if there aren't consequences for their behavior?

Zwilich sneered: Who respects the law? Whose behavior has consequences? Politicians, mega-corporations?

He'd said, "Hell, this is a child who's been arrested. Look at him, he's so small."

Now in the counseling room, Zwilich wasn't so sure. Fury quivering in César's tight-coiled little body, halfway you expected him to spring up at you, like a snake baring its fangs.

"... want to hurt your mother, César? Your little brother? You love them, don't you? Tell me."

"Din't hurt nobody! Shit what Mama says."

"I think you love them. Sure you do. Why'd you want to scare them, César? Tell me."

César shrugged, sniggered. *You tell me.*

In César's file it was noted that his father, Hector Diaz, was deceased. Zwilich said, in a confiding voice, "My father died when I was a little boy, César. I was just six, I know what it's like."

César looked interested, briefly. His shiny eyes shifted with caution, a kind of adult shyness, wariness. As if, like the offer of pizza, this might be some sort of trick.

Zwilich said, "I still miss my father, César. But I talk to him, in a way. Every day, I talk with him." Zwilich paused, wondering if this might be true. He certainly talked with someone, in a continuous tape loop of improvised, pleading speech; but that someone seemed not to be listening. "Do you—with your father—too?"

César shrugged, evasive now, downlooking, wiping at his leaking nose. Zwilich had several times offered him tissues but the boy disdained them, preferring to wipe bloody snot on his fingers and his fingers on the table. Zwilich tried another father-question but the boy wasn't responding. You had to suppose that this was a misguided tactic: probably the kid hadn't ever known his father, or if he'd been told that somewhere he had a father, that the father was dead.

Father *deceased*. One problem out of the way.

When Zwilich proceeded to ask César about the thefts from the 7-Eleven store, the boy became animated, agitated. Now he began to chatter incoherently in an aggrieved voice. The 7-Eleven clerk must have been an Indian, César muttered a racist slur. There was indignation in his little body and he eyed Zwilich insolently as if to say: So what, man?

The boy was mimicking older boys he admired, neighborhood punks, dope dealers, the slatted rat-eyes, jeering laugh, junior-macho swagger. In a boy so young the effect was comical as a cartoon that, upon closer inspection, is pornographic.

Zwilich knew these kids. Some were "juvies," others were adolescents, "youths." Their souls' deepest utterances were rap lyrics.

He pitied them. He was sympathetic with them. He detested them. He feared them. He was grateful for them: they were his "work."

You would wish to think that César Diaz, so young, could be saved from them. Removed from his neighborhood, which was poisoning his soul, and placed—where—in a juvenile facility? But the youth facilities were overcrowded, understaffed. Zwilich admired some of the administrators of these facilities for he knew of their idealism—their initial idealism, at least—but the places were, in effect, urban slum streets with walls around them.

César continued to chatter, agitated and aggrieved. Zwilich glanced at his watch, worn with the dim digital clock face on the inside of his wrist as if the exact time were a secret Zwilich didn't wish to share: 6:55 p.m. The date was June 30, 2006.

Each day, each hour. Equal to all others. If God is in one of these, God is in all of these.

He believed this! He wanted to believe.

Yet: *If God is absent from just one of these, God is absent from all of these*.

The pizza would be arriving soon, the Cokes, these would help. One of the guards would rap on the door: "Mr. Zwilich? Delivery." César would observe the counselor paying for the meal, bills removed from Zwilich's wallet in a gesture of easy generosity. Sharing a meal with a client, in these cramped quarters, was a technique of Zwilich's, a friendly maneuver, intimate, yet not overly familiar. You felt the urge to feed, to nurture, a kid like César, who had to be famished.

At the thought of pizza, Zwilich felt a mild stirring of nausea. Beer fat, whisky fat in flaccid flesh at his waist, a secret fat, for Zwilich was a lean, lanky, still-young-looking man, five feet ten inches, one hundred and seventy pounds, given to small gestures of vanity—smoothing the bristly hairs of his beard, running his fingers through his brush-like hair, checking to see if—yes—was it evident?—the deep bruised indentations beneath his eyes suggested insomniac nights, or late-drinking-nights, restlessly surfing TV. The first mouthful of gummy pizza cheese, greasy Italian sausage and scorched-but-doughy bread would repel him and his thirst wasn't for syrupy-sweet Coke.

She loved him, she'd said. But didn't want to go down with him and he'd said but I thought you loved me in the most piteous voice and she'd said backing away so he couldn't touch her, pull her off-balance toward him as in a clumsy dance, I love you! but Goddamn don't intend to drown with you.

Alcohol, addictions of any kind including nicotine, the most common painkillers, more difficult for women to overcome than for men, must be biochemical, genetic. Zwilich hated it, that his wife feared him when, first time he'd met her, at a bar in New Brunswick, in a gathering of medical students, Sofia had been drinking whisky, straight. He'd been stunned by her beauty, her strong sensual mouth and vivid physical presence. The sight of a woman drinking whisky aroused Zwilich for it was rare in his experience and often the prelude to a sexual encounter as it would prove with this woman even after she'd become his wife.

Nine years! Since he'd first met her. Of these nine years they'd been married seven.

If they'd had a baby. Babies. What then? Zwilich had no idea but couldn't think that having babies was the solution to a riddle that taunted you every time you looked into a mirror: You? *Why?*

Here was César Diaz: a young woman's baby. It had to have seemed little César was someone's answer, a temporary answer, to the riddle *Why?*

Freely César was speaking, boasting to his friends. Lots of friends, César's friends, to look out for him. If he went "inside'— if he was "kept here." No clear transition then to a story about someone who'd fired a gun into the air, they be drinkin', this guy brother home from "Ee-rock" he in the army he have this gun shoot this gun, bullet go high in the air then fall, hit some old guy, poor-old guy next-door backyard he hit, poor-old guy he have bad luck the bullet hit him neck, he don't get to the hospital he die in ambulance you see on TV?—everybody talkin about it but nobody know who shoot the gun. César grinned, laughed. He'd been tapping his neck to indicate a bullet entering, shaking his head, laughing. Nobody know.

Zwilich was listening now. He knew of this incident, which had been widely reported in the Trenton area: a random bullet fired into the air that had fallen and killed an elderly man in the Straube Street project back in April, and the shooter had never been identified. Zwilich tried to interrupt the chattering boy to ask who the shooter was—an Iraqi war veteran?—but César laughed, saying it wouldna happen if God din't want it that way, nobody damn fault how the gun go off, how you blame it?

"César, did you tell your mother about this?"

César sniggered, vastly amused. Had to be Mr. Zwilich was a real asshole to ask that.

"An elderly man dies, nobody cares? What if that man was your grandfather, César?"

"Hey man, he *not*."

Zwilich felt a throb of dislike for the boy. The mimicry of older boys, men, in his voice, his vocabulary, his mannerisms, the contortions of his small body. Zwilich would be meeting with César's mother, not the next day, nor the next, but sometime on Monday, at which time César would appear before a Family Court judge, in the company of a court-appointed public defender. He saw in César's file that Gladys Diaz, twenty-eight, had moved to Trenton four years before, from Camden, New Jersey; she was a diabetic who received Mercer County welfare payments for her sons and for herself; in Camden, she'd been arrested for trying to cash forged checks and had been sentenced to two years' probation. At 3:30 p.m. on June 30, 2006, Mrs. Diaz had called 911 reporting her son César for "threatening" her with a fork—not an eating fork but a long, two-pronged fork like you use for turning meat—screaming he was going to kill her and his six-year-old brother. He'd been sniffing glue, Mrs. Diaz couldn't control him. But when Trenton police officers arrived at the Straube Street apartment, and César ran away panicked, crawling to hide beneath a bed, Mrs. Diaz relented saying maybe they

shouldn't take her son away, then she'd relented again saying
yes! They should! This time she wasn't going to come with him
to the precinct, César is on his own this time, though again changing her mind as the officers hauled the boy shrieking and stumbling to the street, to the waiting patrol car, wrists cuffed behind
his back and the officers would note on their reports a strong
smell of red wine on Mrs. Diaz's breath. César was speaking excitedly of Mama as if Zwilich must know her. César was furious
with Mama but César was desperate for Mama. César was saying
Mama been wantin' to scare him, now Mama sorry. Callin' the
damn police, Mama done that before, sayin' she gonna call them
to scare him, and his brother, too, lots of times, to scare them,
Mama afraid to beat him now, he too big, damn police come for
him at school too but he'd never been "kept in" this place he'd be
let go now, Mama comin to take him home. Why this was funny,
Zwilich didn't know. The boy's laughter was sharp like shattering glass and getting on his nerves. If the boy was made to spend
a single night in the juvenile facility, he'd be punished for that
shriek of a laugh. He'd be punished for his runny nose, and for
his smell, and for being a runt, a loser.

César was demanding to know where's Mama? Was Mama
here yet? And Zwilich said his Mama wasn't here, and César
said, his voice rising, where's Mama? I want Mama to take me
home, and he wasn't laughing now, tears of indignation shone in
his eyes, and Zwilich said, "César: your Mama told us to take
you and keep you here as long as we want to, your Mama said, 'I
don't want César in the house anymore, I'm done with César, you
keep him.'"

Zwilich was a perfect mimic of Mama's furious voice. Fixing
his somber-counselor's eyes on César's face.

In fact, Mrs. Diaz had said something like this. The mothers
of kids brought into juvenile custody invariably said something
like this or more extravagant despairing things but Mrs. Diaz
had also said she hoped her son could come back home that
night, she wanted to take him to stay with a relative in New
Brunswick, get him out of the neighborhood for a while, and

Zwilich, who'd spoken with the distraught woman on the phone said yes, that sounded like a good idea.

César stared at Zwilich now in stunned silence, his mouth quivering. César couldn't be more respectful than if Zwilich had slapped him on both cheeks, hard. You didn't tell an eleven-year-old that his Mama didn't want him, not in Zwilich's profession you didn't, but the impulse had come to him, not for the first time in circumstances like these but for the first time with a child so young, an impulse strong as sex, overpowering, irresistible, a wish to create something—even misery, even self-disgust—out of nothing. Zwilich felt a sick thrill. Zwilich smiled. Zwilich was overcome by shame. Luckily the interview wasn't being taped, no surveillance camera in this airless cubbyhole and outside in the corridor the Mercer County guards stupefied with their own boredom hadn't the slightest interest in what transpired in the room unless there'd been a call for help, an adult's cry for intervention and restraint.

Zwilich relented: "César, hey." Stood, and approached the stricken boy. César's eyes shone with tears that gave him the look of a fierce little dog. When Zwilich touched him, to comfort him, the boy cringed. "César, your Mama didn't mean it. She called us—just a while ago, she called and left a message for me—'I love my—'"

So swiftly it happened then, Zwilich would live and relive the assault and never quite comprehend how César grabbed his right hand and bit his forefinger, before Zwilich could shove him away. Bit down hard, tendons taut in his grimy neck, in an instant he'd become a deranged animal. Zwilich struck with his free hand, his fist, on the side of the head, knocked the boy from his chair onto the floor yet he wasn't able to pry the boy's jaws open to free his finger, Zwilich was shouting, screaming in pain, oh God the pain was terrible, the mad boy had bitten Zwilich's forefinger to the bone, at the first joint, only when the guards rushed at him did the boy release his pit-bull jaws and Zwilich staggered away. The guards cursed the boy trying to crawl beneath the table, he was lifted, thrown down, scrambling frantic and crab-like on the floor, shrieking as if he were being murdered. Quickly now the guards subdued him, cursing him, laughing at the size of him, couldn't weigh more than seventy-five pounds, they had him on his belly on the linoleum floor, on his face, wrists behind his back and cuffed and lifted for maximum pain, wouldn't cease struggling so the guards cuffed his ankles too, marveling Jesus!—the size of the little bastard. Zwilich showed the guards his wounded finger, which was bleeding thinly down his hand, down his arm to his elbow and seemed somehow to have become smeared on the front of his white shirt. He hadn't known he'd been shouting for help. Trying to laugh it off, the kid was quick as a snake, Zwilich hadn't seen the attack coming. He was white-faced, dazed. In a state of shock and his heart pounding crazily. The panic rush, the adrenaline rush, had to be as powerful as any heroin rush Zwilich had had, years ago when he and Sofia had experimented with injecting heroin into their veins, not seriously but just to see what it was like, and they'd backed off from it almost immediately, at least Zwilich had, and never tried it again. Zwilich was stammering at the guards telling them to take César Diaz away, he couldn't bear the sight of the boy any longer. The evaluation would note the abrupt termination *assault on a Family Services counselor*.

In the skirmish Zwilich had nearly lost control of his bladder, Jesus! the guards would've been witnesses, he'd never have outlived such a professional humiliation.

Now you're fucked, *little cocksucker, for life.*

Not for life, surely: only just remanded to juvenile detention for thirty days.

Pitiless glaring lights of the medical center where in a cubicle screened off from more serious traumas Zwilich's wounded forefinger was given a thorough cleansing, disinfecting. The young Korean resident doctor examined the finger as if he'd never seen anything so curious. "You can see teeth marks all round. These are human teeth?"

Human teeth had the ring of a joke punchline. Zwilich laughed, a hot flush in his face. He was still shaky, edgy. But yes, he had to concede: human teeth.

"Small, though? A child? 'Child teeth'?"

"Not so small, the child is eleven."

Zwilich waited for the young doctor to inquire if the child was Zwilich's own child, it seemed a natural question, Zwilich was a normal man yet might be the father of a crazed demon-child, but already the doctor was deftly bandaging the finger. Strangely, for all the pain, that still throbbed like a flashing neon, the wounded finger hadn't bled much.

In a staff lavatory at Family Services he'd run cold water onto the wound, washing away the blood and numbing the finger. He'd have improvised a clumsy gauze bandage for the finger out of a near-depleted first aid kit in the office but his supervisor insisted that Zwilich go to the medical center immediately, to get professional medical attention for the bite. For insurance reasons, Zwilich supposed: if such a wound became infected, if for instance the finger had to be amputated, Family Services would be liable for a large settlement.

Before Zwilich left the clinic holding his thick-bandaged finger at chest-level to minimize the throbbing, the young Korean doctor insisted that he have a tetanus shot.

Zwilich laughed irritably: he was fine, he didn't need a tetanus shot, he was sure. Or rabies.

The doctor said, somberly, "Yes but the inside of a human mouth can be dangerous as an animal's mouth. Teeth caries contain infectious microorganisms, you'd be surprised."

Zwilich thought: Would I! In his dazed state, nothing could surprise him.

The needle bearing the transparent tetanus vaccine entered Zwilich's left bicep cleanly and with little pain but shortly afterward as he left the clinic it began to throb. And the clumsy bandaged forefinger throbbed with pain. A jeering sort of pain it seemed to Zwilich, recalling the demon-child's look of feral hatred. If he'd been able, César Diaz would have torn out Zwilich's throat with his teeth. Zwilich shuddered, stumbling as if he'd been drinking, badly needed a drink and so stopped by the Dorsey Hotel, the romantic-seedy bar like the interior of a cave Sofia had said and that cave undersea and muted where frequently he'd met up with her after work. For a while, Sofia had been a therapist at the hospital a half block away, her specialization was pediatric oncology. Wistfully she'd said, If we're going to start a family, and her voice had trailed off, and he'd said quickly, We can. Soon. We will. When things are more in control. He'd meant to say (hadn't he?) under control. When things are more under control. His father had often used the expression, to placate Zwilich's mother. When things are more under control.

In this way months pass. Years.

At the bar, in perpetual twilight, a ghost-figure barely visible in the mirror behind rows of glittering bottles, Zwilich drank a beer, and a second beer with a shot-glass of whisky, drinking with calculated slowness telling himself that he was early, Sofia wasn't late, he was waiting for her to appear, this pleasant interim of merely waiting, Sofia would be breathless from having hurried, a smell of rain in her loose hair. Sofia's hand on his shoulder, a light claiming touch: "Hey." And the pressure of her wide, warm mouth against his that quickened his heart, that was shriveled to the size of a peach pit, with hope. "Hey. Where've you been?" Already he'd forgotten the interview, the assault, the evaluation, abhorrent to him, he would not remember, an aberration in Zwilich's life not to be shared with Sofia, not ever. Half consciously counting four men at the bar beside himself and there was the bartender and, it's a law enforcement officer's habit, you see that their hands are in sight, and you see where the entrance, exits are, where you might need to take cover, in an emergency. For such things happen, you can't foresee. One of the older drinkers at the bar had the large gravely heraldic head of Zwilich's father, who'd been a rich Hartford, Connecticut, stockbroker who'd died not when Zwilich had been six but when he'd been twenty-six and so long estranged from his father and in so undefined a phase of his life, geographically as well as otherwise, Zwilich hadn't known that his father had had a massive stroke and had died pleading to see his son until several days after the death when Zwilich's distraught mother had finally been able to locate him in an outlying district of Brooklyn where he'd been, temporarily, "living with friends." Zwilich must have been staring at this man unlike Zwilich's late father unkempt, unshaven, for at last the man squinted over at Zwilich, with a faint frowning smile as if trying to determine who Zwilich was and a sensation of cold terror washed over Zwilich *I am not one of you, I don't belong here.* Hurriedly Zwilich paid the bartender what he owed him and fled.

Another Trenton bar, on lower State Street, Zwilich looked into: but Sofia wasn't there. Nor was Sofia at the Bridge House where the bar was crowded, the air dense and combative and Zwilich called to the bartender, "Has Sofia been in here tonight?" and the bartender cupped his hand to his ear amid the din and Zwilich raised his voice, "I'm looking for my wife, has my wife been in here tonight?" and there was a momentary hush, the Bridge House was a tavern in which there is a moment of respect when a man in a blood-splattered white shirt and with a bandaged finger announces in a raw uplifted voice that he's looking for his wife yet still the bartender said no, hadn't seen Sofia that night, in fact hadn't seen Sofia for some time. Zwilich thanked him and departed and now at sunset crossing the Delaware River to Morrisville, Pennsylvania, hot rain splashing against the windshield of his car, Zwilich is possessed by the thought that he will drive to Philadelphia, he's convinced that he knows where Sofia might be staying, and with whom. Driving across the familiar bridge he's made to notice the strangeness of the fading sky, below the bridge there is mostly darkness but much of the sky remains in patches of light, the sun melting into the horizon like a broken egg yolk, the effect has to be the result of chemical pollution yet it's luridly beautiful. Below are the old shuttered mills, warehouses, the decaying Trenton waterfront but at the Pennsylvania shore a string, as far as Zwilich can see upriver, of glittering house lights. His heart beats with a forlorn eager hope: sun spilling its light onto the bridge, onto the river like a slow-motion detonation in which, though many thousands are destroyed in a fiery holocaust, no one feels any pain.

Equality Before the Law

Walter Mosley
THE TRIAL

1.

I was out of breath by the time I'd reached the fourteenth floor of our building. Because of the steep hike I rarely visited the apartment of Milan Valentine anymore. I usually talked with him on the stoop of our building or out in front of the QuickShop down on MLK. We called each other regularly but our business that night was important enough for me to make the climb.

The elevator had broken down two and a half years before but the landlord had yet to fix it.

"What do you expect?" Ferris Burns, the super, had told me. "City's put a cap on rents. There's just not enough left over to pay for luxuries."

"Luxuries? What about Cilla Sanders?" I had asked Burns.

"What about her?"

"She's nearly ninety. She could die of a heart attack climbin' up to floor nine."

"If it's too hard for her she can move," the super replied.

I could have argued, I guess. Anybody might wonder how an eighty-plus widow living on three hundred dollars a month could move anywhere. Who'd carry her belongings? How would she pay first and last month's rent plus the security deposit, plus the real estate agent's fee?

I could have argued but Ferris wouldn't have cared. He had his own problems: one autistic child, an asthmatic daughter and a nineteen-year-old boy serving a seventy-two-year prison sentence for aggravated assault. Ferris's wife hadn't broken a smile in eight years and his girlfriend on the third floor had him running errands day and night.

The super was a Black Man like the rest of us and, like the rest of us, he had little time for charity or kindness.

I knocked because Milan's ringer was busted. His daughter, Angelique, opened the door immediately, as if maybe she was waiting for me.

Angelique was seventeen but looked a couple of years younger. She was slender, black as a human being can be, with features that hinted at the roots of the African American physiognomy from a long time ago and a long way gone.

"Mr. Wayne," she said extending a hand.

I shook the hand and smiled.

"My father is waiting in the kitchen, sir."

"Mister? Sir? I'm not that old am I?"

She grinned and moved her head toward her left shoulder in response.

"Where's your mother?" I asked.

"She went to stay with her sister," the young woman said. "Mama doesn't approve of this."

I nodded and showed myself down the dark hall and to the right.

Garish yellow light illuminated part of the small, disheveled kitchen. Big-bellied, broad-faced, black-skinned Milan was standing at the cracked tile sink drinking water from a red plastic tumbler. At the table in the corner, under the shadow of a burned-out lamp, sat Wilfred Arna, his hands in his lap, on top of a greasy brown paper bag, and his head hanging down. The close-cropped haircut and brown, brown skin marked him as a laborer from the South Side of town. Like millions of others he was a poor man who had worked hard every day of his life.

Milan smacked his big lips and nodded at me.

"They'll be here in forty-five minutes," he said abandoning the usual pleasantries.

"And the witness?"

"She's in my room."

"Who's standing for Lark?" I asked.

At the sound of that name Wilfred looked up, misery squirming under the flesh around his eyes.

"I will," Milan said. "I got almost as much college as you and I went to a good high school in Accra. A Christian school with high morals."

"You know this doesn't mean anything," I said to the Ghanaian born grocer.

"Or it is everything," he replied and then smiled broadly.

Valentine's smile could populate the whole South Side with children from willing mothers' loins. When he smiled you felt that there was some chance at happiness—there was the proof beaming right there in front of your eyes.

"You can use Angelique's room," he told me. "She's going to sit beside Wanita for the night."

After that he walked away leaving me in the half-lit kitchen with the wretched man.

I pulled down a blue tumbler from a yellow plank above the sink and poured myself a glass of the mineral-laden, pharmaceutically enhanced city water. I drank a bit and poured the rest down the ancient porcelain drain.

"I guess we better get started, Wilfred," I said trying to infuse my tone with a certain lightness.

For a moment he sat still as if maybe he hadn't heard. Then he stood up without raising his shoulders, like a condemned man making his way toward the noose.

2.

I had him tell me the entire story from beginning to end; starting with the day that Lark Thinnes had taken over apartment 6G and leading up to the events in the early hours of that very morn-

ing. We went through the documents and forms in his paper bag
and he handed me a small .25 pistol.

Wilfred perched at the edge of Angelique's pink bed while I
sat on a padded stool she had for her makeup table. There were
pictures of athletes and singers on her walls. She was a child like
other children but, as in the case of her father, she was also something else.

"What was in your heart?" I asked Wilfred at one point, and,
"Do you believe that you are above the law?" at another.

We went through his story again and again. Now and then he
wept softly but I said, "I don't want any of that. Your tears don't
mean anything here tonight."

We went over the story so many times because even though I
was aware of the circumstances I wasn't there to have an opinion
of my own.

"Why me?" I had asked Milan when he came down to my apartment
that morning to recruit me for this job.

"Because you have a college degree but still you live in the
Ida B. Wells projects," he'd said. "Because you have studied
the problem from both sides of the table. We need people like you
to keep us honest."

"They'll call it a conspiracy," I said.

"They can call it what they want. You and I know what it's
like to live here. You and I know that justice is not only blind but
deaf and dumb when it comes to this building and these people."

There was something majestic about Milan. He believed in big
things. It didn't matter that we lived in a tenement where gangs
and drugs, prostitution and irrational rage reigned over our lives.
To Milan these were just temporary impediments, momentary
lapses in the advancement and ultimate achievement of our
people.

And when Milan spoke of *our* people he didn't mean Americans or Africans, blacks or whites. He saw in the suffering of any
one person the affliction in us all. If anyone else had come down
to me and suggested what he did about Wilfred and Lark I would

have run away. But I couldn't say no to the Ghanaian. That would have been tantamount to a condemned man turning his back on a chance for redemption at the hour of his execution.

After we'd gone over Wilfred's story six times I turned to the records he kept—from the complaints he'd registered with the police and the petition that he'd circulated only five weeks before to a large portrait-photograph of Josette taken when she graduated from Emmett Till Middle School two years earlier. There were also pages torn from his journal and her diary.

It was very sad. I could have used a few more days studying the papers but I was relieved when the knock came on the door.

Angelique stuck her head in and said, "Daddy says that it's time, Mr. Wayne, I mean . . . Robert."

"Okay," I said. "We'll be right out."

"Okay." She grinned at me then closed the door.

Putting my hand on Wilfred's shoulder I said, "It's time to go."

He waited again and then looked up at me.

"I appreciate what you doin," Bobby," he said. "I know that it'd be bettah for you to just call the cops and wash your hands of it."

"Better's not always best," I said, quoting a fellow I once knew named Marquis.

Remembering Marquis Brown and all of his little aphorisms gave me a moment of elation. This feeling confounded me. I wondered, what was the cause of this errant jubilation?

Wilfred stood up clutching his paper bag and swallowing hard.

"Let's go, Brother," he said.

3.

Angelique was waiting in the hall. She led the way toward the living-room chambers. It was very formal. She wore a white dress and had her tightly woven braids tied back with yellow ribbon. As we were passing the front door a loud banging came from outside.

"Another member?" I asked.

Wilfred was trembling.

Angelique shook her head.

"No," she said, "they're all already here."

Wilfred retreated back toward the girl's bedroom. He didn't go in, just stood there at the doorway grasping at his paper bag.

Angelique put the thick chain in its slot and then opened the door as far as it would go, maybe four inches.

"Yes?"

"Police," a man's unfriendly voice announced.

"Yes?"

"Is your mother home?"

"No."

"Your father?"

"He's at work."

"We're looking for a man named Wilfred Arna. Do you know him?"

"Yes. I know Mr. Arna. He lives on the twelfth floor."

"Can we come in?"

"I'm not supposed to let people in when I'm alone."

"Do you know Wanita Cousins?"

"She's my friend. She lives on the nineteenth floor."

"We think that she may have witnessed a murder."

"I haven't seen Wanita for weeks, officer. My parents don't want me to be her friend. They say that she's a bad influence."

"Why's that?"

Angelique shrugged but said nothing.

"Can we come in?" the policeman asked.

"No."

The door rattled then from someone on the other side pushing hard. But Milan had used a reinforced chain with wide brackets anchoring it. The door itself was solid.

"Do you have Wanita Cousins in there?"

"No, sir."

"It's against the law to lie to the police."

"Yes, sir. I know it is. But I can't let you in because that's my father's rules. Never let anyone in the house when I'm home alone. I have to obey my father too."

There was a brief lull in the conversation. Angelique stared into the opening with no discernible expression on her face.

"When will your father be home?" the policeman asked.

"Later on tonight. He and my mother are at church."

"I thought you said that he was at work?"

"My mother is meeting him there," she said without hesitation, "and they're going on to church. They do that every Wednesday."

Again there was a pause.

"You tell him that we were here."

"Yes, sir."

"Don't forget."

"No, sir," she said and then after a brief moment she pushed the door shut.

Angelique leaned up against the wall for a moment and then regained her composure. She began walking down the hall again. Wilfred had come up behind me and we followed the brave child.

4.

There were nine people in the living room when we got there. Milan was sitting at the left side of the pink couch, his daughter took the center position and poor sad Wanita Cousins sat at the far side. In the big brown sofa chair next to Milan sat Cilla Sanders, by far the oldest person in the room. The others sat in straight-back and folding chairs set around the front of the sofa in a semicircular fashion.

"You sit over there, Robert, I mean . . . Mr. Wayne," Angelique said as light-skinned Wanita glared at the slump-shouldered Arna.

The chairs Angelique pointed out were padded white affairs that Milan must have borrowed from some neighbor. These seats were opposite the couch. I took the place next to Kenya

Broadhouse, who had her baby in her arms. Wilfred wound up next to Milo Stone, the elderly deacon from Third Street Baptist International Church, known in the community as 3BI.

"How you doin', boy?" the charcoal-colored, rail-thin churchman said to the killer.

Wilfred nodded and looked down at his paper bag.

Meanwhile Milan was letting his big eyes roam around the room.

His gaze settled upon Anthony Porter and Gina Gores, who were to his right. Tony was a pharmacist's assistant, in his mid-forties, six years out of prison on a conviction for second-degree murder. He would be on parole for the next twenty years. Gina was on disability because of a drug she was given at the emergency room when she was delivering her baby. The child died and she almost did. She'd made friends with Tony at the drug store and now they were inseparable.

On the other side of the circle was a wise-mouthed kid named Bells. I never knew his real name. Bells was an orphan who stayed with various families in the projects and was always talking about joining the army or robbing a bank. The girls seemed to like him. He was twenty years in the body and a year or two younger than Angelique in his mind. Next to Bells was Reggie Simms. Reggie hung plaster walls for a living. Every day he'd go out to MLK and 147th Street and pick up seven or eight Hispanic, mostly Mexican, workers and go to jobs that he'd set up with construction bosses.

"I got the mouth, the Mexicans got the umph and the white boss got the green," Reggie would say.

If the government came down on the bosses they could blame Reggie. He didn't worry about it. He was a businessman and entanglements with Uncle Sam were just occupational hazards.

Milan took in the crowd and nodded.

"You all know why we're here," he said, "but I'll go over it anyway. Lark Thinnes was killed up in apartment six-gee at about three-thirty this morning. We got us a witness and a suspect and I say we should have a trial."

"We not the cops, Valentine," Reggie said. His dark face was both blunt and brutal. "Why the hell we stick out our necks for sumpin' like this?"

"We're not the cops," Milan repeated, "but we are the people. The police will arrest, the prosecutors will arraign, but who will speak for us?"

"The court will," Reggie said. He turned in his chair but did not rise.

"The cops arrested Lark seven times," Cilla Sanders said loudly and with the rasp of old age. "And seven times the court let him go. Now Josette is dead and so is he. The courts don't give a fuck about us."

"What you gonna do if we say the mothahfuckah's guilty?" Bells said with an arrogant sneer on his youthful face. "What you gonna do if we say he should die?"

"Do you want to pull the trigger, son?" Milan asked. "Do you want to kill somebody?"

"I'm just askin'," the boy said, a little put off by the intimacy of the question.

"If we find him worthy of death and no one else will do it then I will," Milan said pausing after every few words.

"I'll shoot him," Wanita cried. "I'll kill the man killed my baby."

Wanita broke down crying and Angelique put her arms around her, cooing into her ear.

I glanced at Wilfred then. His head was hanging almost to his knees and tears were dripping down.

"The first order of business," Milan said, "is to say whether or not we are qualified and responsible to hold this hearing."

He looked around the circle again. For a few moments there was a pensive silence.

Then, "I've been livin' in this buildin' for seventeen years," Milo Stone said in his soft deacon's voice. "I seen so many people die here that it's a shame. Young people shot an' stabbed and slaughtered for nuthin'. They shout about it in my church. The police tell us that if we do what they say we'll have justice. The courts say that they'll make it right. And politicians say vote for me. But the people just keep right on dyin'. So I say maybe we should at least see how it go."

"Anybody else?" I asked.

"What about you, Bob?" Reggie said.

"I'm here, Reggie. I'm ready to stand for Wilfred. I'm ready to say that we are the law. 'Cause, brother, you know that it sure ain't the man in blue and them wearin' black robes."

"Amen to that," Cilla said.

Tony and Gina, while not speaking, each nodded.

"At least we should hear it out," Kenya Broadhouse said. Her baby, Leonard, cried out at hearing his mother's voice.

"Okay," Milan said. "Let's get to it."

5.

"Robert," Milan Valentine said. "How do you suggest that we go about this?"

"Why him?" skinny brown Bells asked.

"He's got a master's degree in political science," Angelique replied.

Bells sat back twisting his lips as if to say, "Whatever."

My heart was pounding. It wasn't until this moment, I realized, that I was taking this trial thing seriously.

"Well," I said. "Well, I . . . I think we should hear the charges and then the plea. After that we can have what testimony there is and then we can, all of us, including Wilfred, make a ruling."

"Why he got a say!" Wanita cried. "He the one killed Lark!"

"He came to me of his own free will," Milan said. "It's only one vote out of twelve, child."

"Bastard," Wanita spat at Wilfred.

He tried to look at her but it was as if she were the sun blinding him with her insane light.

"Hold up a minute there, Bob," Reggie said. "I said I would come and listen but that don't mean I won't walk right outta here an' call the cops. You know this ain't no legal thing in here. We ain't been made the judges of nuthin'."

"And even still," Milan said with infinite grace and patience, "we judge every day."

"What's that s'posed to mean?" Bells whined.

"It means," I said, "that Reggie here hires illegal workers six days a week. He pays them and protects them and never turns them over to the law."

"That's business," Reggie complained. "That don't count."

"Isn't it our business to make these halls safe our chirren?" Cilla spoke out.

Kenya nodded. So did Gina.

"I said what I got to say," Reggie intoned.

"Well then," I said, "let's get on with it. Milan."

"Yes?"

"Let's hear the charges."

For this the stocky man stood up. He pulled a folded piece of paper from his khaki pocket and read it over. Then he refolded the paper and shoved it back into his pants.

"At three-thirty this morning the accused, Wilfred Arna, went to apartment six-gee, knocked on the door, told Lark Thinnes that he needed drugs and, when Lark turned his back, Wilfred shot him seven times. He then reloaded his pistol and shot the victim seven more times."

Wanita screamed as if in physical pain. Milan looked down on her and then sat.

"Fourteen times?" Anthony Porter asked.

"Yes," Milan replied.

"And did Lark have a gun?"

"No!" Wanita shouted. "All he had was the cocaine that Wilfred asked for."

"No," Milan concurred. "In a court of law it would be called first-degree murder, premeditated homicide."

Tony glanced at Wilfred, who was looking down.

"Is that everything?" I asked Milan.

"Yes."

Wilfred mumbled something.

"What was that?" Reggie asked.

"He killed Josette," Wilfred said a little louder.

"That's a lie!" Wanita screamed. "My baby ain't killed nobody. Nobody."

"He sold her drugs. And when she couldn't pay he made her do things wit' men from the street. He turned her into a dog an' then he turned her away. He might as well have pushed her off 'a that roof."

"He wasn't nowhere near her," Wanita hissed, staring death at the pitiful worker.

"What happened, Wilfred?"

"He killed Lark that's what," Wanita cried.

"We're going to let him speak, Wan," I said. "Then you can tell us what happened."

Angelique put her arms around her young friend again.

"Well, Wilfred?"

The man stood up straight and looked directly at me. He addressed me the whole time he spoke.

"Thursday last I came home and somebody, I don't even remember who, told me that my dead brother's child, Josette, had fallen off the roof. They said Josette was dead. Said the cops had come and the ambulance had come and all that was left was a grease stain in the street. And Ferris Burns had washed that away with a green hose. My dead brother's child was dead. Dead. She hardly ever wanted to stay with me an' Linda and then, after Linda left, she acted like I was some kinda enemy. I'd see her goin' up to the sixth floor, to six-gee. I'd see her staggerin' down the halls and the streets. I seen her comin' from apartments and corners and the alley behind the buildin' with men hitchin' up their pants aftah her.

"Police wouldn't even tell me what happened for three days. They said I had to prove she was my blood. How was I gonna do that? Finally my minister agreed to talk to 'em. An' they told me that she committed suicide. Suicide. I told 'em that it was Lark Thinnes and his drugs killed my niece. It was him that made her into a whore and a soul so sad that she couldn't, she couldn't . . ."

For a moment Wilfred hovered at the threshold of crying. But he pulled himself back.

"So I got me a gun and a box'a bullets and I did just what the little girl said. I knocked on his door and said I wanted some crack cocaine just like they say on the news. I said I wanted some and he smiled at me and turnt his back. I just started shootin'. He run to one side and I shot him and then he run to the other side and I shot him again. I shot him till there wasn't no more bullets in the gun. But he was still movin', tryin' to get away. So I loaded up again an' shot him some more. I shot till all the bullets was done and he wasn't movin' no more.

"Aftah that I walked away down the stairs. I was sittin' outside this apartment when Mr. Valentine came out to go to work.

"You know I went to the police to try and get them to kick Thinnes outta there. They went to see him now and then but they didn't do nuthin'. One cop told me that I should move. I should move outta my own house.

"I went to social services over Josette but they said that she was too old and by the time they got to her she'd already be eighteen."

"Did you mean to kill him?" I asked.

"Yes I did."

"Is that what you planned to do when you went to his door?"

"Yes it was."

"Did it feel good?" Bells asked out of nowhere.

Wilfred was still for a moment and then he shook his head.

"Is that all you have to say, Wilfred?" I asked then.

He nodded and sat down.

Everyone in the room, even Wanita, was quiet and looking at the miserable man.

It was a shattered moment of grace.

6.

"But that ain't all of it is it, bastard?" Wanita said then. "You ain't told 'em how you loaded up your gun a third time and pointed it at me, did you?"

I remembered that the gun was loaded when Wilfred gave it to me. There were also fourteen spent shells in the greasy bag. He had known enough to keep the shells so that the police couldn't use them as evidence.

"I forgot that part," he said. "I suppose I didn't wanna remembah . . . that."

"But you did," Wanita said vindictively. "You loaded it up and came aftah me."

"Oh Lord," Cilla said.

Milo Stone grunted and shook his head.

"Are you hurt?" Kenya asked.

"He was gonna kill me like he did Lark," Wanita said. "He followed me down into a corner and pointed the pistol at my head. It wasn't till I cried and said that I was gonna have a baby that he stopped. If I wasn't pregnant he would have killed me for sure."

Wanita started crying again.

"You're pregnant?" Milan asked.

"Yes, Daddy," his daughter replied. "I went with her to the doctor last Tuesday."

"Is what she says true, Wilfred?" I asked.

"It wasn't 'cause she was pregnant. I was crazy. I wanted to keep on hurtin'. I saw her in there. I knew that she helped him sell that shit. I was crazy mad. I wanted to kill her too but when I saw her cryin' I thought about Josette and I knew that I couldn't do it."

"Well that's it, right?" Reggie Simms said. He even stood up. "The girl saw it and the man confessed. Now it's for the law to decide."

"Sit down, Reggie," Milan said. "We aren't nearly finished here."

"Why?"

"Because we're having a trial and you're part of the judging body. You're here and you will stay here until we have finished."

I was surprised that Reggie obeyed. He was a man who lived

outside the law as far as his profession was concerned but that was because he felt that the laws were stacked against men like him. But Wilfred was something else altogether.

After many long months of considering his decision to stay, I decided that it was because, in a way, Milan was offering him citizenship, membership in a group that would make up their own minds about what was right.

"But he confessed," the kid Bells said.

"That's only the first part of the trial," I said. "And Wilfred says that he did it out of passion over his niece's death."

"Lark didn't kill her," Wanita said.

"Did he get her hooked on that shit?" sand-colored Cilla asked Wanita.

"No," the child said petulantly. "Uh-uh. Josie used to come up there to party and Lark just sold her what she wanted."

"But did he make her into a whore?" Kenya asked.

"He didn't make her nuttin'," Wanita said. "He didn't tie her down. That was her own decision. You can't blame us for that. Lark was a businessman just like Mr. Simms."

"I ain't no drug dealer," Simms said. "What I do help peoples."

"But if one'a the Mexicans work for you get sick or get in trouble that ain't your fault," Wanita argued.

"That's different."

"No it ain't. If your people get sick or get killed comin' here or tryin' to go back home they cain't blame you."

Reggie didn't answer because he might have said the same words.

"And, Bells, you worked for Lark before," Wanita went on. "You even sold shit to Josette before when she was sellin' her ass down in the alley."

Wilfred raised his head to gaze at the young Bells.

"So?" the boy replied.

"So if Lark killed Josie then you did too."

"Tell these people how old are you, Wanita," Gina Gores said.

"What that got to do with anything?"

"She's turned fourteen two months ago," Gina said. "I know. I'm her godmother."

Wanita pouted and looked away from the circle.

"What does her age have to do with this trial?" I asked, to keep us on track.

"If you sayin' that Lark killed Josette because he supplied her with drugs and put her in danger then you need to see if he did it anywhere else. I think that if he was with a thirteen-year-old girl and got her pregnant in a apartment where they sold drugs and sex then that might be one thing we should look at."

The deacon nodded and grunted.

Bells looked scared.

"Okay," I said. "Why don't we talk about Lark's life in apartment six-gee."

7.

That discussion went on for over an hour. Everyone had stories about knifings and robberies, drug overdoses and people that Lark and his cronies had beaten for not paying. There were four girls and two boys in the building that had turned to prostitution to pay the handsome young drug dealer for his little vials.

The only people who didn't speak were the young ones. Wanita glared at the conversation. Angelique was stoic and Bells was sullen listening to the long list of indictments against the murdered man.

"Do you have anything to say?" I asked Bells after the jury had begun to repeat themselves.

"I ain't on trial," he told me.

"I just wondered if you have any stories for or against the victim."

"You mean Lark?"

"Yes."

"I dunno. I mean he was a drug dealer, yeah. But I don't know how you gonna blame him for that. The police go up to him an'

Wan's place ev'ry other week but they left without arrestin' him. They just got they little envelope and walked away."

"He was payin' off the cops?" Cilla asked.

"He was payin' some of 'em. I don't know about 'em all. But you know if he can do his work an' nobody from city hall wanna do nuthin' I don't know how you can sit here an' say it was his fault."

Unconsciously Reggie Simms nodded.

"An' if you wanna blame somebody about Wan you might as well ask Miss Gores about her mother."

"Don't you say that!" Wanita yelled. She leaped up from the coral sofa but was held back by Angelique. For a moment there Angelique's eyes and mine met. I realized that I was attracted to her.

"Well?" I asked Gina.

"I don't have nuthin' to say on the subject. And I think that boy should keep his mouf shut."

"No," Milan said. "This is a room where anyone can speak. This is a room where we aren't going to be silenced."

Something about Milan's tone affected Bells. He sat up straight and stared defiantly at Gina.

"Wan's mother was one'a the first ones to come down to six-gee. Matter'a fact she the one send me down there the first time to get her stuff. She give me ten dollars an' told me to go give it to him. And then she started goin' down there on her own. And sometimes he'd go up to her place. That's where he met Wanita. He was with her mother first."

Wanita buried her face against Angelique's shoulder. Angelique was looking at me.

"So you sayin' that Wanita's mother sold her to Lark?"

"No!" Wanita's scream was muffled by Angelique's white dress.

"No," Bells agreed. "It's just that she ended up down with Lark and her mother got her drugs at discount."

I had never seen Milan frown like that. He seemed lost in the complexity of broken hearts and promises.

"Wanita?" I asked.

"What?"

"Is what Bells says true?"

"What if it is? I still loved Lark. He was too young for my mother anyway."

"And too old for you," Kenya said flatly.

"I'm havin' his baby. I ain't too young for that. Lark loved me. He loved me and I loved him and that man killed him."

"So why didn't you go to the police?" Reggie asked. He was sitting at the edge of his folding chair by then, fully engaged in the discussion.

Wanita froze for a moment staring into the eyes of the construction boss.

"I . . ." she said. "I was scared to go."

"Why?" Milo asked. "You had a right. He murdered your man right there in front of you."

"Her mother been workin' for a friend'a Lark's," Gina said. "The cops would'a taken her to some kinda foster home or sumpin'."

"So you wouldn't have gone to the police?" I asked.

Wanita looked down.

"I was hopin' I could get justice here," she said and I began to understand just how complex Milan's project really was.

8.

"So, Wilfred Arna," I said rather pompously, "are you guilty of having wilfully murdered Lark Thinnes with malice aforethought?"

The trial had gone on for hours. We had discussed the crime and the victims, the law as we saw it, and the law as it saw us. Cilla Sanders stayed with us in spite of her age. Reggie Simms stayed with us in spite of his doubts. Milo Stone stayed with us in spite of the conflicts with his vows to 3BI.

We had come to the final moments of the first part of the trial.

"Yes," Wilfred said sitting up straight and looking around

what came to be known in later trials as the Circle of Judgment. "I murdered him right there in his room. I almost killed the girl too. I was crazy but I knew what I was doin'. I killed him. I shot him until he was dead."

"And do you," Milo asked, "want to be turned over to the police or have us judge you here in this room?"

"You," Wilfred said with certainty that he hadn't shown earlier.

"What if we find you guilty?" I asked.

"That's all right."

"What if they say you should die?" young transient Bells asked.

Wilfred stared at the young man who had admitted selling drugs to his niece. He stared but said nothing.

It was close to two in the morning but no one seemed tired.

"Let's go around the room," I said, "and take a poll."

"Before we do that I have a question about procedure," Milo Stone said.

"What's that?"

"How do we know if he's guilty?"

"The vote will tell us."

"But suppose that some think he's innocent?"

"If nine or more vote guilty," Milan said, "then that's enough for the verdict. Does anybody have a problem with that?"

I expected Wanita to speak up but she didn't. She looked at me and curled her lip but said nothing.

"Cilla," I said.

"Guilty," she replied.

"Milo."

"Guilty."

"Tony . . . Reggie . . . Kenya . . . Angelique . . . Bells . . . Wanita . . . Milan . . . Gina . . ."

"Guilty," they all said.

"And so say I," I added. "We are in unanimous agreement. Now the only thing we need to do is come up with the sentence."

"Cain't we just turn him over to the law?" Bells asked. "I mean they got jails and shit. What we gonna do? Send him to his room without his dinner?"

"Wanita," Milan said.

"What?" The child was in deep pain. Her eyes had heavy marks under them and she couldn't sit up straight without Angelique's help.

I was falling in love with my friend's daughter all through that trial. She had been a child to me before that night but seeing her stand up against the police and for her friend had shown me a woman.

"What do you think the punishment should be?"

"Don't ask me."

"But you knew earlier," he prodded.

"He's guilty but he was crazy too," Wanita said. "I can see that now. I can see how hurt he is. Lark used to go upstairs an' beat my mama sometimes. Mama Gina right, he made her a ho. He did Josie too. Mr. Arna was just mad. I mean he broke my heart an' took my baby daddy but that don't mean he have to die."

"What about you, Reggie?" I asked the builder. "I don't even know why you came or why you stayed. Do you have a verdict?"

"Just 'cause you went to college don't mean you know shit, Bobby," Simms said. "I known Wilfred here since we were boys in high school. We played basketball together. I used to go out with his sister. So when Milan came down to me I couldn't just say no. I mean I think this is wrong, that the law should judge us. But Cilla's right, they don't do it. I know I said different but I just wanted to make sure you people meant what you said."

"If you're such close friends why didn't you say he was innocent?" Tony asked.

"We ain't close. We hardly ever even talk. But I know who he is. He ain't no criminal. And I voted him guilty because he said he was. He had a good reason but that don't make him innocent."

Kenya's baby was asleep on a big pillow on the floor next to his mother.

"Anybody else?" I asked.

"An eye for an eye and a tooth for a tooth," Milo Stone intoned.

Cilla and Gina nodded their agreement.

Wilfred stared straight ahead as if he had not heard. My heart grabbed at my ribcage. Angelique looked at me beseechingly.

"No," Milan's daughter cried. "That's wrong."

"He admitted to the murder," the ex-con Anthony said. "It's not a mistake."

"But why didn't you get together to try Lark?" she reasoned. "If you had done that Josie might have lived and Mr. Arna would never have had to get that mad."

"We can't take back the past," her father said, "only look at where we are today."

"But you can't, Daddy. It would be murder."

"Wilfred?" I asked. "Will you accept the judgment of this court?"

"Yes I will."

"Then," I said, "we have a motion for the death penalty on the table. I second Milo's motion. How many agree?"

Cilla and Milo, Gina, Kenya, Milan, Bells and Reggie agreed.

"Against?"

"I am," Angelique said but everyone else declined to respond.

I called for the vote again with the same results.

"Eight to one," I said. "Should we discuss the manner in which he should be executed?"

9.

"What about the baby?" Angelique asked the assembly.

"What about it?" Milan replied.

"Mr. Arna killed the baby's father. Isn't he responsible for that child's life?"

There was a long silence among us then. The men, all except Wilfred, sat forward while the women sat back considering the question of the woman I was coming to love.

"Child's right," Cilla said. "He has to make restitution for Lark's baby."

Milo Stone said, "Amen to that."

"Do you have any money, Mr. Arna?" Milo asked.

The condemned man opened his mouth but his voice was gone. He shook his head to answer the question.

I noticed that he was sweating heavily.

"He cain't pay for no child if he don't have the money," Reggie Simms said.

"He could pay if we let him live and work it off," Angelique said. "We could put off the penalty or change it to be that he will have to work the rest of his life payin' for the baby whose father he killed."

"What kind of punishment is that?" Bells complained. "Here he kill somebody an' we tell him that all he have to do is go back to work."

"It's justice not revenge we're after here," Anthony Porter said. "We're all guilty here. All of us and the police too. None of this had to happen but now that it has we need to find the balance. We need to try and make things right."

Bells squinted as if trying to peer into some far-off image or mirage.

I felt a smile crossing my face.

"What about you, Kenya?" I asked.

"He murdered that boy," she said thoughtfully. "What if he does it again? What if he's crazy and goes out and shoots Bells next? He know that Bells sold junk to his niece. What if he kills again?"

"He already said that he's willin' to die," Gina argued.

"But now if we let him live then maybe he'll let the anger grow again," Kenya rebutted.

"You wanna kill me, Mr. Arna?" Bells asked then.

"No," the murderer whispered. "I'll never do sumpin' like that again. You know it was just all that stuff all at once. I was crazy."

"I vote to let 'im do what he need to in order to care'a Wan's baby," Bells said. "I ain't afraid'a him."

The rest of the assembly mumbled their agreement. All except Kenya.

"Bells ain't worried 'bout him now," the young mother said. "But what happens when you broke again an' out in the alley sellin' drugs to some other child? What happens when Wilfred see you gettin' another girl to drop her draws to pay you?"

"I'll give him a job," Reggie said then. "You wanna work for me, Bells?"

Everyone was watching the boy as if he were the key to the trial.

"Yeah. Okay. All right. I'll work for you if that's what it takes to save Mr. Arna's life an,' an' Wan's baby."

"An' you can come live with me," Gina said to Wanita. "I got a little room you could sleep in. You could stay with me until your mother gets better."

Wilfred was looking around, a little bewildered it seemed because the attention was no longer on him and his crime.

"So it's either you put me to death or I pay for Wanita an' her child?" he asked.

"Yes," I said. "Do you accept?"

Wilfred stared at me with the reality dawning on him. After another moment he nodded.

"Let's vote on it," I said. "Everyone willing to commute Wilfred's sentence if he agrees to pay for Wanita and her child say aye."

They all, even Wanita, responded.

"That's about it," Anthony Porter said. "And you know this some serious shit here. I mean if my parole officer even hears that I was in a room like this, havin' a talk like this, I will be back in the penitentiary in less time than it took you to kill that man."

"Yes," Milan said. "The law is blind when it comes to Lark Thinnes selling drugs from his front door. The police don't see the prostitutes and muggers that breed around a place like that.

But they will see us. They will see men and women taking the law into their own hands. They will arrest us and convict us for passing judgment where they failed to act.

"So we have to make an oath here that tonight never happened."

"What if we have to meet again?" Reggie said. "What if a new drug dealer takes over Lark's apartment?"

"If he refuses our judgment we will have to bring the whole building together," I said. "We will meet in the laundry room and make up our minds where the law serves us and where it does not.

"If a criminal comes to us and asks us for justice we will give it to him. If he preys on us we will stand together and act accordingly."

"That's vigilantism," Milo Stone observed.

No one contradicted his words nor did anyone say he was wrong.

"What about Wanita?" Bells asked.

"I'll go live wit' Mama Gina," the child said, "at least until my mama is bettah."

"What about the gun?" Kenya, the pragmatist among us, asked.

"We'll leave that with Milan," I said, "and never mention it again."

That was a few minutes after three in the morning. After that everyone left and went to their beds. Wanita, avoiding looking at Wilfred, left with her godmother. Wilfred went to his lonely rooms to brood over what he'd done. Milo walked Cilla to her door and Tony left with Gina as usual. I walked Kenya and her sleeping baby to her apartment and then made my way back up to Milan's door.

Angelique was waiting there again. When I walked in and offered her my hand she leaned forward to kiss my lips. We shared three more kisses and then Milan cleared his throat. He was standing a few feet away down the hall. Wilfred's loaded pistol was in his hand.

Angelique rushed away to her room and Milan gestured with the gun hand shooing me toward the room where we'd held the trial.

I sat on Cilla's cushioned chair and Milo took the couch. He laid the gun next to his thigh.

"What if we decided on the death penalty?" the royal Ghanaian asked.

"First, I guess," I said, "we could offer him suicide. And if that didn't work, you and I, prosecution and defense, would have had to do it together."

"It will never last," Milan said. "Sooner or later the police will get us."

"But it's the right thing," I said, pretending I was him. I even tried to approximate his broad smile.

"But is it worth it?" the master planner asked me—his acolyte.

"I used to know a guy back in Oakland named Marquis Brown," I said. "I've been thinking about him all night. Marquis used to always say that the black man in this country carries his chains with him as if they were made out of gold.

"'If only the black man would drop them chains,' he used to say to me. 'Then maybe he could stand up proud and make a difference in his life.'"

"Have we made a difference?" the usually confident African asked.

"Wanita has a home," I said. "Bells has a job and Lark's baby's got a chance. You know Cilla was feeling good tonight and I'm sure 3BI will be affected by us too. Yes it's worth it. Anything is better than us believing that the lies of the law will bring us justice."

Milan gave me a weak smile and picked up the pistol.

"About my daughter," he said.

My heart flipped in its cavity and the room seemed to pulsate once, twice.

"She will be eighteen in seven weeks," the African continued. "If you still want her then I will not shoot you."

He handed me the gun and we both laughed and laughed.

10.

Wilfred was arrested but there were no witnesses or a weapon. Wanita claimed that she had been staying with her godmother. Gina and Bells testified that he had visited them that night.

I gave the pistol to Cilla telling her that she could turn it over to the police if Wilfred decided that he didn't have to pay for Wanita's child's needs.

Since that day things have begun to change in the Ida B. Wells building. No drug dealer has been able to keep a base of operations there and the police have paid us closer attention which has also cut down on crime.

Angelique and I dated for a while but then she moved to Accra to become a teacher. We are still the best of friends. I am her son's godfather. She came out to attend Cilla's funeral and once or twice when her father asked her to come and sit on one of our Circles of Judgment.

ARTICLE 8

A Legal Remedy

David Mitchell

CHARACTER DEVELOPMENT

It's a steaming mess and Jesus Christ only knows what'll happen.

Mine's a Jack Daniel's. Double.

Well, since you insist, Brother-of-Mine, here's the backstory.

The day before I flew home, I was on guard duty in the Eski— that's the interview room at the base. Hot as hell during the day, the Eski . . . Used to be a storeroom, and still looks like one, but we put in a one-way window. Come night, you freeze your tits off in there. Toseland—*that* Toseland—was interviewing this local doctor, with Sergeant Bax. The doctor's name was Shariba, and he'd been brought in about a militiaman who'd been killed a few days earlier. The militiaman's face'd been . . . Well, "dismantled by spanners" was one phrase that cropped up. After being tortured, he'd been shot in the heart, and left for dead. But the bullet, see, just grazed the heart, so he didn't die straight off. This taxi driver, who'd just stopped for a piss in a ditch, found him and took him to the hospital. Doctor Shariba'd operated on him, but his hemorrhaging was too chronic. But just before he died, he said the crew who'd done him over'd been taking orders from a British officer who'd looked like—I josh not—David Beckham.

With me so far?

Doctor Shariba'd trained in frigging Canterbury, of all places.

Spoke English better than me, and knew a foreign journalist or two.

He'd spoken to one of them about his mutilated patient.

So this hack, being a hack, sniffed around till he'd unearthed a few witnesses who'd seen—or claimed to have seen—the militiaman being bundled into an armored Red Cross vehicle, and before you know it, there's a piece in a paper back home asking if the War on Terror now includes Death Squads, and one of the minister's aides'd cut short our Major Dane's beauty sleep with orders to "establish the facts."

Which is why Doctor Shariba was sitting there in the Eski.

Thing is, the facts Toseland and Sergeant Bax wanted weren't the same as the facts the minister was after. They'd cuffed the doctor, like a common prisoner, and were asking him how many militiamen he'd patched up and sent on their merry way to slaughter innocent civilians and our peacekeepers.

"Slaughter is your business," says Shariba, "medicine is mine."

Toseland says that's very saintly, very Martin Luther King, but had he forgotten that the hospital he worked in was paid for by Coalition funds?

Shariba asks Toseland if *he*'d forgotten that the hospital he *once* worked in was razed by Coalition bombardment?

Bax asks Shariba if he'd enjoyed his five minutes of fame in a British newspaper.

Shariba says no, the article'd made his stomach churn.

"'Cause it misrepresented you?" checks Bax.

The doctor replies, "Because it represented the facts on the ground so well."

Toseland asks why he'd "germinated" rumors of "death squads" instead of raising the matter with the appropriate authorities?

Shariba half laughs, and is like, "'Appropriate authorities'? *Where?*"

Then Bax says, dead casual, he understands Shariba has twin boys.

Bax looks, and sounds, and *is,* a 100 percent frigging ASBO from an inbred rat nest on the Isle of Man. He'd often boasted he'd be serving life somewhere if a reformatory officer hadn't steered him to the army recruitment office.

But Shariba wasn't intimidated.

He'd seen so much death, I s'pose. Even more than us.

Calm as you please, Shariba just asks Bax if he is threatening his family.

Toseland says of course not, oh of course not, my colleague was merely pointing out that *if* the good doctor wants his children to grow up in a lawless shithole run by crazed Allah-intoxicated thugs answerable to no one, elected by no one, then inciting violence against the forces of reason is the right way to go about it.

Shariba just raises his wrists and rattles his handcuffs.

"Standard procedure," says Toseland, "for everyone's protection."

"My point," says the doctor, "precisely."

Bax asks Shariba who put him up to it. Which faction. Which cleric.

Shariba says, "Does my conscience count as a faction?"

Toseland tells him he's being used as a propaganda pawn.

Shariba says he's got a duty to highlight abuses, and a right, as per, he says, "the Universal Declaration of Human Rights."

Bax is like, "Come *a*-frickin-*gain*?"

The Universal Declaration of Human Rights. Then Shariba actually starts reciting it. There and then. This legal document.

Toseland and Bax are stunned as mullets. Then they shit themselves laughing. Toseland's like, "*We* thought this was the ninth century, camels and opium and ragheads with AK-57s as far as the eye can see, but no: it's High Court at the Old Bailey. What's next? An application for legal aid and a frappuccino?"

Just then Toseland's cell phone goes off.

He and Bax're required elsewhere, he says, for a little while.

So out they go. The Eski door clangs shut. Bolted.

With some interviewees—ones with murder instead of eyeballs—you keep your hand near your gun. Doctor Shariba, though, is not low risk, he's no risk. So I just stand in my corner and watch a foot above his head.

A minute passes.

Maybe there's the sound of a Hercules coming in, maybe not. Insects sort of tick in the walls, like clocks.

Doctor Shariba speaks. He says, "What part of the Disunited Kingdom are *you* from, Private?"

I tell him sentries can't speak with interviewees.

He guesses, "Somerset? Dorset? I went to Stonehenge, once."

I can't reply and I don't.

He says, "I expected stars and druids. I found fog and a motorway." Then he tells me how one time a Sikh physiotherapist from Newcastle upon Tyne came to work at his hospital. Nobody in the place understood a word he said. A nurse from Glasgow had to be his interpreter till all the staff got used to him.

Then I coughed. I'd waited for this cough to clear up for a month, but it'd never. Didn't want to gob it out on the floor, so I sort of spat it into a bit of paper.

Shariba says, "Bronchial infection is my guess, Private."

I s'pose I said, like, "Oh yeah?"

He says it's probably viral, but precautionary antibiotics wouldn't hurt.

I mutter, "Okay."

Some more minutes go by.

We was sweating like roast pigs. The midday heat there, is . . . like the sky is one massive sun, one massive . . . halogen bulb. Swear to God, you piss through your pores. There's a ceiling fan, but it's a pile of shit that just paddles heat around. There's some bottles of mineral water on a shelf, and Doctor Shariba asks, "May I have some water? Otherwise your medic will have to use a solution of electrolytes, ideally via a drip . . . assuming a clean needle would be spared for a raghead."

I brought him a bottle, unscrewed the cap and held it to his lips.

He glugged down half of it, and thanked me.

He'd seen my wedding ring and asked if I was married.

If Bax or Toseland was in the Observation Room, they'd've flayed me, so I daredn't answer.

Next up, Doctor Shariba asked if I knew Canterbury.

Again, I did my Coldstream-Guard-ignoring-a-tourist bit.

"Nice place, Canterbury," he said. "No IEDs hidden in ani-mal corpses. No illegal checkpoints. No *legal* checkpoints. A park for football and frisbees, the cathedral, a cinema, a nice Sainsbury's with a clever roof. Good place for children. You have children, don't you, Private?"

He clocked my surprise and said how our "Enlistment by Nature"—being a father, he meant—shows up, even on young faces. He asked if I'd got a boy or a girl. He wasn't expecting an answer, but that was cool. Separation from a wife and child is hard, he said, like he meant it, and knew it . . . maybe it *was* lucky we was in the Eski, 'cause if we was . . . *here*, say, in a cubby hole in the Black Swan, I might've ended up telling this Muslim stranger all about the twins, all about Chloe, all about Chris-in-Sales, Chris-on-42K, Chris-Who-Lives-in-Worcester-and-Not-in-a-Portakabin-in-a-War-Zone, and how Chloe says, "Oh, he's got a heart of gold but he's not my type at all," but won't meet my eye.

Fuck it, none of this is about that.

Another Jack Daniel's, Brother-of-Mine. A double, yeah.

If Doctor Shariba sounds cocky, he weren't: he just had guts.

Or p'raps he was talking ten-to-the-dozen to keep him-self calm.

Wish I'd just risked it and asked him why he hadn't stayed put. In Kent.

Why wasn't he playing football with his kids in a park in Canterbury?

Most of the Western-trained professionals got out before the invasion.

Had he come back just to help, where his people needed him most?

'Cause if that ain't heroism, what is?

Anyway, the Eski door's unbolted; in tromp Bax and Toseland.

Toseland orders me outside with a nod, and follows me.

I'm shitting my cacks he's going to bollock me for giving the prisoner some water, but no, he just takes me next door, to the Observation Room. Toseland says how Shariba's acting the cunny funt just 'cause he speaks a bit of legalese. He says how Sergeant Bax is now going to perform his Oscar-winning role of Uniformed-Thug-on-the-Edge-of-Breakdown.

Total eedjit *I* am, I ask Toseland what *is* the Universal Declaration of Human Rights?

Toseland just mutters, "Who *gives* a rat's turd, Private Yew."

He nods at the observation window. "Watch a Master at Work."

Sure enough, Bax is already flashing his MK1.

Toseland says this technique *is* permitted, sort of, as long as the cartridges are blanks. "Like water-boarding," he says, "without the water."

"The beauty is," Toseland adds, "Raghead *thinks* they're live."

Bax is faking losing it *really* well. His veins're bulging. Over the crackly intercom, he's all effing and blinding and *I do this for a living and I* know *when you're lying 'cause I've heard the* same fucking lies *day after day after day after fucking day and I've had it up to* here *with your bullshit excuses and your bullshit country.*

Doctor Shariba doesn't take his eyes off the gun.

"Where's your 'declaration of human rights' now, sunshine?" murmurs Toseland.

Toseland asks me if I know what dramatic irony is.

I say No, Sir, but the captain doesn't enlighten me.

Bax sort of . . . *wags* the pistol, like it's a stubby finger, going *you, you, you* . . .

Doctor Shariba says, "Is this what you call 'winning hearts and minds'?"

Then Bax's gun goes off.

The doctor's still there, his eyes shut in shock, and I'm like, *Okay, it's okay, he's okay, it was only a blank* . . .

But then why'd Bax give away his own bluff so soon?

This red hole in the doctor's forehead opens up, like a new eye.

His chair sort of squeaks . . . and his head cracks the table.

A live round'd got mixed up with blanks.

Bax is . . . y'know . . . like . . . something half melted in Madame Tussauds.

Toseland sort of hisses, like a puncture. He says, "You Royal Fuck-up."

Time for my therapy with Doctor Jack Daniel's: cheers.

Well, what a strange beastie is the British Army.

It'll issue us with binoculars so *shit* that I have to get you to buy a decent pair from Argos in Malvern sodding Link and send them out. It'll patch up VHF radios twenty years older than *us*—I josh not—so we have to use our mobiles. Great security, that. It'll order five hundred men from A to B but forget ground transport, so we have to scav Unimogs—think of a tin box on a tractor—off of the *Estonians* for Chrissakes. But give the British Army a nice cover-up, give it a rash of suicides at Deepcut Barracks, give it a juicy Bloody Sunday, then oh, just *watch*—world-class gold medal performances all round.

First thing Toseland did was to lock me in a cleaning cupboard.

Straight up. "View this as a Pause Button, Private," he said.

Two hours later, he brings me into the Eski. It stinks of disinfecting fluid, and it's spotless. Toseland tells me how Doctor Shariba left the base alive and well and cheerful at 16:00 hours after helping us establish the facts.

Toseland made me repeat it, three times, like we was Freemasons.

Alive and well and cheerful.

Toseland isn't a man who gives, like, explicit threats.

Explicit threats are for pussies.

My leave gets shoved forward. My clobber's even packed for me, so I can't mingle with Brooksy and the others: not so much as a "See ya in a month, Cocksuckers." Waiting for the transport plane, sat on a pile of tents in a hangar, humble Private

Yew gets a visit from Major Dane. Major Dane tells me how some truths are—get this—"curative" but others are "toxic," and he'd heard I'd witnessed a truth of the toxic variety, a "toxin" what'd "exacerbate tensions" if it ever reached certain quarters of the media. Do officers go on a special course, "How to Speak Utter Wank?" There are journalists, says Major Dane, who'll exhibit war's uglier faces, say "What a fearless fellow am I" and then fuck off to a tenured post in a College of Journalism *before* the retaliatory mortars come raining down on the regiment—not to mention the civilians, "as innocent in all of this, Private Yew," he says, "as Chloe, Jim and Jess."

Major Dane said their names like he was their uncle.

Me, I just wanted to belt the smug git one.

Three days and three planes later you, Brother-of-Mine, and Dad meet my train at Worcester Shrub Hill. A month's leave. Bosom of my Darling Wife. Home comforts. That afternoon in the Eski was all a bad dream, cleaned up and taken care of, and everything's hunky-dory, right?

Right?

Fast-forward to this evening when I'm doing Jimbo and Jess's bath. Jimbo's on about Chris-in-Sale's Toyota Landcruiser and their day at Legoland for the gazillionth time, and I'm like, *That's nice Jimbo*, and my mobile rings. It's either you or Dad 'cause this phone's new and nobody knows the number.

Captain Toseland is who it frickin' is.

He sort of . . . sings, deadpan, *Knowing Me and Owen Yew; Ah-haa; There is nothing we can do*. When I'm not exactly laughing my tits off, he asks what Abba ever did to me. I tell him I heard the joke a few times in my life, Sir, and he says, "I'll bet you have, Private, I'll bet you have." He's phoning from the base to keep me in the loop, he says, prior to my "homecoming" next month. Sergeant Bax is reassigned: that's Intelligence-heads, here today, gone tomorrow. Sadly, the valued member of the medical fraternity, Doctor Shariba, who left our base alive and well and cheerful was abducted and shot through the head. Some gang of ragheads did it. Wouldn't be the first time they'd killed a doctor for being a stooge of the Occupiers. Or for being educated. Or speaking English. Or shaving. Take your pick. Toseland then asks me if I share his fascination for linguistics.

I said I gave up French when I was fourteen 'cause I was crap at it.

Toseland says it's always fascinated him how there's so many words for the same thing . . . "whistleblower"; "informer"; "grass"; "backstabber"; "Judas." Didn't I find that fascinating too?

I say, "Yessir."

He says I've got a promising future. End of call.

Chloe comes in, sees my face, and asks who it was.

I said it was you, saying you might be a bit late.

Sorry, Bro. You might have to lie for me.

Swear to God, Toseland's a mind reader, even halfway round the planet.

I mean, look. This is all wrong.

It's so wrong, it's not even wrong. It's . . . poison.

It's here . . . under my ribs. I can feel it. It's a stone.

What happened *was* an accident . . .

Stupid and terrible and tragic, but to pretend it never happened, like, for *my* regiment, for Granddad's regiment, just to say, *No,* we *never did nothing, Sir, we never saw nothing, Sir, it was one of the other boys, Sir* . . .

That's what a coward does.

Who gives Doctor Shariba's twins *their* bath, now, eh?

S'pose I *do* keep my mouth shut?

What's the difference, then, between me and Bax?

But s'pose I speak up?

S'pose I find that same reporter and tell him, "Sergeant Bax shot Doctor Shariba by mistake and the army covered it up?"

Will that bring anyone back from the dead?

Maybe make an article in *The Guardian,* below the sudoku.

The news guy on Radio 4'll say, "How awful, army running amok as usual, and now, with news of Liverpool's first serious title challenge since 1991, here's Colin . . ."

Toseland made it pretty plain what he'd do to me.

He'd make sure Brooksy and the boys'd know what to think, too . . .

We'd die for each other. We *do* die for each other. Remember Granddad banging on about how your platoon's the tightest family you'll ever have? Dead right: that's why so many of us end up divorced. Back home, when you talk about the shit, the *bad* shit . . . and the *bad* dreams that go with the bad shit, people—civilians—Dad, Chloe, even you—you *say*, "It's okay, Owen, I understand" . . . and you ain't lying, you think you *do* get it, but *No*. You fricking don't. Sorry. You can't. Pray to God you never *do* know. Only other squaddies get it.

Were things this fucked-up for Granddad, in Egypt?

P'raps it's easier to justify shitty means in a clean good-versus-evil war?

Uncle Tom in the Falklands, even. Bad start, nasty middle, clear end . . .

What would *you* do?

'Cause I just dunno, Brother-of-Mine. I do not know.

Looked up the Universal Declaration of Human Rights.

Learned it off by heart, I did.

Want to hear it?

No One Shall Be Subjected to
Arbitrary Arrest, Detention, or Exile

Ariel Dorfman

INNOCENT PASSAGE

For Alvaro Varela and Eugenio Ahumada, with thanks. And
also, of course, to Pepe.

It was because of planes, that's why.

I saved your father because I was in love with planes since I can remember, perhaps before I can remember. No, I'm not exaggerating, young man. My granddad saw me—I must have been seven years old—playing in this very garden where we now sit, playing in what was then his garden, playing with my hands and the sun and shadows, the shadow of my hands dark and soaring on the grass, pretending I was a plane, a helicopter, a blimp, but not a bird, not a bird because my mouth was not chirping or singing, my mouth was buzzing like an engine. My granddad was sitting exactly where you are sitting now, young man, with your teacup filled with—What's that you're sipping? *Boldo,* I think you asked my wife for *boldo.* Your parents must have given you a fair share of Chilean herbs in Berlin, they must have steeped your adolescence in every taste they could muster, but nothing can compare to drinking what is homegrown in the country of your birth, nothing can compare to *boldo* grown in this very garden.

Over there, grown in that clump. Where I found myself, all those years ago, young man, I was over there, by those bushes, a seven-year-old kid steering his imaginary plane through the fo-

liage, trying to avoid a crash. My granddad called me over. He
called me over and grabbed my hands. They wanted to cut loose,
my hands, itching to reascend into the summer skies of Chile—
oh, there was no pollution back then; Santiago was still a magical valley, few cars, no *autopistas,* no smog, no fascists—and the
old man looked at my hands for a while as if trying to remember
something, someone, not letting them go, my hands, and then
he said: "*Quieres ser aviador.*" Not a question, just stating a
fact, that I wanted to be an aviator, and I nodded, yes. "And do
you know why, Benjamín Alonso," my granddad asked, "do you
know why, Benjy, why you want to be an aviator?"

I felt like pointing up into the air, down at the soil of that garden trapping my feet with its gravity. It was so obvious, so clear,
why wouldn't anyone want to fly a plane, why wouldn't anyone
want to be a plane, free oneself from the earth? But I said nothing. I had learned by then that when my granddad knew something I did not know he wouldn't pass it on to me unless I
showed patience; he was already teaching me that, contrary to
what most folks think, an orphan should never be in a hurry,
never try to make up for lost time, lost parents. Like you, young
man, you're not in a hurry at all, are you? You don't mind if
what I'm telling you does not seem to have the most remote connection to why you are here, the response to the question that
brought you to my house and that your father never once asked
me, never got around to asking me, and now here you are,
straight from the airport just like you said in your letter, tracked
me down and came to see me before saying hello to anyone
else in Chile, and even so, I can tell you're not the impatient
sort, you've waited for—what? thirty years? and you can wait a
bit more.

Patience, a difficult thing to learn, at any age. But I was seven
and owed everything to my grandparents, had no one but them
in the world. So I calmed my hands, let my *abuelo* hold them in
those large gruff paws of his that I had not inherited, I just
waited. "You were almost born on a plane," my granddad said.
"My daughter"—that's how he always referred to my long gone

mother, *mi hija,* never by her name, never Carola, never said
your mother, your mom, your *mamá,* only that: "*mi hija,* my
daughter was coming back home from Buenos Aires to have her
baby, to have you," my granddad said, "and I had written to
her quite sternly and your father had also warned her, six and a
half months pregnant is no time to take a trip and certainly not
by air, but she loved airplanes, like you do now, Benjy, and she
was stubborn, like you will be, Benjy, I can already see it. And of
course, my daughter began to feel those pangs as soon as the
plane breached the cordillera, when it was too late to fly back
safely to Mendoza, land in Argentina and have the child there,
on the other side of the mountains," my granddad gestured toward the mountains and I looked up at them, only for a second
and then back at him because he was already telling the rest of
the story. "As soon as you and she entered Chilean airspace,
Benjy, that's when the *parto* began. You wanted to come out into
the world up there, in the air, thousands of meters above the city
where the plane finally landed and where you were ultimately
born, where my daughter died a few hours later. Maybe if you
had been born on that plane, she would be alive today. But that's
not the point, neither here nor there. Here's what matters, Benjy:
before you took your first breath, you wanted to be an aviator."

But you haven't even tried your tea, young man.

Good. Even a sip must be comforting on a day like today, one
sip at a time, that's how we survive, people like you and me, orphans like I once was, like you are now, young man.

I want you to understand that all this is true, what I'm telling
you, what my granddad told me, about planes, I mean. My
mother had managed to hold on for an hour on that plane, two
hours, my granddad said, but he probably was adding some
color to the picture, spicing up the story. The plane circled the
overcast skies of Santiago and all my mother could do was suffer
and pray, trying to persuade God to open a patch in the clouds so
the pilot could land without smacking straight into the Tupun-
gato. "And do you know why I am telling you this now?" my
granddad asked. "I'm telling you this," my *abuelo* said, "because

you need to know now, right now, before you dream anymore about it, you need to know that you will never be an aviator, I will never allow you onto a plane while you depend on us, while I am alive to stop you. You are going to be a lawyer, Benjamín Alonso," my granddad said, "just as my daughter wanted you to be, just as your father always said, a lawyer like him, a lawyer like me, those are the skies you will fly: juridical skies, my boy. Because like the air we breathe, the law is everywhere and there is nothing better than to serve the law and make sure justice is done. Do you understand?"

Yes, yes, I understood. The law and justice and the air we breathe, it was a litany he liked to repeat to me, over and over. I went back to my game and he just watched me as night fell, did not try to stop me from playing, allowed me that small act of defiance against the planeless future he had outlined for me. I don't think he suspected that, as I swooped and looped and landed and took off in his garden, I was already hatching plans. I was only seven but I began to figure out, right here, right on that grass and next to those bushes that *está bien*, okay, I'd be a lawyer, fulfill the wishes of my dead parents, but if the law was everywhere, as my *abuelo* had so often proclaimed, then what about planes? Some lawyers had to be involved with planes, there had to be rules for those planes, how they come, how they go, where they alight, what happens if they crash, or if there's a crime, say, a murder, someone kills a passenger way up in that air that doesn't belong to anyone, then what, who investigates, who arrests the murderer, where do they put him on·trial? I can even remember, young man, wondering what would have happened if I had been born on that plane instead of Chile, what nation would claim me, what the law of the air mandated, I can remember asking myself that twisted question.

Years later, I found out the answer, to that question and many more. Because in law school there was, in fact, one course, an elective, in the last year of studies, Derecho Aeronáutico, and I told myself that maybe it was worth navigating the whole career of *abogacía* only in order to attend that class, that one class.

And I was the only student! I came into the *sala de clases* in March of 1973 and looked around and there was nobody else sitting there, not one soul. And I wondered if I had made some sort of mistake, but patience, patience, and it paid off, my patience, because a few minutes later, precisely as the hands of the clock on the wall ticked into the twelve o'clock noon position, Don Jacinto Prado waddled into the room. He had a briefcase in one roly-poly hand and a bundle of the day's newspapers under his arm. He nodded at me and carefully balanced the papers on the desk and sat himself down and said: "I read all the dailies, every one of them, from all sides of the political spectrum, from top to bottom, I keep informed. And I expect my students to be informed as well, to read at least two newspapers a day." And then he suggested that all the students should introduce themselves, every one of them, he said, as if there were ten of me, a hundred students sitting in that vacant room.

"I'm Benjamín Alonso," I said, almost in a hush, afraid of how solitary my voice would sound in that empty space, afraid that the echo would betray my nervousness, that he'd cancel the class, given that it was only me and no one else who would listen to his lectures.

"Benjamín Alonso, eh? I knew your father, I know your grandfather. Fine lawyers, both of them. And now you seem determined to follow in their footsteps. If you approve this course, naturally. Until then you are, let us say, up in the air."

And at that moment, as if to prove how precarious everything was at that time in Chile's history, a stone came hurtling through the window, splattering glass on the blackboard. Don Jacinto did not acknowledge the interruption. He merely joined his two pudgy hands quite serenely together and said: "Before I can admit you to this class, I need, however, to ask you one question, Sr. Alonso, to see if you are worthy of being my student, to ensure you will not abandon ship, parachute away, let us say, when the going gets rough, when we encounter some turbulence."

I was about to placate him, explain that this was the one class I would never dream of abandoning, that I had waited more than six years for this chance, that—but my professor raised a lone index finger, surprisingly long and slender, and waved it, shushing me. "Paris," he said, "1919, Sr. Alonso. Why should you know, why should I be asking you anything about that city, let us say, and that date?"

Outside I could hear shouts and chants, skirmishes, another stone colliding with another window pane. The right-wing students had been threatening to take over the Escuela de Leyes, one more coordinated attack on the normal activities of the university, one more disruption of life in Chile as the conflict with the Popular Unity government escalated, one more attempt to create chaos in every last corner of Santiago and bring down the government of Salvador Allende, our president, my president, *mi presidente*. I should have been out there, with my comrades, defending the grounds of the law school, defending the government the people had elected, defending our revolution, our peaceful, our legal, our different revolution, our right to radically change the laws that ruled our lives. I knew that Don Jacinto Prado was an ardent supporter of the Popular Unity government, a friend of Allende himself, I had heard, and I almost made the mistake of presuming that this meant that he would understand if I stood up, excused myself for the moment, suggest that I respond to his question later, next class, next week, I almost said to him that what mattered was to defeat fascism, that our lives hung in the balance, peace and justice and—but he seemed, despite his own political convictions, oblivious to the need for his one student to rush out into the courtyard and join the battle for democracy, the battle for the future of Chile.

Don Jacinto Prado repeated, "Paris 1919. What do you say, Sr. Alonso?"

A torrent of words rushed out of my mouth: the Convention of Paris, the first international treaty regulating aeronautics, the establishment of the Comisión Internacional de Navegación Aérea, the urgent need to distinguish between public and private planes, the discussions about how to certify pilots in one country and have their diplomas recognized in another one.

Signed in Paris on October 13, 1919. And none too soon, as on August 25 of that same year, London and Paris had been joined by the first commercial air service on a daily basis.

Don Jacinto smiled for the first time that day and his bald head seemed to shine as he pursed his lips and smacked them together approvingly, jutted out his chin, making me notice a slight dimple that reminded me of Kirk Douglas, you know, in *Spartacus*. And then imparted his verdict.

"*Muy bien*, Sr. Alonso. You have gained admission to this very exclusive seminar. Given the extraordinary circumstances that this university and our *dulce patria* are living through, I will adjourn until one week from today. Here is the pertinent bibliography. Your assignment: the freedom of the air, Sr. Alonso. Its doctrine, its predecessors, its limits. Next week, Sr. Alonso. Regardless of what happens out there, do you understand? Even if the government is in peril, even if democracy is about to founder, even if there is an earthquake that levels this city or a Boeing crashes onto your grandfather's estimable house, Sr. Alonso, I expect those ten pages, typewritten, double-spaced, fully annotated. With at least a reference to hijacking and the jurisdictional dilemmas that ensue from such acts of piracy. Is that understood?"

Adults keep on asking you that, if you've understood. As if I had no ears, no eyes. But there was always a stray rebellious streak in me, so I couldn't help it, I had to ask, I had to throw him a question sharp as a stone, I wanted to see if anything could shatter the austere window of words he seemed to have erected against the unruliness and confusion of the world.

"Even if the government is overthrown?" I asked. "Even if there's a military coup?"

I saw him hesitate, I think I saw him hesitate, something clouding over in his eyes, some surfacing of future or past grief deeper than I was able to comprehend at that point. But if it was there, he recovered rapidly, fondled the bibliography as if it were sacred, handed it to me. "No matter what happens," Don Jacinto Prado insisted, and his brown frog eyes watched me snatch those pieces of paper and scurry for the exit; he must have heard me shouting at the top of my lungs in defense of the government and the revolution and his friend Salvador Allende, my voice allowing itself to avoid politeness as soon as I had left the temple of his classroom. I like to think that he stayed there for a while listening to his lone student enter the fray so that the air of my land and his land would remain, in effect, free.

But when the coup came, young man, when September of 1973 descended upon us and the military took over the country, he did not come to class. Don Jacinto Prado did not return to that classroom; he never stepped inside university grounds ever again. Like your father. Your father never set foot again in one of those barracks he loved so much; once he closed the door behind him on that September 11, 1973, he didn't return to them, not ever. Lucky for him, I guess, because that postponed his capture, that may have saved his life. After all, if they'd caught him early on, I never would have been—well, ready, you know, to have offered help; you wouldn't even be here, young man, not ever have come visiting, not have had the chance to ask someone like me why and how I saved someone like him, like your father. In those first days and weeks after the coup, I wasn't thinking of saving anyone but myself, oh yes, I was on the run.

I didn't really need to hide, but my granddad thought it prudent. He didn't approve of my political activities, even if they were not that strident compared with some of the others at the law school. He said I should lay low while he made some *averiguaciones,* he said, inquiries from his military friends as to what sort of trouble I might be in. A false alarm, it turned out. They were going to expel me from the university, that was obvious, but they had bigger fish to fry for the moment. My granddad received that message from some adulterous colonel whose patrimony he had saved when the wayward officer's wife had tried to strip him of house, automobile and children when she'd caught him in bed with the maid, something of that sort. At any rate, my *abuelo* told me I was safe for now, but César Ruiz Danyau, the air force general appointed by Pinochet as the new *inter-*

ventor y rector of the Universidad de Chile, would start eliminating students one week from today, that I had seven days to graduate. "Go," my granddad said. "I've set up an appointment with the dean of the law school. Yes, I know, you haven't always hit it off well with him, he's a conservative, he sees you as something of a troublemaker; but Mariano's an old classmate and is willing to lend a helping hand. Go!"

My *abuelo* saw me waver. People were being rounded up in stadiums, executed in the night, bodies were floating down the Mapocho, and I was going to try and finagle myself a certificate? Graduate? What for?

"Benjamín!" my granddad exclaimed. "I swore to my daughter that you'd be a lawyer, and I swore to your father that I would take care of you, and I'm not going to let you ruin your life. I wasn't going to tell you this till you graduated, but I had a surprise for you and now—listen, if you get that certificate, the next day you're on a plane to Madrid. You can complete your law degree there."

I was astonished. Hadn't he sworn he would never approve such a move, hadn't he repeated each time we saw a plane flying over our garden that my mother would not have wanted me to board one of those infernal contraptions, hadn't he—

As if my *abuelo* could read my thoughts, he said:

"She'll forgive me, when I meet her in the next life, I'm sure my daughter will forgive me," that's what he said. "You want to travel, Benjy? The ticket is waiting for you. Your dreams, your whole life, everything is waiting for you. Go!"

Dean Mariano Canales was as affable as my granddad had said he would be. No reproaches, no resentment, no lectures. All my grades were in, he said, everything was in order, except, he said, for . . . Derecho Aeronáutico. The last course, the only one I had to finish up, that's all I needed, Derecho Aeronáutico with Don Jacinto Prado.

Who was probably dead, or arrested at the very least, who had not shown his face at the law school in a month, who—

I lowered my voice:

"Haven't they . . . ?"

The dean lowered his voice even more.

"Arrested him?" the dean said. "No, he's gone into"—and here his voice slipped into a whisper, such a faint wisp of a whisper that I almost had to read his lips to realize what he was saying—"into clandestinity."

No, young man, I'm not tired, not at all. Thanks for asking. Perhaps this is a polite way of suggesting that you're the one who's tired? You must be wondering where this is leading, when I will reach the part of this story that concerns you, but now that you've come to this garden in Chile from thousands of miles away, I think you'll just have to trust me. Like your father did, like your mother did. This story does lead to your father and the day he thought he would die, the day he thought he would be facing a firing squad.

So. Where was I? Oh yes, Don Jacinto Prado. I had always known, of course, that my professor was political, you know, a friend of Allende and all that, but Don Jacinto Prado had, in fact, or so the dean implied, been far more important than anyone had suspected, was the unlikely recipient of all sorts of lists of names and safe houses and contacts and who knows what else. If the military caught him, well, your father may have told you that some months after I saved him I was—but that's neither here nor there, I'm sure he explained that they were rather good at dragging information out of prisoners. He probably didn't like to talk about those things; maybe you never asked him. Because we don't need to ask about things like that in this country or abroad either; we don't need to, do we?

Not back then either. Not what the dean wanted to talk about, not what I wanted to talk about.

"Bring me your grade and his signature," Mariano Canales said, that's what he said. "I don't care if it's on a napkin or scrawled on the inside cover of a book or even if you get it tattooed onto your arm. Just bring back the grade, man, and the signature—no, no, don't worry, I'd recognize Jacinto's signature anywhere. Just bring the damn thing to me—and I'll have your certificate issued. You've got seven days. Because I don't think I'll last in this job for more than a week; I'll be out the door soon enough. Hurry, man, there's no time to lose."

Hurry? Where? How to find a man who didn't want to be found, that the police couldn't find, with all their resources? And I had nothing to go on. Not one person at the university, friend or foe, wanted to talk, to even meet my eyes: everybody, a potential enemy, everybody silent, everybody I knew had been carted off or was in hiding or, worse still, they pretended they had renounced politics, had turned over a new leaf. Jacinto Prado? Who's Jacinto Prado? It was as if my rotund professor had ceased to exist. I managed to wangle his address out of the dean, though he told me it would be useless, there would be no one there: Jacinto Prado was a widower, no children, no immediate family. I paid a visit anyway, crossed the city in the midst of a late October drizzle. I didn't like that neighborhood, took it as an ominous sign that he lived in Recoleta, near the cemetery where both my parents were buried, just around the corner from where my father's car had slid into a tree, on the way to the airport, of course; it would have had to be in the pouring rain on the way to the damn airport, and of course I had to pass that very tree that still had the gash of a long scar on its bark, pass that scar, that tree, on my way to Don Jacinto's house, and of course, of course, his house had to be a wreck. The secret police had raided it and burned the books, smashed the door to splinters and left all the windows open, and thieves—or the soldiers themselves—had done the rest. Some kind soul had left the water running. I waded in, as if I could find some clue on the walls, something, anything, floating on the liquid surface of room after flooded room.

I picked up a photo, drifting by on the waters, backside up, I scooped it up and turned it over and it was of Don Jacinto Prado, little Jacinto it was, when he was a child of seven, holding aloft a model airplane in both of his chubby hands, in a garden not unlike the garden of my grandfather.

I looked at him, at the boy who would someday be my professor, the boy who was now as gone and lost as my professor and I followed his gaze upward and that's when I saw it, another photo. Up on a wall. A photograph that had been spared. Behind a jigsaw web of glass that had been cracked open, probably by a rifle butt, a faded group of men in top hats, all of them with beards, all of them solemn. The date: October 13, 1919. The place: Paris. And fastened to the ornate, old-fashioned black frame, a little bronze pin and an attached shield inscribed with the words, 2ND PANAMERICAN AERONAUTIC EXPOSITION ATLANTIC CITY MAY 1919. Not one of those men in the photo—I counted twenty-six of them—could conceivably be alive today, but they were murmuring to me from the past, they were telling me how to save myself now that the air I was breathing, that Jacinto Prado was breathing in some anonymous attic of this city, now that the air of our Chile was no longer free, now that the air of Chile was awaiting the departure of my plane. Do you know what I did?

I went to every newspaper in Santiago and bought an ad in each one of them, an ad that would run for five days: HAVE YOU LOST A PHOTO OF THE PARIS AERONAUTIC CONVENTION OF 1919? IF YOU WANT TO RETRIEVE IT, PLEASE CALL 43640; that was our phone number at my grandparents' house. That phone I had grown up next to, hearing it ring and rushing to answer in case it was for me, a girl or a friend or someone who wanted to speak to my granddad, my grandma. I loved being the intermediary, the messenger, and now, here I was, waiting for the call that might change my life. Patience, patience. Merely sitting there, hoping that Don Jacinto Prado still read all the papers, top to bottom, still kept some of his old habits alive in clandestinity. Hoping he would understand. Patience, indeed, because the first four days passed and . . . nothing. Not even crank calls.

On the fifth morning, the last morning the ad was running, the phone rang and I recognized the voice on the other end. He recognized mine as well.

"Sr. Alonso? Have you now become a pirate who plunders houses? Is that what you have gleaned from my classes?"

"Don Jacinto, I need to speak to you."

"You're not the only one."

"I'm aware of that, sir. I would not have sent you this message if I were not desperate."

"And that photo, do you really have it?"

"Yes, sir. And the pin. I can bring them to wherever you wish, I can—"

He gave me a street corner where we could meet the next day. Tomorrow, he said, Huérfanos con Ahumada. At twelve noon, he said. Sharp, he said.

I was pacing up and down those streets by eleven—not the best tactic if I didn't want to call attention to myself, but at that point I knew nothing about the rituals of clandestinity and repression. I was the bearer of several pieces of paper, all possible sizes, three or four pens I had tried out, scrawled and scribbled with to make sure none would fail me. In my briefcase, next to all my notes, six months of coursework, the bibliography and copies of all my assignments, anything, everything I could think of, so agitated that I missed seeing from where Don Jacinto Prado had materialized when he abruptly hooked his arm into mine and started to walk down Ahumada. Not that he was that recognizable either. He had dyed his hair, shaved his sideburns, lost something like eight kilos, was sporting a beret that concealed his bald pate, but he still rolled with the same duck-like gait, still the same voice, dry and concise and vaguely self-deprecatory, even once I handed him the photo of Paris and the pin, even after I told him why I needed him so desperately that I had enticed him out of the shadows. Tomorrow, I said, I had till tomorrow afternoon to get his grades in and receive my certificate. Told him that my life depended on it.

"Your life?" Don Jacinto Prado repeated my phrase back at me, a certain bemused severity in his voice, stopped briefly to adjust a scarf he was wearing in spite of the hot October noonday sun and that served to conceal his prominent Kirk Douglas chin. "If you think your life depends on something like this, then we're in—let's just say, you're in trouble."

"I am in trouble, sir."

"In trouble, eh? Tell me something, Sr. Alonso. Once you receive this certificate, if you receive this certificate, that is, well then, what happens next?"

I told him I would be leaving the country. "My first plane," I told him, "I've never been on a plane." I didn't offer him the circumstances of my accidental relationship with aircraft, my mother, my birth, her death, my granddad, my father slamming into the tree on the way to the airport, my hands in the garden just like the one he had once played in. We were in the *centro,* teeming with *transeúntes* and spies, strolling up and down that crowded street full of wretched Chileans looking down at the pavement, passing by beggars and prostitutes and shoppers and armed policemen, a squad of soldiers on a jeep steeling their gaze on each passer-by from behind a mounted machine gun; it was not the moment to entertain him as I am entertaining you, young man, there was no time, as we have now, to spool out the whole story, but the urgency in my throat, the distress in my arm he had hooked into, all of that must have convinced him.

"Yes," he said, "some of us must leave, I suppose. I suppose there will be many who will leave and will not come back. Yes, I suppose so. I suppose that is a solution. Though I would like to state that I have never been abroad, never stepped on a plane or been up in that air we have both been so assiduously studying for the last six months."

I had no idea what he was talking about. Just as I guess you, young man, have not the slightest inkling of where this story is going, of why I am telling you all this, what I have never told anyone. Anyone but Marta, that is, and that's as if I had told it to myself, the other part of myself. But talking of Marta, she should be with us any moment now.

Perhaps you would be so good as to wheel me into the dining room? Yes, through the terrace. Marta has prepared lunch for us, something special with you in mind. As soon as she received your letter saying you were coming, she said: that young man deserves something special. No need to thank her, or me, no need at all. It's a pleasure. She loves doing it, believe me. She loves hosting people, taking care of them, of me.

You won't mind if I don't eat very much. I haven't been hungry as of late, things that happen to men like me as we grow older, I'm sure you have seen this before, doctor's orders, you know, that sort of thing. Here, try this Sauvignon Blanc. It goes well with these *empanadas,* right, Marta? *De queso y de pino y de pollito con choclo y también de espinaca.* I've heard that exiles eat endless *empanadas,* but those are nostalgic *empanadas,* young man, saddened by distance, while these—eat them, go ahead, they're all for you, piping hot, delicious.

Where were we? Oh yes, Don Jacinto said I was in trouble and then mused about not having ever traveled outside Chile, never having boarded a plane, right, and I told him this was an emergency and he nodded, yes, he was aware that everything nowadays in Chile was an emergency, but that still didn't solve his main problem, my main problem. "Let's say, for the sake of argument," Don Jacinto muttered as we paced up and down that street like two conspirators in a play, "let's just say that I had completed the syllabus, finished the course material, so to speak, taught you all that you need to know. Not the case, but let's just say it. There. I said it. I still couldn't assign a final grade to you, attest to your expertise; I mean, Sr. Alonso, there has been no exam." And now he stopped in front of the Café Haiti and those frog eyes of his which he could not disguise took a good long look, from below those overhanging and unmistakable lids he searched the window pane for an answer, but all that came to him were the two of us reflected back. I saw myself so tall by his side that we seemed like two cheerless clowns, Abbott and Costello, Laurel and Hardy, he was fat and small and I was elongated and almost emaciated with worry—you may not realize it, now that I'm in a wheelchair, that I used to be considered a tall man, especially by Chilean standards. And there we were, *el gordo y el flaco,* both of us equally glum, and for some reason our relentless despondency made him laugh, the first and the only time I heard him as much as chortle.

And then he said: "The question is whether you are ready. Ready for the exam, I mean; Sr. Alonso, are you in any intellectual condition to show me what you have learned during the last six months?"

"Do you mean now, sir? Here, sir, here and now?"

"I've a good mind to fail you right away for the very thought that I could interrogate you without having given myself time to prepare or given your own person fair notice. Now? Of course not. Tomorrow, man, if you are so inclined. It will have to be an oral exam, of course, I can't stay put in any one place for very long, for obvious reasons. I'll tell you where you should meet me. Not here. Never come back to the same place. I'll tell you where."

I studied all night long. The next morning, bleary-eyed from reading, full of dates and definitions, overflowing with my grandfather's favorite coffee and my grandmother's favorite cookies and possible and improbable questions—Why did the surveillance agreement negotiated in Geneva in 1955 between Bulganin and Eisenhower ultimately fail? How do territorial waters differ from national airspace? How can we differentiate the International Civil Aviation Organization from the Civil Air Navigation Services Organization? What major revisions to the Chicago Convention of 1944 were introduced in 1969 and what areas of transportation do they regulate? and on and on—the next morning at ten o'clock sharp I walked onto the platform of the Estación Mapocho and, not finding my professor there, stuck to his instructions *al pie de la letra* and clambered onto the second compartment of the train going from Santiago to Valparaíso. "Get a round-trip ticket," Don Jacinto had ordered, "and don't worry if I'm not on board. Oh yes, one more thing: make sure nobody follows you."

He wasn't on board and, as far as I could tell, I hadn't been followed. Who would want to follow me anyway and what did I know about resistance to Pinochet? I was just a mildly left-wing law student about to graduate, a young man who was scared shitless by his first experience with death and was being given the chance to finally step onto that flying machine he had been dreaming about since before his birth.

Or maybe not. Maybe I would never earn that ticket my granddad was holding in abeyance, maybe the exam would never take place, now that the train was leaving the Estación Mapocho and there was no sign of Don Jacinto, maybe something had happened to him, maybe I had slogged away all night in vain, maybe this and maybe that, the clackety-clack of the tracks punctuating my thoughts, puncturing them, until all of a sudden he was standing in front of me, swaying back and forth to the rhythm of the train.

"Change places," was the first thing he said before I could even greet him. "I get dizzy if I'm not facing the direction the train is going in." And then, as soon as he was warming the seat I had just occupied: "*Está bien*, Sr. Alonso. Let's see. Innocent passage. What do you say if you define it, demarcate that concept, develop it, so to speak."

Ha! I knew that one. Innocent passage. The right of all ships to engage in continuous and expeditious surface passage through the territorial sea of foreign coastal states in a manner not prejudicial to its peace, good order, or security. Passage includes stopping and anchoring, but only if incidental to ordinary navigation or necessary by *force majeure* or distress, or for the purpose of rendering assistance to persons, ships or aircraft in danger or distress. There! I had remembered the whole thing.

"And force majeure," Don Jacinto said calmly, as if distress were entirely foreign to him, as if nothing could be more ordinary than to examine a student on a train barreling quite expeditiously through the territorial surface of the Santiago countryside, "what is *force majeure* and how does admiralty law influence the laws that govern the air and not the water?"

The interrogation went on and on. Don Jacinto winged me up and down each article of each treaty, each subordinate clause, nuance and ambiguity. I don't think you would be interested in his questions or my answers, young man. I think you're ready for the next course. Marta? Yes, oh yes, a *mariscal*. I'm sure you know some of these. *Machas*, we now export, so you may have eaten some from cans, there in Berlin. That is a *loco,* I'm sure you've heard of it, the famous Chilean abalone, but you can't have ever tasted one, nor that *picoroco,* those *cholgas*, *ostiones*— and that, over there, that's *chapalele.*

Good. I like young people with an appetite. There was nothing like that on the train, young man, I can assure you, and I wouldn't have dared to even buy a sandwich—though there were vendors at each stop hawking their wares from the platform, but neither Don Jacinto nor I were in a mood to eat anything. Back then it took more than two hours to get to Valparaíso by train, and when we arrived there, he did not want us to descend—for the first time, I remarked on a hint of anxiety in his demeanor. He peeked out the window and then clumsily, like a snail, withdrew back into the safety of the carriage. "We'll stay here," he said, "and resume the exam once the train departs for Santiago."

We remained idly on those sweaty seats for a long while and I had trouble keeping my eyes off a stain on Don Jacinto's collar, just below the scarf still adorning his neck, still hiding his chin, I troubled myself by wondering if he had been wearing that shirt for many days, who washed it for him now that he was on the run, where did he sleep, in what sort of unfamiliar neighborhood had he awoken this morning, where would he go once this interrogation on aeronautical law was over. I did not like those thoughts and yet could not avoid them, no matter how I tried to displace them by going over in my mind all the information I had swollen into my brain throughout the long night. So it was a relief when a whistle split the air and the locomotive started up. The train lurched forward and Don Jacinto stood up and switched places with me again, still concerned about his bouts of dizziness. As soon as he was reseated, my professor was at it once more with even more enthusiasm, but this time, during this second stage of the journey, my performance began to, well, falter.

Maybe I was tired, maybe it was that stain—of some sort of tomato sauce, perhaps a drop of blood, some reddish smear—on
his collar, maybe that's what distracted me, the thought of his
pudgy hands scrubbing away the blot, in some dismal place
where he could only spend a night and no more, and maybe it
was that image of him in nothing but his undershirt, scrubbing
away, but by then I was flubbing the answers. I had started out
full blast a few hours ago, like a plane roaring as it took off into
the open skies, up, up and away, but now my wings were wob-
bly, I was losing altitude and pressure and my engines were folding, I was diving down into an abyss, and just when I thought,
that's it, I've come all this way, I've studied for almost seven
years, I went from the law school to his ruined house, from the
newspapers with the ad to the phone call and the rendezvous in
the center of the city, and all that cramming last night and now
these hours of grilling and that blemish on his collar and all for
nothing, all so my professor could say, sorry, you need to come
back next year and repeat the whole course, really exert yourself,
be worthy of my trust, just as I was about to crash land, just as
we were chugging in to the station of Til Til, he said: "*Está bien,*
Sr. Alonso. I believe that is sufficient. Do you happen to be carrying a piece of paper and a pen?" And I was so dumbfounded I
almost didn't hand them over to him; I wasn't sure where I had
put any paper, any pen, what with so many questions and notes
and cross-examination and errant thoughts. "Hurry up, man. I
have to get down here in Til Til and you have to get back to law
school before the day is done." And then I remembered where I
had deposited that ballpoint pen and that piece of paper, lodged
inside a copy of who knows what international treaty, next to his
photo as a child that I had not dared return to him, which I intended to give back as soon as the exam was over, concerned that
he might think this was an invasion of his privacy, and now was
not the time, either, I had to get that signature, on a paper napkin even, Mariano Canales had said, and I passed pen and paper
to Don Jacinto and he wrote out my name as the train began to
brake and hiss, wrote out a five out of seven—not bad, not a

terrible grade at all, generous indeed, given my increasingly poor and frantic performance—and then his signature, with a flourish that a king would have envied.

"Thank you, thank you."

"No need to thank me. I was only doing my duty. I want you to know, Sr. Alonso, that all year long, you have been by far, yes, by far the best student in the class."

And, without another word, not a handshake, not an explanation, he stood up and walked to the end of the carriage and I saw him descend onto the dusty platform of that station halfway between Santiago and Valparaíso.

Why was he disembarking there? How would he get home? Was he going to take the next train, a few hours hence? Amble into the nearby sleepy town of Til Til and grab a bus to Santiago? Or had he arranged for someone to pick him up at this unexpected stop? Was he worried that he might have been identified at the Valparaíso station?

And then I realized that, all this time, I had never given more than a fleeting thought to the danger he had been facing since the coup, the further danger I had thrust him in, it suddenly dawned on me what it meant to have phoned me and set up our meeting and then walked arm in arm through the bustle of downtown Santiago and how many hours he had splurged on this train to examine his only student, the thought hit me at the precise moment when the train started up again, just as I saw Don Jacinto Prado on the platform, his hands in his pockets, I saw Don Jacinto Prado at the exact mathematical moment when I noticed and he noticed the two men who were sauntering toward him, I saw him turn without any sign of haste, almost nonchalantly, and behind him were two other men, not advancing, merely cutting off any possible escape. The train was accelerating now and I managed to catch a glimpse of his face still half hidden behind that scarf, or maybe he was the one who caught a glimpse of my face gone pale as the wagon passed him by, passed his solitary roly-poly figure waiting for the two men, the four men, to reach him, only bid me farewell by not looking at me anymore, not indicating to anyone who might be watching the scene that he had not been alone on that train, that someone like me was speeding to Santiago.

Here, try this Cabernet. None for me, I'm afraid. Those days are gone. But the red will go well with the next course, Marta's going to offer you a choice. Here they are, *gracias, Martita,* here, look: *pastel de choclo,* smell that brown surface of sugar so toasted that it makes the air crackle, and here's a *cazuela a la chilena,* look at this breast of chicken splashed down in the middle of this succulent soup, with its potatoes and carrots and slivers of onion, you must have had this many times over in Berlin, your mother must have cooked this for you and your father every Sunday, like so many other families far from home. Friends of mine, in letters from abroad, they'd ask for ingredients, recipes, there were tears on those pieces of paper that had traveled so far, we sit down every Sunday to a *cazuela,* a *pastel de choclo,* the one meal no child far from his land is supposed to miss—and you can't have been an exception, young man. Well, at least try it, a bite out of each dish and you'll see, you won't stop until you're done, you finish that *cazuela* or that *pastel de choclo* or both and I will finish this story where I'm heading for Santiago and Don Jacinto Prado—where was he, what would they do to him? It was not something I wanted to think about, there, on board on that train, not then, not yet. My first question was more selfish, impatient: What about me, what will happen to me? Am I in danger? Did they follow me? Are they following me now? Were they on the train all this time; are there two, four men, still on this train? What if they search my briefcase and find the photo of that little boy with the model airplane; what if they recognize him as little Jacinto; what if, what if, what if? And, of course, another question only half formulated under my fear, because it would have made me focus on what was happening to him at that very moment: what would he tell them, when would they extract my name from his lips? Would they be waiting for me as soon as my train arrived in Santiago?

But there was no one there—at least, to my inexperienced

eyes. Only the usual crowd at the Estación Mapocho, the usual gray Santiago afternoon. But what did I know? What if they were only *al acecho,* waiting, *agazapados,* hoping that I would lead them to someone else, someone even more vital than Don Jacinto, what if they had been keeping me under surveillance ever since I had ventured into that flooded house in Recoleta and walked away with that photo of the Paris Convention of 1919, the photo and the pin that were now inside his briefcase, that were now being examined by those four men?

Not the right time to think those thoughts. Only time to rush to the law school. My deadline was upon me, not to belabor the fact that the latest events had made it even more crucial that I hand the dean the sheet of paper with that flourish of a signature attesting to my everlasting knowledge of the intricacies of the laws that governed the air and space I had so wanted to explore before I could even remember and that I needed to explore again, soon, get the hell out of Chile if they were looking for me, soon, soon, before Don Jacinto Prado offered those men my name to stop them from doing whatever they were doing to him in some nearby cellar. That was all that cluttered my panic-stricken mind: accompany Dean Mariano Canales down the marble corridors of the law school to the registrar's office and get that five out of seven officially recorded and take the transcript of my brilliant university career and hurry into the main office and watch the dean browbeat the employee there into filling out the papers and then receive the document certifying that I had completed my studies, that I was on my way to being the lawyer my mother had wanted me to be, the same certificate my father had once held in his hands, the profession my granddad still practiced. And then, it happened, that's when it happened.

I guess I could call it a revelation.

Because I didn't go home. I didn't go and show my certificate to my granddad, didn't collect my ticket, didn't pack my bags, didn't head for the airport, didn't board that plane that had been waiting for me since before my birth. I didn't leave Chile.

Clutching the certificate that stated that I was almost a lawyer, a man who had been trained to see justice done, to see that laws, new and old, were upheld, armed with that piece of paper tendered to me by Don Jacinto Prado, I went to Santa Mónica Street, went to see a friend. Pablo Leighton had been by far the brightest of our generation—a few years older than I, he had made a name for himself in the Allende government working out the details of the nationalization of the copper mines—and I had heard that, after the coup, instead of seeking asylum or going into hiding or just lying low, he had been one of the founders, the head lawyer, in fact, of the Comité de Cooperación Para la Paz; your father must have told you how the churches, different Christian organizations, plus the head rabbi of Chile, had set up the—but of course you know this, your mother came to the Comité as soon as she heard they had captured your father and were going to put him in front of a military tribunal, you—

Marta, could you hand me the certificate? Yes, that one, thanks. And you need to decide something, young man, if you'll have some coffee or some more *boldo* with your dessert or perhaps after the dessert. No, we insist. *Leche nevada* or flan or maybe something else? Marta bought a *torta de lucuma* at the Café Tavelli—please, no bother, no bother at all.

The certificate. Here it is. That's what I placed in front of my friend Pablo, on his desk. I was a bit out of breath, had run up the four flights of stairs, taking two steps in one bound, those were the days, when I could use these legs, before that night when—

But Pablo and the certificate, Pablo looking at the certificate, across from me, as close as you are now, young man. "Congratulations," he said. And after looking more closely at the date on the certificate: "Double congratulations. The deadline for students like you, I'm told, was today. But I don't think you came here to receive a hug from me, Benjamín. Everybody who comes here is in trouble. What sort of trouble are you in?"

At that moment, from the next room, a sudden wail went up, a long wrenching howl of pain, as if someone were tearing out their entrails, almost like a vomit of pain, the throat seared by something worse than sobs, worse than screams.

"She just found out," Pablo said. "The mother. About her boy. The body they found, just yesterday, it belongs to him, to her boy." Pablo paused. "I can't tell you how glad I am that this time I wasn't the one who had to tell her, that it was Ana María's turn."

We waited for the howl to subside. It did not. It only began to grow weaker when we heard the woman next door being led out of that room, led down the corridor and the stairs, taken downstairs to a kitchen or a bathroom—I knew nothing about that old house that looked like a castle, with two towers and an attic where I now sat with Pablo, I knew nothing about that mansion except that it was owned by the Archbishop of Santiago, that it was being used now to receive women like that mother, young men like me.

"So you're in trouble," Pablo repeated.

And I took a deep breath and said no, I wasn't the one in trouble. The one in trouble was someone else, and I wanted to know what I could do to help that man, what could be done, I said there had to be something legal, a writ of habeas corpus, something, anything, there had to be something we could do, he had no relatives that I knew of.

"Who is it?"

"Don Jacinto Prado."

"Oh. Damn. You know, I almost took his course before graduating, but then—other interests, that sort of thing. I'd heard he was on the run . . . So they got him?"

"Yes."

"And you think I can help?"

"I don't know who else I can turn to."

Pablo gazed at me for a long while. I was soon to find out how many others, men and women, had sat in front of his desk before I had made my own hasty visit. I was soon to find out that a habeas corpus had already been presented on behalf of the ministers of Salvador Allende captured on September 11 and that the Court of Appeals had rejected that habeas corpus, had refused to even consider that petition or any other recourse. I was soon to find out that Pablo was already debating with his colleagues whether it made sense at this point to present a collective writ of habeas corpus on behalf of a growing series of men like Jacinto Prado, youngsters like the son of that wailing woman, whether the lawyers of the Comité should act publicly now or wait until more evidence and documentation were available, whether it was better to work silently behind the scenes for the moment and get the junta to just as silently release the prisoners it had already acknowledged were in custody rather than provoke and exacerbate the authorities into disappearing even more citizens. In the years ahead I was to find out many things. But I knew nothing then. Only that the fear that had been crawling inside my stomach had not abated, but that it could be controlled, that was what I was learning, that was what I would learn in the days and weeks and months that were to come.

Because Pablo said: "Maybe we can save Don Jacinto, maybe we can't. I'll try to find out who has him, where he might be. But meanwhile, there are others in need of assistance and you, you've got that certificate. We need people like you," Pablo said. "Some people are killed outright, their bodies dumped on a street or in a ditch, and some people are kidnapped and we can't find even a trace of them, can't tell if they'll be freed, if they're alive or dead. But others, more and more of late, are dragged in front of a military judge and tried and then, well, most of them are being executed. And when the sentence has been commuted, that's still no guarantee they will survive, because someone higher up in the military flies in on some helicopter and orders them killed anyway. And recently, a few who have been let go, well, they end up murdered in their homes or on the street. There is no pattern to it yet, except sheer terror. But in the midst of the chaos, a few can be saved, perhaps more than a few, things can be done, small things, big things; we can't really know yet what works and what doesn't work. A couple of trials that are about to take place, military tribunals, things of that sort. Would you like to help?"

And that's how I met your father. A few weeks later. As he

hadn't been captured the day of the coup, like the rest of the group he belonged to, his was a special case, different from the other air force officers loyal to Allende who had been arrested and accused of treason and sedition. It was absurd, a legal travesty: they were being accused of being enemies of the state because they had defended the constitutional government, defended the state, in fact, one could say. Though everything was absurd back then. Those officers were all in terrible trouble. But your father, when the secret police nabbed Captain Emilio Meneses, you can believe me that he found himself in even more of a fix. The fact that he had gone into hiding was taken as proof of his guilt, proof that he had been engaging in subversive activities after the military takeover. He was my first case. And I was, incredibly, successful. I got his sentence reduced to three years and I also persuaded the judge to expel him immediately from the country. Beginner's luck. I know, I know, in your letter you said your father called it a miracle; your mother spoke of me as some sort of saint. But I never got to explain to him how it had happened, that's how quickly they deported him.

And somehow, he never asked. He just sent a message, sent me one message each birthday of mine, just a card with the word *Gracias* on it, that was all, just that word, regularly coming on my birthday; who knows how he found out what day it was, but there it was. And I kept expecting him to turn up on my doorstep when democracy returned and some of the military men loyal to Allende came home. I wondered if some day he wouldn't appear himself, sit there where you are sitting, young man, but he sent his son instead; he never made it back home, did he? Never wanted to ever again see his native land, step on this soil. And never found out from me, face-to-face, why and how I was able to save him.

Shall we go out again into the garden? Yes, I'd like that. Yes, that's where I'd like to end this story. Yes, here is a perfect place, here is where my grandfather sat all those years ago as I dreamed of lifting my body up, up, up into the air.

Planes. I told you it was because of planes.

That air force judge was a colonel who had studied with Jacinto Prado, had been obsessed all his life, just like me, with the laws surrounding aeronautics. He somehow found out about my interest, maybe Pablo Leighton, crafty fox that he was, slipped that information to that judge. At any rate, after one of the sessions he was holding to try your father, he suggested we share some coffee in his chambers—not really chambers, just a room with a desk and some files in an air force barracks, but in Chile we like to call things by names other than what they really are. So we got to talking about this and that, the last course he had taken at the Escuela de Leyes, he had also been the only student of Don Jacinto that year. And I mentioned our professor's penchant for reading all newspapers from top to bottom and the judge mentioned Don Jacinto's fascination with the Paris Convention of 1919, and then we chatted about his jutting Kirk Douglas chin and the difference between maritime law and the law that governs the air above and around us. And I did not say a word about the exam on that train or those men in Til Til, not one word, because that judge knew perfectly well that Don Jacinto was missing and in custody, or maybe already dead, I said nothing because my client was not my missing professor but the very present Captain Meneses, and my patience paid off, patience, patience, that is what I have tried to learn, what Pinochet taught me better than my grandfather and better even than Don Jacinto, Pinochet forced me to be patient, and as I said, it paid off, not rushing in, not forcing anything, just praying that my tactic would work, my aeronautical connection—and it did, it did, because the day before sentencing, the colonel said to me— he wasn't whispering, just telling me how things were, very matter of fact: "I can do nothing for Don Jacinto, have no idea who has him or why or anything at all. There are things even I should not ask. But I can do something for your man, I can do something for him, in the name of Don Jacinto, in his name and memory I can do something for your officer."

And that was it. No miracle. Nothing heroic. It just happened. I didn't choose your father, I hadn't met him before, I wasn't ever prepared for that sort of career. I didn't do anything other than show up and know more about planes than any other lawyer in Chile except for Don Jacinto Prado and that air force judge. That's how life is at times. One man dies, one man lives. One man leaves, one man stays. That's how it is at times. One day you're a boy of seven playing with your hands like a plane in a garden where your grandfather watches you and then, in what seems like the snap of a finger, there is someone else standing there by that clump of bushes and I am here in the same chair where that old man used to sit.

You know, I never did travel, young man. I've never set foot outside Chile. The closest I ever got to a plane was Marta. A stewardess, she used to be a hostess on LAN Chile, met me when I was convalescent, let's put it that way, her cousin was the doctor who took care of me, my legs, after, you know . . . She's tried to convince me that we should take a trip, get on one of those planes droning up there, see the world, but she knows and I know that there's only one man who could persuade me to travel and it's not likely that man is still alive, not after thirty-some years. So I guess I'll just stay here in Santiago. I'll keep working as a lawyer and be glad that I don't have to defend anyone like your father, that those days are over.

And now, yes, of course, you must be going, you have so many other people to visit, so many places you have not seen since you were a child and forced to leave with your mother and your father, so much to do and here I am, I've just spent your first whole day telling you this story.

I'm only sorry that I never got to speak to your father before he died. I would have liked to have had a chance to tell him what I've now told you, what I've only told one person in the world before you, only told this to Marta, Marta and now you.

What's that?

Why you?

Why should I trust you, why have we prepared all this food, brought you into our home, treated you like a son?

It's really quite simple. You're the first. Nobody else, my boy.

Nobody else ever asked me; you're the first person in the whole world to come to my house and ask what happened, how I came to be the man I am now, the man I became.

And talking of now, I wonder if we might go inside one last time. There's a photo I'd like you to see. The photograph of Don Jacinto, the one I rescued from those waters and never managed to return. Maybe you'd like to take a look at Don Jacinto when he was a child, so proud, that boy, of his model airplane, there in his own garden and dreaming of being a pilot, we could do that before you leave, maybe, while we drink one long last cup of herb tea, you and me and, of course, my Marta, maybe we could do that together before you leave, before you say goodbye.

The Right to a Fair Trial

Amit Chaudhuri

ANIRUDDHA: THE LATEST INSTALLMENT

"The mind is restless, O Arjuna."
—The charioteer Krishna addresses the great warrior
Arjuna in the Bhagavad Gita

Then there's Aniruddha, who can't help doing what he isn't supposed to—not because he is subversive, but from being helpless. Or it could be quite the opposite of subversiveness, a sense of meek, silent, pure-hearted obedience to a mysterious impulse, a mysterious thought, which has come to him suddenly and has no clear provenance. And since there's no rational cause to deny that impulse, it seems like superstition to disobey it: it's like abandoning education—and we know how educated Aniruddha is—and beginning to believe the universe has its own ordained purposes.

Aniruddha has, of course, been trying for a while now to transplant a Bengali domestic scene onto England—onto North London to be exact. He's been quite successful in this; the fact that he's Bengali and his partner English, the fact that he's gay—these facts shouldn't distract us from his continuance of an essentially Bengali tradition: the island-like, delicately cultivated microcosm in an English city, neither of the city nor out of it. Here, as in the old relationships between the Indophile and the exotic, quixotic, shy object of adoration, the adorer from the former colonizing power would seem to be the stronger partner, and to be in control; while, actually, it was usually the other way round—the

slightly scatterbrained and vulnerable expatriate held, inscruta-
bly and finally, the key.

It was the same with Chris and Aniruddha. The Bengali depended
completely upon the Englishman (who worked at a newspaper, but in marketing); and the Englishman's life would have
fallen apart if the Bengali ever left him. It was, in other words, a
typical—even completely conventional—Bengali intercultural
marriage.

Except that they were not married; and Aniruddha's relatives in Calcutta (of an ancient, century-old Brahmo family, lost in their inbred decorum and nervous gentility, and of which Aniruddha is
the perhaps last unwitting protagonist) didn't know about the
true nature of the arrangement. Or—who knows; anything's possible these days—they may have guessed, and felt no reason, in
their remoteness, to disturb or question it.

In all the acceptable ways, Aniruddha was a "good" Bengali
spouse and son. He'd taken a first in history from Oxford; he
was now researching on recurrent homoerotic tropes in the stories of migrant indentured labour in nineteenth-century India.

Besides all his winning, youthful, Bengali qualities—his in-
genuous bookishness; his undemonstrative but sure instinct as
a shopper; his charitable and accommodating ways as a com-
panion, especially regarding space on the king-size bed and
the possession of the duvet; his sweetly undemanding but frail
apparition when he fell ill—in addition to all this he was a ter-
rific social asset. His modesty and his Bengali-inflected erudi-
tion were augmented by his culinary proficiency, which went
almost logically with his thinness; he had not only picked up,
perfected, and bettered Bengali recipes for cabbage, daal, and
goat's meat from his mother and various ancient, indubitable
sources; he made spicy Moroccan lamb with couscous, and scal-
lops in wine.

More important, neither he nor Chris had any time for the gay
scene. In fact, if you hadn't known, or noticed, that Aniruddha

was gay, you might have thought he was slightly, irksomely homophobic. Even in the first discovery of the truth of his sexuality in Oxford and suburban London—in those bewildering, rapid, euphoric years—he'd had no time at all for gay pubs, cruising, cottaging, camp soirées, or earrings: all these made him shudder and balk delicately as they would any other bookish, serious, mother-loving, conservative, marriageable Bengali boy. He and Chris wanted, strongly, conventional happiness; and because, to a large extent, they had it, they could impart to others—their friends and colleagues—the deep, immovable tranquillity that conventionality can have.

And yet there were those moments when he lost control and became a bit reckless—"stupid" is probably a better word. They were subtle, undermining and in the end (thankfully) not serious. At most, they were recurrent and unfathomable; you could call them a sort of stubborn perversity. For instance, that time when Aniruddha and Chris decided to go to East London for an Indian meal in early November. It had turned cold, and Aniruddha wanted to wear his silk scarf. It was very subdued and becoming. But he decided not to wear a sweater, because the scarf looked best with a jacket and shirt. Before going out, Aniruddha had worn the sweater, tucked the scarf in, and then, in a swift decisive movement, taken the sweater off. That night, he caught a cold that in three days turned into a hacking bronchitis, and finally debilitated and punished him for two months.

There was also the time, long ago, when Aniruddha was still a student and picked up, probably for the first and last time, a young, oddly radiant stranger on the Tube, a charming, slightly scruffy man whose name, I think, was Will—and (more at Will's gentle insistence) kissed him. Aniruddha escaped quickly once he reached his stop—Marble Arch—but, although he'd never looked back once over his shoulder, couldn't stop worrying for more than a week later of what he might have contracted from that touch—the liquid, ineffable touch—of wet saliva.

* * *

I could point to other, similar examples. The question is: why
did Aniruddha do these things—give in to what wasn't even a
temptation, but almost an impulse, a small tremor and doubt and
irritation that does no more than disturb and partly dislodge the
furniture? Especially when he knew—even diligently invented,
in his head—the consequences? Someone else would hardly have
suffered comparably (in terms of worrying and remorse) as a
result of their actions, would have been hardly aware of an aberration or a slip. He was, after all, a staunchly peace-loving, law-
abiding boy with academic intentions: why do things—not even
real transgressions, real wrongdoings or lapses—that made you
shiver with disproportionate, almost visible, anxiety later?

This brings me to a rather silly but revealing anecdote that will bear
out to you, I think, what I've been saying about Aniruddha. It
was just a week after the 7th July bombings; train services had
just resumed at King's Cross. Every person who lived in London
or had anything to do with it or used the Tube had had a week-
long orgy of "It could have been me or my wife" or "I could have
been on that train" or "My cousin usually takes that train at that
time" convulsions, recriminations, and epiphanies. Hours had
been expended watching, on television, images of the provoca-
tively burst bus on Tavistock Square, the mysterious samaritan
leading by the hand the nebulous, inhuman bandaged woman on
the curb of Euston Road, and especially the CCTV footage of the
homegrown, matter-of-fact, occasionally almost jaunty young
men who seemed to have congregated in the morning to go out
together somewhere—clearly nothing important or official about
their purpose, but something vaguely interesting—and were
now, with an almost seductive dreariness and unthinkingness,
pushing their tickets dutifully into the ticket machines. That in-
termediate world especially turned out to be fascinating and at
once chilling and unthinkably remote and deceptively familiar,
that little world between the ticket desk and the barrier where
people hover with something between indecision and purpose-
fulness before they disappear down the escalator. Everyone wit-

nessed, on BBC news and Newsnight and Channel 4 and ITN, and sometimes all four, again and again and again these humdrum episodes that would lead to the irrefutable quality of what happened later; "everyone" included Aniruddha.

Then an announcement was made, amusing and dispiriting and democratic in its own way: "Please refrain from carrying rucksacks on the Tube." Everyone heard about this and laughed; or protested, as if it were an infringement of their personal freedoms; or nodded dourly and profoundly. Aniruddha read about it, or saw a large sign somewhere, large letters scrawled on a board in a bold marker pen. He resolved at once—"I must not carry a rucksack"—because he hated, and studiedly steered clear of, trouble.

Anyway, he wasn't a rucksack-carrying sort; he had an expectedly elegant London Review Bookshop cloth bag and a large translucent plastic one from the British Library; he didn't even enormously mind tottering about with a pile of books in his arms. Which is why what he did the next day is difficult to understand; it was silly and, as Chris said, it was "annoying." Aniruddha was planning to go to the British Library to write his second chapter, the first day he'd resume his research after the small holocaust and desperate spectacle of 7th July. He thought to himself, "Let me take my books in my Samsonite zip-up shoulder bag"—because he had an exceptional load that day—*The Erotics of Labour, Journey to Guyana, The Falling Body,* and other scholarly excursions in the fields of history and cultural studies—and then he thought: "Chris's rucksack might be better." Why he didn't put that thought out of his mind is hard to tell; but it's also typical of the Aniruddha we know. The next thing that came to him was a sort of ornamental caveat, a prevarication: "No, it's best to avoid rucksacks for a while now." Then, trouble returned the next moment, posing as logic and objectivity: "No, there's more space in the rucksack—easier to lug around (and what's wrong with rucksacks?)." And then he busied himself in a flurry of activity, retrieving the ugly object from Chris's cupboard, emptying it,

filling it with his clumsy, necessary tomes. None of those state-
ments that occurred to him in that last spell of reflection, before
he embarked on his decision, are really refutable; but you can see
why, in hindsight, they are infuriating.

Off he went, then, this "good," unsuspecting, clean-conscienced
Bengali youth, emerging into King's Cross, slightly bent and ancient, along with the booming, still mildly nervous, stream of
commuters. He was near the ticket barrier, about to merge form-
lessly with the queue, when a policeman-type came near him and
murmured: "Sir, could you step aside for a minute?" Aniruddha
is used to obeying orders; and this kept him from being entirely
flustered and unhappy. But it led to embarrassment, the polite
policeman looming over Aniruddha and speaking sideways into
his radio while the Bengali stood there with his thin, slightly famished, indeterminate air, and others glanced and then looked
away while pushing steadily toward the barrier. My point is:
none of this was really necessary; if one were to be cruel to
Aniruddha, one might claim it was so premeditated as almost
to be a performance; but one can also predict with a certain
confidence—that Aniruddha will of course do this kind of thing
(self-delaying tactics, really) again, and again, and possibly again.
No lessons are, or can be, learned by Aniruddha; his brain's just
wired that way. They took him to a small, fluorescently lit neigh-
boring room, where two other apologetic-looking young men
(noticeably less scholarly than Aniruddha) were seated. Chris's
rucksack was solemnly scanned and then (because the men at
work were almost equally embarrassed)—but I won't bore you
with what are quite tedious details. You can picture the scene in
the room.

"What do we do with Aniruddha, though?" That was the
question that circulated later, among Chris's friends, as well as
Aniruddha's Bengali and old Oxbridge ones, after they'd heard
what had transpired from Aniruddha's own sheepish admission.
"You have to be a tiny bit more careful, more sensible," is the
consensus. Also—these were Chris's stern but forgiving words—

you shouldn't go out of your way *looking* for trouble, should you? Then Chris laughed, and Aniruddha's particularly charming when he's mortified.

That's the latest dispatch on Aniruddha, but you're probably right in concluding that another is imminent.

Presumed Innocent

Petina Gappah

AN INCIDENT AT LUNCHTIME

No matter how many times they go back and forth between the city center and the Dales, Gazza can never feel comfortable. As the van glides along the crushed purple carpet of jacaranda petals and moves past the manicured lawns and high walls of Borrowdale, Greendale, Colne Valley and Highlands, Gazza longs for the chaos of the townships, where something happens when you least expect it and there is no knowing what incident the day will bring. And so it is that whenever they leave the suburbs and reach the outskirts of town, he expels a loud and relieved whistle. The sight of Harare's twenty-floor skyscrapers makes him feel relaxed enough to raise his voice. The distant sight of the building reminds him of something he read recently, he cannot be sure where he read it, but he remembers the main point.

"Do you know, *Mukoma*Prosper," he says to the driver, "that the Reserve Bank building is the highest building between Johannesburg and Nairobi?"

"That's because there is nothing else, no large city, between Johannesburg and Nairobi," Prosper says.

Gazza accepts this assertion without question: as always, he bows to Prosper's superior knowledge. Prosper stayed at school right up to O level, and when it came to things that come out of books, he always knows what he is talking about.

The sight of the city center is also Gazza's cue to start collecting the fares.

"Eh, ngatibatanidzei tione vabereki nevaberekesi."

In obedience to his command, the passengers prepare to pass their fares. The sign placed prominently on the inside of the windshield says 12 PASSENGERS ONLY, but what applies in Japan does not necessarily do for Zimbabwe. Extra seats have been built in to make room for an additional eight, so that twenty passengers sit balancing each on one buttock, not falling over only because they are so tightly packed that they do not need seatbelts.

It is a death trap, this vehicle; the fire extinguisher under the seat is a merely decorative object, as its contents have long been emptied and were never replaced. The doors no longer have the original glass from the van's factory in Japan; instead, thick sheets of semi-transparent sheeting are the only thing that prevents the wind from blowing the heads of the passengers against each other. The floor is rusted with bits of it sticking out in dangerous spikes. Just last week, a woman cut herself on the rusty door, which has long since lost the rubber coating that hid its sharp edges. The driver's seatbelt is no longer capable of adjusting to suit the size of its wearer, so that whenever they spot a police checkpoint, Prosper has to sit on the extra length to make it appear as though it fits. As for the passenger seatbelt, it is a memory as distant as the front indicator lights, which disappeared even before Gazza started working in this van. The first thing he noticed about Prosper when he met him was how dark his right arm was compared to the rest of his body; no small wonder, as it was the arm that did all the indicating.

And so from the outside, this van is a hazard on wheels. To Gazza on the inside, it is his kingdom. In here he reigns supreme. He has mastered the skills of the good *hwindi.* A good *hwindi,* he knows, is more than a conductor, more than a collector of fares. He is a necessary part of the driving: because he does his job well, Prosper can concentrate on the job in hand, on driving, knowing that Gazza will shout out their destination and collect passengers, collect the right amount of fares, bully the maximum number of passengers into squashing next to each other in the small space available and generally maintain order in the taxi.

And none is more fitted to occupy the small space available for a *hwindi* than Gazza, the light-footed boy whose future once glittered, perhaps not as brightly as that of the real Gazza in England, the football hero from whom he had taken the name, but it had shone all the same. On the football field of Zengeza High One, Gazza had forgotten his stammer, forgotten hunger even, as he dribbled and passed and headed for the goal. Now, as he yelled out "Mbare Nash, Mbare Nash, *one ariega, handei ku*Greytsome Park, *one more Kamfinsa handei tione*," he scarcely remembered that his dreams had died with his mother. She was replaced by a woman who thought it entirely reasonable that all his father's resources should be focused on educating their two children and the three she had brought from a previous marriage, and so Gazza's schooling had stopped, and with it had ended his bicycle kicks, and his gifted ability to head from any angle. No more school and no football for Gazza, and all that remained was the name.

He whistles now, Gazza, and calls out again to the passengers to pass him the fares. He cannot move around himself for this purpose, the car is too tightly packed for that, and so passengers do this for him; his only job is to ensure that the twenty passengers all give him the right amount.

The notes are passed to him, he counts them, whisking them expertly without so much as lifting a finger to his mouth to lick the notes. That is done by the less expert *hwindi;* he is an old hand, Gazza, and knows just the right way to move his finger to separate each note from the next.

"Wait a minute," he says after counting twice. "There is not enough here. We are five million short."

The passengers mumble and look sullen.

"We are five million short," he says again.

There is no response until Prosper says from behind the wheel, "Just give the money back, and each will take what they had."

A woman in a blue woolen hat looks up. "Five million short?" she asks.

"Yes, *ambuya,*" he says. "I should have two hundred million, but I have one hundred ninety-five million, which means that I am short five million."

His use of the customary form *ambuya* is a formality, she is just a woman in a blue hat to him, a passenger who is about to become an irritant, as her next words prove.

"How much is the fare?" she asks.

"*Ambuya,*" his voice is laced with impatience now, "how can you board a taxi when you do not know the fare?"

"*Hezvo,* my son," she says with asperity, "there is no need to talk like this to your mother. All you need to do is tell me how much it is."

He has the grace to look slightly ashamed, and with less impatience says, "It is ten million."

"But I thought the fare was five million."

"No, it is ten million."

"It was five million this morning."

"That was this morning, *ambuya.*"

"But I paid five million just this morning," she argues. "Things can't just change in three hours."

"They can and they do, *ambuya.*"

"And they did," laughs Prosper.

"And I only got on *pa*Grain Marketing."

The impatience is back in Gazza's voice as he says, "Do you see that sign?"

The woman looks at the signs above the driver's head. In addition to the one specifying the optimum number of passengers as twelve, there is another that says JESUS IS MY DRIVER, another that says 100 PERCENT TALIBAN, and a fourth that says SAME FARE FOR EVERY DISTANCE.

"If you drive ten meters in this car, you still pay ten million," says Gazza.

The woman gives up, and, mumbling, digs into her bag, counts

out her millions as if they were so many precious jewels, and hands
them to the man in front of her, who passes them on to Gazza.

"*Pa*corner," says a voice.

Gazza bangs on the roof to stop the van. Two people jump out
to be replaced by two more.

"*Handei, handei*," he says, and the van moves off again in a
cloud of petrol and exhaust fumes.

One of the new passengers is a young woman whose perfume
now fights the exhaust fumes to fill the van. Gazza has to push
against the man next to him to let her pass. He stumbles and collapses into the man.

"Sorry, sorry, *vakuru*," he says, as his arm brushes past the
man's jacket pocket. He then turns to the woman and says, "*Ko-*
sister, smart as you are, where are you off to?"

The woman ignores him, takes out her mobile phone and begins to type out a text message.

"Did you see this smart sister of mine?" Gazza calls out to
Prosper.

"I can smell her from here," Prosper says.

At the back of the van, an old man lets out a sneeze that startles the child sitting just in front of him.

"*Maiwe* sister," Gazza says in mock horror, "look what you
have done now, you have made that poor old man sneeze from
your perfume."

"Maybe it is the ancestral spirit in him that does not like modern times," says Prosper, as he chuckles.

"And modern women," adds Gazza.

The sneezing man scowls and says, "*Munataura zvamunoziva
mhani, mazvinzwa*." He sneezes again.

As the words are spoken in the sing-song voice associated with
Malawian farm laborers and domestic workers, it is the cause of
much laughter for Prosper and Gazza.

Prosper says to Gazza, "You had better watch out now that
watsamwisa ava SekuruMuChawa. You have made him angry, and
you know how these maBhurandaya are with their medicines.

Now you won't hear the end of it. You will probably find a little Malawian *tokoloshi* waiting for you at home."

"*Achimwene*," says Gazza to the old man. "This is how city women smell, you had better get used to it, this is not the reserves."

"Who said I have come from the reserves?" the old man says. "And who said anything about Malawi? You should know what you are talking about before you just start to talk-talk for nothing. You *hwindi,* that is all you know how to do, you just talk-talk for nothing."

But Gazza's mind has moved on, and he now entertains Prosper, and by extension the entire van, with a story of a *n'anga* from Mufakose, a man of Malawian origin, who restores lost property and removes the male organs of adulterous men who use them on women that are not theirs.

"*Havaiti kani*," Gazza says, "*Mumwe mu*face felt a strong urge to urinate after a long drinking session, so he goes to the toilet, *waketa*, and he looks down, and there is nothing there, can you imagine? Nothing at all. Like a doll, *waketa*, he was just like a smooth doll."

The woman whose perfume had been the cause of this conversation raises her voice to speak up.

"*Pa*Holiday Inn," she says.

But Gazza is concentrating on describing just how the man with the missing appendage reacted to his missing appendage, and he does not hear.

"I said I am getting off at the Holiday Inn," the woman says again, just at the moment the van drives past the Holiday Inn.

"Why didn't you ask me before?" Gazza says with irritation. "You know we can't stop here now."

"She did ask you," the man over whom he fell says to him.

"Who exactly are you, and what's it to you?" Gazza says.

The man gives him a look of pure loathing but subsides into silence. The van stops at the next permitted corner, just before the traffic lights, and the woman gets off, leaving her perfume lingering in the van. As she crosses Samora Machel Avenue, Gazza shouts, "That's why you do nothing but spend time just looking at yourself in the mirror all day and combing your hair."

"Your mother is uglier than Joseph Chinotimba's arse," the woman shouts back.

Gazza makes as though to go after her, but the light changes, Prosper laughs and the van moves forward. Gazza now abandons the story of the man with the missing genitalia to describe in graphic detail just what he would do to the departed woman if he got the chance.

"A woman like that," he concludes, "just needs a good seeing to, that's all she needs."

On this triumphant note, he starts to whistle a Macheso tune.

They are now in the center of the city.

As the van passes Second Street, Gazza spots a familiar face at the steering wheel of an omnibus that has stopped on the other side of the street.

"Wait, *Mukoma*Prosper, he says. "I have to give something to that *mu*face."

He jumps out and weaves his way in the traffic, a fleet-footed blur in his white Arsenal shirt, evading the cars as he once dribbled past opponents to score the winning goal on the fields of Zengeza High One until he reaches the other side of the street. He stops at the driver's window. The passengers cannot see him; his back is to them as he talks to the driver. In less than five minutes, he is back, running through the traffic, and banging on the roof as the van moves off.

He seems even more cheerful than before and turns to the man sitting next to him. "Why so glum, my brother?" he says. "Are you still sore because I fell on you? Sorry *zvenyu blaz*, but *inotambika*. Don't worry, be happy."

And with that, he starts to sing, *don't worry, be happy*.

The sound of a ringing phone cuts into Gazza's song. It belongs to a woman in the back, who says hello, will call you back in a low voice, and hangs up. The man seated next to Gazza, who had put his hand to the inside pocket of his jacket when the phone started to ring, now pats his jacket pockets.

"My phone," he says.

He tries to stand up and fails. With difficulty, he pats his trouser pockets.

"I don't have my phone," he says.

His voice begins to rise in panic.

"My phone," he says again.

Gazza shakes his head.

"*Aiwa vakuru*," he says. "It will not come just because you call for it. A phone is not a cow, you know, or a dog."

"Maybe you left it at home," Prosper calls from the front.

The man turns his accusing eye on Gazza. "It was you," he says. "It was you who took my phone."

"What?"

"You took my phone," the man says again.

"You must be mad," Gazza says.

"Yes, that's right," says the woman in the blue hat. "He brushed against you, he pretended to fall, I saw him."

"And me," says the man with the Malawian accent. "And me, I saw the whole thing."

Another voice comes from the back and says, "All these *vanah-windi* are thieves, we all know that they will take anything if given the opportunity. He must have taken it when he brushed against you."

Prosper now drives the van into the taxi rank, where it halts to allow the passengers to disembark. They get out of the vehicle, but no one moves away from the van; instead they crowd around Gazza.

"I did not take your phone," he says. "I don't have a phone on me, look."

He holds out his empty hands.

"I have nothing in my hands or pockets apart from the money I collected from you all."

The man searches him roughly, but finds nothing.

"He must have given it to someone," the woman in the blue hat says.

"Yah, that's what happened," says the man with the Malawian accent. "He gave it to that man, the one he talked to at Second Street."

"I saw him pass something."

"It was nothing," Gazza says.

"I saw it all," says a voice.

"It wasn't a phone, what I gave him. It was, that is, it wasn't. It wasn't a phone. It was . . . I took nothing."

Gazza's eyes are round with fear now, his thoughts run confused, faster than speech allows, and his stammer, so long conquered, is back.

"We are going to the police." The man with the missing phone takes Gazza by the upper arm and begins to march him away. He is almost shaking with anger, but his grip on Gazza is tight.

The commotion has now attracted a crowd around the rank. What has happened, what has happened, whisper the onlookers. The answer sweeps across the rank. A thief has been caught, a *hwindi,* you know how they are, such thieves, all of them. He has been caught red-handed, actually caught, just imagine, with his hand in someone's pocket.

"*Mukoma*Prosper," Gazza pleads. He is no longer the cocky brazen Gazza of a few moments before, but a frightened, stammering boy.

"*Mukoma*, please, tell them, I have not taken anything. I swear on my mother who is buried at Serima mission, I did not take anything from anyone."

Prosper tries to prize him out of the man's arms. "*Varume,*" he says, "we will go to the police and sort it out."

"You are in it together." The man with the missing phone rounds on Prosper. "He took it, I know he did."

"But how can you be so sure, can you prove he took it?" Prosper asks.

"He has to prove he did not take it."

"How do I prove that I did not do something I did not do," Gazza says. "I swear on the dead, I swear, I swear on the grave of my mother, I swear on her grave, I did not do this."

"Take him to the police, they will beat all sense into him."

"That is the only good thing about our police, they really know how to sort out thieves, they will beat him up until he tells the truth."

A short man in a green dustcoat who has been watching from a short distance is so incensed by Gazza's denials that he approaches Gazza and gives him a ringing slap across his face. Prosper tries to intervene, but he is pushed away. Gazza breaks free, and tries to flee, but he is stopped by three ice-cream men, who shove him against a pile of rubbish that has been allowed to gather for weeks. Gazza falls against rotting vegetables and ice-cream wrappers. It is not certain where the next blow comes from, but it is struck, and a second, and a third, and a fourth. When Gazza collapses to the ground, the crowd kicks him. A punch lands on Prosper too, and another. He turns and flees in the direction of the police station. A few stragglers try to chase him down, but they are soon caught up again in the real matter before them.

The news of the captured thief streams across to Copa Cabana, where a crowd is waiting to board taxi vans to Kambuzuma and Mbare. It reaches the corner of Kaguvi Street and Kwame Nkrumah Avenue, and all the way to the flea market, as people rush to see the thief.

"Watch my box," a woman called *Mai*Whizzy says to her young daughter. She is on her way to her stall at Mbare Musika, but that can wait, for now. She hurries to where everyone is headed, brow perspiring with the effort of running, and joins the crowd that swells now with anyone who ever had a grudge against a *hwindi,* anyone who has ever had anything stolen, and anyone who has nothing to do but enjoy the spectacle of a man being beaten by a crowd.

*Mai*Whizzy pushes her way to the front, she has to fight to get in, her face is scratched, and the sweat of bodies almost defeats her, but she pushes on until she is within sight of Gazza, and just as he raises his head, she kicks him back with her left foot. She almost loses her balance, but rights herself, and with a surge of triumph, she lets others take her place.

There is a shout of *mapurisa, mapurisa*, and there are the familiar brown tunics of two policemen headed in the direction of the crowd. With them is Prosper, now holding a towel to his head. As quickly as it had gathered, the crowd melts to leave the broken and beaten body of Gazza lying among the stink of rotting vegetables in his bloodied Arsenal shirt.

The angry horde becomes individuals again, and each person continues on to the business of the day. *Mai*Whizzy walks across to her daughter, eager to recount to her friends the kick she gave the thief. She finds her daughter flirting with a *hwindi,* and scolds her for smiling at thieves. She continues scolding her daughter almost halfway to Mbare, until the incident is forgotten as she tells the story of the beaten thief to her friends, giving the starring role to the kick she gave the thief. The story of *Mai*Whizzy and the thief is the sensation of the day and attracts more people than usual to her stall to buy vegetables.

The man with the missing mobile also walks away from the crowd. He has seen the man beaten up, he saw him lying bloodied and unconscious, but that is not enough, he wants him dead, he hopes he is dead. He heads up Speke Avenue towards Cleveland House. As he walks past the building, he hears a voice call his name.

"*Ba'm'kuru*Joe."

He is not sure that he really has heard himself called—was it him, or perhaps it is another Joe who is meant?

He moves on.

"*Ba'm'kuru*Joe," the voice comes again.

He turns to recognize his young niece, Mazvita. She is breathless, and has been running, she says. She was headed for his office, she explains.

"*Maiguru Mai* Selina sent me to find you, you left your phone behind," Mazvita says, "She said you would not be happy unless you had it with you, so she sent me after you, I left just thirty minutes after you did."

Mazvita holds out the phone to him, and he takes it without knowing that he does so.

"Did you know," Mazvita says, "I heard at the rank that a thief was beaten up. *Anzwa bhata shuwa*. These thieves are such a problem, I wish I had been there, but I always miss such things."

Now he has to buy her a Coke, she says, or maybe she should have a Creme Soda in one of those nice cans from South Africa. And she needs money to go back home, she says.

They walk on the flyover across Julius Nyerere Way as Mazvita chats brightly on. He holds his phone in his hand for a long time before putting it in his jacket, where it rests comfortably in the inside pocket of his jacket, right next to his heart.

Privacy and Reputation

Milton Hatoum

TORN

Have you always been a coward? asked M.A.C.

M.A.C. was trying to convince Ângelo to take part in the protest on W3 Avenue, but Ângelo, standing beside his bed, was eating biscuits his mother had sent from Belo Horizonte. He chewed them anxiously, looking from time to time at a spider's web in the corner of our room.

We can go together, I said, but I don't think Ângelo even heard me.

Cowardly or afraid? M.A.C. went on, with a contemptuous laugh. Ângelo lay down on the bed, stopped chewing and looked at the ceiling; he seemed to be choking, on the point of crying. I gestured to M.A.C. to stop pressing him.

At school they made fun of Ângelo and M.A.C., saying the two of them were frightened rats, but now M.A.C. had emerged from his hole, and who knows, in the next demonstration Ângelo might go with us. Then M.A.C. decided to walk to the central bus station: he'd eat a pasty and then go to W3.

An afternoon like this, dry and sunny, made you want to walk, but I decided to get the bus an hour before we'd agreed to: I'd get off near the National Hotel and go down W3, going round the semi-detached houses on the avenue. Brasília was still a strange place to me; I'd not yet got used to this space, too empty and grandiose for human beings, nor to the identical buildings, all the same height, surrounded by a muddy, grassy area that spread out toward the surrounding scrubland. It was Thursday. Students from the high school were coming out from the badly kept buildings in the north wing of the city; from the campus came older people: university students, teachers, ancillary staff, already experienced in these things. The student leaders would appear at the agreed moment, make their speeches and disappear. It was said they spent the night in different houses, outside the planned center of the city, maybe in Goiânia or Anápolis, or in one of the satellite towns; one of the leaders had been arrested there on Republic Day, November 15.

On that afternoon of protest, the crowds gave us support. At five o'clock we listened to the lightning speeches, roared out the usual slogans, daubed graffiti on the walls and distributed pamphlets at the doors of houses and shops. The dispersal began before darkness fell. The army and police vehicles had surrounded the area leading off W3 Avenue and set up barriers on the city's central axis, where the congress and the ministries stand, blocking off all escape routes from Brasília. No one would go to the Beirute, a bar watched by the police, nor the bus station, which was a war zone. In the chaos, with people running hither and thither, I left W3 and got to a street at the back of the shops and bars; I tried to walk calmly, whistling a song; then I started nervously humming the same song, my voice trembling, but nerves and fear were taking hold of me. The sky was still blue, and it was still a landscape of possibilities.

I followed the instructions to avoid suspect gestures: never look back or join other demonstrators, pretend that friends are strangers. Up to now there were no faces I knew, and the cathedral and the National Theater looked like gigantic unfinished statues. I'd wait there for the night to come, signaled by the lights on the tower at the hub of the central axis. The dispersal and the running were still going on, and the most sensible thing to do was to sit on the grass of residential block 302 or 307 and watch the kids playing football. Saturday I'd go for a boat ride with Liana on Paranoá lake, on Sunday I'd read *Huis-clos* again for a rehearsal; on Tuesday were the final exams for literature and physics. If only that were all living was, and if only someone hadn't called out my

name two or three times. Frightened, I recognized M.A.C.'s
voice, and his body was staggering in my direction. There was no
time for conversation; block 302 was invaded by police as if in a
nightmare—to have tried to react or escape would have been
equally disastrous. My schoolmate and I were pushed into a vehicle
with darkened windows. M.A.C. asked where we were going, and
a faceless, menacing voice said: shut your face, hands behind your
back and lower your head. We went toward the unknown. The
van took a winding route, with lots of turns so we lost any sense of
direction, maneuvers we'd only imagined and were now happening somewhere in Brasília. M.A.C., one of the poorest students in
the second year, was an enigma, cornered like a strange animal. He
was shaking beside me and seemed to be crying when the vehicle
stopped in front of a three-storied building. I couldn't make out
where we were, perhaps near the airport or the air force base, because of the intermittent noise of motors and aircraft engines. I
heard my mate's terrified voice: *I'm a minor,* then a slap, and M.A.C.
was dragged into a room. He managed to turn his face
toward me, his look pleading for help.

I didn't see him again all that long night. I'm a minor too, I said to
the man who took me to a small room. He ordered me to strip
and took everything away: my clothes, the money for the bus, my
identity card and student pass. I remember that one or two hours
later another man opened the door and threw a plastic bottle and
an empty can onto the floor. I drank a little water, and only later
understood the reason for the empty can. A small window covered with a piece of black paper made a hole in the upper part of
one of the walls. I lay down on the cement floor, nodded off and
woke up again several times that night, a Thursday in December.
I don't know what time in the small hours it was when I heard
screams of pain coming from the other side of the wall. Somewhere near me, someone was suffering, might even be dying, and
that idea terrified me. The screams lasted for some minutes and
stopped, but I heard them again later, perhaps at dawn or in the
early morning. I felt hunger, drank a little more water and wished

I could see my mother, who lived in the north of the country, some two thousand kilometers from Brasília. She could do nothing for me, but the letters she sent me, four or five a month, helped cure my homesickness. I knew I would find a letter from my mother in the room where I was living, in the north wing of the city. Ângelo would keep the letter for me, and that bucked me up. To kill time and not just think of the solitude, I tried to remember what my mother had written in her last letter. I remember she'd mentioned one of Machado de Assis's stories, a story she loved, and even knew bits of it by heart. I could see the hardback volume, blue, a 1957 edition; I could see the collection on the shelves there in the room, and saw my mother reading the story out loud, standing up, and suddenly, with a shock, I heard her voice saying: *It wasn't just a Christian Sunday, it was an immense, universal Sunday.** Just those words, then her voice and image disappeared, and I murmured Today is Thursday, a sad day, I've got to do something or I'll go mad. I walked slowly in the darkness, not knowing what time it was. Little by little you can get used to an enclosed, dark space. I walked a few paces— four or five—till I touched a wall; I did it again with my eyes open, then changed direction and shut my eyes. I felt dizzy, looked for the empty can and urinated into it, knocked in vain on the locked door, heard the noise of a plane, and lay down so as not to fall. I didn't feel cold; what bothered me most was the smell of urine. I was numb, more from fear than exhaustion. In the night (since everything was dark), someone unlocked the door and threw my clothes onto the cement floor. Two men took me to a car and gave me a sandwich; one of them, the taller and bulkier of the two, said I should eat with my head lowered, looking at my feet. I couldn't see the men's faces. It really was nighttime, or the end of the night, when they left me at the side of a road. Seated, I waited for dawn. I remember a flat horizon, and the colors of the sky. I saw low-growing trees, their twisted branches with few leaves and no flowers. My mouth was dry. I got up with a strug-

---

* From *"Uns braços"* (*A Pair of Arms*) by Machado de Assis (1839–1908).

gle and saw the asphalt road, a wide, straight strip that ended in a vanishing point. A desert torn by an asphalt strip. I knew I was somewhere in the Federal District of Brasília, but outside the central, planned area. Then I imagined something was finishing and murmured these words: something has ended forever. Dawn was breaking. In front of me was the beauty of the scrubland landscape and the sky of Brasília. And my youth was coming to an end. A car stopped and the driver offered me a lift to the bus station. With a weak voice, I asked where we were and what day of the week it was. Today is Saturday. We're on the road from Taguatinga to Guará, said the driver. I got in the car and avoided looking at him. When he was going to stop at the bus station, I told him I lived in the north wing and had no money to get a bus.

You must be a student. Where are you studying? he asked me.

In the White Elephant College, I lied.

Did the party end up on the road?

I was going to say: it ended with a lot of booze, but I thought it best to keep quiet and wait a little to let out a forced laugh. He left me at the entrance to my block; I went slowly up two flights of stairs and saw the door was open. M.A.C. and Ângelo weren't there. Ângelo's bed had no sheets on it, and there was a note on the pillow: *I've gone to Minas. I'm going to live with my family.* M.A.C.'s possessions were scattered over the floor: a few clothes, a flask, two old history books, an algebra manual. When I was going to lie down on the bed, I noticed that my case was open; someone had rummaged through my clothes and piled my books up in a corner of the room; next to an open novel, I saw bits of paper; I put the pieces together, trying to recompose the sheets of a letter; the paper was so torn and crumpled that I could hardly put a sentence back together, but I saw it was my mother's handwriting. I managed to read the words *rain*, *storm* and *love*, and only three phrases: *your grandfather's coming from Panama City tomorrow*; *Sunday at the Tarumã waterfalls* and *your uncle's been fired by the Federal interventor* in Amazonas. Under the bed I found a

---

* The temporary governor of a state, sent in by the military dictatorship to impose direct rule.

torn photograph; the hands that had torn that photograph in which my mother appears—a photo she'd put in the same envelope as the letter—had left her face intact, but the body and the background had been torn to pieces. More or less, I was able to put the pieces of the photo together and stick them onto a sheet of white paper. It's the only picture of my mother in a bathing suit, sitting on a stone beside the Tarumã waterfalls. She was looking at the camera lens with a serious, worried look.

I never mentioned my imprisonment or the letter that had been violated and torn, not even when she asked why I'd never replied to her; I kept my mouth shut, imagining the questions I hadn't been able to read—or that I'd been stopped from reading. And only much later, not long before she died, did my mother repeat the questions that had been torn by criminal hands. She told me that in the letter she'd asked if I wouldn't like to come back home, to Manaus. For she'd regretted allowing me to go and live in Brasília, alone, at the age of fourteen. She'd interpreted my silence in several ways, but she didn't tell me how. And she died without knowing I'd been detained by the police the same week she'd written to me, voicing her regret and her desire to see me back home.

That Saturday in December 1969, I waited for my other roommate, but M.A.C. didn't come back. On the Monday, he didn't go back to school, nor did he appear at the final exams. One more disappeared person in that year-end, when I left Brasília forever and went to live in São Paulo. For some time I dreamed that Brasília was a desert lit by sunset or sunrise; the soundtrack to the dream were the screams of pain I heard in the first hours of my detention, screams that followed me and wouldn't leave my memory. When I forgot these sounds, I remembered the letter and the picture of my mother. It all seemed like one thing. Sometimes M.A.C.'s frightened face came to my mind, and I even thought the screams were his, that a body was dying a few yards from me. And if they were his, maybe he was dead, or mad, his mind and body destroyed.

* * *

Thirty-two years later, on my first trip back to the capital, I met Carlos Marcelo, a friend from 1969 who still lived in Brasília. I asked about M.A.C.

He's living in São Paulo, he said. He might be your neighbor.

I thought he'd died.

For a long time he did die. He disappeared from the school and the city; then he was resuscitated and amnestied.

Exile, I murmured.

Betrayal, Carlos Marcelo corrected me. M.A.C. squealed. He informed on lots of people and vanished from sight.

Freedom of Movement

Ali Smith

THE GO-BETWEEN

You know what Spain is? It's a bird's flight from here. I don't mean a long flight. I mean, use your eyes. You see those lights across the bay? That's Europe. You see that fence? The other side of it is Europe. I lost the top part of my ear on the fence. The top part of my ear is in Europe!

The first thing you learn to do is to make a ladder. Your passport is your ladder! You need two passports, one for up and one for down. A ladder consists of plastic, rope if there's any rope, wood, good knots and a row of rocks. The rocks must be small enough not to be too heavy and heavy enough for ballast. The plastic has to be thick. You need a mat or matting to go between you and the wire at the top. A mat can be anything thick enough to stop the wire getting to you.

My ear got caught, the place where it curls at the top. My third finger off this hand? Underwater. There are underwater fences as well. But my ear first. It was the second time we went over. Five hundred of us, they didn't expect that, and it was a police holiday, so double surprise! The man next to me phoned Lagos, his family. He had a phonecard with Beckham on it, Madrid. He had been saving it. We stood at the foot of the fence, I was all blood from my ear but I was happy, and he was shouting down the phone, I'm in Europe! I'm in Europe! I had no one to phone but our ladders were hanging behind us like long decorations all along the fence, the bright colors of the plastic. Over his shoulder I saw them running toward us all with the guns. Europe! I said.

So they opened the big gates and rounded us all up with dogs and threw us all out. We were in Europe. They were meant to process us, even if we didn't have the papers. They were meant to give us new expulsion papers. These would mean we would be processed. What they did, instead, was they chased us with dogs, sticks, electric shock sticks and guns, and a boy near me fell down, he had a bullet in the leg, and then a guard was beating the boy on this same leg with a stick. And others had worse before they threw us out of Europe and locked the gates.

I phoned the French doctors. You know what Europe is? It's a phone signal! It's the moment on the screen in your hand when MarocTel changes to Vodafone Espagne. Sometimes just standing still in Africa we look down at our phones and we're—in Europe! I rang the number. I let it ring three times. The French doctors phoned straight back. We got into Europe, and they are shooting at us, I said. The French doctors can be Italian, Spanish, French, English, for instance. I speak these, and also some others. I was a microbiologist, before. I worked in the university. Mycology. Virology. "A man is always to be busy with his thoughts if anything is to be accomplished." That's a quote from Van Leeuwenhoek. Now, there was a man who knew how to use his eyes. There was a man who knew how to make what's invisible be visible. There was a man who knew the great power in what looks, to the human eye, like nothing at all.

These days, here, in this city, with its new buildings all along its new waterfront, with its new palm trees, its new look of Europe even here in Africa, I help the French doctors. Borders are not always visible! I can go between people and places. I can go to the bits of the city they can't, or the buildings they can't, or the people they don't know about, or the people who don't wish to be seen. I can take them with me, I can tell the people it's okay. I can go out to the camps with them and out to the bush. I can translate for the people who don't know what it is they're saying, or don't believe what they're saying is true.

I take them to the new arrivals and take the new arrivals to them. This month, November, I took them to where the man whose legs were broken under the train was. I took them to the woman who'd been raped, first by the Network, then by the police. At first she wouldn't talk to anyone. Then she talked to me. Then she talked to the doctors.

I went into the bush with them to find the man with the scalds after the water pot, and I took the boy who was dying. He had infected kidneys. I can do a bit of doctoring. I can do a bit of translating. It's my very learned profession! I'm a born border crosser. I'm MarocTel. I'm Vodafone. Without the connection, nothing.

The second time over the fence was just a couple of weeks before the border police—you know, there's more than one kind of police—came into the camp. They slashed the tents so they were useless when it rained. They burned the blankets. They collected up the mobiles. They took them away. They took all the food they found. They collected up some of the people from the camp when they went into the bush to get food, and drove them to the desert in a truck, and left them there. I mean left them with no water. That was us, warned. We had made a football pitch in that camp. We had a market, we had a restaurant, we had our own law system and our own police. We had our own police! We had a currency. It wasn't euros!

You can use things all sorts of ways. You can play chess with the tops off water bottles. You can make ladders, tents, matting, beds, carpets, out of plastic. It's better than sleeping on nothing under nothing. I think of the girls sitting in the mud at the openings of the tent; they were cooking rice and they were using hair straightener, beautiful, sitting in the mud, straightening their hair. Girls get to Spain a lot easier. (If they're not pregnant and don't have TB.)

A building is better than plastic. I'm happy to live in a building now. I have gone up in the world! I live on the roof! From the roof, a bird's flight away: Spain. One of the men in the other room—there are six in his room, three in mine—has covered the photos of his wife and his children in thin plastic. They're still clean and fresh, and the certificate of his son's birth, sealed in this plastic too, all inside another plastic bag, under his sleeping mat.

All the men in this building suffer from it, Spanish blindness. All you can see is Spain. All you can think is Spain tonight, Spain tonight. They've paid all their money to the Network, and the Network has promised a boat, maybe tonight. This boat never comes.

Myself, I don't have the Network. I don't have this particular blindness. My blindness is for what's behind me. I would like to go back. I want to go back. But I have to go forward. I can't go back. Back's not possible for me.

I've nothing left except a shirt, the Cameroon team colors. Cameroon World Cup!

Don't you understand? Nobody leaves home unless home is the mouth of a shark.

I was telling you about the fences. They're three meters high. Sometimes when I'm asleep I dream the barbed wire is frothing at the top of the fences like the froth on a pan of urine.

The first time I climbed it my second ladder wasn't so good, the plastic didn't hold, and when I hit Europe I fell too hard on my feet. Three of us went, one made Spain, one was thrown back, and Professor Me, I climbed at the place where there was a stretch of earth and a road being built—they were building the second layer of fence right there! I landed in no-man's-land! Wise Professor Me. But I lasted there six weeks, because the fence builders had a hut, and each day when it was a working day a different man came and gave me his lunch. Their village was splitting in two. One side of the village would be Africa, one side would be Europe.

In the daytime I hid in the trench and at night I crawled into the hut, it was winter, pretty cold. It was kindness, those lunches. I lay in the cold between the lengths of fence and most days, for several weeks, I ate like I was in a world with no fences.

I don't know who told the police. Maybe no one did. Maybe they just found me. They didn't beat me up, because I made them laugh. I said, wait, this isn't Africa! This trench is Europe! This mud is my home! I've always lived here! I'm a European! They laughed. They patted me on the back. They gave me cigarettes. They helped me walk to the gate and they threw me out. The French doctors treated the foot for me. It was a long walk with a sore foot, that short walk to the gate. Walking the Africa I've walked wasn't nearly as hard as that walk to the gate.

Professor of walking, me. First to Agades, where I got on a lorry for Libya. I was shut in the lorry for two weeks. There were eighty of us in there. We'd no food, a few biscuits, they were good! We'd just enough water. I know about men who drank their own urine to survive. We were luckier. The desert is beautiful. But it's dangerous. The desert's full of corpses. In Libya I was the wrong religion so I walked to Melilla in the dark, I slept in the daylight in the snow. I crossed the border at night in the mountains and nobody saw me. Then I walked to Ceuta. I've walked six hundred kilometers. No one leaves home unless home is a mouth full of teeth. Why would he? Why would she? No one leaves home unless home is going to devour him.

Lucky Professor Me, no sharks in the water round Ceuta. Bel Younech is a lit-up fence so I went by sea. That's what the posters say on all the buildings in Tangier. La Mer. Votre Plus Belle Route. I swam it twice, the plus belle route. I'm the Cameroon swimmer! Olympic! I was picked up by the patrol boat both times. The second time I was bleeding. The fence goes right under the water. My hand caught on the razor wire. The third finger of this hand is still swimming the Mediterranean!

I dream when I'm asleep that I'm walking down the big streets of Madrid with their fine white stately buildings, and then this is what happens. First this arm, and then this other arm, and then this leg, and then the other leg, one, two, three, four, drop off me as I move. Behind me I'm spilling a litter of myself. It's spoiling the streets of Spain.

This new waterfront is very fine. The governor of the city has been planting a flower for everybody, it makes it look pretty. A flower will be planted for every single person in Tangier. But not

us. Not me. I'm not here! A miracle, no? A real border crossing!
I'm speaking to you and I'm not really here!

Call me Blaise. It's not my real name. All I have left from the
time I was called my real name is a Cameroon team shirt. Blaise
is the first name of the philosopher Pascal. "Our nature consists in
movement; absolute rest is death." That's Pascal. And: "The
smallest movement affects all nature, the whole ocean is changed
by the shift of a single pebble." Pascal. And: "You get tragedy
when the tree, instead of bending, breaks." Wittgenstein. And:
"If a lion could talk, we wouldn't understand him." Wittgenstein.
And: "Whenever I found out anything remarkable I knew it was
my duty to put it down on paper, so all ingenious people might be
informed thereof." Van Leeuwenhoek. Van Leeuwenhoek was a
philosopher too. Microbiologists are also a kind of philosopher.
And: "Hope is a waking dream." That's Aristotle.

I'm a small, slight man. I'm not a big man. I'm lean and slight.
My stature is slight. My coat is a bit too slight—here comes the
winter! I'm thirty-three years old. I'm a mature old man, me! I'm
not noticeable. I'm quiet.

The Cameroon swimmer. Philosophical Professor Me. Border
Crosser Extraordinaire. You would walk past me in the street
and not see. I've only a slight limp, not noticeable. I wear my
hat down over my ears. I keep my hand folded so no one sees the
loss in it.

David Constantine

ASYLUM

Prison more like, said Madeleine.
　　Come now, said Mr. Kramer.
　If I run away, they bring me back, said Madeleine.
　Yes but, said Mr. Kramer.

Mr. Kramer often said, Yes but to Madeleine. Something to concede, something to contradict. Now he said again how kind everyone in the Unit was, all his visits never once had he seen any unkindness and couldn't remember ever hearing a voice raised in anger against any girl or boy. So: not really like a prison.

Then why's she sitting there? said Madeleine, nodding toward a nurse in the doorway. The nurse did her best to seem oblivious. She was reading a women's magazine.
　You know very well, said Mr. Kramer.
　So I won't suddenly scratch your face and say you tried to rape me, said Madeleine. So I won't suddenly throw myself out of the window.
　That sort of thing, said Mr. Kramer.

The window was open, but only the regulation few inches, as far as the locks allowed. Mr. Kramer and Madeleine looked at it. She'd get through there, he thought, if she tried. Not that I'd ever get through there, said Madeleine, however hard I tried.

* * *

The walls of the room were decorated with images, in paintings and collages, of the themes and infinite variations of body and soul in their distress. A face shattering like a window. A range of mountains, stacked like the hoods of the Klan, blocking most of the sky, but from the foreground, in a red zigzag, into them went a path, climbing, and disappeared. Mr. Kramer liked the room. Waiting for Madeleine, or whoever it might be, he stood at the window looking down at a grassy bank that in its seasons, year after year, with very little nurture or encouragement, brought forth out of itself an abundance of ordinary beautiful flowers. At this point in his acquaintance with Madeleine it was the turn of primroses. The air coming in was mild. Behind the bank ran the wall of the ancient enclosure.

Asylum, said Mr. Kramer. What is an asylum?

A place they lock nutters up, said Madeleine.

Well, yes, said Mr. Kramer, but why call it an asylum?

Because they're liars, said Madeleine.

All right, said Mr. Kramer. Forget the nutters, as you call them, and the place they get looked after or locked up in, and tell me what you think an asylum seeker is.

Someone from somewhere bad.

And when they come to the United Kingdom, say, or to France, Germany or Italy, what are they looking for?

Somewhere better than where they've come from.

What are they seeking?

Asylum.

And what is asylum?

Sanctuary.

Sanctuary, said Mr. Kramer. That's a very good word. Those poor people come here seeking sanctuary in a land of prisons. An asylum, he said, is a refuge, a shelter, a safe haven. Lunatic asylums, as they used to be called, are places where people disordered in their souls can be housed safely and looked after.

Locked up, said Madeleine. Ward 16, they took Sam there last week.

So he'd be safer, said Mr. Kramer. I'm sure of that.

Madeleine shrugged.

Okay, said Mr. Kramer. A bit like a prison, I grant you. Sometimes it has to be a bit like a prison, but always for the best. Not like detention, internment, real prison, nothing like that.

Madeleine shrugged.

Mr. Kramer's spirits lapsed. He forgot where he was and why. His spirits lapsed or the sadness in him rose. Either way he began to be occluded. An absence. When he returned he saw that Madeleine was looking at him. Being looked at by Madeleine was like being looked at by the moon. The light seemed to come off her face as though reflected from some faraway source. Her look was fearful, but rather as though she feared she had harmed Mr. Kramer. Rema says Hi, she said. Rema said say Hi from me to Mr. Kramer.

They both brightened.

Thank you, Madeleine, said Mr. Kramer. Please give her my best regards next time you speak to her. How is she?

Can't tell with her, said Madeleine. She's such a liar. She says she's down to four and a half stone. Her hair's falling out, she says, from the starvation. She says she eats a few beansprouts a day and that is all. And drinks half a glass of water. But she's a liar. It's only so I'll look fat. She phones and phones. She wants to get back in here. But Dr. Khan says she won't get back in here by starving herself. That's blackmail, he says. She might, however, if she puts on weight. Show willing, he says, show you want to get better. Then we'll see. She says if they won't let her back she'll kill herself. Thing is, if she gets well enough to come back here, she thinks they'll send her home. Soon as she's sixteen they'll send her home, her aunty says. But Rema says she'll kill herself twenty times before she'll go back home.

Home's not a war zone, if I remember rightly, said Mr. Kramer. Her family is, said Madeleine. They are why she is the way she is. So quite understandably she'll end it all before she'll go back there.

Rema told me a lovely story once, said Mr. Kramer.

Did she write it?

No, she never wrote it. She promised she would but she never did.

Typical, said Madeleine.

Yes, said Mr. Kramer. But really it wasn't so much a story as a place for one. She remembered a house near her village. The house was all shuttered up, it had a paved courtyard with a sort of shrine in the middle and white jasmine growing wild over the balconies and the wooden stairs.

Oh that, said Madeleine. It was an old woman's and she wanted to do the haj and her neighbors lent her the money and the deal was they could keep her house if she didn't come back and she never came back. That story.

Yes, said Mr. Kramer, that story. I thought it very beautiful, the deserted house, I mean, the courtyard and the shrine.

Probably she made it up, said Madeleine. Probably there never was such a house. And anyway she never wrote it.

Mr. Kramer felt he was losing the encounter. He glanced at the clock. I thought Rema was your friend, he said.

She is, said Madeleine. I don't love anyone as much as I love her. But all the same she's a terrible liar. And mostly to get at me. Four and a half stone! What kind of a stupid lie is that? Did she tell you she wanted to do the haj?

She did, said Mr. Kramer. Her owl eyes widening and taking in more light, passionately she had told him she longed to do the haj.

So why is she starving herself? It doesn't make sense.

I told her, said Mr. Kramer. I said you have to be very strong for a thing like that. However you travel, a pilgrimage is a hard experience. You have to be fit.

Such a liar, said Madeleine.

Anyway, said Mr. Kramer. You'll write your story for next time. About an asylum seeker, a boy, you said, a boy half your age.

I will, said Madeleine. Where's the worst place in the world? Apart from here, of course.

Hard to say, said Mr. Kramer. There'd be quite a competition. But Somalia would take some beating.

I read there are pirates in Somalia.

Off the coast there are. They steal the food the rich people send and the people who need it starve.

Good, said Madeleine. I'll have pirates in my story.

Madeleine and Mr. Kramer faced each other in silence across the table. The nurse had closed her magazine and was watching them. Mr. Kramer was thinking that from many points of view the project was a bad one. Madeleine had wanted to write about being Madeleine. Fine, he said, but displace it. Find an image like one of those on the wall. I have, she said. My image is a war zone. My story is about a child in a war zone, a boy half my age, who wants to get out to somewhere safe. Asylum, said Mr. Kramer. He seeks asylum.

Tell me, Madeleine, said Mr. Kramer. Tell me in a word before I go what feeling you know most about and what feeling the little boy will inhabit in your story.

The sleeves of Madeleine's top had ridden up so that the cuts across her wrists were visible. Seeing them looked at sorrowfully by Mr. Kramer she pulled the sleeves down and gripped the end of each very tightly into either palm.

Fear, she said.

Mr. Kramer might have taken the bus home. There was a stop not far from Bartlemas where that extraordinary enclosure, its orchard, its gardens, the grassy humps of the ancient hospital, touched modernity on the east-west road. He could have ridden to his house from there, almost door-to-door, in twenty minutes. Instead, if the weather was at all decent and some days even if it wasn't he walked home through the parks and allotments, a good long march, an hour and a half or more. That way it was late afternoon before he got in, almost time to be thinking about the cooking of his supper. Then came the evening, for which he always had a plan: a serious television program, some serious reading, his notes, early to bed.

On his walk that mild spring afternoon Mr. Kramer thought about Madeleine and Rema. It distressed him that Madeleine was so scathing about Rema's story. How cruel they were to each other in their lethal competition! For him the abandoned house had a peculiar power. Rema said it was very quiet there, as soon as you pushed open the wooden gates, no shouting, no dogs, no noise of any traffic. The courtyard was paved with colored tiles in a complicated pattern whose many intersecting arcs and loops she had puzzled over and tried to follow. The shrine was surely left over from before Partition, it must be a Hindu shrine, the Muslim woman had no use for it. But there it stood in the center of the courtyard, a carved figure on a pedestal and a place for flowers, candles, and offerings, and around it on all four sides the shuttered windows, the balcony, the superabundance of white jasmine. The old woman never came back, said Rema. It was not even known whether she ever reached Mecca, the place of her heart's desire. So the neighbors kept the house but none had any real use for it. Sometimes their cattle strayed into the courtyard. And there also, when she dared, climbing the wooden stairs and viewing the shrine from the cool and scented balconies, went the child Rema, for sanctuary from the war zone of her home.

Mr. Kramer was watching a program about the bombings when the phone rang. Such a program, after the cooking and the eating and the allowance of three glasses of wine, was a station on his way to bed. But the phone rang. It was Maria, his daughter, from

Ukraine, already midnight, phoning to tell him she had found the very shtetl, the names, the place itself. He caught her tone of voice, the one of all still in the world he was least proof against. He hardly heard the words, only the voice, its peculiar quality. Forest, memorial, the names, he knew what she was saying, but sharper than the words, nearer, flesh of his flesh, he felt the voice that was having to say these things, in a hotel room, three hours ahead, on a savage pilgrimage. The forest, the past, the small voice from so far away, he felt her to be in mortal danger, he felt he must pull her back from where she stood, leaning over the abyss of history, the pit, the extinction of all personal relations. Sweetheart, said Mr. Kramer, my darling girl, go to sleep now if you can. And I've been thinking. Once you're back I'll come and stay with you. After all I cannot bear it on my own. But sleep now if you can.

Mr. Kramer had not intended to say any such thing. He had set himself the year at least. One year. Surely a man could watch alone in grief that long.

The Unit phoned. Madeleine had taken an overdose, she was in hospital, back in a day or so. Mr. Kramer, about to set off, did the walk anyway, it was a fine spring day, the beech trees leafing softly. He walked right to the gates of Bartlemas, turned and set off home again, making a detour to employ the time he would have spent with Madeleine.

In the evening, last thing, Mr. Kramer read his old notes, a weakness he always tried to make up for by at once writing something new. He read for ten minutes, till he hit the words: Rema, her desire to be an owl. Then he leafed forward quickly to the day's blank page and wrote: I haven't thought nearly enough about Rema's desire to be an owl. She said, Do you think I already look like one? I went to the office and asked did we have a mirror. We do, under lock and key. It is a lovely thing, face-shaped and just the size of a face, without a frame, the bare reflecting glass. I held it up for Rema. Describe your face, I said. Describe it exactly. I was a mite ashamed of the license this exercise gave me to contemplate a girl's face while she, looking at herself, never glancing at me, studied it as a thing to be described. Yes, her nose, quite a thin bony line, might become a beak. Pity to lose the lips. But if you joined the arcs of the brows with the arcs of shadow below the eyes, so accentuating the sockets, yes you might make the widening stare of an owl. The longing for metamorphosis. To become something else, a quite different creature, winged, feathered, intent. Like Madeleine's, Rema's face shows the bones. The softness of feathers would perhaps be a comfort. I wonder did she tell Madeleine about the mirror. Shards, the harming.

The Unit phoned, Madeleine was well enough, just about. Mr. Kramer stood at the window. The primroses were already finishing. But there would be something else, on and on till the autumn cyclamens. It was a marvelous bank. Then Madeleine and the overweight nurse stood in the doorway, the nurse holding her women's magazine. Madeleine wore loose trousers and a collarless shirt whose sleeves were far too long. She stood; and toward Mr. Kramer, fearfully and defiantly, she presented her face and neck, which she had cut. Oh Maddy, said Mr. Kramer, can't you ever be merciful? Will you never show yourself any mercy?

The nurse sat in the open doorway and read her magazine. Madeleine and Mr. Kramer faced each other across the small table. All the same, said Madeleine through her lattice of black cuts, I've made a start. Shall I read it? Yes, said Mr. Kramer. Madeleine read:

Samuel lived with his mother. The soldiers had killed his father. Some of the soldiers were only little boys. Samuel and his mother hid in the forest. Every day she had to leave him for several hours to go and look for food and water. He waited in fear that she would not come back. There was nothing to do. He curled up in the little shelter, waiting. One day Samuel's mother did not come back. He waited all night and all the next day and all the next night. Then he decided he must go and look for her or for some food and water at least because the emergency supplies she had left him were all gone. He followed the trail his mother had made day after day. It came to a road. She had told him that the road was very dangerous. But beyond the road were fields and in them, if you were lucky, you might find some things to eat that the farmers had planted before the soldiers came and burned their village. Samuel halted at the road. It was long and straight in both directions and very dusty. A little way off he saw a truck burning and another truck upside down in the ditch. But there were no soldiers. Samuel hurried across. Quite soon, just as his mother had said, he saw women and girls in blue and white clothes moving slowly over the land looking for food. Perhaps his mother would be among them after all? At the very least, somebody would surely give him food and water.

Madeleine lifted her face. That's as far as I got, she said. It's crap, isn't it? No, said Mr. Kramer, it is very good. Crap, said Madeleine. Tell me, Madeleine, said Mr. Kramer, did you write this before or after you did that to your face? After, said Madeleine. I wrote it this morning. I did my face two nights ago, after they brought me back here from the hospital. Good, said Mr. Kramer. That's a very good thing. It means you can sympathize with other people's lives even when your own distresses you so much you cut your face. I know the rest, said Madeleine with a sudden eagerness. I know how it goes on and how it ends. Shall I tell you? Will you still be able to write it if you tell? Yes, yes. You promise? Yes, I promise. Tell then.

She laid her sleeves, in which her hands were hiding, flat on the table and began to speak, rapidly, staring into his eyes, transfixing him with the eagerness of her fiction.

In among the people looking for food he meets a girl. She's my age. Her name is Ruth. The soldiers have killed her father too. Ruth's mother hid with her and when the soldiers came looking she made Ruth stay in hiding and gave herself up to them. That was the end of her. But Ruth was taken by the other women and hid with them and went looking for food when it was safe. When Samuel came into the fields, Ruth decided to look after him. She was like a sister to Samuel, a good big sister, or a mother, a good and loving mother. When it was safe to light a fire, she cooked for him, the best meal she could. After a while the soldiers came back again, the fields were too dangerous, all the women hid in the forest but Ruth had heard that if you could only get to the coast you could maybe find someone with a boat who would carry you across the sea to Italy and the European Union, where it was really safe. So that's what she did, with Samuel, she set off for the coast, only traveling at night, on foot, by moonlight and starlight, steering clear of the villages in flames.

Sounds good, said Mr. Kramer. Sounds very exciting. All you have to do now is write it. You've looked at a map, I suppose? The nearest coast is no use at all. That's where the pirates are. You need the north coast really, through the desert. And crossing the desert is said to be a terrible thing. You have to pay truckers to take you, I believe. Yes, said Madeleine, I thought she'd do better on the east coast, with the pirates. A pirate chief says he'll take her and Samuel all the way to Libya but it will cost her a lot of money. When she says she has no money, he says she can marry him, for payment that is, until they get to Libya, then he'll sell her to a friend of his, who will take her and Samuel into the European Union, which is like the Promised Land, he says, and there she will be safe, but she'll have to marry his friend as well, for the voyage from Libya into Italy. I asked Rema would she do it and she said she wouldn't, she couldn't, because of the things at home, but she said I could, Ruth in my story should, it would save the two of them, they would have a new life in the European Union and God would mercifully forgive her the sin. She says Hi, by the way. She asked me to ask you are you all right. She said it seemed to her you were a bit lonely sometimes. Thank you, said Mr. Kramer, I'm fine. And guess what, said Madeleine, she doesn't want to do the haj anymore, not till she's an old woman, and she doesn't want to make Dr. Khan have her back here either. No, she's decided she'll be a primary schoolteacher. Plus she's down to four stone. So it's all lies as usual.

A primary schoolteacher is a very good idea, said Mr. Kramer. But of course you have to be strong for that. As strong as for a pilgrimage.

I told her that, said Madeleine. So she's still a liar. Anyway, another thing about Ruth is that when she's with the first pirate, as his prostitute, all the way up the Red Sea he sends her ashore to the markets—Samuel he keeps on board as a hostage—and she has to go and buy all the ingredients for his favorite meals. I've researched it, baby okra and lamb in tomato stew, for example, onion pancakes, fish and peppers, shoelace pastry, spicy creamy cheeses, all delicious, up the coast to Suez. So she makes her Lord and Master happy and Samuel gets strong.

Will they stay in Italy, Mr. Kramer asked, if the second pirate keeps his word and carries her across the Mediterranean? No, said Madeleine, breathless on her story, they're heading for Swansea. There's quite an old Somali community in Swansea. I've researched it. They've been there a hundred years. At first she'll live in a hostel, doing the cooking for everybody so that everybody likes her. Samuel goes to school and as soon as he's settled Ruth will go to the CFE and get some qualifications.

Madeleine, said Mr. Kramer, it's very hard to enter the United Kingdom. Ruth and Samuel will need passports. I've thought of that, said Madeleine. The first pirate chief has a locker full of passports from people who died on his boat and because Ruth is such a good cook he gives her a couple and swears they'll get her and Samuel through immigration, no problem.

Rema should go to the CFE, said Mr. Kramer. I believe the Home Office would extend her visa if she were in full-time education. And if she trained as a primary schoolteacher, who knows what might happen?

She's a liar, said Madeleine, very white, her face almost translucent through the savage ornamentation of her cuts. She's supposed to be my friend. If she were really my friend, she'd come back here. Then we'd both be all right like we were before she left me.

You want to stay here?

Yes, said Madeleine. It's safer here.

Why overdose? Why cut yourself?

The nurse was watching and listening.

Because I'm frightened.

My daughter was frightened, said Mr. Kramer, and she's twice your age. All the time her mother was ill, four and a half years, she got more and more frightened. And now she's gone to Ukraine, would you believe it, all on her own and not speaking the language, to research our family history. She phoned me the other night from the place itself, a terrible place, I never want to go there, all on her own, at midnight, in a hotel. Write your story, won't you? You promised me. Somalia is very likely the worst place in the world and Swansea is a very good place, by all accounts. What an achievement it will be if you can get Ruth and Samuel safely there!

Madeleine's white hands with their bitten nails still hid in her sleeves. All the animation had gone out of her. I'll never get to Swansea from Somalia, she said. Never, never, never. I can't even want to get out of here.

First the story, Madeleine, said Mr. Kramer. First comes the fiction. Get Ruth and Samuel out of the killing fields, get them by the cruelty and kindness of pirates into a holding camp on the heel of Italy, get them north among strangers, not speaking a word of the language—devise it, work out the necessary means. You promised. Who knows what might happen if you get that lucky pair to Swansea?

The Right to a Nationality

Jon Fosse

HOMECOMING

Why did he cry like that, the old man, as he stood there. He had gone through the kitchen door from the hallway of his house, an old white house, not big, not small, an old house on an old farm where he was born, had lived all his days and had been away from now for a few months but had come back to today. And now he stood there, on the kitchen floor, with a crammed holdall in one hand, in his best suit and a firm knot in his tie; he stood there with his big and heavy body, with his bald head, and held his zipped holdall in one hand and in the other he held a stick which he was leaning on; he stands there, stooped, with his big heavy head bent forward and she who stands by the kitchen table, in her blue dress, and her knitted gray cardigan, her thin gray hair falling across her frail face, she too is looking down and then she says you're home again now, Peter, she says and he says yes that I am, Signe, he says, yes it's been a while, it's a long time since I've seen you, she says, yes, he says, but now I've come back home, he says and she says that he should sit down, he should go and sit down at his place at the end of the table, and she will get some coffee and a bite to eat, she says and he walks slowly across the floor and he sits down at the end of the table, with his holdall in his lap and his stick leaning against the table

You've been fine then, she says

Yes, he says

and then he just sits there

You were gone a long time, she says

I could've been gone longer, he says

Yes you could have, she says

and then they are silent, he sits there and perhaps he is ashamed
in a way and doesn't quite know what to say, and she stands there
and perhaps she too is a little ashamed and she doesn't quite
know what to say either, and then his thick stiff fingers fumble
with the loop of the zipper on his holdall, he pulls it open and he
takes out a bag and there are a few half-rotten bananas in the bag,
and he puts the bag on the table

I think they've gone off, he says

Is it a while since you bought them, she says

Couple of days, he says

and she comes over and takes the bag and opens it and then she
puts the half-rotten bananas on a tray, and she puts the tray down
by the sink

And now everything's fine, she says

Now you're well again, she says

That's what they say, he says

The doctors, she says

Yes, he says

You are well now, she says

So they tell me, he says

and she goes and sits in her chair, close to him, at the long end
of the table

It was so awful when you were sick, she says

and she looks straight ahead and then she glances up at him
and then she looks down again and he nods

It's one of the worst things I've lived through, she says

Yes, he says

But now you're well again, she says

That's what they say, she says

No more mad thoughts, she says

No, he says

And no more mad actions, she says

No now I'm back to the way I used to be, he says

That's good, she says

and then they sit there, on their chairs, where they have sat untold times, at untold meals, and everything is a little odd, they are
both ashamed the way they were when they first went out together
and they each had these thoughts, they don't quite know what to
do with themselves, they don't know what to say

You felt bad, he says

Yes, yes I couldn't help it, she says

Yes it's shameful, it's very shameful, he says

Yes, she says

To lose your mind, yes, he says

and once more they sit there in silence

But now you're home again, she says

And now you're well again, she says

Yes, he says

And is that why you're crying, she says

Because you've come home again, she says

Yes, he says

Because now you see your house again, she says

And the farm, he says

Everything, she says

Yes, everything, the farm, the mountains, the fjord, he says

I've lived here my whole life, he says

Always here, he says

This is where I was born, and this is where I have lived, my
whole life, I've looked at the fjord, at the mountains, I'm not
quite myself if I can't see the fjord, see the mountains, he says

Yes this is your land, she says

Yes, he says

And I can't be anywhere else, he says

And, well, that was, she says

and she breaks off and she sits there and looks down at the
table and regrets it

That was why I became sick, he says

Yes, yes in a way, she says

Yes, in one way it was, he says

That you thought the house and the garden would be taken from you, she says

Yes, he says

Although no one was going to take it, she says

No it was just something I thought, he says

Are you hungry, she says

Not especially, he says

Now why didn't I put some food on the table right away, I'm not quite myself either, now that you've come home, she says

And coffee, I haven't even put the kettle on, she says

No oh no, she says

and finds some pleasure in her forgetfulness

It'll wait, he says

and he too takes some pleasure in sitting there without coffee and then they fall silent again and don't know what to say

But, she says

Yes, he says

I did get a bit, yes a bit scared, when I saw you standing there and I saw tears on your cheeks and you wouldn't look up and look at me, and I thought, yes perhaps, she says

That I wasn't well, he says

Yes, she says

But it was only because you'd come home again, that was why you were crying, she says

Yes, he says

And now you're home again, she says

And now you're going to stay at home, she says

You'll stay at home for the rest of your life, she says

Yes, he says

and he puts his holdall down on the table and he stands up, slowly and laboriously, he takes his stick and pushes himself up and he stands there and looks down, and she gets up and stands there at the table, and then he opens the door to the living room and he goes in and he goes over to the window that looks out on the fjord, with the mountains on the other side, and he stands

there, with bent head, he stands there leaning on his stick looking
down, and she stands there, in the doorway, and he lifts his head
a little and throws a glance at the fjord, at the mountains, and
then he turns toward her and he looks at her and she sees that his
legs give way at the knees and then they fold beneath him and his
whole heavy body sinks down and his stick slides along the floor
and then he lies there on the floor with his hands and feet all tan-
gled, his tie lies across his stomach all crooked and his eyes are
staring and she goes over to him and she bends down and throws
her arms around him and she presses herself against him. And
then she sits up, on her knees. And she puts her hand to his mouth
and cannot feel any breath, and she puts her hand on his heart,
and cannot feel any beat. She stands up. She stands there in her
blue dress and her knitted gray cardigan, her thin gray hair falling across her frail face, and then, as she always does, she walks
into the kitchen.

Translated by May-Brit Akerholt
Sydney, September 27, 2008

ARTICLE 16

Marriage and Family

Kate Atkinson

THE WAR ON WOMEN

So it was really going to happen then. Geoff phoned from the office (the "Holy Office," as Tina called it) to say that there would be an announcement on the midday news—announcing the announcement, as it were. Trust Geoff to know ahead of time. He had always liked to think he was standing right on the edge of the future. With Tina it was the other way round, hanging on to what had been and even to what might have been.

Before Geoff had slowly worn her away, like water on stone, Tina Soutar, formerly Peck, had been a woman of the eighties. (She hadn't wanted it all, just some of it.) Twenty years old and armed against the world with only her RSA certificates, a power suit from Next and a Chanel "Rouge Noir" lipstick and already thinking with nostalgic fondness of the drunken and careless youth she had exchanged in order to be tethered to a Dictaphone (*Dear Sirs, In regard to . . .*) in the cramped back office of MacGregor and MacGregor, an ancient law firm down a dank close off the Royal Mile. The two MacGregors were not related to each other, were not in fact actually alive anymore and the practice was in the hands of their equally elderly successors. Sometimes Tina came into work in the morning and found mouse droppings on her desk and wondered if this was how it was going to be forever and if there was anything she could do about it.

Geoff was the harbinger of a brighter future. At MacGregor and MacGregor, Tina worked on a big upright Olivetti machine that had been built to survive a nuclear war. Then Geoff came along and seduced her with his exotic talk of microchips and word processors. ("*The Amstrad 1512, Teen—it's the future!*")

The first time she took Geoff to meet her parents ("your beau," her father called him) he turned up in a fashionable but funereal suit and tie from Topman, which made her parents anxious. Tina's mother, Carol Peck, was eager to get her daughter off her hands so that Tina's father could take early retirement and the two of them could caravan around the south of England in their Sprite Alpine.

Carol Peck served up her signature tuna and pasta bake and Geoff said, "Very tasty, Mrs. Peck," with a bonhomie that he was still in the process of learning but would soon perfect. The tuna and pasta bake, on the other hand, found itself somewhat wanting when faced with a cocky twenty-two-year-old with a (mediocre) business degree from Napier and a strange way of selling himself to her parents through mysterious slogans (*I believe in commitment to growth* and *Profit must be the businessman's mantra*).

Geoff was in at the beginning of computers, selling PCs out of a converted shoe shop on Dalry Road, and it turned out that he was right about the coming revolution. Within the year even the musty old solicitors Tina worked for had succumbed to the lure of the future and she found herself typing out deeds and divorce papers on a word processor with a little blinking cursor that followed her every move like a jealous emerald eye.

The tuna and pasta bake was followed by a Viennetta ("*Go on, Geoff, spoil yourself*"), after which Tina's mother invited Geoff to a reconnaissance of the Peck family photo albums.

"Just like Madonna," Geoff said, looking at a photograph of Tina primped and preened for the school prom—black lace fingerless gloves, footless tights, frou-frou skirt, a huge bow in her hair and strings of cheap beads round her neck.

"Done up like a Christmas tree," Tina's mother said.

"Thanks," Tina said. Tina had always liked clothes and makeup. Always would.

"Oh, I don't know," Geoff said, squaring off ever so slightly against his future mother-in-law (even though in that future they would frequently side with each other against Tina). "I think she looks very nice."

Her mother moved on to baby photographs, going backward in time. "Christina Jane," she said with a sad smile as if the Tina now sitting on the sofa were a completely different and (let's face it) disappointing person. "I always wanted a boy," her mother said wistfully.

Geoff proposed a few months later, offering a ring with a tiny chip of a diamond. "Buy you a bigger one when I make my first million, Teen," he said. Neither of these things had come to pass. They were married the following May, confetti falling like petals on Tina's pearl-coroneted head and her enormous wedding hairdo.

Geoff had not managed to hang on to his earlier Thatcherite promise and he now worked, as a regional sales manager, for someone else, someone who had a better grasp of the concept of growth and profit. Undeterred, he embraced his job with an evangelist's enthusiasm (a 1,000 gig serial ATA II hard drive with a 32 megabyte cache!). There was, however, something increasingly brittle about Geoff, and Tina wondered if one day soon he was going to realize that his relentless, often absurd, optimism had caused him to spend his life fighting his way upstream to nowhere.

Tina had also moved on, from the Old Town to the New Town, working three days a week for a real estate agency on Dundas Street, where her immediate boss, a leery, beery fifty-something in a broad pin-stripe suit, was always trying to get his hands on her in inappropriate ways (*"What's the matter, Tina? It's just a bit of fun"*). The rest of the time she was an Avon lady. *Ding-dong*. She could be enthusiastic about cosmetic products in a way she never could about leases and surveys. (*"That foundation really suits you."*) "I'm a people person," Tina always said. And she was.

"And what will happen after the announcement?" Tina puzzled.

"Oh," Geoff said airily, "I doubt that you'll notice much change at all." This seemed a ridiculous statement; surely the whole point of the thing was change, but before Tina could pursue this argument the doorbell rang and she said, "Well, I'll see you tonight then," and Geoff said, "You can bet your bottom dollar on that!" in that strangely chipper way he had, like a Spitfire pilot about to take to the skies (*Chocks away, Teen!*).

As soon as Tina opened the front door, Shirley and Laura pushed their way into the house. Both women were neighbors in the well-heeled, well-groomed suburb of Edinburgh, where Geoff and Tina were clinging to their expensive mortgage like shipwreck survivors.

Shirley was clasping a Waitrose carrier bag to her chest as if it contained the Holy Grail. "Gin," she said. "Mother's ruin."

"No, mother's little helper," Laura corrected cheerfully. She was a consultant in the emergency room at the Edinburgh Royal Infirmary. Laura had a lovely daughter, Clare, and Tina had made the cake for her eighteenth birthday, a triple-layer chocolate cake with fudge icing with fancy piping and "Happy Birthday, Clare!" spelled out in tiny sugarcraft roses that Tina had also made. (Tina had done an "Advanced Cake Decoration" evening class.) Clare was a medical student now. Tina tried to imagine her own spiky, resentful daughter turning to her and saying, "Mum, I want to be a doctor!"

Faced with the crème de la crème of the Grange bourgeoisie, Tina had a confused moment when she wondered if she had got the day of the week wrong (not to mention the hour and the week itself) and it was her turn to host the book group. Tina had only recently been persuaded to join the "Grange Book Group" but the others (all women, of course) had been meeting for years, gathering on the first Thursday of every month at the church of fiction, clutching their bottles of wine and their copies of *Atonement* or *The Time Traveler's Wife* (and twice a year, a classic). Tina would have been quite happy with just the wine, novels not featuring high on her list of life's necessities. And then not only to read a novel but to talk about it afterward! Double trouble, as it were.

It was Shirley, Tina's next-door neighbor, who had asked her to join the book group. You had to be invited by a member; it was like the Masons. Shirley was a journalist with *The Scotsman*, makeup plowed into her wrinkles and deep into the drink but slap-dash maternal with it (her son was a financial adviser, bespectacled, quiet). Tina used to read the *Mail* but in a halfhearted way; now she read *The Scotsman* so that she could say, "That was a good piece, Shirley." It only seemed polite.

Shirley had reached bus-pass age but still kept on working (*Going out feet first*). When Tina got her bus pass (a while to go yet, thank goodness), she was going to catch the first bus that came along and see how far she could get.

The first time Tina went to a meeting of the book club was at the home of a woman called Virginia who was an accountant with Deloitte and Touche—nice house, fresh flowers everywhere, cream carpets. No children, needless to say. Virginia was stringy, as if she spent a lot of her time in the gym. She was single, a divorcée, which she pronounced the French way so that it sounded like an even more alluring state than usual to Tina. When the girls were a little older and she could find enough energy (and it would require a lot), Tina was planning to leave Geoff. She could imagine the acres of arguments ahead of her ("*Come on, Teen, we've made it this far*") but she really didn't want to make old bones with a man who in the middle of (very mundane) sex would suddenly stop and say, "Damn! I forgot to e-mail in my expenses."

As soon as Tina walked into Virginia's cream-carpeted living room she had sensed the other members of the book club bristle to attention. Something to do with her high-heeled mules and low-cut top, she supposed. Or the big earrings like chandeliers. Or her blond hair, piled on her head like an ice-cream cone. Everyone in the book group seemed to have high-powered jobs. They were the kind of women who employed women like Tina.

"Ladies," Tina said, putting on her Avon smile. "I'm Tina."

Someone called Catriona, who was a lawyer, said to Tina, "Oh, wonderful, about time we had some fresh blood!" but Tina knew they were looking at her clothes and thinking, "Uh-oh, not the brightest button in the box." It was true she wasn't as educated as they were; school for Tina had been about getting a social life not an education. The only subjects she had liked were domestic science and games—producing a perfect Victoria sponge or belting up the wing on the hockey pitch (occasionally hacking an opponent's ankles) had always seemed more enjoyable than knowing about algebra or the Declaration of Arbroath.

"Why don't you tell us a bit about yourself, Tina?" a fat woman called Julia ("freelance radio producer") said, as if Tina were a particularly intelligent dog.

"Wife and mother," Tina said. "Beth's fifteen, Zoe's twelve, Geoff's old enough to know better. Ha, ha. Always been a secretary. I like cooking and sewing and gardening," she added defiantly. Tina and Geoff had assigned themselves traditional roles as soon as the confetti-like petals had been brushed from their hair—Geoff went out and sold computers, Tina did everything else. The other women all smiled encouragingly at her, waiting for more. There wasn't more. It was enough, in Tina's opinion. It was more than most people had in the world. "And a dog," she added. "An old one."

She didn't mention the Avon lady thing although there were one or two of them who looked as if they could do with a good makeover. Nor did she mention the way that Beth had rolled home at one o'clock this morning, stinking of alcohol and cigarettes, her pupils like black holes that led to another, dangerous world. ("*Fuck off and leave me alone, Mum.*") Her school reports were worse every term and she found every sly opportunity to truant. She visited websites about suicide and anorexia; she treated Tina like dirt on her shoe. She would come through it, Tina reassured herself, through to the other side where obedient adulthood beckoned. Geoff said that this was "exactly the kind of pressure he could do without."

Tina imagined a future Beth—a lawyer, a doctor, a journalist—sitting in a cream-carpeted room discussing the latest Booker winner while in a playpark in that same future Tina was baby-sitting her grandchildren. The future, like the past, was prefera-ble to the present.

Beth was darkness, Zoe was sunshine. She was in her first year at Gillespie's. She would still cuddle and kiss Tina (when had Beth last let her touch so much as a finger?). She liked horses and *High School Musical* and anything pink and still liked to tell silly jokes (*Knock, knock, who's there? Arthur. Arthur who? Arthur any more at home like you?*) Tina was currently em-ploying the global scientific community to find a way of keep-ing her like this forever. "Just joking."

"Great," said a woman called Margot ("in advertising"). She was wearing exactly the wrong shade of lipstick for her coloring. "Really great, Tina."

"No," Tina said. "Not great, just ordinary."

The book they were discussing was *Memoirs of a Geisha,* which Tina had watched on DVD so she hadn't needed to read it. Tina thought it was a shame that no one served food at these meetings. When it was her turn, she would lay on a feast.

"It's so hard for us to understand," Catriona said, "what it would be like to live the life of a geisha. To be so constrained, economically, socially, politically."

Well, Tina thought, I think I can understand.

"Right," Shirley said, chinking ice into glasses and pouring the gin. "Let's get settled in front of the TV." Tina put out a dish of salted peanuts. You would think they were about to watch *EastEnders,* not a proclamation that was (no matter what Geoff said) about to transform their lives. And not in a good way. Not a bit.

The screen filled with a shot of Big Ben that immediately com-menced its solemn *bonging* and Laura said, "No need to ask for whom it tolls. Thee and me, I fear, ladies."

Laura reached out to Shirley sitting next to her on the sofa and grabbed her hand so that the pair of them looked as though they were planning to drive off a cliff, like Thelma and Louise. Tina looked out of the window. The blossom trees on the street were bare and stark against a winter sky.

A disembodied voice, the kind they used to announce royal deaths, said, "And now, live from Westminster, the prime minister is to broadcast to the nation on a matter of national importance . . ."

"Here we go," Shirley said as the prime minister's mellifluous tones rolled around the kitchen.

"*I am speaking to you from the Cabinet Room at 10 Downing Street . . .*"

"That's that, then," Shirley said, staring like a fortune-teller at the ice cubes in the bottom of her empty glass. "We're the enemy now."

"What about the book club?" Laura said suddenly. "We're still allowed that, aren't we?"

Considering it was a day of such "national importance," life continued in the same old humdrum vein. Macaroni and cheese for tea, clean plates all round, except for Beth, of course, who said she had given up eating for Lent. Geoff said that her self-obsession (as he called it) was a travesty of religion, which was one way of putting it, Tina supposed. Tina didn't believe in God, didn't believe in much really, apart from being kind to small children and old dogs. Teenagers and cats she could take or leave.

Geoff, though, believed in a robust, manly Church of Scotland God, the sort who kept schedules and inventories and who knew all the words to *Address to a Haggis* and probably played golf when he wasn't sending down laws from mountains. When did Geoff start believing in God and why hadn't Tina noticed?

"God is the Law," Geoff said pompously as he dug into an "apple streusel crumble" of Tina's own invention. "And the Law is God."

Tina passed him the custard.

* * *

After tea, the girls went to their rooms, Zoe to do her homework, Beth to sulk. Tina sat in front of the TV and watched a repeat of *Agatha Christie's Marple*. She had the remains of a box of chocolates from Christmas on her knee, as well as the dog, making strange creaking noises as it slept. Geoff came into the living room, a large glass of Talisker in his hand and, toasting thin air, said, "Well, today's the day when life in Britain changed forever," and Tina said, "I thought you said that this thing wasn't going to make much difference?" Geoff looked at her and said quietly, with a funny look of distaste on his face, as if he were thinking through his teeth, "Not thing, Teen, it's the Law. Why do you have to be so irreverent?"

"Don't be such an idiot, Geoff," Tina said and Geoff said, "You wait, Christina Soutar, you just wait."

Nothing happened for a while.

"Phony war," Shirley said. "Don't worry, they're biding their time, waiting to make their first move." And so it was.

"A headscarf?" Tina had never worn a headscarf in her life. You couldn't wear it the way the Queen did, horsy and loosely tied, you had to wrap your head up like a parcel. Crazy. And black, for heaven's sake. They were all going to look like Sicilian widows. No way was Tina going to spend good money on a headscarf, so she threw an old sheet in the washing machine with some black dye and when it was dry she cut it into squares and hemmed them on the machine. What about Beth and Zoe? Did they have to wear them? There were many unanswered questions. There was a site online that you could go to, www.scottish.parliament.co.uk/newlaw, where it said that all girls who had entered puberty had to wear the scarf. Zoe's periods had started a couple of months ago, but she was only twelve—a child—and Tina would like to see someone trying to get Beth to wear a big, ugly, black headscarf—it would be like veiling a tiger. There was a PTA meeting at Gillespie's tonight about changes to the uniform rules. ("No way, Mum, am I wearing that fucking thing.")

Shirley had written an article about the introduction of the headscarf for *The Scotsman*. It was scathing but funny and Tina said, "That was a good piece, Shirley," and Shirley said, "Sexual apartheid. We have to fight back. They can't silence us all, there are too many of us. We are women, hear us roar."

The struggle had begun, Shirley said. There was a big demonstration being organized, thousands of women marching through Edinburgh "*sans* headscarves," wouldn't Tina join them? "Well, I don't know," Tina said, "I've never been what you would call political."

Instead she put on her Avon face and made a call on a client, a woman called Fiona who bought only an eye shadow palette because Tina had to spend most of the time giving her a tutorial on how to wrap up her head like a parcel. "They mustn't see our hair, apparently," Fiona said. "They'll become inflamed by desire and be unable to control their lust."

"Yeah, any excuse not to be responsible," Tina said.

Tina left Fiona practicing packing her head into the scarf. On the drive home Tina noticed that all the blossom trees were now in fat bud. She loved driving around in her little car, "tootling about" her father would have called it.

When she got home, she made a pot of tea and watched the demonstration on the TV news. Shirley was right, there were so many women, there was no way that men would be able to impose the new law. The whole thing was absurd.

"Give up work? What are you talking about?"

Geoff hauled his golf clubs out of the boot of the car. There was a new cheerfulness about him, the same as when he'd pulled off a big deal.

"You know, stop work," he said patiently, as if she were a child or an idiot. "Give up your job—jobs—and stay at home to look after your family. A woman's place is at home, after all."

"Says who?"

"Says the Law. Get used to it, Tina."

Tina went inside and downed a glass of wine as if it were medicine and then started on a chicken casserole, but her heart wasn't in it.

The latest thing was a kind of robe (black, naturally) that they had to swaddle themselves in from top to toe. Eyes, feet, hands were all that were left. They were being erased, blacked out inside their blankets.

Beth would have ripped hers off the minute she was out of sight but then she would never have been allowed into school. ("Modesty!" Beth spat the word out as if it were poison on her lips.) Geoff wanted her to stay home, he had already pulled Zoe from school, but every morning Beth marched out of the front door as if she were going into combat.

"Nobody's going to stop me going to school," she whispered fiercely to Tina. Not words Tina had ever expected to hear Beth say. They were allies now, with Geoff as their common enemy.

Beth smuggled textbooks out of school for Zoe, and Tina sat with Zoe at the kitchen table every day after Geoff had gone to work and made her do her lessons while she prepared the elaborate, labor-intensive meals that Geoff had decided were his due when he came in at night. The joy had gone out of cooking for Tina.

It was dangerous on the streets for young girls, and Tina would have driven Beth to school but Geoff had sold her little car because "You don't need it anymore, after all." Apparently the Law said that Tina was only allowed to drive the car if she was accompanied by a male relative. Tina didn't have any male relatives. Apart from Geoff, of course, but he had refused to be driven by her even before the Law was passed.

"How am I going to do the shopping without a car?" Tina complained. "How am I going to get to the supermarket?"

"I'll do the shopping," Geoff said.

"You?"

No online shopping, either. Geoff didn't allow any of them to use the Internet. "Too much stuff that's inappropriate for you."

"Are you sure the Law says we can't use the Internet?" Tina asked. It was funny but the Law seemed to be pretty much whatever Geoff decided it was.

It was ridiculous.

"This is ridiculous," she said, and Geoff punched her in the face.

The book group met at Margot's house. Again no food.

"This feels like a secret society," Julia the radio producer said, as they divested themselves of their black robes.

"Where two or three are gathered together," Catriona murmured.

The book this month was *A Thousand Splendid Suns* and Tina had managed to read a few chapters when she was stuck in the kitchen with Zoe. At least Geoff hadn't banned reading. Not yet anyway. Catriona said, "It's so hard for us to understand what it would be like to live the life of an Afghani woman. To be so constrained, economically, socially, politically."

Well, Tina thought, I think I can understand.

"I want a divorce," Tina said.

"In your dreams," Geoff said.

Casualties began to mount. There was an article in the *Evening News* about a woman who was flogged at the Tron for being seen in public with a man. Soon they would be tying them to stakes again and burning them.

"They never stopped," Shirley said.

Eyes, hands, feet were still too much, apparently. Now they had to wear a garment that resembled a circus tent, with just a little grille to look through. It was like being inside a post box and no matter how hard she tried Tina couldn't get the hang of wearing it. She felt suffocated inside the stuffy folds of material and because she was blinkered she kept tripping over the hem.

They had disappeared completely now. They were invisible women.

* * *

Shirley wrote an article about the new garment. It was angry and not at all funny. "That was a good piece, Shirley," Tina said and Shirley said wearily, "We must keep trying."

Tina wondered what it was about women that made men so angry. Women disappeared every day. They were kidnapped and beaten and imprisoned and raped and whipped and murdered for talking to a man in public. One girl (younger than Zoe) was killed by her (male, of course) relatives for having an unknown number on her mobile phone. Five girls and one of their teachers were gunned down outside Gillespie's. Tina was terrified for her warrior daughter but then she didn't have to be terrified anymore because the school announced it was closing to girls. Now all three of them sat in the kitchen and read books, like people under siege. The next book for the book group was *Persuasion*. Tina never thought she would enjoy reading Jane Austen. It just went to show.

"This is ridiculous," Tina said and Geoff punched her twice in the face.

The Law was unclear on the subject of book groups but it seemed that it wasn't in favor. That was the nature of the Law, it could be interpreted in any way that suited. Tina volunteered to hold the next book group at her house while Geoff was in Aberdeen at a sales conference. She felt as if she were in the French Resistance, all the planning, all the secrecy. Although the French Resistance probably didn't eat a warm roasted pepper salad, lemon chicken (Swiss onion tart for the vegetarians) and a chocolate and brandy mousse, which is what Tina spent all morning preparing.

She stood on the doorstep and watched as the women careened along the street toward her house, carried on a stiff spring breeze. They looked like a flock of giant, ungainly birds. They brought a flurry of petals into her house with them, pink thumbprints on their shrouds.

"I could get a three-ring circus under here," Virginia grumbled, shucking off the sea of material.

The Law didn't actually say they had to wear it, but no one wanted to risk the consequences if they didn't. ("Safer in than out," Margot said.) They had become their own jailers.

"Well," Laura said, pulling off her own tent, "at least I don't have to worry about anyone seeing my cellulite." She smiled brightly and flapped her arms up and down in an indecipherable gesture. Tina wondered if she was trying to fly away. She was demented, of course. Something terrible had happened to her daughter, the lovely Clare (*Happy Birthday, Clare!*). She had been walking by the Meadows when four men jumped from a car, pulled her into it and drove off. They beat her and raped her and later threw her out on Niddrie Mains Road like rubbish. Now she wouldn't leave her room at all. "That's what they want," Julia said.

A breathless Shirley arrived and said that she had heard that a woman was going to be stoned on Mull for adultery.

"We should protest," Margot said.

"We should demonstrate outside the Parliament building," Catriona said.

"A silent vigil," Virginia chipped in.

"Won't you join us, Tina?" Shirley said.

"Well, I don't know," Tina said, "I've never been what you would call political. Shall we talk about the book? We're a book group, after all."

"It's so hard for us to understand what it would be like to live the life of an Austen heroine!" Catriona said. "To be so constrained, economically, socially, politically."

"I think we all understand now," Tina said.

Shirley went to Mull and, under the cover of her big-top garment, she managed to witness the stoning of the woman taken in adultery and wrote an article about it for *The Scotsman*. She described how the woman had been placed in a sack and then she had been put into a pit that had been dug in the ground and how the pit was then filled in, leaving only the woman's head and shoulders free and then how people threw rocks at her head until she was dead.

"That was a good piece, Shirley," Tina said.

Shirley was dead. Two men broke into her house and shot her as she lay sleeping. The sound of the gun woke Tina but, not knowing what it was, she fell back to sleep.

There was a kind of armistice for a while. The economy slumped while women stayed home and read books. And then a new front opened up and hostilities recommenced.

"Another wife?"
    "Yes."
    "You're taking another wife?"

She was called Gina. She was eighteen years old, the daughter of a work colleague.

In many ways it was a relief for Tina to be relegated to the small, musty attic bedroom that was, appropriately, full of unwanted objects. She heard Geoff's inchoate cries in the night and felt almost sorry for his new bride.

"I want a divorce," Tina said to Geoff and he said, "That's what the woman on Mull said."

Geoff got into an accident on the bypass (bit of a shunt). He ended up "writing off the other guy's car," and it turned out that Geoff had let his insurance lapse. "Dying under the weight of all the bills, Teen," he said.

"That's because there's only one wage coming in," Tina said, but managed to keep the words safely inside her mouth because she was tired of being a punchbag.

It was OK, though, Geoff said. He had "come to an arrangement with the guy."

"That's good," Tina said.

"Yeah," Geoff said, taking Gina by the elbow and guiding her up the stairs.

"You're <u>giving</u> him Zoe?"

"Don't start arguing, Teen."

"You're giving him your *child*?" Tina howled. "To settle an insurance claim? Our *baby*?"

"She's not a baby. Zoe's twelve, old enough to be married, according to the Law."

"How old is he? This man?"

"Fifty-two," Geoff said.

Zoe danced into the room and said, "Knock, knock, who's there? Major."

"Major who?" Tina sobbed.

"Major open the door, didn't I? What's wrong? Mum?"

Tina wondered if this was how it was going to be forever and if there was anything she could do about it.

Tina did her hair and makeup. She applied extra blusher and lipstick. She put on her armor—the shortest skirt and the tightest, lowest-cut top in her wardrobe. She hitched up her breasts and showed off her cleavage.

"I want to come with you," Beth said and Tina said, "You have to stay. You're the future. The fight's yours now. I love you. Don't forget to moisturize. You'll thank me when you're forty. I love you—did I say that already?"

Tina stepped into a pair of spike-heeled shoes. Her legs were bare, her arms were bare. She stood on the doorstep and felt the warm breeze on her skin, on her face. She shook her hair free.

She walked down the path and turned into the street. She didn't look back. She reached the Meadows. She saw her life behind her—baby Christina Peck who should have been a boy,

Tina Peck racing up the wing, hockey stick like a weapon, the young bride Tina Soutar, brushing confetti from her hair.

Tina stepped out of her shoes. She removed her top, her skirt, her underwear and let them fall to the ground.

She was no longer invisible. Tina walked naked across the Meadows. The sky peeled back. The light was blinding. The trees that lined the path dropped their petals on her, like confetti. She wondered how far she would get.

Marriage and Family

Banana Yoshimoto

A SPECIAL BOY

What made him different from the usual six-year-old was his ability to quit whatever he was doing right away.

If the aunt who was raising him said, "It's time to go" or "Dinner!" he would stop immediately, even if he had reached a crucial point in a game or the best part of an anime.

All the other Japanese children that I know would grumble and try to keep playing the game. They would stay planted in front of the TV set, tearing themselves away—complaining all the while—only when Mother started to yell. I never realized that such ordinary moments of discord, such scenes that occur without fail in every house, are symbols of happiness.

"Why do children have to be like this?" "Why is this one so stubborn?" "Why do parents have to get mad all the time?" "I'm having so much fun! Why do I have to stop?" I never knew that such feelings of resentment on both sides of the parent-child divide are themselves what constitute happiness.

What I mean is that the process of repeatedly finding the precise point where both sides can come together is itself a form of nurturing, a form of mutual love and interdependence that takes shape only because each side learns to accept the other in the course of acting out these far-from-rosy scenes, these tedious collisions that form such a large part of how parents and children interact throughout the world.

His aunt was by no means too strict with him, but the boy always followed her orders as if struck by lightning.

The boy's mother went off and left him. Only after a year had gone by did any word come of her whereabouts. By then she had had a child with, and married, another man.

Apparently the boy's father had often beaten his mother. When they split up, the boy and his elder brother were taken in by the father's parents. By then the brother was old enough to be less of a burden for his father and grandparents, but the little boy was too much for them, and one day all of a sudden, it seems, he was dropped in the laps of his mother's parents.

People who marry are supposed to be grown-ups, I thought. And when two grown-ups have a child, they're supposed to take care of it until they can present it to society in some kind of decent shape. Nowadays in Japan, though, it seems that children often marry children, and when *they* have children, they find these new ones too much trouble, so they let them go. They're like the kind of idiots who buy dogs because they think they'll make cute pets, and kick them out when the barking annoys them.

The mother's parents—the boy's other grandparents—were not eager to have him, either. They were too old to be raising a child, they said.

The boy's aunt couldn't stand to see what was happening to him and decided to take him in herself. She told me, "I didn't want to tell him that we were going to start living together from now on, or that he'd be leaving Grandpa and Grandma's house. I figured that, at some point while I was playing with him, I would just say that we'd be going to another house, or maybe when we were all eating together I'd just say I wanted to take him home with me and not make a point that he would be leaving Grandpa and Grandma's place for good."

Finally, though, how painful could it have been for him to leave the home of grandparents who couldn't raise him? To me, that made him all the sadder, all the more pitiful. Of course the grandparents were probably not devoid of feeling for him, either, nor had they treated him badly, I suppose.

The boy had clothing, shoes and toys. He could watch TV, eat three meals a day and go to kindergarten. Some might conclude that he was a lot better off than many children around the world living in misery.

But something important was missing from the boy's world—a secure sense that things would go on as usual and little things allowed to pass, an atmosphere that let him feel, "I can stay here."

Japan may well be full of such children these days.

I kept my thoughts to myself, but they went something like this:

If it had been me, I would have liked her to let me know what was happening. As painful as it might be, I'd rather have her tell me the truth. Your father and mother abandoned you, and though your grandpa and grandma do love you, they simply can't raise you. So now you're going to be leaving their house. From now on you're going to live with me, your aunt.

I would have wanted her to say it that clearly.

I wanted to tell her that it might be more painful for him to learn the truth, but that at least he wouldn't have to deny anything.

But each family has its own way of dealing with such things. He would at least be better off than he had been. He would be able to live in the same house with the same person. This was nothing for me to be giving opinions on.

One night shortly after he had started living with his aunt, the boy came to play at my house. He and my son enjoyed playing games, talking endlessly, and sharing the names of each other's friends. He was thoroughly delightful—a bright, lively, wide-eyed little fellow.

Like other children, this boy had so far grown up with someone to change his diapers and give him his milk every day. What had happened to ruin things? How could a person just walk away like that, decide one day to cast aside this smooth-skinned little creature who wants nothing more than to enjoy life with wide-open eyes, a little creature who, moreover, gives his protector such unconditional love? And all because of what? Not genuine poverty or hardship, but just some irresponsible *thing*.

The boy's aunt said to me with understated love, "I made his mother sign a document so that I would absolutely never have to give him up if all of a sudden on some whim she decided she wanted to take him back."

This was both terribly sad and terribly important as a final lifeline for him now.

Once he started living with her, she said, he had started smiling more often, and stopped having pointless fights with his friends or fits of temper. It seemed that he was finally starting to feel somewhat secure.

I couldn't help wishing that all children might have someone to appreciate them in this way. But there must be so many, many children in the world for whom that never happens—children who die unnoticed, unloved children who turn to violence because they don't know what else to do. Parents who toss their children aside are incapable of realizing that each and every such child is a treasure for all the world.

"Time to go home."

When his aunt said this, the boy stopped playing the game and jumped to his feet. Only my son stayed sprawling on the sofa. He still had no idea how fortunate he was to be able to do this. Sadly, he might never in his life realize that he was too fortunate to recognize his own good fortune.

"Gotta pee," the boy said. The three of us waited for him at the front door. He came out of the toilet with incredible speed, still zipping his fly. "Oh, good," he whispered to himself the moment he caught sight of his aunt.

Clearly, this meant, "Oh, good, she's still here."

Only a child who had been dumped in numerous places without warning could have said this.

They went off down the dark street hand in hand. They would probably go on living together as peacefully and happily as they appeared to be at this moment. The painful memories of abandonment would no doubt fade for him, and his life with his aunt would become indistinguishable from that of any ordinary mother and son. As in any family whose children had not experienced abandonment, they would have their fights and their moments of tenderness and would overcome the many obstacles encountered on the road from childhood to adulthood.

But still, that little whisper, "Oh, good," would probably never fade away completely. The right to utter those words was a thing of value that belonged to him alone.

It was like a tiny diamond, painful but precious, that he would keep inside. Even if he forgot about it, it would always be there, sparkling, long after the parents who had abandoned him forgot his very existence.

Translated by Jay Rubin

Owning Property

Alexis Wright

BE CAREFUL ABOUT PLAYING
WITH THE PATH OF LEAST RESISTANCE

When his grandfather spoke on his traditional country, the boy knew he was listening to the voice of Aboriginal Government.

There are many, many paths in your country, good boys and girls. Good stories. Good life. Go take the right one. Plenty of good ones. People here, all of your family can tell you which one. Play wherever around here all right, but never go anywhere near one bad story. Try to be the right story.

He already knew that many people in his community were calling him naughty boy, but still he went, nice way, "Yes, oh, hello Aunty, hello Uncle," so on and so forth, styling up—he greeted them all accordingly. He knew how to be respectful, as he was supposed to be, to each and every one of dozens of relatives stopping to look, and muttering, "the house of smart alec," seeing him sitting outside in the front yard of his parents' house, "watching television like some lazy whatnot."

Watching his relatives filing into the house to talk to his parents about his behavior, he felt as though his brain had been transformed into a savage dog. His head was on fire and the dog was locked behind clenched teeth. He was bursting at the seams to break out and scream at the world that nobody's words would bother him. Yeah! Well! You got to love him, the relatives say, after trailing in and out of the house to see if he was still there, once they had finished warning his parents about what the government would do to them. His ears pricked up, and he turned down the TV a notch or two, to hear the heated conversation inside the house.

The loudest voices were saying, "Don't you people here have ears? Haven't you heard what the government in Canberra is talking about on the radio and the TV and all that?

"Well! The government, you know, has gone mad—more mad—madder than before—when it comes to Aboriginal people. It is all on the news. They are sending the army in to all of the Aboriginal communities to take control of your kids if they don't go to school. It will be the army who will be telling parents what to do. Didn't you hear about that?

"All you get is this government mob in Canberra bellyaching about Aboriginal people and the whole country *big-note-ing* itself—wanting to make a *blackfella* story into a white story. You want to get that television set off of your son once in a while and listen to a bit of news, because the government said that they will be giving us orders from now on about how we spend our own money."

His eardrums were burning—he really was on fire—and he honed in, listening more closely to the conversation inside the house. "The army are already on the way." His parents were warned that the government was sending the army in to storm into all of their homes.

"Just like you have seen armies pushing around all of those other poor people on the earth, like in the war on terror over in Iraq and Afghanistan."

And there it was, you could bet on it every time—a plague of fearfulness in the atmosphere flaring up, and simply by osmosis he was hit by a silent twang, and his spirit slapped back inside his parents. He thought it was a trick, that their fear was joined to him by invisible elastic that could be pulled by either of them in an instant, to make him feel what it was like inside of their skin. He knew that they were frightened of the police, frightened of the government and frightened of officials, which meant they were frightened of any white person in the vicinity, and any others in a proximity that radiated outward and onward until it encompassed the entire continent. A shiver disconnected him. He did not want their fear.

"They will be searching you to see if you are abusing your kids."

He strained to hear the whispering stuff and muffled voices talking about the news of how Aboriginal men were sexually abusing all the children.

No, nobody knew which men, but it looked like all Aboriginal men were doing it, even here and everywhere, according to what was being said on the radio and on the TV, too. *"We are just finding out about it now."*

He heard his parents being told that all of the children would be forced to have medical checks to see what was wrong with them. "The army will be arresting all of the children and taking them to see a doctor to see which ones are being abused, and they might find out something else too, why they are not going to school." The voices became shrill, saying, "You got to make him." He should be flogged and flogged solid, until he went to school.

He heard them say that everyone in the whole community would starve more now, because parents would lose all of their welfare money if he didn't go to school. *You can't make me!* The voices shouted so he could hear what they were saying, even from where he was, sitting outside of the house.

"Tell him that the government's intervention into the Aboriginal communities in the Northern Territory will make him go to school everyday, or else they will clear the lot of us away from our traditional land again. We won't be able to live here anymore. Tell him they are going to take him away, along with everyone else's children too. Parents will all be separated again from their children, just like the Stolen Generation days."

He knew that many of his relatives had too many people living in their homes just like his place, which was called overcrowding, and most of their children were not going to school either. Why were they trying to force him to go to school?

"No! Don't tell him, just flog him and make him sit at school, or everyone will starve to death in this place."

"You tell him all this is the government's law now, and we are telling you that the government's law wants you to flog him until you kill him if he doesn't go, otherwise they will close this place down."

He thought all the talking about the army coming into his home had to be some kind of joke, but he could tell by the way that his parents were screaming that they were pretty shaken up and the fear in their voices really confirmed in his mind once and for all that this was no joke. They were responding in the only way that they knew, by telling everyone to get out and leave them alone. The country's ghosts only knew how he wanted the whole community to explode when they heard him say exactly what he thought about the government to their face when they turned up with the army.

He punched himself for bravery, commanding himself that he was not frightened of any government. If they wanted to make war—*Well, go for it!* He would give them war. He imagined himself falling from the sky like a high-speed missile, which he would steal from the army—*Whoa!* His hands were joined high above his head, and he dived straight through the air, and down, *BANG!*

He had set up the television in the front yard by running a thirty-meter-long yellow extension cord out through a window of the house from a broken plug in the wall that he had played around with until he made it work. He wanted to show everyone how he looked after himself. He felt that smart about fixing the broken plug, he thought if he ever got an education the first thing he would do would be to make the biggest missile in the world to protect his grandfather's traditional country so nobody could take it away again.

All of his relatives had now come by, even the ones who were visiting and camping at his parents' place in the backyard, and he thought by now they would have exhausted themselves after spending all morning just talking about how the Federal Government Intervention Policy would work, and he reckoned that, altogether, they had not missed one single thing that they wanted to say to his parents for the final time that day. You know how they had looked when they left? You could see their tongues hanging out for water.

Their message had been made clear: *We fought for our land rights for years before we got it back.* If *smart alec* decides not to go to school, they said, he will be forcing the whole community to leave their country forever, and they will all have to go and live like dogs, fighting with all the drunks on the fringes of the town, which was about four hundred kilometers away from their traditional land. He could still hear their voices fading into a settled place in his brain that lived, just to keep reminding him: *Who will be left to look after the country? No one will know the songs. We will not be allowed. We will not be able to come back. It will be too hard. Everyone will forget. The government will be the winner. They have always wanted to take our land rights back. It will just take one smart alec going about doing the wrong thing.*

The school was a showcase the government built to help a politician win votes in his electorate. The lime-green color of the school was very nice. It was the only building that had been replaced in his community for years. It was an achievement so rare, so everyone claimed, they had started calling the building *rapid-quick time*—compared to anything else that they had tried to work for with the government. The community was proud of the school—but not him. He thought the school was an eyesore amidst the few dozen houses in the community that were so old the wind had blended the color of the walls with the red earth, and this was the predominant color he had grown up with since he was born, twelve years ago.

He wished the school could teach him something radical and brand new—something that would be useful for a boy living there to know, like how to fix up his mum's stove. Or just imagine if they taught other miracles. He would have liked to know how to fiddle with the broken fridge and fix it up because nobody had seen a repairs and maintenance man in years. He contemplated how he might be able to go down to the rubbish bin and find some electrical bits, but he reckoned he still needed to know how to do the job. What else did he need? Tools! Money! Dream on! His mind traveled through a litany of malfunctioning plumbing and electrical wiring until he was exhausted from the thought, and he disentangled himself from the suffocating wires and pipes that invaded the consciousness of the entire community.

The schoolteachers loomed large in his mind and now, after what he had heard from all of the relatives bothering his parents, they had become the centerpiece of his contempt. "You know," he snapped at a children's presenter on TV, "if they are so smart, how come those losers don't teach anything useful?" He did not know what was worse—the boring television presenter or the teachers who talked about nothing all day and were to blame for making him feel mad.

He imagined the teachers flying above him in flights of white-winged unreachable clouds that plowed on regardless in words that were just clouds, moving in the opposite direction from where he was sitting down below. His head felt hot under his mop of hair sticking out like a nest of straw. He could not get these teachers out of his mind.

Well! Take a look at him. There he was in the classroom day after day until he could not stand another moment of not understanding one single thing they were supposed to be teaching him. He felt his day had turned into a pile of rubbish like yesterday, and the day before that, and he reached further back in time until he could remember not feeling demented like mad, drunken people.

There was nothing worthwhile to watch on kids' TV that stopped the secret moving in the pit of his stomach. It was the secret he had not been able to tell anyone. It was about what was happening to him at school. In his loneliness, he brought the bundle up to his throat, where it became blocked, and he sent it back down. Once this ball started bouncing up and down it would make him feel sick. He would not allow himself to think about what he knew and did not want to know, that he had failed before even reaching the years ahead to finish his schooling in the ugly, slimy-green school, where he felt as though he was a toad, sitting in vomit.

Nah! He would not do that. He was not going to waste his time. *I want to stay feeling clean.* He could not think of any teacher giving him a clue about what he would do with their education. *Why waste having a good shower on them?* He flicked the TV flicker around for the sake of flicking. He shoved his bad thoughts out from the classroom and into the schoolyard. He cast his mind over the little trees that clung to life in the heat of the day, or the winds of winter, and had never grown at all, having remained like little sticks with a few half-dead-looking leaves. Schoolteachers were not smart about that, making a garden on his country, *were they?* He looked around at his country's landscape of red, browns, gray and yellow, olive and blue, and thought it looked good just the way it was already. It was full enough with too many plants like spinifex grasses, eucalyptus trees and all the scrubs with their own spiritual stories. The flicker was working overtime, pushing the bad thoughts between images of cartoons on two TV channels.

He left the TV on full static and walked down the road, dreaming about the hunting dog he wanted to own. He decided to visit his grandfather because he had dogs. "Give me one of your dogs." He had asked his grandfather the same thing every time he saw him. There were plenty of dogs living with the old man, but his grandfather loved all of them. He waited for the same answer while wondering which one he would choose between the biggest or even the littlest, but he would not take the *ugliest* one, even if old grandfather changed his mind and gave it to him.

"Maybe I will give you a dog one day when you grow up a bit."

"I know how to look after a dog and I need one now because I am leaving here to live in the bush before the army gets here."

The old man laughed.

"I don't know what is going on in that young mind of yours about the army and all that stuff, but I will give you my best dog one of these days, but not now."

The boy played with a few of the younger dogs, teasing them with sticks while he was deciding what to do next, and what occurred to him was the little game he kept playing with himself, and he thought of everyone talking about him once they had heard what he had done.

"This boy, skinny one with rubbish head," his grandfather would say, "already knew that he was not supposed to take that one old overgrown path at the back of the community, but you know, from plenty of tracks he could have chosen—all of them with big stories of the epics he belonged to from the beginning of time, he did what? *Why did he go and do that for?*" Then he thought of his parents, his mother and father crying that they have been *perplexing themselves silly* to understand what mystery sickness he had that had drawn him like a magnet to that one overgrown track—*the one over there*, lying beneath a covering of dry grasses. He even knew it would be impossible to count the number of times he had been told not to go near that track.

He felt the bad story about the track stirring him inside, which kept him noticing the way the grass grew like a door at the entrance to where this story began, and this was the reason why he kept going back to watch the phenomenon, of how the grass had almost concealed the path. Soon, he thought, the path would disappear altogether if nobody walked on it, and if he had not been any the wiser, even he would never have known that it ever existed. The memory would be gone forever and he would have forgotten the reasons for the country taking over the footprints that had been made from children who had gone there to commit suicide. All of it will be gone when the grass covered the stories his people had condemned to die, to never be spoken of.

Hey! Itchy! Titchy! Feet so Itchy! In the game of daring the children played, teasing one another to find out which one of them would be game enough to go to paradise, and he let their words float while they grew larger in his mind, to energize him until he was under the spell. The thought of traveling had always been locked inside of him like a colossal force, and now it pulled him through a pathway created from children's rumors that had been embellished from whatever may have once been true. The idea of being dangerous, of leaving, made him feel strong. It was even better than thinking he could steal a missile. A volcano in his lungs spilled lava and its heat was driving him crazy with wishing, and he felt like this each time he went near to the barely visible, abandoned opening between the dry grasses. He liked playing this game that kept singing him to a wild volcanic dance in his imagination, pulling his eyes further in to where the track ended some distance away to a sunlit opening among a circle of ghost gums with white trunks and a canopy that was held in an embrace—a glen he should never go to at the end of this path, in fear that his life might disappear forever, because no child who went there had ever come back.

This game had become something special to him, and he was beginning to feel ambivalent, and he did not care, because his attraction to what he ought to avoid was growing lovable through a fiery argument that he controlled and owned. His wishing was becoming his soul mate; a strange friend to run to from the secret he knew about himself of a learning, a knowledge of his future, that he had lost his way already in the classroom while the voices of teachers reverberated through the air as sounds that told him that he would not succeed in life without an education.

He slipped from the knowledge of failure, unable to capture a picture of himself in the future that he could love, nor could he retreat to the past and begin again like a little child, and he slipped further into this special relationship with the path that stood apart from anything else that he knew, and let it fuel him with the power of destiny. He felt stronger, as he was once before he could no longer understand the lessons of school. He was thinking alone with his own fiery secret, which was as precious as the one other abandoned dream of owning hunting dogs.

This was the game of a conqueror, the way he casually walked in a roundabout way toward the path, so he would not be noticed, and stood at the entrance of the track, kicking the grass aside with his bare feet. He felt the warming blood of a warrior, a soldier, or a rich man at the wheel of a new car. He saw himself inside a television, hunting for a future inside a boy, and racing toward invincibility among the spirits. The call came to him through the wind rattling the leaves, or it came through birds beating on the hardwood of a tree trunk, or from among the branches scraping against one another. All called of knowing him. He felt the need growing stronger, and it was as if he already knew that just to exercise his own willpower would change his life, for the better, to make him rich, who only knew what would happen then. He did not care.

The thought occurred to him that he would go through the path in a flash, and he believed he would be back in a minute. This short journey to the glen among the trees where for no other mysterious reason at all he just wanted to stand in the lovely shade amongst the ghost gums. Nobody would ever know if he went there, if he took one, or two, steps farther along the path. One time, when he was about to try after making a decision he could go forever, a cloud of yellow butterflies crossed in front of him, stopping him in his tracks. Then an owl swooped at the idea one night. Another time, when he had made up his mind that he did not care whether he came back, an eagle had arrived in front of him, landing among the branches, as though warning him to stop.

He wanted to run headfirst into the place where children he had known had asked for invincibility in their death, and had their spirit freed, only leaving the memory of a child who had taken his own life behind for the families to mourn. He stood in front of the path ready to go as quickly as if he were at the starting line of a race, so that he could run to the rest of his life. Suddenly, instead of the loud shrill of the whistle, he heard his grandfather's voice quietly speaking behind him.

"You are going to our Aboriginal land council meeting today to learn all the important business of looking after our human rights, our culture and our ancestral land. It is time you learn to make sure nobody takes that one away from us."

He ran off quickly, surprised that his grandfather was not worrying about the government or the army, and even dispelling his own thoughts, nagging: *Path! Path! What about the path?* Forget that path. Nobody questioned his grandfather. When his grandfather spoke, he knew that he was talking for the spiritual ancestors who had created their country. He was not going to be left behind. He would have to pack the swag, to go with his grandfather, who said that they would travel for many, many hours, maybe even two days.

"Now, don't muck me around. I am going to show you plenty of stories for the country along the way. You will remember all of them."

He knew he would now be one of the people who came home telling stories of traveling through their country in all the seasons of scorching heat, or extreme cold, or maybe big starry nights, moving over very rough roads, and what happened on the way when the car broke down. He would talk about the big meeting of elders that took place in another community—a place on an open plain close to the sky dreaming, or another place that was resting against a rocky range that was the body of an ancestor lying in the spinifex grassland of the vast Aboriginal-owned land governed and cared for by the tribal nations and language groups of his own people.

"You are old enough to start learning about the big responsibility of looking after the stories for the country now, and maybe if you listen and learn something, you might even become responsible for looking after the country one day."

The boy sat between his grandfather and his best dog on the long journey of stories, and his grandfather showed him their big argument, which was where the miners were digging up and breaking the spiritual resting places on their traditional land.

"This is why I want you to be strong and to get a good education. So you can fight all of that one for me with a proper pen-and-paper job."

The boy nodded truthfully, because he would walk over hot coals for his grandfather.

When they arrived home after several months of traveling with the other senior Indigenous law people for some of the important religious ceremonies to honor the country, he found that his parents had left the community. Many of his aunties and uncles had gone away, too. He was told that they had gone to live in town because they were scared of the government and the army.

The government in Canberra had changed again, and now the Intervention laws affecting his people were called *Closing the Gap*. It still meant that if you were an Aboriginal person living in a remote community on your traditional land, then you had fewer rights than other people in the country, and were forced to live under special laws that ruled over your life. The only choice his parents had was either to stay on their land and live under these laws, where they had very little control over their lives any more, or to leave.

Over at his grandparents' place it was really chock-a-block with all of the children who had been left behind so somebody else could try to force them to go to the slimy-green school that still looked the same, and still meant nothing in the lives of any of these children. He thought of the silent grandmothers, and grandfathers, and old aunties and uncles anyway worrying for some money for tucker, with nowhere else to go and all they wanted to do was to stay with their country to look after it, and now looking after all of the children, including the ones they were already caring for, like the ones whose parents were handicapped, or a long way away sick in hospital, or had passed away, or were serving time in some distant jail, or had gone now for any of a hundred reasons that call people away for ceremony and looking after the country because that was their responsibility.

He thought there had to be somewhere where he would find some money to buy his grandparents food when the government and the army came and took all of their welfare money away for three months, as they said they would do, because they could make a law to starve them all if the kids were not going to school. He would not let them starve. He would rob someone, and he pushed the thought away that kept occurring to him that he would go somewhere . . .

Freedom of Conscience

Helen Dunmore

WHERE I KEEP MY FAITH

When we were children and our badness jumped out of our hidden hearts and showed itself in bold words, Grandpa would raise himself from his chair. His shadow would fill the doorway as he went into the yard to cut a switch. When he had found the right one he would call us outside. Five strokes on our calves, no more. Each one was a sharp, hot, single pain. I would stare down to see if my badness was flickering away across the dust like a snake. Maybe if I looked hard enough I would see the moment when the shadow of it left my body and slipped to the earth.

My grandpa never hurt us hard. My mind was always quick and alive, not swallowed up in pain the way I know that a mind can be beaten until darkness overcomes it. But Grandpa made me think about badness: where it came from and how it could be seen in a person's eyes or in his voice or in his smile. It might be hidden but it would never be hidden enough, not from my grandpa or from the eye of God.

One night Grandma showed me something that looked like a star. She got me to fix my eyes on it and then she told me that it wasn't a star, but a satellite made of metal and plastic.

"Who put it there?"

"The Americans put it there."

"Why?"

My grandma shrugged. "Who knows?" she said. "They could do it and so they did."

I wondered if one day a satellite might take out God's eye. If so, he would be able to see nothing. I thought about God seeing nothing and waiting blindly to be told what had happened in the world.

I was grown up before I knew that it was the other way around. Something had taken out the eye that would show us God, and only faith would help us in our blindness.

And I was grown up some more when all this changed again. Blindness and hiddenness were in me and all around me. The words I had stood up for in church were far away. The sound of my voice praising the Lord was silent.

Where is a person's faith? Where does she keep it? I have been thinking about this question. You might answer that it is obviously kept in the soul, and then we can talk about what the soul is made of, and whether we can see it, and where it goes after death. Or perhaps it is in the heart. The heart is closer and more familiar. We are used to it knocking against the ribs when we are afraid, or melting tenderly at the curve of a baby's head. Perhaps faith is in there too, sometimes knocking and sometimes melting.

But I don't think so. I've had a long time to think about it, and many alternatives have presented themselves to me.

Firstly, the hair. Unlike the heart and perhaps unlike the soul, hair continues to grow long after we are dead. It is not a pleasant thing to imagine hairs pushing through the skin, wriggling out into the white shroud. Even if a woman has always colored her hair, she won't be able to fool anyone after her death: the hair that grows will be gray. Sometimes I imagine all the hair that is growing all over the planet, from the recent dead.

Hair is not a safe place to keep your faith. It can be cut off against your will. It can be torn from your scalp. But on the other hand hair can be plaited so tightly that the pattern endures for weeks. Perhaps faith would be happy there, planted deep in the maze of the pattern.

It is a long, long time since anyone plaited my hair, although I can remember sitting between my grandma's knees while she combed and separated and twisted. She had strong fingers but she never hurt me.

"What's the hurry? We have all the time in the world," she used to say. My grandma liked to stroke the curve of my cheek. She told me that I was like land after rain had fallen on it, because I was young.

"Look at my face. This is how land becomes when rain refuses to fall."

She laughed and all the gullies in her face crinkled, exactly like the channels that ran down to the dry river.

You might think it would be possible to keep faith in my grandma's lines. Surely it would be safe there. An old woman's lines will only grow deeper and provide a better shelter. But even apart from the fact that my grandma is dead, I don't think it would be possible. We shed our skin every seven years.

I am supposed to sign a letter, renouncing my faith. I have spent a long time thinking about what this means. If you renounce something, then it goes away from you. But where does it go? The letter has been written on a computer. If I renounce my faith, will it go into the fibers of the paper, or will it lodge in the hard drive? Where exactly will it go?

What is supposed to happen is this. They bring me out of my cell, into a room where I have been brought many times before. It is a small, dirty room with a desk and a chair with a man sitting in it. He is dressed in his army uniform. The uniform is clean and stiff and his boots are also clean. His boots and his face gleam like land where rain has fallen. My feet are bare. The skin is gray and the veins are knotted. I have no mirror but I know that my hair does not shine. I have an infection in one eye which refuses to clear. I am not clean and so my body smells. I see his nose wrinkle. I am forcing him to do things he doesn't want to have to do. All that is necessary is for me to sign his piece of paper and then sensible things can begin to happen.

Each time it happens I look down at my feet. On my right foot the big toenail has gone. Obviously I did not keep my faith in that toenail. I almost smile, but without changing the expression on my face.

It is stupid, all of this. It is so stupid. They make that so clear to us. There are four of us keeping our faith not in our souls or our hearts or our hair or our toenails or our grandmothers' wrinkles. Sometimes we are kept separate and told that all the others have signed the piece of paper and gone away. They have been given food and a shower and shoes and clean underwear and even a small roll of notes so they can buy a bus ticket home.

When the men say this, we just wait. We don't look believing and we don't look disbelieving. Even though I know it isn't true, my stomach hurts because of the thought that it might be only me left. I fear that the others have been killed. I see them so rarely and we never have time for more than a few words. It's better if we aren't together, in case we give something to one another. Our badness maybe, or else our faith, which we ought to give to the white sheet of paper.

I think of a thousand falling at my side, and ten thousand at my right hand.

I am not the material of which martyrs are made. I have always known this. The others say that they are the same. It's just that we took a step, and then another step, and these steps brought us here. But in fact it's not possible to count the steps. And you can't take them back again, because in order to do that you would have to unmake everything. I would have to become a woman with ten toenails and ripe, moist skin and hair the color of earth after heavy rain has fallen on it.

Sometimes I imagine myself lying on the ground, clinging to the big shiny boot of the man who brings in the piece of paper. Rubbing my cheek against the leather. Saying that I will do anything he wants.

But what would be the good of that? I would have to get rid of my faith first, and I am unable to do that until I find out exactly where it is.

In my skull perhaps. I have a bony cave of secrets under my

scalp, just like everyone. They could dig their way into it, but that would be the end of me. No chance of a pen in my hand then. No words on paper. *I give up. I renounce. I have no faith anymore.*

I understand completely that it would be gratifying to kill me. I am an annoyance, as well as a source of undesirable odors. I get in the way of what ought to happen next. Sometimes I find myself completely in sympathy with their point of view.

Perhaps my faith is in my elbow. Elbows are awkward things, jabbing out into the world, making space for themselves. They are also far from beautiful. The only elbow it's possible to love is the elbow of a baby, so soft and dimpled that it fits into your mouth like a plum.

My elbows are dry. When I hold my arm out straight in front of me, wrinkled skin hangs. Sometimes it seems very funny to me that once I had those plum elbows too. At other times I feel as if time has stopped moving in a straight line and is zigzagging back and forth like a snake on the floor. I feel my grandmother's hands in my hair. I hear her voice vibrate against the back of my head. I watch my grandfather throw his switch onto the earth and walk back inside.

Without question I am lucky that I have no children. My little son with the plum elbows was never born. But sometimes I forget it. I feel the tingle of milk beginning in my breasts. I feel my belly lift and tighten as if someone is about to be born. After a while I come back to myself and I am glad that I am alone, that my grandparents are dead and that everyone in my family has signed the piece of paper. Or have they? Perhaps they never needed to, because they were clean of faith.

I remember everything about when I was taken away. There were six of us in a room, and the Lord was with us. Wherever two or three are gathered together in my name.

This is why they keep us alone most of the time, so that two or three cannot gather together. But being alone does other things as well. It makes time whip backward and forward like a snake about to strike. It makes a baby come to me.

Of course I pray. I say words, as if my faith were in my mouth.

The others tell me: I will pray for you, and I say: I will pray for you. It makes our prayers sound like wheels, rolling across the world and touching on one another.

But my faith is not in my mouth. I pray less than I ever did.

My voice was beautiful. I was a praise singer. I used to rise up, and then raise them up. The sound would grow from deep inside me and swell richly until my forehead was slick with the dew of praise. I sang for hours and never tired. My voice was a gift and I gave it back to the Lord seventy times seven.

Yes, I thought a lot of myself, the way a woman does when her skin is ripe and soft and her voice sways a roomful of hearts.

Now I look back at that singer with her blaze of a smile at the end of a song and I'm watching a child dance in imitation of a grown woman. My voice has dried up. All last winter I had a cough from lying on the ground. I don't worry about it too much. My voice will come back, or else it won't. I used to think that my faith was in my voice. It made people turn to me like flowers. They called my voice a gift from God.

I won't sign the piece of paper. It's not something I've decided, it's just come to be true for many reasons which are all one reason. My missing toenail, my knotty hair, the veins on my feet, my disinclination for prayer. The sound of the switch and the slam of my head against the wall. The gray hairs that'll still be growing after I die. My elbow joint, working away like a knuckle under the flesh. My brain that says that the men are right, what I am doing is not sensible.

The Lord refusing to be with me, then suddenly giving me a child.

The smell of myself.

The fact that I can't, anywhere, find where I keep my faith.

Freedom of Expression

Héctor Aguilar Camín

COMRADE VADILLO

Before his arrest in 1968, the writer José Revueltas spent two months living in hiding in the house of a friend by the name of Cantú, a stone's throw from the Mariscal Sucre bandstand in the center of Mexico City. The bandstand has long since gone from the city, but not from my memory. In my nostalgic vision I can still see its green roof, dark in among so many trees and plants, with its granite steps and bronze lions guarding the noisy peace of children playing all around it. A maternal, bovine happiness reigned within its floral confines, shielding it from the violent, reactionary truth outside in the same way that we were shielded by the events of '68, and Revueltas' dreams of the future.

Cantú worked on *El Día,* a newspaper that, thanks to support from the president, was set up in part by the senator Manuel Moreno Sánchez to provide some criticism of the government and break the conservative stranglehold on the rest of the national press, which went in for solemn commentaries on the blindness of the oligarchy and confirmed its prejudices at cocktail parties in the U.S. embassy. Cantú edited *El Día*'s cultural page and was the secret author of one of the most natural palindromes in the Spanish language:

Sana tigre vas a correr rocas a ver gitanas

If we discount Cantú's latent madness, provoked by his early abuse of alcohol and its abysses, it is difficult to see why Revueltas chose his mansion for a hiding place. Wanted as a dangerous criminal since the September '68 military occupation of the university, hunted by all the police in the Mexican capital, perhaps Revueltas was merely putting into practice the crazy detective truth outlined in Poe's story, namely that the best place to hide something is where everyone can see it. The fact is that Cantú's mansion housed Revueltas' clandestine existence in the most ostentatious and overt manner. The small study where he installed himself, built by Cantú over the garage in a concealed corner of the building, became the most visited hiding place in the history of modern Mexico. It turned into a kind of lay sanctuary, receiving a stream of fugitive student leaders and foreign journalists, all desperate to get an interview with the persecuted writer, the born-again guru of Mexican dissident thought.

Revueltas' adventurous heart had effortlessly identified with the anarchic undertow of the sixties youth movement, that sudden need to react that not only moved the constipated bowels of the "Mexican miracle" but also heralded its end. Thanks to Revueltas' permissive, tolerant presence, the most extreme personal necessities of the movement's members were satisfied in Cantú's mansion. Its clandestine welcome was extended not only to political meetings of the highest level, but also to the amorous needs of couples who came there in search of a broken-down bed where they could obey their bodies' demands. In less than a fortnight, in addition to Revueltas, four or five other transient lodgers slept there regularly. Their faces and attire changed each night, but their way of occupying the territory did not. This occupation expanded daily—from the study to the bedrooms, from timidity to familiarity, from occasional interruptions to permanent invasion. After three weeks of useless resistance, Cantú's family decided to retreat, and traveled a thousand kilometers north to Monterrey to await the outcome of the strange role history had called upon them to play.

Once the only remaining representatives of normality had been removed, the mansion surrendered its turrets to the social upheavals of the moment and openly celebrated its erratic freedoms. These were presided over by Revueltas' festive spirit and his eloquent genius. He worked all day long, talking and writing non-stop: he gave interviews, stimulated debates, wrote manifestos and pamphlets, newspaper articles, letters to comrades whom other comrades would be seeing that day, and all the while carefully copied in his shorthand notebook everything that anyone said, suggested or proposed. In this way, talking or writing, he gave free rein to the words that were the true lubricant of his protean brain. He was capable of the entire register, from effervescent to precise, from playful to solemn, theoretical to narrative, from introspection to looking outward at the immense pull of the real world. At eight in the evening, freed from his daily routine, Cantú would return from the newspaper to the occupied house. He would buy a bottle of tequila at the nearest liquor store and then prepare for the only indispensable ritual of the day: to drink and talk with Revueltas and whomever else was there until eleven o'clock—at which time Revueltas, with the Calvinist rigor of a field commander, would declare the proceedings at an end and withdraw to type out the latest outpourings of his indefatigable mind.

In those days, Revueltas was a living myth, the Mexican writer who came closest to embodying the innocence of our libertarian dreams. He was fifty-four, and in our eyes was the quintessential embodiment of a mature writer who had always swum against the tide. All alone, he had fought and lost the battles on behalf of heterodoxy that we could have wished to have been part of. As a punishment for his communist militancy, the government had made him suffer misery and years of imprisonment. And within the strictures of Mexican communism he had also been made to suffer calumnies, expulsions and ostracism for his heretical tendencies. In the 1940s, after criticism from his comrades in the Mexican Communist Party, to which he belonged all his life, especially the years when he was not an active militant, he withdrew a play (*El cuadrante de la soledad*) from circulation and submitted himself to a Stalinist self-criticism for one of his major novels, *Los días terrenales*.

His unique voice had won out over both exclusion by the
government and communist orthodoxy. By the sixties we had
learned to contemplate the desolate, profound world of his
writing, but read it wrongly as an extension of the character we
admired, the José Revueltas who had discovered in '68—late
and alone once more, at a time when what all his contemporar-
ies were looking for was fame or a life of habit—an opportunity to pit his desires against the petrified forces of the
established order, to once more risk everything in favor of
change, life and revolution.

His voice had other qualities: the echo of an ancient world
we knew little of, with its religious tribulations and a rare non-
religious quest for the absolute in that forest of phantoms with
which, according to Novalis, mankind peopled the heavens
after the death of God. It was thanks to this kind of misunderstanding that I, like many others, felt for Revueltas the kind of
crazy infatuation I have not since felt for any other writer: the
almost physical need to meet him, to be with him, hear him, to
greet him, study him up close, to get his autograph, keep the
napkin he had scrawled something on while he was talking or
listening. Therefore as soon as I heard—thanks to an indiscre-
tion by Adolfo Peralta, the precocious Trotskyist and philosopher from Atasta (Campeche)—that Cantú was hoarding this
treasure in his house, I embarked on a tedious strategy that
eventually led me for the first and only time into Revueltas'
presence.

This strategy consisted of the most ridiculous of excuses: I
wrote for the cultural pages of *El Día,* and so three times a week
I took my article to Cantú. I usually went to see him around
midday, calculating (usually correctly) that the piece would be
published the next day, because it was between one and six in
the afternoon that Cantú chose what was to go into the paper.
When I heard his house had been taken over by Revueltas'
clandestine circus, I changed the time I went to see him. I
started taking my articles later in the afternoon, half an hour or
so before Cantú finished for the day. The abject reason behind

this change was so that I could leave the newspaper office with
Cantú and catch the bus home with him, in the hope that as I
was getting off, a few stops before him, he might suddenly say:
"Oh, by the way, since we're only a few blocks from my house,
Revueltas is there at the moment, and I know you admire him,
so why don't you come and see him?" I started inventing inter-
minable conversations about anything under the sun a block
before I reached my stop. I hoped this would mean that we
went on talking until we reached Cantú's stop and that would
give him the chance to say: "Oh, by the way, since we're only a
few blocks from my house, and as you know Revueltas is there
at the moment, why don't you come and meet him?" I remember this once led me to start a conversation about *Muerte sin fin,*
José Gorostiza's most important poem, on which Cantú was a
renowned expert. We went on talking about it not only as far as
Cantú's stop but also on the street corner for another half an
hour. But still Cantú did not pronounce the magic words: "Oh,
by the way, José Revueltas is at my house: I suppose you'd like
to meet him. He knew Gorostiza and has lots of stories about
him. Why don't you come with me and we can carry on our
conversation at home with him?"

I continued with my feeble efforts throughout the following
week. I twice invented conversations just as I was about to leave
the bus. I stayed on board and got off with Cantú, but he never
said the words I was hoping for. He simply looked at me with
that charming, intelligent expression of his that gave him a far
too adult appearance beneath his broad forehead, as if he knew
perfectly well what I was angling for and was playing me along.
The fourth or fifth time I employed my strategy I tried to engage Cantú in a discussion about the relevance to Mexico of
Naphtha and Settembrini's argument in Thomas Mann's *The
Magic Mountain*. At this point Cantú said to me straight out:

"What you want is to meet Revueltas, isn't it?"

"Yes," I said.

"Why didn't you say so straightaway?" he asked me. "What
was all the metaphysical rubbish on the bus for?"

* * *

So it was that, humiliated but happy, and carrying the obligatory bottle of tequila and two cartons of grape juice as tribute, I finally arrived at the table where Revueltas was installed. He was accompanied—with a less worshipful attitude than seemed to me appropriate, and in such a natural way that it seemed to me disrespectful—by a Trotskyist couple who were endlessly fondling each other, and by Roberto Escudero, a student leader from the Faculty of Philosophy and Letters with whom many years later I shared a passion for Malcolm Lowry. Revueltas was waiting with almost adolescent anxiety for Cantú's arrival with the nightly sacrament. I was struck above all by the playful, earnest way he received the tequila: the frank, down-to-earth gesture from someone we considered a terrible, frightening monster, well-nigh sacred in his superhuman majesty. He took the bottle in both hands and unwrapped it from the brown paper bag like a child unwrapping a sweet in such a careless but contented way that he immediately won my democratic support.

"If God were to exist, comrade," said Revueltas, waving the bottle I had given him in front of my face, "he must have created the agave tequila is made from solely to win us over to his cause. Because God, comrade, if he does exist, he lives in a sacred place somewhere in the life that tequila offers us. To-night you are the emissary of that mineral god the poet Jorge Cuesta was searching for in his *Canto a un dios mineral.* And your gift reminds us why Cuesta never found what he was looking for: he was looking in the mineral world for something, comrade, which, if it exists, does so in the vegetable world. More precisely, in agave from whose bountiful depths you have brought us this perfect, transparent sample."

It was a clear tequila whose white transparency made Revueltas' words seem even brighter, so that they had the same transparency as the God of which he was speaking.

"You talk of God as if you had slept with him, Pepe," said Escudero in a sacrilegious tone that made Revueltas laugh. "Didn't we agree that God doesn't exist?"

"You're right, he doesn't exist," said Revueltas. "But if he did, he would live in some vegetable corner of the world of tequila."

"But does he exist or not, Pepe?" asked the young girl, stroking her boyfriend's mop of hair in her lap.

"No, he doesn't exist, comrade," said Revueltas, starting to pour the tequila into the glasses Cantú had fetched, "but we have to concede him the metaphysical possibility of existing. If we have an idea of him in our heads, then something of him already exists. The fact that we can imagine him is proof that we cannot dismiss him out of hand, without at the same time dismissing something which we know exists, namely the idea of his existence inside our heads. Your health."

Then, at Revueltas' request, Cantú told us all the latest news from the paper. I cannot remember exactly what this was, but it involved the repercussions of the so-called Silent March, when hundreds of thousands of young people marched through the streets of Mexico City without shouting a single slogan, in complete silence.

"It was the longest-lasting demonstration so far," said Revueltas.

"The one on August 27 was bigger," said Escudero. "It took the columns four hours to file into Zócalo Square."

"Agreed, comrade," said Revueltas. "But I'm not talking about physical time, or the arithmetical dimensions of the demonstration. I'm talking about real time, about the internal, deep-down duration. We were only on the streets for two and a half hours for the Silent March, but inside us it felt like a century had passed. We never saw the face of the city so clearly as on that day, and we had never seen one another's faces in the way we did then. We had all the time in the world to do so. To think to ourselves: 'Oh, after this street we're marching down, from that corner to Mascarones, that's where Insurgentes Street starts.' And we had time to think: 'What a wonderful name for a street: Insurgentes.' That demonstration lasted much longer inside all of us than any of the others. Compared to that, the

August 27 one was like an orgasm. It gave us more pleasure, but it was all over in a moment's shout. This time thing is very complicated. It's like Mexican politics: completely different on the outside and on the inside. From the outside, it looks like a straitjacket; from inside it's pure lacework."

Roberto Escudero explained how perplexed he was that it took only seconds for memory to recall events which had in reality taken hours, and how he sometimes woke up in the middle of the night with the impression of having lived a century in the two months since the start of the student movement of which he was a leader.

"That's because it's a novelty," said Cantú. "Life goes by quickly when all the days are the same, and slowly when it is full of novelty and adventure. We say of someone who is constantly having new experiences: 'He lives too quickly.' In fact, it's the opposite: his life is longer-lasting than a couch potato's. He lives two or three times more than the other person, and therefore remembers two or three times as much. If memory is the yardstick of time, you could say that the adventurer has more of these yardsticks stored in his mind."

"But memory is a lady with a mind of her own," Revueltas objected. "She remembers only what she wants to. You might say she is the politburo of our soul. Constantly erasing Trotsky from history. There are some intellectuals here in Mexico, such as the more clever than beloved don Octavio Paz, who are horrified at the way Trotsky has been erased from Soviet history. They are right—but here in Mexico we've done the same with no less a historic figure than Iturbide. I don't know how we do it, but in the history of Mexico's fight for independence, Iturbide only figures as a villain. It's the same as if the Soviets had not merely erased the memory of Trotsky, but of Lenin himself. What I'm trying to say is that one of the fundamental characteristics of memory is that it gets rid of everything it doesn't like or finds inconvenient. Every time I think of that and of comrade Freud, I remember comrade Luis Arenal."

"Siqueiros' brother-in-law?" asked Cantú.

"Yes, the one who attacked Trotsky's house in Coyoacán alongside Siqueiros," said Revueltas.

"What happened with Luis Arenal?" Cantú wanted to know.

"Well, this did," said Revueltas. "For two years I tried to get that silent fellow Luis Arenal to tell me about the attack on Trotsky's house. I tried everything I could to get him to talk. I took him to eat, to drink, to dance. I invited him to La Bandida's brothel in the Condesa neighborhood. I had him listen to revolutionary songs, northern dance music. I was always buying him drinks, because he liked to get drunk at other people's expense, to see if I could soften him up and get something out of him. Finally, one night we went to the *Leda*. I had finished that book one day—I mean I had finished a book that day. All of a sudden one morning, when I thought I still had two chapters or so to go, I wrote six pages without stopping. I suddenly hit upon a paragraph that rounded everything off: it came out from my mouth to my hand as if it had been dictated. I came to the end of the paragraph and told myself: 'You've finished it, Pepe.' I was so amazed I walked all round the room. I argued with myself: 'You're just fooling yourself. You don't want to do any more work on it, so you've invented an ending.' But then a third, even more powerful and convincing voice inside me said: 'No, you've finished, that's it.' I believed this voice because it sounded so sincere, even if it was a false sincerity. So I went into the kitchen and had a tequila. It was only eleven in the morning, so after the first tequila I had another one, to see if it helped me get through the day. It seemed to me, comrade, that day was going very slowly. It needed a helping hand. I used the tequila to help it along, and so time went by quite smoothly until lunchtime, when I went to eat with Luis Arenal. Contrary to what I had done until then, that afternoon I talked and talked, without stopping. I didn't let him get a word in edgeways, not even that typical phrase of his: 'Not even Stalin could do that.' He used it for everything. For example, if you told him you had made love twice the night before, or had read *War and Peace* the previous week, comrade Arenal would reply: 'Not even Stalin could do that.' It was his favorite comparison: what Stalin could or could not do. Anyway, we went on drinking until ten at night, when we ended up in *Leda*. I was still talking twenty to the dozen, telling him about the book I had just finished, and about the one I wanted to write next, until there came a moment when Arenal could not bear his own silence any longer, and protested: 'Not even Stalin could talk as much as you do. I'm going to tell you something you'll never be able to talk about if you don't listen to me.' And then he proceeded to tell me what I had been trying to worm out of him for the previous two years: how he and Siqueiros had attacked Trotsky's house in Coyoacán. He finally told me the whole story. But life is more than a match for those of us living it, comrades. By the time Luis Arenal began telling me the story, I had already drunk more than my fair share of tequilas and aniseed liquors. While I was listening to him, it seemed like the most incredible story I had ever heard. But the next day, I couldn't remember a single word of what he had said. I remembered being amazed at the story but could not recall a single detail. Like someone who remembers being amazed by *Don Quixote* but cannot remember that Sancho Panza had a donkey. Arenal's story made a huge impact on me as literature, but I wanted its historical impact. I wanted all the real details of what had happened, not the magical effect that the normally silent Arenal had created. I'm telling you all this to show how memory functions as a politburo. I have never been able to remember anything but the fact that Arenal opened the gates of hell for me that night, but I have no idea what it was like, nor how many demons were roasting young children at the entrance. I erased this visionary insight in a way I can only compare to the one Comrade Vadillo refused to give me on another occasion. But I'll keep that story for some other time."

"We've got time today," Escudero said.

"It's a non-story," Revueltas said apologetically.

"By definition there's no such thing as non-stories," the Trotskyist said, confusing rudeness with sincerity.

"Yes, there are," said Revueltas. "Like the Mexican revolution, which was a non-revolution."

"It may have been a non-revolution," Escudero conceded reluctantly. "But they don't half beat us over the head with it."

"In the same way I at least am bothered by Comrade Vadillo's non-story," said Revueltas. "Cantú knows it all."

"If you tell it again, I'll remember it properly," said Cantú.

"It's a forbidden story about Mexican communism," Revueltas said. "You need to know that communism in Mexico is also full of its Trotskys and Iturbides. We've kept quiet about almost as much as we've done—perhaps more, because we haven't done an awful lot."

"So, what is the story?" the girl asked, still caressing her partner as if the last thing on her mind was to erase him from her memory.

"What is the *non*-story," Revueltas insisted. "What's most important about it is that it was never told. I mean, we know things around it, we know its beginning and end, but don't know the details, the inner secrets. It's as though we had the gun barrel but not the steel shell inside it."

"How did you meet Vadillo?" asked Escudero.

"In the eye of the storm that was the communist youth in the thirties," said Revueltas. "The start of the thirties. We used to be sent out together on missions for the Party, which in those days had a presence in some rural areas, especially Veracruz. We used to go out regularly from Mexico City. To organize a strike, take a top-secret message to comrade Laborde's family, to 'enter into discussions,' as we used to say, with the thugs from the CROM, who had corralled our cadres in Puebla. We never stopped. I have even sometimes wondered if the communist youth of that period had any other militants besides Evelio Vadillo, Miguel Angel Velasco and me. As soon as any complicated matter arose, one that demanded travel outside the capital and involved some risk, it was Comrade Revueltas, Comrade Vadillo or Comrade Velasco who was called upon to carry out those highly important missions for the Party. We went and joined the struggle without a word of protest. More than that: we were delighted to do so, we were pleased to be of service, we could sense the euphoric current of history flowing through our own minuscule biographies, as though we were in direct contact with the future of mankind. I now think it was an abuse on their part, and yet I cannot recall a happier time, one when we felt in harmony with the universe, than those years when the Party was entrusting us with impossible tasks. I remember one of those missions. It was a typewritten order, neatly typed with wide margins on both sides. It said more or less the following: 'Comrade Revueltas is ordered to travel as soon as possible to the region of Pátzcuaro, in Michoacán, where proletarian unrest has recently become evident among peasants and indigenous peoples. He is to make contact with the popular leaders of the region, set up a new organization for their struggles, affiliate a majority of the peasants to the Party and organize a powerful demonstration that will show the peoples of the world that the flame of the proletarian struggle is spreading unstoppably throughout Mexico, in solidarity with the movement for world revolution.' I received the order and set out for Pátzcuaro in a broken-down bus, with three pesos in my pocket. When I got there or elsewhere, I would try to make contact with the 'proletarian unrest,' which almost always consisted in some boundary dispute or other between communities that had been fighting over the same issue for centuries. That was enough for me to launch into an explanation about the dangers of the people fighting among themselves, of the historical need for peasants to acknowledge the urban working classes as the revolutionary vanguard who would resolve the fundamental political questions affecting the struggle in the countryside. Despite this, some of our audience always seemed to take to us and invite us to eat or sleep in their huts. Then as soon as we began to trust one another, with that unerring wisdom and gentleness so typical of Mexican peasants, they would ask us: 'What are you doing out here, when you could be in Mexico City? Why don't you go back there? Your parents must be worried about you.'

The upshot of all this would be that we would write a report to the Central Committee, informing them that we had made contact with the local movement and that the work of awareness-raising, although slow moving, would inevitably lead to a higher level of struggle. It was all very frustrating because what we wanted as twenty-year-olds was really to promote the revolution, to establish communism in Mexico. In our minds, these words were synonymous with the fulfillment of man's destiny on earth. We wanted to make a Soviet revolution here. Literally. The Soviet revolution seemed to us the most glorious event in human history."

"But Stalin had already seized power in the USSR," the young Trotskyist objected.

"Not in our minds, comrade," said Revueltas, more amused than irritated by finding himself in the dock in this way. "The Stalin you are talking about had not even seized power inside Stalin himself. I'm talking about 1934, only five years after the global crash of capitalism and the Great Depression. At that time, it seemed as if Marx's prophecies about capitalism were coming true, that it was well on the way to self-destruction. The only alternative we could see in the world was the Soviet revolution. The Stalin you are talking about did not yet exist, although he was on his way. The Moscow show trials were a few years in the future, and Trotsky's murder was another six away. More than anything else, comrade, those were years in which we wanted and needed to believe in something. And as we know, faith can move mountains, in part because faith is blind and does not distinguish mountains from plains."

"But what was going on in Mexico?" asked Escudero.

"Here there had already been a revolution," said Revueltas. "We young communists felt an irresistible desire to keep the Mexican revolution going. You might say we were born a generation too late. We had been caught out by the historic events. I was born on November 20, 1914, the day we celebrate the Mexican revolution. On the day I was born, in Durango, the forces of Pancho Villa took the city. I've always thought that if

I had been born fifteen years earlier, I could have been a member of Villa's troops when they took Durango. But when I first opened my eyes, everything had already happened. What I and a lot of others of my generation wanted was for the film to start all over again. This time to make a real revolution, the socialist revolution. We desperately wanted something heroic to happen to us: that was why we went to the villages wherever the Party sent us, looking for what they said was there and what was not. So it was that, searching for tits on snakes and sleeves on waistcoats, as they say, Comrade Vadillo and I got involved in the mess that brought us together for the rest of our lives."

"In Monterrey?" asked Cantú.

"In Monterrey," Revueltas concurred. "In 1934. The Party reckoned that a workers' revolt was about to break out there. Naturally, they sent Comrade Vadillo and me to investigate. Our modest mission was to bring the insurrection under the control of the Party. What we found was a group of farmers who were upset because they had been thrown off land on the banks of the River Santa Catarina, which they had taken over illegally. By the time we arrived, they had already been given land somewhere else. They had even published a letter thanking the governor in the local newspaper, so there was nothing for us to do. We could not bear to go back to the capital without having steered any mass movement in the right direction. We were still worrying about this when we heard that in a place called Camarón, in the same state, a strike of fifteen thousand agricultural workers had broken out. They were demanding the minimum wage. We set off determined to direct the efforts of the confused masses. But this was a serious affair. The striking comrades were very well organized and lots of them had weapons. They also had the tacit support of the state government, which had let them go ahead without doing much to get in their way. As soon as Comrade Vadillo and I saw the situation, we sent a report condemning what was going on to *El Machete*, which was the Party newspaper. It was so powerful it was published the very next day. Only three days after we had first come into contact with this agrarian struggle in Nuevo León, the forerunner of a worldwide agrarian revolution, our text was being passed from person to person and being read out loud at meetings by those who could read to those who could not. The landowners immediately claimed the strike had been infiltrated by communist agitators and had lost its way. Anti-communism was the favorite sport of the politicians of the Calles government. That Senator McCarthy who appeared years later in the United States would have seemed like a half-hearted kid compared to the rabid anti-communism of the Mexican regimes of the early 1930s. So, no sooner had the land-owners said there were communists behind the Camarón strike than the authorities identified us as the agitators: we were the only two people in the protest who were not from the region and were obvious outsiders. One night they arrested us without saying a word and put us on a train under guard. All that night we were scared they might shoot us and say we had been trying to escape, but the next morning we arrived in Querétaro, where still without a word they put us on another train heading north-west. When we reached Mazatlán, I understood what was going on, because I had made that journey before. I told Com-rade Vadillo: 'Don't worry, comrade, I think they're taking us to the prison on the Islas Marías.' Comrade Vadillo asked: 'Why to prison, Pepe? What crime have we committed?' He was a stickler for the law. 'It must be a really serious one,' I said, 'because we're being taken to the highest security prison in Mexico.' They were taking us to the Islas Marías, a prison where the sea was the walls. I wrote about it later in a novel: it was the prison where the most dangerous criminals in Mexico were sent. I had been there a year before on similar charges to the ones we were accused of now: 'agitation,' 'incitement to violence,' 'disloyalty,' 'treason.' The same charges as always, the same ones they're accusing me of right now. I would have been better off devoting my life to robbing banks. To cut a long story short, we ended up in Islas Marías, Comrade Vadillo for the first time and me for the second. We were still not twenty years old."

"What charges were brought against you?" asked Roberto Escudero.

"We never found out," said Revueltas. "We were never put on trial and never sentenced. Which was all to the good, because when we arrived and the prison governor saw us, he came up to me and asked: 'What are you doing back here, my lad? Did you really do something this time, or have you just been stupid like before?' The governor was General Gaxiola. He was an excellent fellow. The first time I had been on the islands he had treated me well and given me a job in his office. We had ended up talking a lot about the revolution and socialism. He had set me free at the first opportunity of pardon, so that I had only spent five months on the Islas. I can't say they were the worst months I've spent in my life. That second time on the Islas, with Comrade Vadillo, things were not so easy. I was put to work, but so was everyone else, so I can't complain. It was backbreaking work, though. We had to chop wood and unload the boats that came with cargoes of salt and provisions. We worked eight hours a day without stopping, including Saturdays and Sundays. My hands were calloused and bleeding most of the time, but at least the work prevented me thinking about what a mess we had got ourselves into. In the evening we had a few moments when we could read in the prison library. We asked General Gaxiola to order books and filled the library with subversive literature. And Comrade Vadillo and I talked. We talked at night, as if we were singing each other lullabies, until we were overwhelmed by tiredness. For months, the whole ten months we spent in the prison, the last voice I heard at night before I fell asleep was Evelio Vadillo's, and he heard mine. I can hear it now, in the midst of all our troubles, almost like the soothing voice of a mother, a substitute for that essential voice which when we were children used to keep us safe from demons and ghosts, protecting us from fear and harm, leading us gently back to the earth's secure, warm bosom. We did not talk about ourselves, but about the revolution, the struggle of the peoples of the world, the future. I was worried sometimes about how my family must be suffering because of me. Comrade Vadillo was not even concerned about that. But the topic of our conversations was unimportant. What mattered most was to be able to listen to each other in the boundless night of the Islas, to know we were next to each other, lost but supporting each other in the vast, inhospitable world. As I think I said, we spent ten months on the Islas Marías. We left thanks to the amnesty the Lázaro Cárdenas government decreed. Almost as soon as we had got out, we were given our reward, the sweetest, most amazing one we could ever have imagined: we were invited to be part of the Party delegation to the VIIth Congress of Comintern, the Communist International, held in Moscow. Moscow! The capital of the new world. And to the Communist International, no less, the meeting place of all those who represented the future of the world."

"When did the Congress take place?" asked Escudero.

"In July 1935," Revueltas replied. "We arrived in Moscow on July 25, the day of the opening. Three of us: Comrade Velasco, Comrade Hernán Laborde and me. Comrade Vadillo had travelled two weeks earlier and was waiting for us. Moscow was one huge fiesta, the universal celebration of communism. Stalin spoke at the opening ceremony. His speech marked the beginning of the period of popular fronts, the anti-fascist alliance, world solidarity to ensure the survival of socialism in the USSR. After his speech, every country sang their national anthem: Italians, Argentinians, Spaniards, Peruvians. We hugged one another, cheered everyone. We lived the amazing, incomparable experience of solidarity, of belonging to the battalions setting mankind free. I can still remember how moved I was at seeing the march-past of the young communists in Red Square, my absolute conviction that I had seen the truth of history in their glowing cheeks, their banners and their salutes to the presidium, which for me was the incarnation of wisdom, honesty, rectitude, the communion of the individual with history. Always history, wasn't it? The sense of history was everywhere: every event was historic, every speech was a historic declaration. It was like being inside a perfect sphere, where everything was meaningful and harmonious. When the celebrations were over, Comrade Vadillo and I stayed on in Moscow, invited by the city Komsomol, the organization of communist youth. We exhausted ourselves in meetings, in our admiration for our Soviet comrades and in endless talks about what Comrade Vadillo and I would do to create a reality like this one back in Mexico. We visited museums, work centers; we walked round the Kremlin. Every day we sat in a bar on Pushkin Boulevard to drink and go on talking, endlessly, about how we could transfer everything we were witnessing back to Mexico. On one occasion, blushing with embarrassment because he considered it such a privilege, Comrade Vadillo told me of a decision he had made: he had been offered a grant to study at the university, and had decided to accept. I felt betrayed: first because I had not been offered a grant, then because Comrade Vadillo had not suggested I be offered one, and thirdly because he had not refused the offer if I were not included as well. As the days went by, I realized my resentment was absurd, because there was no way I could have stayed on in the USSR. I wanted to get back to Mexico, to fight to bring socialism there. Also because back home there was a female comrade whose eyes were almost as appealing as the thought of a socialist homeland. Also because I had just received one of the worst bits of news of my entire life: my brother Fermín had died in Mexico City. His was a stupid, unbearable, premature death—like all deaths. I arranged my return. I spent the last night of my stay in Moscow drinking beer with Comrade Vadillo in what had become our second home in the city, the beer cellar on Pushkin Boulevard. 'I envy you, because you are going back to our suffering country,' Comrade Vadillo told me as the night dragged on. 'I'd love to stay in the land of Lenin and Stalin,' I replied, 'but somebody has to do the work to bring the kind of socialism flourishing

here to Mexico.' 'You carry on the fight over there, and I'll do
my best over here,' Comrade Vadillo told me. 'Someday we will
meet again, satisfied in the knowledge we have fulfilled our
duty, in a world that is more just than the one we inherited. We
will know we have dedicated our lives to the noblest of causes.'
That was how Comrade Vadillo always talked, looking to the
future, sure of his mission on earth. We said goodbye on that
already cold night in Moscow with a long embrace that masked
the lumps in our throats. That was at the end of September 1935."

With this, Revueltas fell silent, as though to drink his tequila. But after he had swallowed a glassful, he remained quiet,
staring at the floor.

"What happened then?" asked Escudero, also emptying
his glass.

"I don't know," said Revueltas. "I did not see Comrade Vadillo for another twenty-three years, until October 1958."

"What?" exclaimed the young girl, still stroking her Trotskyist partner's hair.

"What you heard," said Revueltas. "Neither I nor anyone
else in Mexico saw Comrade Vadillo again until he came home
in 1958, twenty-three years after our last beer on Pushkin Boulevard in Moscow."

"What happened to him?" asked Roberto Escudero.

"Twentieth-century history happened to him," said Revueltas, twisting his goatee beard into a nervous stalk. "We know
now what that meant. We sensed what was coming toward us
even while we were enjoying those beers on Pushkin Boulevard
in the autumn of 1935. I mean, Stalin's steamroller had already
started up. The first important victim had come with the assas-
sination of Comrade Kirov in Leningrad at the end of the previous year. Then the great purge of the old Bolshevik guard
began, which led to the Moscow show trials, the alliance with
Hitler, the Second World War, the Stalinist terror, the concentration camps, the personality cult, socialism in one country.
Things we all know about, although I'm not sure we know all

there is to know about them. That doesn't matter: in general, we know enough about that atrocious history we were the innocent accomplices of for so many years and which now offends our communist morality in much the same way as the history of the dissolute, bloodthirsty popes of the past makes well-brought-up Catholics feel ashamed. What we don't know is the impact of that history on the minuscule, invisible life of an individual like Comrade Vadillo."

"Wait a minute, Pepe, you're going too fast," said Roberto Escudero. "What did happen? Some things must be known."

"Yes, a lot is known," Revueltas admitted. "Lots of dreadful things. But they are the broad outlines, or suppositions, guesses—not the precise, detailed story of what twentieth-century history did to Comrade Vadillo."

"What are the broad outlines?" Escudero wanted to know.

"Shortly after I returned to Mexico, Comrade Vadillo was arrested in Moscow," Revueltas said. "Apparently this was because one morning the dormitory where he slept at the university was covered in Trotskyist banners and slogans written in Spanish. The dormitories were houses where six or seven students lived. Nobody apart from them could get access. The authorities concluded that the person responsible for such a terrible plot must be someone in the dormitory. They could not discover who it was, so with that innate logic the political police have, they proceeded to arrest all of them for interrogation. Nobody knows what happened next, except that they were all eventually sent to work camps in the eastern provinces. As we usually say: 'They were sent to Siberia.'"

"What happened next?" asked the young girl, who for the moment had stopped stroking her partner's hair.

"That we don't know," Revueltas said. "There is some evidence to show that Vadillo spent the Second World War in various work camps in the north and east of the Soviet Union."

"But didn't the rest of you here in Mexico ask what had happened to your comrade?" protested the young girl, who seemed more shocked by the story than anyone else present.

"Thousands of times," Revueltas said. "His family did, and so did we, his comrades and friends. We always received the most glowing answers. According to one, Evelio Vadillo had fought as a volunteer in the Spanish Civil War. He had come back so laden down with honors that he was made an officer in the Soviet army. Afterward, he had decided to become a Soviet citizen and to stay and fight for his socialist homeland, cutting all ties with his previous life. At the end of the war, we were told he had gone off to volunteer in the Chinese revolution. We imagined him speaking fluent Chinese, deciding the course of history once more in the caves of Yenán. Yes, Comrade Vadillo, a Mexican from Campeche, who had not even known enough Russian to be able to order beers on Pushkin Boulevard."

"But how on earth could you believe all that?" asked our Trotskyist comrade, shifting in the warm lap where he had been resting his head all night.

"Because we were good, well-disciplined communists," said Revueltas. "In the same way that the early Christians believed in Jesus' resurrection, and Christians nowadays believe in the historical continuity of the Roman Catholic Church."

"What happened then?" asked Cantú.

"The least gloomy part of the story," said Revueltas. "Stalin died, and then there was the XXth Congress of the Soviet Communist Party, when we learned a little about the horror we had been celebrating. What we know now. The important thing for Comrade Vadillo was that with the thaw he was let out of captivity. He went back to Moscow. Nobody there knew who he was. Sooner or later, somebody asked him for his papers. They searched through his record and were suspicious about this Mexican who claimed to have been one of Stalin's victims. They shut him away again, but this time not far from Moscow and under a less harsh regime, until they could clarify his situation. He spent another five years in this lenient detention: he was able to work as a waiter and to move around within a restricted radius. Eventually it occurred to him to call in at the Mexican embassy and tell them what had happened to him. The ambassador offered to try to secure his freedom. Comrade Vadillo gave his permission, saying he was tired and wanted to go home to Mexico to die. But he still did not say a word about his experiences in the USSR. The formalities took a year, because the Moscow authorities had no record of any Mexican by the name of Evelio Vadillo. The ambassador only vaguely got to hear some of the details I've told you about. Finally, in mid-1958, Vadillo was granted his freedom and allowed to travel to Mexico. He reached here in July 1958. At that time, I had split from the Party. I was in the doghouse and had been ostracized. I only found out Vadillo had come back two months later, quite by chance. I discovered his address and went to visit him. He refused to see me. I wrote him a letter reminding him of who we had once been. About a week later, a niece of his turned up at the offices of *Política* magazine. She told me her uncle would see me the next Friday at six o'clock. She asked me to be on time and to bring some of my books with me. I took him signed copies of all the ones I had. I arrived at five minutes to six. I was shown into a very humble apartment on Calle Alvaro Obregón in a gloomy building that smelled of drains. At six on the dot a hunched old man in a blue boiler suit appeared in the bedroom doorway. 'How's things, Pepe?' he said. When I heard the voice, with a sense of horrified compassion (what the Greeks call *catharsis*), I recognized my old friend Evelio Vadillo. He must have been forty-six at the time, but he looked like a man of seventy. He had lost his teeth and his hair, and the skin of his cheeks hung down from his face like turkey wattles. When I embraced him, I could smell the sour smell of age and neglect. As we sat down in threadbare armchairs, he said to me: 'How long have you been wearing glasses? They make you look like a teacher.' This made me think that I looked as old to him as he did to me, and that the image we each had of the other was of us in our twenties. 'I've been wearing glasses since I was last expelled from the Party,' I said jokingly, 'so that I don't have to go around blind.' He gave a hollow laugh. 'How often have you been expelled from the Party?' he asked. 'More times than I can count,' I said, 'but

I'm still a part of it.' 'I've heard a bit about that,' he said, with a discreet but racking cough. 'I've brought you the books,' I said. 'There's a lot of them,' he replied. 'How many more are you going to write?' 'As many as I can,' I said. 'But that's not why I'm here. It was you I came to see, to find out how you are, to hear what happened to you.' 'You can see how I am—never better,' said Vadillo, with weary irony. 'As for what happened to me, there's no point. No point talking about it.' 'But something really serious happened, didn't it?' I said. 'You vanished for a quarter of a century. There were all sorts of stories here: that you fought as a volunteer in the Spanish Civil War and in the Chinese revolution.' 'I didn't fight in either of them,' said Vadillo. 'Nor with the Red Army, though I would have liked to.' 'Where were you then, Evelio?' I asked him. 'In a fold of history, Pepe, as you would say,' he replied. 'There's no point talking about it. Tell me about yourself. What do you think of the Party? Do we have any hopes for the future?' 'None,' I said. 'In Mexico, the proletariat is headless, it has no vanguard, no real party.' 'I know your argument about that,' said Vadillo, referring to my book on the headless proletariat. 'I don't know if you're being completely fair,' he added. 'Perhaps you're committing the sin of impatience.' 'My sins are my impatience and my conscience,' I said. 'But as I said, I didn't come here to talk about my books, but about you. What happened to you all those years? I want to know.' 'There's no point,' Vadillo repeated. 'That was all in the past, and it's not the past that should interest us, but the future. That is why we have lived, and that is what we will die for.' 'Were you in jail?' I asked, pressing him. 'Let's just say that together with a whole people I lived a historic deviation of socialism,' Vadillo said. 'As a prisoner?' I insisted. 'I wouldn't put it like that,' said Vadillo. 'How would you put it, Evelio?' I prodded him. Vadillo said: 'As Engels used to say: history often walks on the wrong side of the street. It advances taking wide detours, it looks as though it's headed in the wrong direction, but it gets where it needs to in the end. If we want to conquer the future, we have to pay the price of not always aiming straight for it. That is what happened.' 'But what happened to you?' I said, probably already a little agitated. 'To you, not to the history of socialism: what happened to you as a person?' 'I already told you, what happened to me is of no importance,' said Vadillo. 'And you won't hear it from me. We individuals do not matter in all this. That's what I learned in all these years. We are everyone and no one at the same time. Or better: either we are everyone or we are no one, because nobody gets out of it on their own.' "

At this, Revueltas fell silent again, as if forgetting we were listening. Cantú was the one who had the courage to break this imposing, almost ritual silence: "So, he didn't tell you anything?"

"Nothing," said Revueltas.

"In his own way, he told you everything," Roberto Escudero suggested.

"According to his curious dialectic, he did," agreed Revueltas. "But in the real world, the only thing he said, at about eight that evening, was that he needed a rest. He went back into the room he had emerged from. His niece showed me to the door. I never saw him again. He died a month later. Some scoundrel wrote an article in *Excelsior* blaming me and others for having abandoned him in the Soviet Union."

"The Mexican press is shit," said the Trotskyist. He was still nestling in his amazon's lap, but shifted nervously, determined not to let Comrade Vadillo's non-story upset him.

His comment finished us off. We sat staring at the table, spinning our empty glasses between our fingers.

"Talking of the press," said Revueltas eventually, "I have to answer a questionnaire for the student newspaper at Berkeley, and it's one o'clock in the morning. If there is no other business, I propose one last toast. And then to bed."

"There's no more tequila," said the girl.

"An air toast then," said Revueltas. "If air is the soul of the world, let's help it commune with ours by swallowing it."

"I'll drink to Comrade Vadillo, who believed in the soul of history," said Escudero.

"Two big drinks," Revueltas agreed.

He got up, stood to attention and gulped down air twice in succession, concentrating hard as if he really were taking communion.

Two months later, in November 1968, Revueltas was arrested. Accused of every imaginable crime, he made things worse by mockingly confessing to them all and more. He spent two years in jail before he was set free, using his time to write *El apando,* a masterpiece on the horrors of the prison world. Ten years later, he let himself die, weary of fighting a cosmic depression that the doctors did not know how to cure, and he did not wish to.

In July 1980, four years after his death, a slender envelope with no indication of sender arrived at the office of the magazine *Nexos,* where I then worked. It contained a photocopy of the official handover by the Federal Security Directorate (Mexico's political police) of the prisoner José Revueltas to the Ministry of Justice. Together with this document, stamped November 18, 1968, there was a text by Revueltas. This was in the form of a handwritten diary entry for the day of his arrest. In it, Revueltas lamented the death of Vicente Lombardo Toledano, the eternal leader of Mexico's reformist Left, because it had deprived him forever of the chance of arguing with him and "demolishing his ideological positions one by one." Revueltas also wrote that he had no complaints about his arrest, "apart, of course, from the loss of liberty." He said he was happy to have been given the most unexpected books by his captors, including Mao Tse-tung's *The Little Red Book* and the complete plays of Chekhov.

Revueltas' text ended like this:

I'm writing these notes like someone throwing a message in a bottle into the sea. Who will it reach, if anyone? Well, writing itself is a kind of freedom, which even if we have no paper or pen nobody can steal from our head, unless they lodge a bullet in it and end everything.

I know the thought of that bullet echoed round his brain that first night of his last term in prison. I also like to think that, before he fell asleep, he missed Comrade Vadillo's fraternal voice that had once brought him the warm sound of mother and earth, of youth and faith, the uncontrollable voice of hope that had given their lives the religious fire that set them alight until they were consumed by it, and gave their deaths the crepuscular glow of the century where their embers still give off defiant sparks.

Translated by Nick Caistor

Freedom of Expression

Paulo Coelho

IN THE PRISON OF REPOSE

In 1966, 1967, and 1968, I was admitted to a psychiatric hospital—Casa de Saúde Dr. Eiras—in Rio de Janeiro. Medical diagnosis: antisocial, rebellious, incapable of obeying parents. Rather than writing theoretically about the importance of freedom of expression, I would prefer to transcribe here extracts from the diary I kept during my first period of internment.

WEDNESDAY, JULY 20

08:00 I was woken up to have my blood pressure taken. Still groggy with sleep, I thought it was a dream, but gradually, the reality of the situation began to sink in. It was the end. They told me to get dressed quickly. Outside the house stood a car from the Emergency Psychiatric Service. I had never imagined how depressing it would be to get into such a car.

A few neighbors watched from a distance as the thin youth with long hair bowed his head to get into the car. Yes, bowed his head. He was defeated.

09:30 All the necessary bureaucratic documents have been filled out. And here I am again on the ninth floor. How fast things happened! Yesterday, I was happily walking with my girlfriend, a little worried, but certainly not expecting this. And here I am again. If I'd stayed out all night rather than gone home, I wouldn't have had that scene with my parents. I think of my girlfriend sometimes. I miss her.

Here everyone is sad. There are no smiles. Eyes stare into emptiness, seeking something, perhaps an encounter with the self. My roommate is obsessed with death. To tease him, I play the Funeral March on the guitar. It's good to have my guitar here. It brings a little joy into this atmosphere laden with sadness—the profound sadness of those who aspire to nothing in life and want nothing. The only thing that consoles me is that they still know how to sing.

15:00 I was talking to a young man who has been in here for two years now. I told him I couldn't bear it and wanted to get out. And he said in all sincerity: "Why? It's great here. You don't have to worry about anything. Why struggle? Deep down, nobody cares about anything anyway." I felt afraid, afraid that I might start thinking like him. I now feel real anguish, the anguish of not knowing when I will stop seeing the world through bars. It's indescribable. The anguish of the man sentenced to life imprisonment, knowing that one day he'll be given parole. But when will that day come? In a month? Three months? A year? Never?

17:00 Never?

19:20 I can't leave this floor, I can't phone anyone or write letters. A little while ago, I tried (in secret) to phone my girlfriend. She couldn't come to the phone, she was having supper. But what if she hadn't been having supper? What would I have said to her? Would I have complained about my lot, got angry? What would I have said? Who would I have been saying it to? Can I still speak?

I'm shocked at how calmly people accept being shut up in here. I'm afraid I might come to accept it too. If every man is an incendiary at twenty and a fireman at forty, then I reckon I must be thirty-nine years and eleven months old. I'm on the brink of defeat. I felt this when my mother was here this afternoon. She looks down on me. This is only the first day, and yet I already feel half beaten. But I must not let myself be beaten.

THURSDAY, JULY 21

08:00 Yesterday they gave me a really powerful drug to make me sleep and I'm only just coming to. During the night, for no apparent reason, my roommate woke me to ask if I was in favor of masturbation. I said I was and turned over. I really don't understand why he would ask me that. Or perhaps I dreamed it, but it was certainly strange. Flávio, my roommate, normally spends long periods in complete silence. When he does speak, he always asks the same question: How are things outside? He still wants to maintain contact with the outside world. Poor thing. He's proud of his bohemian lifestyle, but now he's in here and admits that he's ill.

I will never do that. I'm fine.

11:30 I've just realized that they've emptied my wallet. I can't buy anything. Rennie, my girlfriend, promised to visit me today. I know it's forbidden, but I need to talk to her. I spoke to her on the phone, but I kept the tone light, to disguise my depression.

The people here like to show me new things. I'm fond of them really. One guy, Roberto, is always showing me things—a way of calculating someone's age, a voltmeter, etc. Flávio is obsessed with knowing important people. There are endless interesting cases here. One man is always sniffing his food, another doesn't eat anything for fear of getting fat, a third talks only about sex and sexual aberrations.

My roommate is lying down, staring into space, looking fed up. They're playing a love song on the radio. I wonder what he's thinking about. Is he desperately searching for himself or is he just drifting aimlessly, lost and defeated?

I talk to some of the other patients. Some have been here for three months, others nine, still others have been here for years. I won't be able to bear this.

"Now from the sixth hour there was darkness over all the land unto the ninth hour. And about the ninth hour Jesus cried with a loud voice, saying: My God, my God, why hast thou forsaken me?"

Music, the sun beyond the barred windows, dreams, all of this brings with it a terrible melancholy. I remember the theater at Teresópolis, where we put on my play *Timeless Youth*. It flopped, but it was still a great experience. Those were happy days, when I was free to see the sun come up, go horseback riding, to kiss my girlfriend and to smile.

Not anymore. Not anymore. Sleep dulls the ability to reason, and I'll end up like everyone else in here.

14:10 I'm waiting for Rennie. My doctor came to my room to bring me an anthology of French poets. That's good, because I'm starting to learn French. He remarked on the fact that I seemed calm, that I appeared to be enjoying myself. And sometimes I do enjoy it here. It's a world apart, where one just eats and sleeps. That's all. But there always comes a moment when I remember the world outside and then I feel like leaving. Not so much now. I'm getting used to it. All I need is a typewriter.

I know that my girlfriend will come (or try to come) today. She must be curious to find out what's happening to me. She'll visit another two or three times and then she'll forget about me. *C'est la vie*. And I can do nothing about it. I'd like her to come every day to cheer me up as only she can, but that won't happen. I don't even know if they'll let her visit me today. Still, it's a pleasant prospect—the enjoyable suspense of waiting.

14:45 It's quarter to three and she hasn't arrived. She won't come now. Or perhaps they wouldn't let her in.

FRIDAY, JULY 22

12:00 I'm beginning to allow sleep to overwhelm me. A heavy, dreamless sleep, sleep-as-escape, the sleep that makes me forget that I'm here.

14:00 I've stopped reading *The Leopard* by Lampedusa. It's one of the most boring books I've ever read. Monotonous, stupid and pointless. I abandoned it on page 122. It's a shame. I hate leaving anything half finished, but I couldn't stand it. It makes me sleepy. And I must avoid sleep at all costs.

14:45 *Conversation with my roommate*.

"I don't want to live here, in Flamengo, in Copacabana, or in any of those places."

"So where do you want to live, Flávio?"

"In the cemetery. Life has lost all meaning for me since Carnival in 1964."

"Why?"

"The person I loved most in the world didn't want to go with me to the Carnival ball at the Theatro Municipal."

"Oh, come on Flávio, don't be so silly. There are plenty of other fish in the sea. [Pause.] Do you still love her?"

"Him. He was a boy. Now he's doing his entrance exams to study medicine and I'm stuck in here, waiting for death."

"Don't talk nonsense, Flávio."

"He phoned me yesterday. He's a bit effeminate. It would make me so happy if he came to see me. I attempted suicide because of him. I drank ether spray mixed with whisky on the night of the ball. I ended up in the Emergency Department. Now he's out there and I'm in here, waiting for death."

He's a strange guy, Flávio. He seems totally schizoid, but sometimes he talks perfectly normally, like now. I feel sad and powerless. He's made several suicide attempts in here. He's often spoken to me about the bohemian life he used to lead, and I've noticed a certain pride in his voice when he did so. I know from my own experience that all bohemians feel proud of being bohemian.

Flávio is crying.

15:00 The patients here can sometimes be very funny. Ápio, for example, who's fifty-six, told me yesterday that the Bolshevik revolution was financed by the Americans. And there's a young man, the only other patient who's about the same age as I am, who makes everybody laugh.

I can't write anymore. Flávio is crying.

SATURDAY, JULY 23

10:00 Last night, I managed to phone Rennie, who told me that she was still my girlfriend and still loved me very much. That made me so happy, and I probably said a load of silly things. I'm a sentimental fool. When I stopped talking, the telephonist butted in and I couldn't say anything else. Rennie's coming here on Monday. I hope I don't spend all the time complaining. It's awful, I feel inferior.

It's Sunday morning. I'm listening to the radio and I'm filled by a terrible sense of solitude, which is slowly killing me. It's Sunday morning, a sad, dull Sunday. I'm here behind bars, not talking to anyone, immersed in my solitude. I like that phrase: immersed in my solitude.

It's Sunday morning. No one is singing, the radio is playing a sad song about love and weeping. A day with few prospects.

Rennie is far away. My friends are far away. Probably sleeping off a night of partying and fun. I'm all alone here. The radio is playing an old-fashioned waltz. I think about my father. I feel sorry for him. It must be sad for someone to have a son like me.

On this Sunday morning, I feel my love for Rennie die a little. I'm sure her love for me must be dying too. My hands are empty, I have nothing to offer, nothing to give. I feel powerless and defenseless, like a swallow without wings. I feel bad, wicked, alone. Alone in the world.

Everything here is at once monotonous and unpredictable. I cling fearfully to my photos of Rennie and my cigarettes. They are the only things that can distract me a little.

I long for you and the nearer the time gets to your visit, the more I long to see you. On Saturday, on the phone, you said that you were still my girlfriend, and I'm very glad to have a girl-friend. It makes me feel less alone in here, the world seems a nicer place, even from behind bars. And it will be even nicer when you arrive. And so this morning, I open myself entirely to you, my love, and give you my heart. I feel a bit sad because you're far away and can't be with me all the time, but I'm a man now and have to survive this ordeal alone.

SUNDAY, JULY 31

13:00 At this hour on this day, in this hospital, I have just received the news that in the poetry competition run by the newspaper *Diário de Notícias* I came ninth out of twenty-five hundred entries in the general category and second in the honorable mention category. My poem will probably appear in the anthology they're going to publish.

I'm happy. I wish I were outside, telling everyone, talking to everyone. I am very, very happy.

Here, behind bars, I wonder if Tatá still remembers me, her first boyfriend. I don't know if she's grown a lot, if she's thin or fat, if she's an intellectual or a member of high society. She might have been crippled or lost her mother, she might have moved into a mansion. I haven't seen her for eight years, but I'd like to be with her today. I haven't heard from her once since then. The other day, I phoned and asked if she used to go out with a guy called Coelho. She just said "Yes" and hung up.

SATURDAY, AUGUST 6

Now that Dr. Benjamin has threatened me with insulin and electroconvulsive therapy, now that I've been accused of being a drug addict, now that I feel like a cornered animal, utterly defenseless, I want so much to talk to you. If this were the moment when my personality was about to be completely transformed, if in a few moments' time the systematic destruction of my being was about to begin, I would want you by my side, Rennie.

We'd talk about the most ordinary things in the world. You'd leave smiling, hoping to see me again in a few days' time. You would know nothing and I would pretend that everything was fine. As we stood at the door to the lift, you'd see my eyes fill with foolish tears, and I'd say it was because our conversation had been so boring it had made me yawn. And downstairs, you'd look up and see my hand through the bars waving goodbye. Then I'd come up to my room and cry my heart out thinking about what was and what should have been and what can never be. Then the doctors would come in with the black bag, and the electric shocks would enter me and fill my whole body.

SUNDAY, AUGUST 7

Conversation with Dr. Benjamin.

"You've no self-respect. After your first admission, I thought you'd never be back, that you'd do all you could to become independent. But, no, here you are again. What did you achieve in that time? Nothing. What did you get from that trip to Teresópolis? What did you get out of it? Why are you incapable of achieving anything on your own?"

"No one can achieve anything on his own."

"Maybe, but tell me, what did you gain by going to Teresópolis?"

"Experience."

"You're the sort who'll spend the rest of his life experimenting."

"Doctor, anything that is done with love is worthwhile. That's my philosophy: if we love what we do, that's enough to justify our actions."

"If I went and fetched four schizophrenics from the fourth floor, I mean real schizoids, even they would come up with a better argument than that."

"What did I say wrong?"

"What did you say wrong?! You spend your whole time creating an image of yourself, a false image, not even noticing that you're failing to make the most of what's inside you. You're a nothing."

"I know. Anything I say is pure self-defense. In my own eyes, I'm worthless."

"Then do something! But you can't. You're perfectly happy

with the way things are. You've got used to the situation. Look, if things go on like this, I'm going to forget my responsibilities as a doctor and call in a medical team to give you electroconvulsive therapy, insulin, glucose, anything to make you forget and make you more biddable. But I'm going to give you a bit more time. Come on, be a man. Pull yourself together!"

SUNDAY, AUGUST 14—FATHER'S DAY

Good morning, Dad. Today is your day.
For many years, this was the day you'd wake up with a smile on your face
and, still smiling, accept the present I brought to your room,
and, still smiling, kiss me on the forehead and bless me.
Good morning, Dad, today is your day,
and I can neither give you anything nor say anything
because your embittered heart is now deaf to words.
You're not the same man. Your heart is old,
your ears are stuffed with despair,
your heart aches. But you still know how to cry. And I think you're crying
the timid tears of a strict, despotic father:
you're weeping for me, because I'm here behind bars,
you're weeping because today is Father's Day and I'm far away,
filling your heart with bitterness and sadness.

Good morning, Dad. A beautiful sun is coming up,
today is a day of celebration and joy for many,
but you're sad. And I know that I am your sadness,
that somehow I became a heavy cross
for you to carry on your back, lacerating your skin,
wounding your heart.
At this very moment, my sister will be coming into your room
with a lovely present wrapped in crêpe paper,
and you'll smile, so as not to make her sad too. But inside you,

your heart is crying,
and I can say nothing except dark words of revolt,
and I can do nothing but increase your suffering,
and I can give you nothing but tears and the regret
that you brought me into the world.

Perhaps if I didn't exist, you'd be happy now,
perhaps you'd have the happiness of a man who only ever
wanted one thing:
a quiet life,
and now, on Father's Day,
you receive the reward for your struggle, in the form of kisses,
trinkets bought with the small monthly allowance
that has remained untouched for weeks in a drawer
so that it could be transformed into a present,
which, however small, assumes vast proportions in the heart
of every father.

Today is Father's Day. But my dad had me admitted
to a hospital for the insane. I'm too far away
to embrace you; I'm far from the family,
far from everything, and I know that
when you see other fathers surrounded by their children,
showering them with affection, you'll feel a pang
in your poor embittered heart. But I'm in here
and haven't seen the sun for many days now,
and if I could give you something it would be the darkness
of someone who no longer aspires to anything or yearns for
anything in life.
That's why I do nothing. That's why I can't even say:
"Good morning, dear father, may you be happy;
you were a man and one night you engendered me;
my mother gave birth to me in great pain,
but now I can give you a little of the treasure
placed in my heart
by your hardworking hands."

I can't even say that. I have to stay very still
so as not to make you even sadder,
so that you don't know that I'm suffering, that I'm unhappy
in here,
in the midst of this quietness, normally only to be found in
heaven,
if, of course, heaven exists.
It must be sad to have a son like me, Dad.

Good morning, Dad. My hands are empty,
but I give you this rising sun, red and omnipotent,
to help you feel less sad and more content,
thinking that you're right and I'm happy.

TUESDAY, AUGUST 23

It's dawn, the eve of my birthday. I'd like to write a message full
of optimism and understanding in this notebook: that's why I
tore out the previous pages, so devoid of compassion and so sad.
It's hard, especially for someone of my temperament, to with-
stand thirty-three days without going out into the courtyard and
seeing the sun. It's really hard, believe me. But, deep down, I
know I'm not the most unfortunate of men. I have youth flowing
in my veins, and I can start all over again thousands of times.

It's the eve of my birthday. With these lines written at dawn, I
would like to regain a little self-confidence.

"Look, Paulo, you can always do your university entrance
exams next year, you've still got many years ahead of you. Make
the most of these days to think a little and to write a lot. Rosetta,
your typewriter, your loyal companion-at-arms, is with you,
ready to serve you whenever you wish. Do you remember what
Salinger wrote: 'Store away your experiences. Perhaps, later,
they'll be useful to someone else, just as the experiences of those
who came before were useful to you.' Think about that. Don't
think of yourself as being alone. After all, to begin with, your
friends were a great support. Being forgotten is a law of life.

You'd probably forget about one of your friends if they left. Don't be angry with your friends because of that. They did what they could. They lost heart, as you would in their place."

THURSDAY, SEPTEMBER 1

I've been here since July. Now I'm becoming more and more afraid. I'm to blame for everything. Yesterday, for example, I was the only one to agree to have an injection to help me sleep, and I was the only one to obey the nurse and lie down; the others, meanwhile, continued kicking up a ruckus. One of the nuns who helps out here took a dislike to my girlfriend and so she's not allowed to visit me anymore. They found out I was going to sell my shirts to the other patients and they wouldn't let me: I lost an opportunity to earn some money. But I managed to persuade my friends to bring me a gun, a Beretta. If I need to, I'll use it.

Interruption for a haircut.

Right, my hair's all gone. Now I'm left with a baby face, feeling vulnerable and mad as hell. Now I feel what I feared I might feel: the desire to stay here. I don't want to leave now. I'm finished. I hadn't cut my hair since February, until the people in this hospital gave me an option: cut your hair or stay here for good. I preferred to cut my hair. But then came the feeling that I'd destroyed the last thing remaining to me. This page was going to be a kind of manifesto of rebellion. But now I've lost all will. I'm well and truly screwed. I'm finished. I won't rebel again. I'm almost resigned.

Here ends me.
With no messages to send, nothing, no desire to win,
a desire that had its guts ripped out by human hatred.
It was good to feel this. Total defeat.
Now let's start all over again.

In 1998, I published my book Veronica Decides to Die, *based on my experiences in the psychiatric hospital. Up until then, even*

though I was well known as a writer, no one knew about this pe-
riod of my life. Senator Eduardo Suplicy read out passages from the
book in Congress and finally managed to get approval for a new
law on arbitrary hospitalization, a law that had been hanging
around in the Brazilian Congress for ten years. Nowadays, Brazil
has one of the most modern and most democratic systems in this
respect.

Translated from the Portuguese by Margaret Jull Costa

The Right to Peaceful Assembly

Mahmoud Saeed
WARRIORS OF THE SKY

A desire to fly would come over him at dawn, right after morning prayers. The light would penetrate everything, slowly and persistently, weaving a diaphanous veil over the vast, endless palm forests on both sides of the Euphrates. How would this look from above? If he had a small plane, he would fly every day above this piece of land that he loved more than any other in the world. Its name was Zargá, Blue! It was a good name. From afar it looked black, closer by it turned green, and in the light of the dawn it appeared blue. Rays of sun were playing games with his eyes, refracting off the surface of the Euphrates. The river was a vast natural mirror stretching to the east and south. He loved to look out on the vista of the dense forest and the river that lay on it like an immense dragon. He dreamed of flying on invisible wings all the way to the curvature of the horizon. His large garden extended to the waters of the river and was demarcated on each side by wire fences. He could see the cars of his followers and members of his tribe. They were motionless but each was enveloped in a cloud of dust that it had raised. He could not see where the end of the line was, nor did he hear the engines. At seven he had seen only four cars. Now there were more than thirty: fifteen in the first row and the rest farther behind. There were other puffs of dust cloud on the horizon, which meant more cars were coming. How many cars would be there at ten in the morning when they would start to move? Maybe a thousand.

* * *

Muhammad smiled broadly and closed his eyes. He felt the presence of Hannan near him. She put her hand around his waist. He put his head on her shoulder and allowed his eyes to fall on her full breasts. She was wearing a loose-fitting, flowery red silk shirt. He never failed to be aroused by her hard body and prominent breasts. He kissed her neck and felt a sudden desire overtaking him. He covered her face in kisses and ran his hands over her chest. She burst out laughing and distanced herself. "Enough of that. The kids are coming!" He stopped but she grabbed him around the waist again. "How long are you going to wait?" He pointed to an area north of the house that was free of palm trees. "Here we will build the kindergarten, the school, the theater and music school."

She laughed. "Aren't you forgetting the dance school?"

He shook his head: "Yes, and the dance school. Our girls will learn to dance the ballet. There will not be a single illiterate child in our tribe. All will go to school." She increased her sensuous pressure on his waist and started to tickle him. He looked in her smiling eyes. He loved her wide smile, her gleaming teeth and the dimples in her gorgeous face. He had an unbounded passion for her. Why would they say passion dies after marriage? After fifteen years his love for her had only increased.

"What else?"

"And a sports complex with twenty standard international arenas for soccer, basketball, volleyball and other sports."

"You have so many dreams."

"Life is nothing but a struggle to realize dreams." He pointed to the south: "That is Ali Kazem coming."

"I wish he would not come."

"Don't hate me."

A four-wheel-drive car was splitting the desert and raising a line of dust. Their middle-aged maid said: "Hajji, the breakfast is served."

He laughed and said: "Don't call me Hajji, Samsama! You know I haven't yet gone to Mecca."

"But you intend to!"

Hannan laughed: "Smart answer!"

The maid laughed, too: "The kids are waiting."

They all went downstairs. The kitchen was huge, thirty-by-fifteen feet, and it featured two refrigerators and a freezer. The living room was lined with bookshelves stocked with copies of a handsome volume decorated with the face of the master of the house wearing a black turban. The title was *Warriors of the Sky: New Iraq, New Departures* by Muhammad Amin. The breakfast table was set along the garden side of the kitchen. A bank of lilies and daisies of various colors led to a forest of lemon, orange and fig trees. Nur and Shehab were waiting at the table. Shehab started speaking in a loud voice, his large eyes shining brightly. "I am coming with you." Hannan responded: "No. You are not coming. Neither you nor your sister. Thousands will be going around the Mausoleum of the Imam. You will get lost. Nobody knows how crowded it's going to get."

Nur was seven and had inherited her mother's beauty in all its details. "I will stay at home with Auntie Samsama." There was a knock at the door followed by footsteps in the vestibule. Samsama was welcoming someone: "Peace, Ali, my son. Come on in. They haven't had their breakfast yet." Ali was in his thirties. His brown eyes were slightly bulging in a dark face that was marred by a slight asymmetry of the jawbone. His bald head was shiny. Ali greeted everyone with a voice that was mixed with a slight enigmatic laugh. The master of the house returned his greeting. He sat at the table as a member of the family despite blushing with embarrassment. He stole a glance at Hannan and sat down.

"Great timing, Ali! We haven't started."

"That was my plan."

"*Yallah*, then."

They sat at the long table with its garden view. Ali stared and smiled broadly at the bowl of dried cream and plates full of various cheeses, date molasses and other delicacies. They started eating as Samsama served them with tea. Ali cut a piece of the dried cream wafer and started to chew on it. Shehab was staring at his uneven jaw. His mother noticed that he had stopped eating. "Come on, boy, eat. Hurry up."

Muhammad asked Ali, "What did they tell you?"

"They agreed with almost everything."

"Since when have you become so diplomatic? Tell me everything," Muhammad insisted.

"They refuse to license a new organization."

"Under the name Warriors of the Sky, you mean?"

"Under any name!"

"All right, then. We'll tender a proposal to form an association, then."

"Tender a proposal? To whom?"

"To the interior ministry. Aren't they in charge of licensing new parties and associations?"

"The minister is one of them. He won't agree to it."

"But our organization is a reality. How can they refuse to recognize it?"

"Ah, that's the point. If they didn't know you, they might have given permission. But now that they know you, they will never agree to it."

Muhammad fixed his eyes on Ali. "They don't have the right. The dictatorship is over. It's been three years. We ought to be able to start our own organizations, whenever we want and wherever we wish. We have a new constitution and new hopes. My tribe has more than ten thousand members. We will all sign the petition. Our tribe will be the ground zero of change for the entire country. We will end sectarianism, fanaticism. We say no to exploitation and to tithing."* He turned and pointed to the rows of his book in the living room.

Ali Kazem took a sip of his tea, looked with his bulging eyes at Muhammad and his wife in turn and started to speak in a loud voice. "And that's the main point. Everything except this! They won't let you challenge tithing. They told me your late father

---

* Shiite Muslims pay a fifth of their net income to the religious authorities as religious tax. This is called *khums*.

used to pay three hundred thousand dollars in tithe every year. In the last two years since his death you haven't paid a penny."

Hannan interrupted the discussion: "But you were the first to read the book and you were very happy about abolishing the tithe."

Muhammad continued:

"Do you know how I'll use the tithe money?"

"Forget about this part. They can't force you to pay the tithe. But they won't allow you to go public with your organization," Ali answered.

"And what about other reforms?"

"What reforms?"

Muhammad's voice was agitated: "Banning self-flagellation, chest beating, chain beating, blade beating, ritual cursing of the enemies of the faith and the regular recitation of the passion of the martyrs. Our organization will unite the Iraqis, the Arabs and the Muslims."

"*Ya Sheikh!* Dear cousin, I've told you several times. The organization is forbidden. The tithe can't be abolished. Passion rituals will go on. You can't change a thing."

"So, you are saying we must remain a bunch of monkeys, hitting ourselves with chains and swords and covering ourselves in mud? No education? No dance? No songs? Are we to stay pariahs forever?"

"*Ya Sheikh!* May God grant you long life! Why all this hurry? Look at life. Modern inventions have entirely changed the world. But human affairs proceed much slower. The stuff that is in your books can bring capital punishment on your head, a death fatwa from religious authorities."

"What stuff?"

"Mixed schools, for instance. That is suicide."

"So what? We had mixed universities before occupation!"

"That is why that system fell. Now, Islam is the rule."

Hannan laughed: "What are they, Muslims now?" Ali bowed his head and did not respond. She continued: "That book explains an enlightened Islam." Muhammad took his wife's hand

and raised it with pride. Her wide, silk sleeve slid to reveal her alabaster armpit. Ali Kazem felt a savage desire for her and averted his eyes. Shehab and Nur were clapping for their mother and laughing.

Muhammad added:

"We want a contemporary Islam that unites rather than divides."

"They have promised special considerations for you," Ali said.

"Like what?"

"Like they will forgive you your tithe."

"As a bribe?"

"You can erect whatever buildings you want. But you must name them for the official religious authorities."

"This is larceny!"

Kazem smiled: *"Ya Sheikh.* May God grant you long life. Oh, father of Shehab! My friend, they are all against you. You have to compromise."

"But they want everything. Do they want to interfere in our educational affairs too?"

"Of course, they will. They want to set the curriculum of the schools."

Muhammad exchanged smiles with his wife and children and started to argue. "Do you mean that I should become a contractor for the powers that be? To build them schools and raise students, so they can claim the credit?"

"Do you want to teach music and dance in an Islamic school?" Ali responded.

"What's wrong with that?"

"Well, then next will come Freud, Marx and Darwin!"

"And what of it? I studied Freud, Marx and Darwin at school! I am the best lute player in Kufah and I am the best dancer as well."

Muhammad took Hannan's hand and looked at his children: "Come on." She got off her chair and held hands with the children and started to dance to Muhammad's beautiful voice reciting a *dabka*:* 'Oh, the eyes of my beloved, the eyes of my beloved."

Ali laughed. "Come, Muhammad, stop." He was ogling Hannan's flexible body as she danced. He was captivated. Muhammad continued to stomp to his beat: "The iron bridge wore out from my constant coming and going to my beloved's house."

What harmony in that supple body! She had always bewitched him. He would never forget the five minutes that he spent on top of her. He still remembered her warmth, the heat of her body as he penetrated it. It was seven years ago and he still recalled it. Oh, how lucky you are, my cousin. This mother of two, thirty-two-year-old woman with the body of a teenager. Everything went to his cousin: the leadership of the tribe, the looks, the higher education in Baghdad and the most beautiful wife in the universe. Oh, and the superior mind and the talent in music and dance! And what about him? He was stuck with an ugly mug, bulging eyes, a balding head and a body to go along with all that. He had failed in everything, including the military service. He was rescued from the drudgery of a private's service to be appointed his uncle's driver. Meanwhile Muhammad had become a university graduate and a handsome, educated millionaire. The only thing left for him was to dream about Hannan and do a hundred different things to get her attention. But he had failed there too.

The only consolation was the hours he spent hatching his dark plot to take advantage of Hannan. Although it was only a thought, he pledged not to miss an opportunity to see his plan through. Seven years ago the opportunity had knocked. He was supposed to go to Basra with his uncle and Muhammad. The owner of a date silo had died and they had to go there to watch over the process of shipping dates to India. He put a hot compress on his face before his uncle woke him up to leave and affected a raspy voice: "I have a fever. Put your hand on my face, Uncle."

---

* A *dabka* is popular Arabic lyrics sung in a dancing beat.

His uncle winced. "Oh, you are burning with it. We will take you to the hospital."

"Not necessary, Uncle. Just let me lie down for a few hours."

It was spring. He was a nervous wreck as he waited for his uncle and cousin to leave. He was all ears.

"Ya-allah."

Nur ran to him to take his hand and drag him to the dance. But the sheikh stopped the dance. "It's nine. We have to get ready."

"Let's drink another glass of tea," said Hannan.

Nur was still in the mood to dance: "Come on, Shehab. Let's dance. Only the two of us." Then she took her brother's hand and sang her father's line: "Oh, the eyes of my beloved, the eyes of my beloved . . . the iron bridge wore out from my constant coming and going to my beloved's house."

Ali interrupted her. "May God grant you long life, my Sheikh. This is what they are objecting to."

"What?"

"How old is Nur?"

"Seven."

"She must wear the hijab at her age."

Hannan screamed: "What?"

"She must wear the hijab, I said."

She laughed with derision, as if she wanted to spit in his face. But she was staring him in the eyes. "You must be the last to speak of hijab." Ali lowered his head in shame. But Muhammad held her hand to calm her. After a while he turned to Ali and said: "I know how to raise my children." Then he rose. "Okay, we have to change. It's time to go."

He quickly climbed the stairs to the second floor, holding his wife's hand. When they entered their bedroom, he said to her in a calm voice: "You were too cruel to the poor guy. He was an orphan. Without my father he would have ended up on the streets. And besides everything he has to bear the difficulty of his looks."

"No. He's not poor. He's capable of doing just about anything. He's spying on you. How does a nobody like him turn up as the driver of the chief security adviser? They trust him. He speaks for them."

"Come, who cares for a driver? Don't give the matter more weight than it deserves. Don't forget he is the ward of this family."

Then Muhammad locked the door and tore her clothes off. She stood there with nothing on but a silk pair of red panties that set off her snowy skin. He attacked her. But she stopped him with both hands: "We have to wait. Today is Ashoora, the most important day of the year.* You are a *sheikh*. They are all waiting on you." He laughed. "Then let me kiss your breast." She pushed him back again, while holding onto her red bra. "Don't damage your leadership by being late. People will talk."

He walked away. "You are right. You are wiser than I will ever be."

Ali Kazem stared at him as he descended the stairs. A black *dishdasha,* a black *aba,* intricately embroidered in gold thread, and a green turban.† Ali was shocked by the change. Wasn't this the same man who played the lute, sang and danced a while back? Now he appeared as a strong tribal leader. He was spontaneously moved to say: "You are the sheikh of all sheikhs, oh Muhammad. If this is not pure charisma, then nothing is."

Muhammad laughed. "Thanks."

Hannan came downstairs in a rich, blue dress that came down to her ankles. She wore a black headband and a silk headdress whose strings came down to her chest. He wanted to say that

---

* Ashoora is the day of the martyrdom of Prophet Muhammad's grandson Hussein at the hands of Yazid, the second of the Umayyad kings. Shiites celebrate the passion of Hussein on this day with processions and public rituals.

† A *dishdasha* is a loose-fitting outfit Arab men wear. An *aba* is worn on the shoulders, like a cape.

even in such heavy covering she was more beautiful than a movie star. But he feared another humiliating rebuke. He asked Muhammad:

"Why are you taking her?"

"Why shouldn't I?"

"Why are you exposing her to danger?"

"Do you mean I am in danger?"

Ali was taken aback: "Who knows."

She didn't look in his direction before heading to the living room. The children were watching the satellite cartoon channel. She hugged and kissed Nur. "Take care of yourself and your brother, dear. Don't do anything without Auntie Samsama's permission."

"No, I won't." Then she hugged Shehab. "Listen to your sister and to Auntie Samsama." Then she left. She did not find her husband or Ali. She went to the front door. In the dirt yard beyond the garden hundreds of cars were waiting for them. The tribal leaders were paying their respects to her husband. Then Ali stopped his red four-wheel drive in front of him and addressed Muhammad: "I forgot to tell you that they sent you two hundred guns and two hundred hand grenades. It's a gift."

"We have no need of weapons and if we did, we would buy them."

"But you are targeted."

"By whom?"

"Al-Qaeda."

Muhammad laughed and other sheikhs followed.

"Return their weapons to them. Tell them we are men of dialogue, men of the future and men of peace."

"Trust me. You are targeted."

One of the aides had opened the door for Hannan. She entered the beautiful silver-colored German car as her husband got in through the right-hand door. They sat behind the driver, who was an old man in his sixties. He wore elegant Arabic clothes

with an *aggal* and a black *ķuffieyeh*.* Muhammad stuck his right
hand out of the window of the car. He patted Ali on the shoulder
and said: "Go in peace." The car started on its way and a line of
hundreds of cars followed it. The caravan raised a huge cloud of
dust that did not settle for quite a while. They were on their way
to Najaf.

Ali returned to the house in extreme agitation. Samsama opened
the door for him and asked him: "Why didn't you go to the
ceremonies?"
    "I am tired."
    "Shall I make you some tea?"
    "That would be great."
    "Five minutes only."
    He stopped in the living room. Nur and Shehab were watch-
ing the cartoons, lying on their stomachs. He looked at them.
Thank God Nur had not inherited any of his ugliness. God alone
had helped him succeed in his dark plot.

As soon as he had heard the sound of Muhammad's car leaving at
dawn toward Basra he had relaxed. He entered Muhammad's
bedroom and was immediately surprised by a pleasant aroma.
The generous, full perfume of a female body suffused the room.
He couldn't see anything, not even the wide bed that he had seen
many times during the day as Samsama made it. He did not even
see the window that opened onto the back garden. He remained
frozen for a few seconds until his eyes got used to the darkness.
Then her image started to appear in front of him. Now he could
make her out completely. She was lying on her left side and wore
only a nightgown. He could not make out its color. It was spring.
He remained frozen for a few more minutes. Her black hair covered her face. He started to distinguish the color of her body, her
slightly full thighs and her bulging right breast. He climbed on
the bed. She felt the movement and rolled on her back. Her knees

---

* The *aggal* is the rope-like headgear Arabs wear, while a *ķuffieyeh* is the
  cloth worn with the *aggal* on the head and shoulders.

were together. He opened them up and touched the wet spot between her legs with his fingers. She sighed and said: "Muhammad." He didn't respond but just murmured: "Mmmmm." Suddenly he was overwhelmed by a wave of irresistible desire. He could not wait. He penetrated her. She sighed: "Go easy. You are hurting me."

The warmth of her body was melting him. Another wave of desire hit him and he could not control himself this time. He came in the blink of an eye. She moved, extended her arm and took a deep breath. Then she extended her hands toward him. Maybe she realized who he was. He wasn't sure. He ran from the room. His penis was still dripping on his thigh. Ali put on his clothes and started to run. She was standing at the door of her room wrapped in a blanket, utterly terrified and deathly pale. She asked him: "Was that you?" He didn't respond. He just kept running.

No one knew where he hid. He returned after four years. He was sure Hannan had not told anyone or else he would have been killed like a pestiferous animal. It was March 1, 1999. He would never forget the day of his escape. He saw Nur after four years and learned that she was born at the beginning of December. His guess was that she was his daughter. But the secret was between the two of them. There was no sign of what had happened between them except for the scorn and loathing that she unleashed toward him in her speech and the clever rebukes that she would serve him in a way that only he would understand.

The cartoons were new. No Mickey Mouse, no Popeye. He sat back and closed his eyes and found himself on a ship, sailing with Popeye on a turbulent sea. Popeye was fighting his giant foe. He tried to make peace between them, but they both ganged up on him and threw him in the water. His mobile phone rang. He looked at the number. It was from the chief security adviser. He didn't pick up. The clock showed two minutes past eleven.

He just sat there. He couldn't believe he had slept for an hour and a half. He touched the glass of tea. It was cold. The kids were not in the room either. Samsama entered: "Did you sleep well? I didn't wish to wake you up. Did you stay up last night?"

"Last night? I stay up every night. Till midnight at least."

"You should have never left this house. Your cousin will take care of you."

"I will return."

"That would be a good thing to do."

"Yes, it would."

He turned on the TV. The voice of the anchor was agitated, insistent: "The chief security adviser at the Interior Ministry has issued a communiqué stating that a group composed of Saudis, Egyptians, Syrians and Moroccans has attacked the pilgrims, killing dozens. They intended to assassinate the great Sources of Emulation.* But the operation was discovered and neutralized in time." The camera panned to show hundreds of dead bodies in and out of their cars on the road. Many cars were overturned, others had been strafed with bullets or blown up by missiles. There was wreckage everywhere. It was obvious that the caravan had been hit from the air.

The camera zoomed in on a silver-colored German car. Only its back trunk and fenders were intact. The body was riddled with bullets. There was no sign of life except a pool of blood outside of it. The agitated voice of the anchor sounded once more: "Look. The car of the Antichrist himself.† This man claimed to be the special envoy of the Saviour Mahdi."

Ali trembled. He could not stop his tears. Then he sobbed. They were both dead. He had not intended for her to get killed.

---

* The highest office for Shiite Muslim clergy. A source of emulation commands the allegiance of very large communities of believers.

† The concept of someone who opposes the Savior of the World after his Second Coming is shared by the eschatology of the Shiite Muslims, where Dajjal is prominent. Like the Antichrist, Dajjal has found literary recognition as the description of things undesirable.

What a disaster! He wanted to keep Hannan for himself. He wanted her to survive, live. She might agree to be with him after the death of her husband. They would take care of the children. But nothing had gone according to the plan.

He surfed the TV channels. On the Iraqi channel a member of the parliament described the Warriors of the Sky as "an anti-nomian sect bent on bringing on the coming of the Mahdi." On the Jordanian channel a professor of fine arts said that Muhammad Amin was a profound intellectual and humanist. On the Karbala channel a speaker with a black turban and an effeminate lilt was saying: "He wanted to be a singer and a composer, too." On the Najaf channel a man was saying dismissively: "He was a pervert, a libertine, given to music and dance." This was followed by a government speaker who announced that after a raid on the Warriors of the Sky terrorist organization 263 people had died, 210 had been injured and 502 had been taken prisoner. Also, a quantity of light and heavy weapons had been confiscated at their headquarters.

Ali heard the sound of helicopters above the house. The wind of the propellers was beating down the trees in the garden. The door of the kitchen was kicked open. Samsama was knocked on her back by the force of the sudden entry. A number of soldiers rushed in and proceeded to turn the house inside out. Some entered the living room and some went upstairs. Ali was staggered, frozen in his seat. Then the chief security adviser appeared in front of him with his wild eyes and unkempt beard. He was angry.

"You lowlife! You pervert! You were supposed to deliver the weapons to them!"

"But they refused, Excellency."

Ali felt the sting of an unexpected slap on his face.

"Where are the weapons?"

"In my car, Excellency."

The chief security adviser turned to a major who was standing behind him. "Get me the keys. Get the weapons out and arrange them; photograph them."

He took a copy of Muhammad's book off the shelf and laughed: "Warriors of the Sky! No, Warriors of Satan!"

Four soldiers were stomping downstairs. One of them was carrying a box full of jewelry in one hand and bundles of dollars in the other. The second had both hands full of swords embossed with gold and silver, and a third carried small frames that he had ripped off the walls. The last soldier was dragging Nur and Shehab along. The children were crying and screaming. Samsama yelled: "They are only kids!" The chief security adviser turned to her: "Shut up! They are the spawn of Satan." Then he stared at Ali, while waving the book. "Falsehoods. May God damn you all. You are all apostates, followers of the Antichrist."

Dozens of soldiers were arranging the weapons in the garden. An old man was carefully filming them from various angles. A general opened the door of the kitchen and said: "We are ready."

"Proceed."

A few soldiers attacked Ali and Samsama, tied their hands and beat them with canes until they fell down. Then they tied their feet and dragged them out. After a few minutes helicopters fired missiles at the house and reduced it to rubble.

Translated by Ahmad Sadri

Free Elections

Richard Griffiths
THE OBVIOUS CANDIDATE

The crowd remains obediently silent, so the click of the sergeant's right boot thwacking into his left—again—is loud and clear. The soldier who's slow-marched out with him presents his rifle for inspection. The sergeant faces him and stops. The two men stare at each other from behind their skull-grip sunglasses.

The intense heat gets worse as the moment extends. I try mind over matter, relaxing into it, taking the toneless scrape of the crickets as a mantra. I try physics, standing straight, letting my clothes hang from the bones of my shoulders and hips to keep them away from my skin. I should have left my backpack at the hotel, trusted them with my passport.

No one else seems to notice the sun. The other tourists, baseball-capped or not, seem unconcerned. Carla, bare-shouldered next to me, is watching the scene steadily. Half her face is obscured by her big sunglasses but the mouth says enough: she can't decide whether to laugh or sneer.

Now the sergeant moves, but as an automaton, as if he's busking, pretending to be a robot, smooth hand and arm movements terminating in abrupt, mechanical reversals. His head tilts forward, his neck extends and his head rotates right then left as he examines the length of the rifle. His white-gloved hand moves quickly, then slowly, to the rifle butt, then stops as if merely showing us that the rifle does indeed end where we think it does, that we are looking at something solid, that this is not illusion. Then he stands still again and the two men resume their mutual stare.

I'm watching carefully now, but I don't see what happens: there's the slap of gloved hands on metal, a movement of arms that's too quick to catch, and again they're motionless and staring, but now the gun is in the sergeant's hands.

Carla rotates her head toward me, stops in the same mechanical way and I'm glad we're on the steps at the back of the crowd because I don't think she'd care if anyone saw her. She raises an eyebrow and rotates her head back. I look away, over the top of the soldiers, past the white box of the tomb toward the city. There is no dramatic view here; this part of the cemetery does not face any of the monuments downtown; I can only see apartments, construction cranes, forest rising into haze.

The guard change takes forever, but it does end, and when the sergeant has finally marched the relieved soldier offstage, the crowd breaks up. The new guard starts to pace down the marching mat in front of the tomb; Carla and I make for the shade of the trees on the far side of the steps.

A couple with a wheelchair pass by.

"It's about respect," the man says.

"But I didn't know," the woman says, "I didn't *know*!"

"Didn't know what?" I say to Carla.

"Maybe she let the flag fall from the stroller mid-ceremony. What did you think of all that?"

"Those guys at the front had their camcorders in the sergeant's face. That's not respectful, is it?"

"Respect! You know they change the guard twice as often in the summer?"

"So? It's bloody hot out here."

"Hot, my ass. They're soldiers. It's so we all get to see them do it. It's so *we* don't have to hang around waiting for the show."

We sit down on a bench under the trees. Carla searches in her backpack, and her concentration face appears. It's such an unexpected face, such a mismatch with everything else she presents to the world, that it still startles, even after all this time. It's the tongue, of course, appearing between her lips, but not just that. It's the momentarily dropped guard, the uncharacteristic, and worryingly sudden, appearance of weakness, as if absolutely everything she is hangs on whatever she's searching for in her bag.

She pulls out two bananas. "Want one?" The face has gone. There was a brief time when I thought it signified the real Carla and that I was the only one who understood that.

"I thought it was water-only in here."

"It's a big cemetery. I'll faint if I don't eat." She holds one out to me.

"No, I just need water."

"Sure," she says, in a tone that could mean anything.

"I just don't like treading on other people's holy stuff."

She shrugs and peels her banana.

"Is it true," I ask, "that some people make a living from running flag shops here?"

"I think so," she nods. "You guys don't do flags much, do you?"

"No."

"Why's that?"

"I think we're embarrassed by them."

"Why?"

"Is there ever one outside your house?"

She shakes her head.

I've been to her house. Just the once. I genuinely don't remember whether there was a flag holder outside. I remember the front lawn, neatly mown and unfenced, identical to all the others on the street. She let me in ahead of her, and when she closed the door behind us, I realized that we had never before been in a space not stolen from work.

"Embarrassment's still a big thing with the Brits, right?"

"Rest assured I'll let you know the minute it isn't."

She'll mention it now, and we can get it over with. When she picked me up at the hotel a couple of hours ago, it was obvious straight away, although I'm not sure how, that we weren't just going to carry on as normal. One of us has to say something. The heat makes the thought of it much worse, and I'd almost prefer to spend the weekend on my own, get myself calm in the privacy of my own head.

"How's your jet lag doing?" she asks.

"Should be all right by Monday."

"Monday, yeah. You ready to take them on?"

"I think so." I wait for her to say more, but after a few moments she stands up.

"Listen, I'm going to check out the view before they get started on that RoboCop stuff again. Stay here and cool off, if you want." She walks away before I can say anything.

I watch her. She's unhurried, doesn't look annoyed, doesn't look anything. I can't tell what she wants from me. Maybe nothing. Maybe I'm less important than I think.

In one way, it's really simple: I got the job, she didn't. If she thinks that's unfair, she can say so. We were both interviewed. Maybe she thinks I've been parachuted in, the foreigner come to sort things out. Well she can say that, too. She usually says precisely what she thinks.

Have I been parachuted in? Is that what it looks like? Maybe it does. In which case, perhaps I should roll my chute and hide it. No, I don't need to come over all faux military, I'm the training manager, not, despite what our new boss says, the vanguard of the shock troops of change. This is mundane corporate life: I'm not going to end up dead in a ditch.

Monday's their annual shindig—the guys who report to me now. They have their convention here. They're the installers; they install the company's stuff and train the customers. The convention is pretty much the only time they see one another; the rest of the time they're on the road, living in hotels, driving rented cars, spending two or three days with strangers and moving on. Overindulging in fast food. On Monday I'll get up in front of them and outline the new world order, the gospel according to me. Carla's thinking it should be her walking up to the stage, me down in the audience. She'll be there, listening carefully to what I have to say, like the rest of them.

Two small things will give it an edge this year. One, their previous and well-liked boss was fired two weeks ago, and no one really knows why. And two, once everyone had got over the shock, and were sure they weren't on the list too, and started talking succession, the favorite was Carla.

My seat in the shade is perfect for observing the principal responsibilities of a tomb guard, which are, apparently, to walk twenty-one steps, turn around, wait twenty-one seconds and walk twenty-one steps back. I haven't been timing his pauses, but he does pause for quite a while, and I'm betting that a key piece of his training is how to estimate that twenty-one seconds accurately and repeatably.

He's guarding the Unknowns, the remains of unidentified soldiers from various wars. There's a special irony about this because he—according to the tour guide—is very much known. Only volunteers with cleaner-than-clean records can get the job, and they can be removed from the job's scroll of honor if ever they should sully their record in any way at all, even after they're dead. That's quite a demand. It makes the objectives I agreed with my new boss last week look rather halfhearted. Successful volunteers will join a rota of soldiers guarding the tomb twenty-four hours a day, seven days a week. In perpetuity. Which is something of a commitment, too.

People are gathering for the next ceremony. I don't hear any foreigners, everyone seems to be American. I imagine this place is somewhere many Americans would want to visit at least once. It occurs to me that if I were in my team's shoes, that's what I'd do: fly in a couple of days early and see the sights before the convention. One or two of them might even be out here, right now.

There's no sign of Carla. She probably won't be back for a while. She's not oversensitive to that kind of thing; she'll assume I can entertain myself.

Sitting next to her on the Metro this morning, it felt like old times. Then I asked her why she wanted to come out here.

"It's the only attraction left."

"What d'you mean?"

"We've seen everything else."

So is that all it was? The kind of thing you'd do for any colleague staying away from home? The thought was so sudden and acute that I knew I shouldn't look at her, because it would be there on my face. But I let myself; I turned toward her. She wasn't looking. I saw only the reflection of her sunglasses in the window.

"The cemetery will be full of Support-Our-Troops folks," she told me.

"Will I be able to tell?"

"Sure. They look like sheep. But they get the vote, same as you and me."

I can't spot the sheep. Some of the visitors seem awed, reverent, but it's hard not to be, the place is designed to make people feel that way. I feel slightly out of sorts myself, and it's not just the heat and the time difference: when I pay attention to the feeling, I realize it's envy. I want to be like them; belong to all this, not be a tourist. When the Metro broke out of the tunnel into the sunshine this morning, and ran alongside the highway, we saw a billboard for the marines: "For country. For honor." Impossible at home but I imagine the visitors here have no difficulty with it. This close to the military, to this particular part—its pride, its family—it is easy to be pulled closer. And to end up here, in this cemetery, would be to belong to a community: gardeners, tourists, guides singing your praises, the company of an adored president, all the comings and goings of twenty burials a day. You might only be a name on a headstone—or a forename on the back of a headstone if you're a wife—but you wouldn't be lonely here, not ever.

Why was Carla the obvious candidate? And who says so? Not that many people, because not many people care. But talking to some who do, I could see their surprise that I'd been chosen, they couldn't quite hide it. So what? What's obvious when viewed from the bottom of the corporate ocean? Nothing. No one should be surprised that things don't happen as they expect.

None of this should matter to me. I'm not sure why it does.

Maybe it's my age, the fact that quite soon it will start to count. Or the fact that I'm a late starter. I should have been here sooner, at Carla's age. And I'm conscious of the age difference now; it hasn't mattered before. She's always offered opinions and asked for mine, but I'm wondering whether she'll bother with the asking part any longer. She probably thinks her ideas are better than mine, more relevant. She uses Facebook, Twitter, has her calendar out in the ether; I prefer anonymity. So far that's been something we've joked about. That and Wikipedia: the reliability of user-generated content. She wants the installers to have their own wiki. She imagines them in the evenings on the hotel Wi-Fi, amending installation instructions with their experiences from the day. I wonder how long it will be before she starts on that one again, now I'm in charge. I don't know how to say it to them, so I'll probably just be blunt: I'm not having that everyone-has-an-equal-say shambles. It won't work. She doesn't take their personalities into account, their long-distance rivalries. What they write will never be free of their own, skewed, too-many-nights-dining-alone-in-the-Tex-Mex take on the world. Someone needs to be in control.

Still no sign of her.

There's a building behind the tomb. We hurried round it to see the main attraction and paid it no attention. It's actually an amphitheater, so I go over for a look. It's enclosed by a twin circle of columns, and in their shade, with my hand on the stone, I can imagine the possibility of being properly cool again later, back in the hotel. There are raked curves of benches in the auditorium, and these are exposed to the full glare of the sun. At their focus is a stage with a kind of throne, upon which a disrespectful child is sitting. His parents are in the front row, taking photographs.

Carla is under the arches on the far side of the circle. She's walking slowly, taking things in, looking like a tourist. She's not looking for me. I know she does this normally, but for some reason, I find it annoying now. Maybe it's the proximity, the fact that she's practically within spitting distance and still doesn't remember that I'm waiting. I've half a mind to hide, but don't.

"Hey!" she says when she finally arrives round my side of the circle. "There you are!" And she's talking about what we might do when we've finished out here, where we could go, what we could eat. She frowns, or at least I think she does behind her sunglasses, "What's up?"

"Nothing's up."

"Boss," she nods. She means it to be funny.

"Boss," I say, "And how does that feel?"

There's a small, but sharp, adjustment to the angle of her head, "Not good."

"I wondered." I want to say I understand, but I'm not sure I do.

"How would you feel?"

"I don't know."

"You can imagine. Can't you?"

"We're a team."

"We were," she says. "Against the rest of them."

The rest of them, yes. It didn't start out like that. Carla and I were assigned to work together on a project and told what was required. We decided to do something else and suddenly a *them* and a *they* appeared. So we maneuvered them into accepting what we wanted, because we knew we were right. People say they hate politics at work, the schmoozing and the backstabbing, but sometimes it's what makes the job worth doing: it creates something to belong to.

"All right, *were* a team. I need that to continue."

"It can't. Not like that."

And she says that last phrase carefully, which catches me out, and it's as if she's making the pause that follows, opening a gap for me. I start to ask *like what*, but I'm not quick enough.

"You know you can fire me now?" she says.

"Why would I do that?"

"You might have to."

"I doubt it."

"So doubt it, but could you do it?"

Could I? It's something I don't want to think about. These last few months, all the work we did together—our careful maneuvering to pick off objectors, our e-mailing on private accounts, the hours in the air over the Atlantic, the feeling of being clever and ahead of the pack—it all seemed to be *for* something, to be leading somewhere.

She moves her head to face me directly. "Well, are you tough enough?"

I look at her. We're just sunglasses and mouths to each other and I remember an advertisement for the army, from years back. The camera's behind the eyes of a soldier facing an armed man guarding a well. The man is waving his gun and shouting. He's wearing camouflage and a beret and large, dark glasses. Then the image brightens: the soldier has removed his own sunglasses. And it all calms down, and everything is OK.

My hand's halfway toward my temple when she says, "Because I'm tough enough. I'd do it. I would."

There's a pause, in which she seems as startled by what she's said as I am. And she rushes on, "You've seen what happens: you come in one morning and you're given a cardboard box and thirty minutes. That's what you have to do if you need to. You can't let me get away with being less good than I should be. Could you do it? Could you fire me?"

"This is ridiculous. It's not going to happen. Where's this 'less good' come from?"

"Nowhere. It's different now. You have to look at me like that."

"And you'd be looking at me *like that*? If you were in my place?"

She doesn't answer.

A voice is raised outside the auditorium. The sergeant is shouting at the crowd in slow motion, requesting that everyone stands. The guard is changing again.

"Why am I giving you advice?" Carla says.

"I don't know. You tell me."

But she doesn't, and the seconds go by until I know she's not going to. She may not have an answer and if she does, she may not understand how she could say it. That time in her house, when there was as much space as we wanted, and we were for once not hemmed in by office cubicles, bright lights, e-mails and flight schedules, when the talk about work petered out and we were faced only with each other, our curiosity failed us.

And so after a minute we leave, and take the road to the exit. It winds down through the open cemetery. One of the Unknowns is out here: they found out who he was, and when they did, he was moved. Now he's a stone in a row of stones, where no one stands guard, and although the grass is cut, the elements are free to get on with their job of smoothing things out and wearing away the names.

Free Elections

Juan Goytisolo
MR. PRESIDENT . . .

DEMOCRATIC REFLECTIONS

I am a past master in the art of inflating budgets, handing out posts and manipulating figures. I lie on camera with consummate ease. The public knows all this and admires me. That's why I was elected President and will be once again, because ordinary citizens identify with my character, my fondness for power and money and the bold pirouettes of my campaign. He's what we'd like to be, they tell themselves. He's inviting us to imitate him. If he now owns factories, companies, television channels, newspapers and football clubs and rakes it in from all sides, we'll adopt him as our model. This is the essence of me on the election trail: recognize yourself, look at yourself in your mirror! In five years your holdings can also increase tenfold, if not fiftyfold! Gone are the days when people talked about honesty, transparency, improved social services and other rubbish from the stupid, empty-headed Left. The man in the street knows what's good for him, elects the clever guy and cuts to the quick. My barefaced cheek and antics boost the popularity and practical appeal of my promises. A vote for me is a vote for you. I'll take up the challenge yet again! I'll be everyone's president because we all belong to the same body! I will continue in the breach for another five years, in the forefront, long live freedom and the nation.

A WARNING TO THOSE
WHO LEAP TO CONCLUSIONS . . .

If the kings and priests of yesteryear flaunted divine attributes in order to strengthen their grip on a timorous flock, today's state-of-the-art tools for spying on people and keeping them in line allow power to be exercised with means that are infinitely more efficient than the sacred, though fallible, invoking of the Lord. The cutting-edge technology at our fingertips enables us to detect, guaranteeing absolute success, the slightest signs of discontent shown by individuals averse to the democratic gains and advances forged by our President, the Father of Our Nation. Microscopic cameras, ubiquitous bugging devices scrutinize and record everything that happens in the domestic space of every member of the citizenry, from the matrimonial bed to the john where they satisfy their most intimate needs. Whoever dares to challenge the Boss and stand as candidate in an electoral contest that they've lost before it has begun, faces the fallout from such rash lunacy. Endless images taken while he settles his buttocks on the toilet bowl, tenses jaws and stomach muscles, sticks his index finger into his anus to facilitate the exit of fecal matter and then checks the weight and size of the final emission will be downloaded on to the Web and put out on peak-time bulletins' breaking news. Countless surfers and television viewers will watch in delight as he punctiliously rubs his rear eye, glances askance at the brown smeared paper and stands up to evaluate his stools with an expert's learned eye. A voiceover will comment sarcastically: do you really want to vote for a fellow like this? You will hear an answer comes in the form of a side-splitting guffaw. This wretch deserves outright rejection by the whole citizenry! Go with the whole people to his house and express your anger! Close-ups of the masses gathered on his doorstep, a frenzied sea of flags and photos of the President, and that voiceover again: Our President anointed will never be defeated! Everyone chorus that to the baton of the Father of Our Nation!

Much to the surprise of our man in exile, dear reader, the Internet message you've just read comes with his e-mail address. What devious spirit is pursuing him through the virtual galaxy of cyberspace?

THE ONE AND ONLY

In the presidential elections periodically organized by my security services and in which I am backed in a plebiscite by 99.999 percent of the population, the scant number of votes against—less than a hundred from a census of more than ten million—convinced me of the triumphant success of my governance from that now distant day in which a providential armed movement hoisted me into the Leadership of the State and put an end to the charade of corrupt politicking rogues performing like puppets before an indignant, mocking public. Since then everything has followed a perfect, orderly routine: the setting of a date for the referendum, a massive publicity campaign—city by city, district by district, household by household—for a yes vote, a formal invitation for alternative candidacies to those who would like to compete against me and don't dare for fear of lasting opprobrium. The humiliating public excuses voiced by some of those pretentious poetasters dissuaded all the others from following their example and losing face in a laughable, pointless contest. But that isn't what happened in the last round of elections. There were no opponents and the count, which was observed and endorsed by a number of international observers, came up with an astonishing result: a single vote against.

After the euphoric official celebrations, telegrams of congratulations from other Heads of State and spontaneous street parties throughout the land, I found the figure disturbing, rather than comforting. It was quite normal for there to be a handful of resentful folk opposed to the great social achievements of my rule: they merely represented themselves and thus revealed their regrettable blindness and lack of understanding. But that solitary, hard-line, recalcitrant vote, cast by someone stubbornly opposed to the generosity of my government, forewarned me of the existence of a new danger, of a latent threat that could surface at any moment.

Who was the enigmatic opponent?

I was obsessed by the question and couldn't sleep. I mobilized the information agencies to get on his trail and identify him: they must scrutinize the electoral district where the vote was cast under a microscope, establish a list of suspects, carefully sieve through the tapes filmed by the spy cameras on that ill-omened day. The search lasted several months and proved pointless. None of the individuals arrested on various roundups admitted their guilt. Should there be recourse to torture of those jailed, as the head of the scientific police advised me? After weighing up the pros and cons, I concluded that would be futile. Once submitted to such treatment, the innocent would confess and, he, the relentless enemy of my good works, would give nothing away. Malevolently, implacably, he would redouble his efforts to fulfill his goal: to finish me off, that's right, to eliminate me.

I summoned my advisers and the underlings in my chain of command to discuss the matter. The ideas they put forward—individualized punishments from first to third degree, the extermination of all those on the electoral lists for that district—seemed to me impracticable and I rejected the lot. I had a dark feeling it was a battle lost in advance. That merciless enemy would survive me. I suffered weeks of anguish, prey to a single idea: a secret, undetectable plot was being put in place, down to the finest detail. As I tossed and turned in bed I had a dream full of foreboding: I saw myself in the polling station while I was casting the damned voting slip. When I woke up, without giving anyone prior notice, I filmed my confession on video, serenely certain that I would be executed immediately and would rest in peace forever.

Translated by Peter Bush

Economy and Society

Yann Martel

THE MOON ABOVE HIS HEAD

I've never liked downhill skiing. The skier's labors are as futile as those of Sisyphus—the same pointless up and down on the side of a hill—only they're done for fun, the ennobling sense of tragedy thus sacrificed on the altar of frivolity. And this, in freezing cold weather. No wonder the sport leaves me as glum as a boulder. But my wife loves skiing and I love her and she had been planning this holiday with friends for months. So the cozy domestic routine had to be interrupted, my writing studio in the backyard boarded up, my current play put on hold and barbaric skiing in the Rockies endured for ten days.

By the third day, I had managed to ease myself out of my wife's icy boot camp of pleasure, waving her and our friends on, and I had retreated to a café bearing the name Shangri-La. It was the highest resting place in the resort, perched atop a bluff just below the top ski lift. The view from its terrace was splendid and the coffee and sandwiches were passable. I found myself a warm, sunny corner and settled down with a book, taking breaks to enjoy the alpine panorama. It was there, incredulous, that I heard for the second time of Abdikarim Ghedi Hashi.

I was reading. A group of skiers gathered at a picnic table not far from my chair. They were in high spirits. I didn't pay them much attention until I heard a young man say, "Did you hear about the guy who was trapped in the can all night?"

His friends seemed to think it was the start of a joke. I pricked up my ears.

"No, I'm serious," the young man continued. "A guy two days ago fell through the hole in the shithouse and spent the whole night there."

The group loudly expressed disbelief and hilarity.

"I swear I'm not joking. He fell through the hole and spent the whole fucking night in the septic tank."

Howls and cackles of laughter.

"Where'd this happen?" a sceptical voice cried.

"Just over there." The young man pointed. The restrooms were not attached to the café. They were directly opposite, across a flat bit of piste. "It was the end of the day and no one heard him shouting."

"Did he hurt himself?" someone thought to ask.

"No. He just spent a miserable night in a swimming pool of piss and shit." The young man couldn't stifle his mirth any longer and burst out laughing. He controlled himself. "They found him in the morning. The ski patrol pulled him out, wrapped him in blankets and brought him down the mountain on a sled."

Their faces were red and they had tears in their eyes. Their laughter boomed across the vast, sunlit space beyond the terrace, rolling down the side of the mountain. The laughter of young gods.

They eventually settled down to their hot chocolates and sandwiches, though the occasional interjection—"I wonder what they did with the blankets?"—set them off again.

As they were leaving, I signaled to the teller of the tale. "You didn't catch the name of the man who had that accident, did you?" I asked.

He shook his head. "No, I didn't."

I went to investigate the restrooms. There were two doors, the one on the left being the men's. Inside, the sink and two urinals were widely spaced to accommodate skiers lumbering about in their boots. A wide door gave onto the large cubicle. The toilet was a long bench made of compressed board that ran the length of the back wall. In the middle was the plastic toilet lid and seat. I lifted them. They fell back easily on their hinges. The hole was larger than I expected, the seat overlapping the wood rim by no more than an inch. Still, not a big hole. I looked down. The smell didn't come through strongly because of the cold air, but the mound of soiled toilet paper and excrement glowed in the penumbra. I couldn't tell how big the tank was, or how deep. I looked at the hole again. Could a person really accidentally fall through it? It seemed scarcely believable.

The restroom didn't have windows. There was no natural light, only that coming from two light fixtures on the ceiling, one in the cubicle and one beyond, where the sink and urinals were. Compared to the shattering light outside, the fixtures shone weakly, giving off a diluted, yellowish light. Stepping outside, I noticed the small panel attached to the roof of the restroom. A solar panel.

I went back to the café. When there was a lull in traffic, I approached the cashier. "Excuse me, the man who had the accident two days ago, who spent the night . . ." I pointed toward the restrooms.

She nodded. "Yeah?"

"What was his name?"

"I don't know."

"You didn't see him?"

"No, I wasn't working that day."

A co-worker came up. "I saw him. I was on the lift coming up for my shift. The ski patrol was taking him down in a sled pulled by a skidoo."

"Did he have brown skin? I mean more than just a tan."

"Couldn't tell you. He was all wrapped up in blankets."

"Of course. Something else: are the lights in the restroom turned off at night?"

"They're never turned off. They're solar powered and it's better for the battery if the charge goes up and down."

"Do they stay bright all night?"

"No, they start to dim. It's not a big battery."

"I see. So, tell me, how could I find the man's name?"

"You could talk to the ski patrol office," said the cashier.

"Do you have their number?"

She let me use the phone and I called. The man who answered couldn't remember offhand. He looked through some papers.

"It was something complicated," he said "Here we go. His name was Ab—di—" He was working his way syllable by syllable.

"Abdikarim Ghedi Hashi," I interrupted him.

"That's right. Not your usual skier name. D'you know him?"

"No, but I've heard of him. Is he all right?"

"Yeah. They had a look at him at the hospital. He got cold, but he's fine."

"Was he angry?"

"No. I mean, he was distressed, but I wouldn't say he was angry. He said it was an accident. Accidents happen. Mind you, this was a real freak one."

"Where is he now?"

"Don't know. He's not staying here, I know that. After the hospital we drove him to a motel in town."

"Do you know which one?"

"I can find out. Give me a minute."

I wrote the name of the motel down, hung up and returned to my seat on the terrace for a think. Accidents happen, they do, but even freak ones have their limits. Because the thing was, two winters ago, at a different resort in British Columbia, on another of my wife's skiing holidays, I'd heard the same story. A short article in the local paper had caught my eye. A man had accidentally fallen through the hole of a toilet at a café on the slopes, had spent the night in the septic tank, had been rescued in the morning. He'd told the reporter that the quality of the light in the toilet had struck him. And another detail had stayed with me: the man was a Somali-Canadian by the name of Abdikarim Ghedi Hashi.

Later that afternoon, after the skiing day was over, I took a moment to call his motel. He was still there. The receptionist put me through to his room.

"Hello?" A soft, accented voice.

"Is this Mr. Hashi?"

"Yes, it is."

"Mr. Hashi, I was sorry to hear about your accident. I hope you're feeling better."

"I am, thank you."

"I'm glad to hear that. I was wondering if we could meet to talk about it?"

"What is there to talk about? It was an accident."

"I'm curious, that's all. I'm a writer. And I was in Somalia briefly, years ago."

"Are you a journalist?" There was suspicion in his voice.

"No, not at all. I write plays. I was in the north of Somalia, a town called Hargeisa. I traveled there by bus from Ethiopia. It was in my hardcore backpacking days. Beautiful country."

"I've never been to Hargeisa. My family was from Mogadishu."

"Well, there wasn't much to Hargeisa itself, I have to say."

"There's not much to Mogadishu, not now. Civil war does a town no favors."

What did Hargeisa no favors was dusty, grinding poverty. I'd found nothing to do there but poke around a few mosques, wander around a zoo that baked in the sun and sit at a tea stall in the market, drinking tea and being stared at by everyone.

"Can I invite you for a tea or a coffee? I could meet you at your motel tomorrow morning."

He agreed, with politeness that might have been reluctance.

The next morning, I drove to the small town next to the resort. I found his modest, roadside motel easily. It was a cheap way to have a ski holiday, staying in town and relying on the shuttle. I called him from the reception. He came over promptly, clutching himself in the cold air in his blue winter coat. We shook hands. He was small and slim and had a pleasant face, with a goatee and a bald, slightly bulbous forehead. He was in his mid-thirties perhaps. I proposed that we go over to the diner that was next to the motel. We walked over.

I had coffee. After some persuasion, he ordered a small fruit salad. We chatted, circling around the accident. He told me a little about himself. He'd come to Canada via a refugee camp in Ethiopia, sponsored by a charity, six years in all it had taken him. He'd ended up in Calgary, had studied this, worked there, and so on. He'd taken up skiing, though he wasn't very good at it, he said.

"So how exactly did it happen?" I finally asked.

He looked away. "I needed to urinate. The ski boots are so big and heavy. I removed them and climbed onto the bench so that I wouldn't get my socks wet in the melted snow on the floor. But I didn't want to make a mess. I lifted the toilet seat. That's when I slipped. It happened so quickly. It was an accident."

I thought to myself, "You slipped with both feet. Into that tiny hole? You didn't manage to catch yourself with your arms or any other part of your body? You fell through as straight as a diver? And it's happened to you twice, and both times at the end of the day, when no one was around?" I didn't let on that I knew he'd had this "accident" once before. He was a very small man. Now that he had removed his coat, I could see that clearly. Still, the incident beggared belief. It was so absurdly implausible. But he had a quiet, mournful dignity. He spoke earnestly. Perhaps he was just a tiny, clumsy man, hurrying too much because he was tired and because he badly needed to pee. Accidents do happen. My heart sank at my disbelief. I wanted to believe him.

"You couldn't climb out?"

"I couldn't see a way."

"No one heard your cries for help?"

"No one."

"What did you do all night?"

"Well, I couldn't sleep. The filth came up past my knees and there was nowhere to sit. So I leaned against the wall and I looked at the round hole above my head and the night went by very slowly."

"And you were rescued in the morning?"

"Yes, a man's head appeared."

What more was there to say? We finished up. He had three

more days of skiing, he told me. He took lessons every afternoon.
He was getting better.

We were in front of the motel. We had shaken hands in farewell and I had moved back a few steps towards my car. Casually,
I asked him if he was here with his family. I only asked so that I
might wish them well. I thought that would please him, me wishing his family well. Instead he came up to me, eyes staring hard,
and it was with shock that I realized that he was upset. When he
spoke, it was with great feeling.

"I remember something from my night in that stinking pit of
filth," he said. "The hole above me, the toilet hole, the way the
light was shining through it, it reminded me of full moons over
the ocean in Mogadishu when I was a child. My grandmother
used to tell me the moon was a hole in the night sky and that's
where God came in. She would hold me in her arms and we'd
look at the moon together. I kept hoping to catch God sneaking
into the world. I loved those moments with my grandmother. It's
the last time I remember being happy. You ask about my family?
I have no family. They all died in Mogadishu in the civil war, all
of them. Goodbye. Thank you for the fruit salad."

And with that he turned around and walked back to his room.
I watched him go. Then I drove back to the resort, put on those
damn ski boots and went off to find my wife.

Chimamanda Ngozi Adichie
SOLA

Sola has disappeared. Today, I walked into his room and saw his father sitting on his bed, crying, back slumped, and in one hand was the red Arsenal shirt Sola always wore when he watched the Premier League. His father never liked me. For the almost two years that Sola and I have been together, his father would ignore my greetings, would mumble that I was a bad influence, a city girl. But when I walked in and saw him crying, he looked up, his eyes full of bewilderment, and I placed my hand on his shoulder and then offered to boil some water to make him atiya.

Sola walks with a limp. The midwife pulled me out too roughly, he said, to explain that hiccup in his gait. He told me this the first day we met. I had gone to the kiosk owned by one of those Fulas from Guinea to buy a packet of cookies and was walking back to my aunty's house when he called out to me to stop. I don't usually have patience for men who stop women on the street to chase them, and I was going to tell him off, but he did not say the usual, "Tell me your name," or "I like you." Instead he told me, "Don't walk so fast. I can't catch up with my three-quarter leg. The midwife pulled me out too roughly." There was a slightly self-mocking smile on his face and I found myself smiling back. Later, I would come to hear him tell this midwife story to many people and would watch them fall under his spell, as I did that first day. It was so easy to fall under his spell.

I walked along the street with him, this slender stranger, talking about nothing in particular, watching him kick a small can along as he walked. He did not profess love at first sight, as many of the men I saw in the neighborhood liked to do, as though a good way to deal with their boredom was to find a girl and tell her you were madly in love with her when you were not. He did not even say he wanted to be my friend. He just walked along with me and talked, with a kind of intensity that surprised me, about small subjects like which brand of milk was better, Peak or Omela. When we got to my aunty's gate, I said I would walk around the street once more with him; I was not ready to go inside. He was a journalist with the *Express* and when I said, "That paper is just the president's mouthpiece," he looked at me and nodded and then changed the subject. I would come, later, to realize how much he resented the restrictions placed on his work, when he would give me articles to help him line edit and then later tell me that his editor, Mr. Mahoney, had killed the story because it might offend the president.

As we walked, he said he had seen me a few times at the kiosk and had heard the people there gossiping about me, calling me a foreign girl, a spoiled rich girl, saying that all I did was read books and take photographs of ordinary things on the street and go to London whenever I wanted to. That was why he had stopped me. He was curious about me. I felt a little dampened by this but I told him my story: I had left the university and I was painting and taking photographs and living with my aunt because my parents had asked me to leave their house until I decided to behave myself. He looked at me, his eyes huge with disbelief. I was so different from what he was used to. I had my camera around my neck so I showed him pictures I took from the last time I visited London. The buildings and pigeons and ducks at Hyde Park did not interest him, but he focused on the only picture of me, taken by a friend. He noticed that I was wearing the same shoes in the photo as I had on then and he bent down, in a swift and surprising way, and touched my black sneakers and said, "Oh, so these have walked in London!" Before we parted that day, he told me, "You are too big for me," and I told him to stop Mahoneyking rubbish. But he was right. I was the silly daughter of big people who owned property all over Banjul and I could afford to loaf around knowing my parents would always support me. He was a boy from the country who had worked hard and come to Banjul to get a job in journalism and was paying his brother's school fees and supporting his father and his sister. Still, only two days later, I was with him in his room, under the blanket, and he was whispering that he loved the sound of the rain on his roof.

Sola has disappeared. Policemen came to his house and took him away. Some people say that he had argued with his editor, Mr. Mahoney, earlier that day, that Sola's voice was raised and that Mr. Mahoney was threatening him. His father and I went all the way to Fatoto Police Station in the east, because we had heard that he was taken there. But the police said he was not there. One policeman called his father an old fool. On the long bus drive back, I began to cry. His father said that he'd liked it when Sola began to work at the Express because working for a paper that had never been anti-government meant that what had happened to Deyda Hydara would not happen to Sola. I remember when Hydara was shot in Banjul, I remember how Hydara wrote so angrily, so boldly, about press freedom, about the excesses of the president. But I felt angry with Sola's father for bringing up Hydara and for linking that brave, doomed man to my Sola.

Sola is an avid self-improver. The first time I saw all his books, collected from secondhand shops, from acquaintances he met through work, many of them without covers, I was very moved and thought about how casually I had always treated my father's library. Sola is always asking me the correct way to pronounce English words. When I told him to stop saying "innit" because it was not the kind of British thing that was good to imitate—all the young people in Banjul say innit and it annoys me so much— he told me he was lucky he had me to explain these things to him.

He has that kind of humility, but he also has a kind of confidence that just pops out when it is needed. When he first told Mr. Mahoney of his plan to write a long investigative piece about his country, Mr. Mahoney told him it was unnecessary, but Sola insisted. Of course, he did not tell Mr. Mahoney what he told me, that he planned to show Mr. Mahoney a tame version but would publish the real thing abroad, that he was already in touch with some journalists in Europe.

Exactly eight days before he disappeared, I met his editor, Mr. Mahoney. "You are Sola's woman?" he asked, in a tone of surprise that was also lazy and knowing. I did not like the way he looked at me, as many men with influence do, as though they already know what is inside you and they own it and they will decide when to take it and you have no say at all. It is small-small men with petty influence like Mahoney who cause the greatest trouble. That evening, as I watched Sola make his atiya, with cube after cube of sugar, and throw his head back slightly as he drank, I was filled with a panicked love. I began to worry about his safety. I told him I did not think he should send that piece he was writing to the European journalists. He looked at me as if I were suddenly speaking an incomprehensible language. I, after all, had encouraged the article from the beginning and it was almost finished now. He had said that it was the best way for him to air his concerns about the future of his country, by publishing his piece abroad, and I had agreed. But now, perhaps because I had met his editor, I was no longer sure it was worth it. It was raining. On Saturday, the Naweetan football league would begin. I was making a bean soup that he liked, that he teased me was very "foreign," just as he teased me about not knowing how to boil water properly unless I had an electric kettle.

He finished his atiya. I watched him, this slender man with a gentle self-composure. He was not a man who needed to be loved, and because of this, he commanded love, he drew love to himself. I came to know of the many women who loved him: the women he worked with, the women he met when he went to conduct interviews. Once, I asked why he was not like his friends who chased many women at the same time—I knew that he was faithful—and he looked at me and shrugged and said it was because he had nothing to prove to anybody. Then he took my hand in his.

Sola has disappeared. Today the information minister sent out a press release, which said this: the government does not have any knowledge of Sola's arrest. A woman whose cousin's wife works as a nurse at the Royal Victoria Teaching Hospital came to tell us that policemen had brought in Sola for medical treatment. I ran to the hospital. He was not there. And I came back and told his father that I had not found him.

Sola has disappeared.

Nadine Gordimer
AMNESTY

When we heard he was released I ran all over the farm and through the fence to our people on the next farm to tell everybody. I only saw afterward I'd torn my dress on the barbed wire, and there was a scratch, with blood, on my shoulder.

He went away from this place nine years ago, signed up to work in town with what they call a construction company—building glass walls up to the sky. For the first two years he came home for the weekend once a month and two weeks at Christmas; that was when he asked my father for me. And he began to pay. He and I thought that in three years he would have paid enough for us to get married. But then he started wearing that T-shirt, he told us he'd joined the union, he told us about the strike, how he was one of the men who went to talk to the bosses because some others had been laid off after the strike. He's always been good at talking, even in English—he was the best at the farm school, he used to read the newspapers the Indian wraps soap and sugar in when you buy at the store.

There was trouble at the hostel where he had a bed, and riots over paying rent in the townships and he told me—just me, not the old ones—that wherever people were fighting against the way we are treated they were doing it for all of us, on the farms as well as the towns, and the unions were with them, he was with them, making speeches, marching. The third year, we heard he was in prison. Instead of getting married. We didn't know where to find him, until he went on trial. The case was

heard in a town far away. I couldn't go often to the court because by that time I had passed my Standard 8 and I was working in the farm school. Also my parents were short of money.
Two of my brothers who had gone away to work in town didn't
send home; I suppose they lived with girlfriends and had to buy
things for them. My father and other brother work here for the
Boer and the pay is very small, we have two goats, a few cows
we're allowed to graze, and a patch of land where my mother
can grow vegetables. No cash from that.

When I saw him in the court he looked beautiful in a blue suit
with a striped shirt and brown tie. All the accused—his comrades, he said—were well dressed. The union bought the clothes
so that the judge and the prosecutor would know they weren't
dealing with stupid *yes-baas* black men who didn't know their
rights. These things and everything else about the court and trial
he explained to me when I was allowed to visit him in jail. Our
little girl was born while the trial went on and when I brought
the baby to court the first time to show him, his comrades hugged
him and then hugged me across the barrier of the prisoners' dock
and they had clubbed together to give me some money as a
present for the baby. He chose the name for her, Inkululeko.

Then the trial was over and he got six years. He was sent to the
Island. We all knew about the Island. Our leaders had been there
so long. But I have never seen the sea except to color it in blue at
school, and I couldn't imagine a piece of earth surrounded by it. I
could only think of a cake of dung, dropped by the cattle, floating
in a pool of rainwater they'd crossed, the water showing the sky
like a looking glass, blue. I was ashamed only to think that. He
had told me how the glass walls showed the pavement trees and
the other buildings in the street and the colors of the cars
and the clouds as the crane lifted him on a platform higher and
higher through the sky to work at the top of a building.

He was allowed one letter a month. It was my letter because
his parents didn't know how to write. I used to go to them where
they worked on another farm to ask what message they wanted
to send. The mother always cried and put her hands on her head

and said nothing, and the old man, who preached to us in the veld every Sunday, said tell my son we are praying God will make everything all right for him. Once he wrote back, That's the trouble—our people on the farms, they're told God will decide what's good for them so that they won't find the force to do anything to change their lives.

After two years had passed, we—his parents and I—had saved up enough money to go to Cape Town to visit him. We went by train and slept on the floor at the station and asked the way, next day, to the ferry. People were kind; they knew that if you wanted the ferry it was because you had somebody of yours on the Island.

And there it was—there was the sea. It was green *and* blue, climbing and falling, bursting white, all the way to the sky. A terrible wind was slapping it this way and that; it hid the Island, but people like us, also waiting for the ferry, pointed where the Island must be, far out in the sea that I never thought would be like it really was.

There were other boats, and ships as big as buildings that go to other places, all over the world, but the ferry is only for the Island, it doesn't go anywhere else in the world, only to the Island. So everybody waiting there was waiting for the Island, there could be no mistake we were not in the right place. We had sweets and cookies, trousers and a warm coat for him (a woman standing with us said we wouldn't be allowed to give him the clothes) and I wasn't wearing, anymore, the old beret pulled down over my head that farm girls wear, I had bought relaxer cream from the man who comes round the farms selling things out of a box on his bicycle, and my hair was combed up thick under a flowered scarf that didn't cover the gold-colored rings in my ears. His mother had her blanket tied round her waist over her dress, a farm woman, but I looked just as good as any of the other girls there. When the ferry was ready to take us, we stood all pressed together and quiet like the cattle waiting to be let through a gate. One man kept looking round with his chin moving up and down, he was counting, he must have been afraid there were too many to get on and he didn't want to be left behind. We all moved up to the policeman in charge and everyone ahead of us went onto the boat. But when our turn came and he put out his hand for something, I didn't know what.

We didn't have a permit. We didn't know that before you come to Cape Town, before you come to the ferry for the Island, you have to have a police permit to visit a prisoner on the Island. I tried to ask him nicely. The wind blew the voice out of my mouth.

We were turned away. We saw the ferry rock, bumping the landing where we stood, moving, lifted and dropped by all that water, getting smaller and smaller until we didn't know if we were really seeing it or one of the birds that looked black, dipping up and down, out there.

The only good thing was one of the other people took the sweets and cookies for him. He wrote and said he got them. But it wasn't a good letter. Of course not. He was cross with me; I should have found out, I should have known about the permit. He was right—I bought the train tickets, I asked where to go for the ferry, I should have known about the permit. I have passed Standard 8. There was an advice office to go to in town, the churches ran it, he wrote. But the farm is so far from town, we on the farms don't know about these things. It was as he said; our ignorance is the way we are kept down, this ignorance must go.

We took the train back and we never went to the Island—never saw him in the three more years he was there. Not once. We couldn't find the money for the train. His father died and I had to help his mother from my pay. For our people the worry is always the money, I wrote. When will we ever have money? Then he sent such a good letter. That's what I'm on the Island for, far away from you, I'm here so that one day our people will have the things they need, land, food, the end of ignorance. There was something else—I could just read the word "power" the prison had blacked out. All his letters were not just for me; the prison officer read them before I could.

* * *

He was coming home after only five years!

That's what it seemed to me, when I heard—the five years were suddenly disappeared—nothing!—there was no whole year still to wait. I showed my—our—little girl his photo again. That's your daddy, he's coming, you're going to see him. She told the other children at school, I've got a daddy, just as she showed off about the kid goat she had at home.

We wanted him to come at once, and at the same time we wanted time to prepare. His mother lived with one of his uncles; now that his father was dead there was no house of his father for him to take me to as soon as we married. If there had been time, my father would have cut poles, my mother and I would have baked bricks, cut thatch, and built a house for him and me and the child.

We were not sure what day he would arrive. We only heard on my radio his name and the names of some others who were released. Then at the Indian's store I noticed the newspaper, *The Nation,* written by black people, and on the front a picture of a lot of people dancing and waving—I saw at once it was at that ferry. Some men were being carried on other men's shoulders. I couldn't see which one was him. We were waiting. The ferry had brought him from the Island but we remembered Cape Town is a long way from us. Then he did come. On a Saturday, no school, so I was working with my mother, hoeing and weeding round the pumpkins and mealies, my hair, that I meant to keep nice, tied in an old *doek.* A combi came over the veld and his comrades had brought him. I wanted to run away and wash but he stood there stretching his legs, calling, hey! hey! with his comrades making a noise around him, and my mother started shrieking in the old style aie! aie! and my father was clapping and stamping toward him. He held his arms open to us, this big man in town clothes, polished shoes, and all the time while he hugged me I was holding my dirty hands, full of mud, away from him behind his back. His teeth hit me hard through his lips, he grabbed at my mother and she struggled to hold the child up to him. I thought we would all fall down! Then everyone was quiet. The child hid behind my mother. He picked her up but she turned her head away to her shoulder. He spoke to her gently but she wouldn't speak to him. She's nearly six years old! I told her not to be a baby. She said, That's not him.

The comrades all laughed, we laughed, she ran off and he said, She has to have time to get used to me.

He has put on weight, yes; a lot. You couldn't believe it. He used to be so thin his feet looked too big for him. I used to feel his bones but now—that night—when he lay on me he was so heavy, I didn't remember it was like that. Such a long time. It's strange to get stronger in prison; I thought he wouldn't have enough to eat and would come out weak. Everyone said, Look at him!— he's a man, now. He laughed and banged his fist on his chest, told them how the comrades exercised in their cells, he would run three miles a day, stepping up and down on one place on the floor of that small cell where he was kept. After we were together at night we used to whisper a long time but now I can feel he's thinking of some things I don't know and I can't worry him with talk. Also I don't know what to say. To ask him what it was like, five years shut away there; or to tell him something about school or about the child. What else has happened, here? Nothing. Just waiting. Sometimes in the daytime I do try to tell him what it was like for me, here at home on the farm, five years. He listens, he's interested, just like he's interested when people from the other farms come to visit and talk to him about little things that happened to them while he was away all that time on the Island. He smiles and nods, asks a couple of questions and then stands up and stretches. I see it's to show them it's enough, his mind is going back to something he was busy with before they came. And we farm people are very slow; we tell things slowly, he used to, too.

He hasn't signed on for another job. But he can't stay at home with us; we thought, after five years over there in the middle of that green and blue sea, so far, he would rest with us a little while. The combi or some car comes to fetch him and he says don't worry, I don't know what day I'll be back. At first I asked, what week, next week? He tried to explain to me: in the Movement it's

not like it was in the union, where you do your work every day
and after that you are busy with meetings; in the Movement you
never know where you will have to go and what is going to come
up next. And the same with money. In the Movement, it's not like
a job, with regular pay—I know that, he doesn't have to tell
me—it's like it was going to the Island, you do it for all our
people who suffer because we haven't got money, we haven't
got land—look, he said, speaking of my parents', my home, the
home that has been waiting for him, with his child: look at this
place where the white man owns the ground and lets you squat in
mud and tin huts here only as long as you work for him—*Baba*
and your brother planting his crops and looking after his cattle,
Mama cleaning his house and you in the school without even
having the chance to train properly as a teacher. The farm owns
us, he says.

I've been thinking we haven't got a home because there wasn't
time to build a house before he came from the Island; but we
haven't got a home at all. Now I've understood that.

I'm not stupid. When the comrades come to this place in the
combi to talk to him here I don't go away with my mother after
we've brought them tea or (if she's made it for the weekend) beer.
They like her beer, they talk about our culture and there's one of
them who makes a point of putting his arm around my mother,
calling her the mama of all of them, the mama of Africa. Sometimes they please her very much by telling her how they used to
sing on the Island and getting her to sing an old song we all know
from our grandmothers. Then they join in with their strong
voices. My father doesn't like this noise traveling across the veld;
he's afraid that if the Boer finds out my man is a political, from
the Island, and he's holding meetings on the Boer's land, he'll tell
my father to go, and take his family with him. But my brother
says if the Boer says anything just tell him it's a prayer meeting.
Then the singing is over; my mother knows she must go away
into the house.

I stay, and listen. He forgets I'm there when he's talking and
arguing about something I can see is important, more important

than anything we could ever have to say to each other when we're alone. But now and then, when one of the other comrades is speaking I see him look at me for a moment the way I will look up at one of my favorite children in school to encourage the child to understand. The men don't speak to me and I don't speak. One of the things they talk about is organizing the people on the farms—the workers, like my father and brother, and like his parents used to be. I learn what all these things are: minimum wage, limitation of working hours, the right to strike, annual leave, accident compensation, pensions, sick and even maternity leave. I am pregnant, at last I have another child inside me, but that's women's business. When they talk about the Big Man, the Old Men, I know who these are: our leaders are also back from prison. I told him about the child coming; he said And this one belongs to a new country, he'll build the freedom we've fought for! I know he wants to get married but there's no time for that at present. There was hardly time for him to make the child. He comes to me just like he comes here to eat a meal or put on clean clothes. Then he picks up the little girl and swings her round and there!—it's done, he's getting into the combi, he's already turning to his comrade that face of his that knows only what's inside his head, those eyes that move quickly as if he's chasing something you can't see. The little girl hasn't had time to get used to this man. But I know she'll be proud of him, one day!

How can you tell that to a child six years old. But I tell her about the Big Man and the Old Men, our leaders, so she'll know that her father was with them on the Island, this man is a great man, too.

On Saturday, no school and I plant and weed with my mother, she sings but I don't, I think. On Sunday there's no work, only prayer meetings out of the farmer's way under the trees, and beer drinks at the mud and tin huts where the farmers allow us to squat on their land. I go off on my own as I used to do when I was a child, making up games and talking to myself where no one would hear me or look for me. I sit on a warm stone in the late afternoon, high up, and the whole valley is a path between the hills, leading away from my feet. It's the Boer's farm but that's not true, it belongs to nobody. The cattle don't know that anyone says he owns it, the sheep—they are gray stones, and then they become a thick gray snake moving—don't know. Our huts and the old mulberry tree and the little brown mat of earth that my mother dug over yesterday, way down there, and way over there the clump of trees round the chimneys and the shiny thing that is the TV mast of the farmhouse—they are nothing, on the back of this earth. It could twitch them away like a dog does a fly.

I am up in the clouds. The sun behind me is changing the colors of the sky and the clouds are changing themselves, slowly, slowly. Some are pink, some are white, swelling like bubbles. Underneath is a bar of gray, not enough to make rain. It gets longer and darker, it grows a thin snout and long body and then the end of it is a tail. There's a huge gray rat moving across the sky, eating the sky.

The child remembered the photo; she said *That's not him*. I'm sitting here where I came often when he was on the Island. I came to get away from the others, to wait by myself.

I'm watching the rat, it's losing itself, its shape, eating the sky, and I'm waiting. Waiting for him to come back.

Waiting.

I'm waiting to come back home.

ARTICLE 24

The Right to Rest and Leisure

Xiaolu Guo

AN INTERNET BABY

Here are the reasons why Weiming and Yuli have to sell their baby on the Internet, a baby who's only seen the light of this world for five days.

Yuli is still at school, in her first year at Chongqing Technical College. For an eighteen-year-old girl from a rural village, the scandal would be huge; she would certainly be expelled and lose all the time and money she and her parents have invested to get her where she is: on the way to some better life. She has lied to everyone—from the dean of her department to her class and dormitory mates. To all of them she said she had hepatitis and needed to stay at home for a while. That's after she'd managed to hide her growing belly in a large coat for five months. And now, in a shabby and dirty clinic in a suburb of Chongqing, she's given birth to a screaming little thing.

Yuli is a determined girl. She will study, get her diploma and start a career in a big city. She won't raise a child now. Therefore she won't let anyone know from her village, in a mountainous region in Sichuan where the only income is from growing chili peppers, and the villagers take family things too seriously. If they learned she'd given birth to a son, they'd come to Chongqing straight away and do everything they could to keep the child. Yuli's mind is clear and certain while the baby is sucking her nipple with a small, wet face. She won't keep it.

Yuli's boyfriend Weiming has one very simple motive for selling their baby: lack of money. Weiming is from the same village as Yuli. They are childhood lovers. As a nineteen-year-old man, he's had trouble surviving in this city ever since he left his hometown to follow her. There's no way he can imagine helping Yuli with her college fees, sending money to his family back in the village and bringing up a baby here at the same time. Not possible. He's already working twenty hours a day, on two jobs: during the day he cleans cars, private ones and government ones, and at night he stands by a door as the porter of a karaoke parlor. He can only sleep from 3:00 a.m. to 7:30 a.m. He's been exhausted from the day he arrived in this city; his sight is blurred from lack of sleep and his mind is as foggy as the permanent clouds hanging on the Yangtze River. But he understands: to help his girlfriend and his poor family in the village, he has to work like a donkey. A donkey can sleep while standing still, and Weiming has to learn to do that too. He has no choice. He doesn't complain either.

So the young lovers agree to sell their baby on the Internet. Yuli studied computer technology at college, she knows how it works. What people normally sell online are machines, things like TV sets, Walkmans, bicycles, cameras, or sometimes a banned book. Selling a real baby is not very usual.

"But what's so different?" Weiming says. "Selling a baby is the same as selling a car, the only difference is the price. If China could sell some of its population to the West, then there would be fewer people starving here, and we would have more money."

Yuli takes some photos of the baby and chooses the cutest one to put online. And after a discussion with her boyfriend, she also puts up a price.

Healthy newborn baby boy for sale—8,000 yuan.
Contact: 13601386243

The number is Weiming's mobile phone, given to him for his night job. Although both of them know 8,000 yuan is really much too little money for a healthy baby boy, they reason that most people in the provinces are not rich and as they are in a hurry to get

rid of the baby, asking for little money could sort things more easily and more quickly. And Weiming also thinks that his girlfriend can always get pregnant again if this one works out.

After putting the ad online, Yuli feeds her son a bit of milk
and changes his wet nappy. What she's worried about is that if
the baby doesn't go soon, she'll miss her end-of-term exam, then
she won't get her diploma.

The Internet ad proves effective. After just a few hours, the
phone starts to ring continually. The first few people want to
know whether the whole thing is just a joke, which makes Weiming shout back at them impatiently. He's got no time to joke
about life, he needs money. Sounding like a snappy businessman,
he yells back that if they're not interested he'll just hang up, while
his grumpy boss is cursing him from behind his back.

But then a woman with a shaky voice explains on the phone
that she's from a seaside town near Qingdao, that she is forty-six
years old, her husband has been very ill, that's why they didn't
have a child, and now he just died, and she would like to buy the
baby, a boy would be ideal. She sounds nervous.

"Can you pay 8,000 yuan cash in one go?" Weiming asks
hastily.

"Yes. But I first need to check whether the baby is really
healthy."

Weiming assures the woman that his boy is in perfect shape
and that he'll call her back after discussing things with his girlfriend. Weiming knows that he shouldn't say yes to the first interested person. Through negotiation, prices can always be
improved.

A few more useless calls later, a couple rings from Wenzhou,
a rich industrial town in Zhejiang province. They want the
baby as soon as possible: "We can get on the first morning flight
to Chongqing and meet you." The couple speaks on two hand-
sets at the same time. Weiming learns that they run a shoe factory in Wenzhou, that they're wealthy but cannot have babies.

"Well, I have some other customers interested. How do you
want to persuade me to go with you?" Weiming asks, a clear hint

that an auction is on. The couple are quick businesspeople; they immediately offer double the price to get the boy.

So the deal is done. Weiming will receive 16,000 yuan in cash. But he doesn't want the couple to come to Chongqing where he and Yuli live. To avoid any risk of being found out by neighbors, Yuli's school friends or his own colleagues, they agree to meet in a city where no one knows them: Shanghai. The meeting point will be Shanghai's People's Park, the next day at 4:00 p.m. in front of the park gate.

The young couple grab a bag, wrap up their sleeping baby and hurry to the train station to get on the next train to Shanghai. Both Weiming and Yuli hardly ever took the train before and they are overexcited, like children, on their seats, eagerly observing every station the train passes, picturing themselves ending up working in Shanghai, thanks to those 16,000 yuan. From time to time, Yuli feeds the baby, but the moody little thing doesn't appear to like the trip and keeps screaming all the time. Every passenger knows them and hates them. At one point the conductor even comes to ask whether they need some medical assistance.

After fourteen hours, the young couple arrive, pale and exhausted, in the shiny city of Shanghai. Yuli is deeply impressed. People here are more beautiful, fashionable, the houses are much taller and more luxurious than in Chongqing. But Weiming is hungry; he can't enjoy the new city, he's starving and feels even more powerless in Shanghai's busy streets than he is in Chongqing. They enter a wonton restaurant and eat two bowls of wonton soup each. Weiming swallows half a roasted duck as well. The food is eaten quickly, brutally and silently, but the baby sometimes coughs in Yuli's arms, no one knows why.

Twenty minutes before 4:00 p.m., Yuli and Weiming stand in front of the iron gate of Shanghai's People's Park. The baby is crying again and Yuli has to swing him in her arms all the time, wearily, until he falls asleep.

The Wenzhou shoemaker couple arrive on time. They both are about thirty-five and look more humble than they sounded on the phone to Weiming. He thinks they look even more sleepless than he is, worn out. But as soon as they see the baby in Yuli's arms, the couple's eyes start to glisten. Their eyes are glued on him as if on a magnetic object. The woman can't help but scream: "What a beautiful little boy! How cute! How sweet he is!" Her husband stretches his stiff finger, which must be overworked polishing his factory's shoes, and touches the baby's red cheeks and caresses his soft hair. He seems to be fond of the boy, too. The woman takes the baby from Yuli's hands, holds him and now starts to feel how a mother feels when her son is asleep in her arms.

The little baby wakes up from his nap, his big eyes stare at the strange woman who keeps kissing him and speaks some incomprehensible Wenzhou dialect.

"What about the money then?" Weiming asks cautiously.

The man opens his leather suitcase, takes out a heavy blue plastic bag, but doesn't give it to Weiming straight away. Instead, he says:

"Let's get into the park. We need to check if the baby is as healthy as you said."

The two couples agree and enter the People's Park. It is May, the willows are green, the bamboos lush, flowers blooming. Some old people are doing tai chi. Kids are flying their kites, with their grandparents running after them.

The baby boy is now in the Wenzhou couple's arms. In turn, both the wife and the husband thoroughly check him, studying him like a pair of newly made shoes; they turn him upside down, check his ears, eyes, nostrils, fingers, legs, toes, as well as his bottom and his front. Oddly enough, the baby doesn't cry this time. He seems to enjoy this sudden attention, and he starts to giggle.

Finally, the Wenzhou woman is satisfied and asks the young couple:

"Do you have a name for him?"

"Not really. Just for the hospital registration we called him Wei Yu, that's a combination of our family names," Weiming answers.

"In that case we will give him a great name, the best name a man can bear!" the Wenzhou man says in an inspired voice.

They find a quiet area of the park, a lake surrounded by leafy willow trees. There, no one can watch and find out what's going on. The water is clear, one can see red carp swimming on the bottom. Lotus plants grow lush, dragonflies are skating on the surface of the water. The Wenzhou woman volunteers to stand guard and leaves. The Wenzhou man puts his suitcase on the ground and takes out the blue plastic bag. Picking up a bundle of money, Weiming starts to count, carefully. From time to time, he also checks whether the notes are fake.

It takes too long, half the money is still uncounted. The Wenzhou man begins to look impatient and Yuli gets restless, too. She lays her baby on the ground, facing the lake, and starts to count another bundle of notes.

After an intense silence filled only with the flicking of the bank notes, they reach their conclusion: exactly 16,000 yuan, no cheating. Weiming starts to gather the money, when suddenly there's a scream.

"Where is my baby?" Yuli is crying in panic.

The three scan the surroundings, but there is no baby around, only an empty suitcase lying on the soil.

The Wenzhou woman is just returning. As she approaches, her face changes color. All follow her look to the quiet lake. As their eyes settle on the water, they see a baby silently drowning, drifting toward the clear bottom of the beautiful lake.

Alice Pung

THE SHED

The shed was always locked.

Right from when I was about four, I was told never to tell anyone about the metal shed. It whirred and hummed like a live thing. It vibrated like a massive machine with a throbbing migraine heartbeat. "If you tell anyone, we could get into big trouble from the government," Mum and Dad always warned. "The government does not know we do this."

"What's the government?" I asked.

"People who are good to us," my father explained, "but who also take our money."

"Isn't that stealing?" I imagined cloaked pilferers stalking our house at night, with crowbars ready to break into the shed.

But there was no money in the shed, just a lot of twenty-four-karat gold. So I thought that the government wanted our gold, the gold my mother melted and molded into shape in that shed. Red dust floated out when the breeze blew, from the gaps beneath the door. In the Australian summer, the shed heated up like a hot poker, and because it did not have any windows that could open, it was difficult for Mum to breathe while she was in there.

Mum spent most of her daylight hours in that shed and I was never allowed to tell, let alone show anyone, what was inside: the wax molds, the plaster casts, the gray filings and tiny hills of gold dust on metal trays—remnants from the filing down of rings. When I was four, I used to poke my finger in those gold hills and spread them flat into strange rivers on the tray. "Aiyoh!" Mum would yell when she saw me. I was not allowed to move or take my hands from the tray lest we lost a bit of the gold dust to the ground. Dad would fill a used ice-cream container with water and soak my fingers in it, so that the gold would un-adhere itself and slowly float to the bottom of the container, where it could be rescued, melted down and reused.

Mum made jewelry in that shed in our backyard. Bespoke jewelry, some of the shops in the inner city would call it. Completely made by hand. Artisan labor, they proclaimed on small tags in the sterling surfaces of the shop counters, and because each item had that little label it could be sold at a hundred times the price of my mother's labor. To make a bracelet, my mother would stretch gold wire until it was almost hair thin. One end of the wire was held in place by a clamp, but sometimes the wire would slip and flick her in the face, and there would be a line of blood. She would then take the wire and sit down at her work desk, which was a white corkboard affair one of our family friends had knocked up for us. Her tools were second- or thirdhand, but she used new blades in the surgeon's scalpel to cut the strand of gold wire into tiny pieces of no more than half a centimeter long. Then she would link the tiny segments together with a pair of tweezers, as children string Christmas paper chains together with scissors and tape. She would treat it in potassium cyanide and polish the surfaces with a piece of jade that was stuck on a wooden handle.

"One dollar a ring," Mum would promise us when we were young, "if you help me polish them." But she never gave us the money—she just counted up all the rings we had polished. "Five dollars," she would tell us, tallying up our halfhearted palely polished efforts, efforts she would always have to fix, "five dollars will get you an umbrella." Then she would come home with one that had Spoony on it, which was the Chinese counterfeit of Charles Schulz's creation; but I didn't want Mum's practical protection from the elements. My seven-year-old self took umbrage at that umbrella. I wanted the five dollars cash in hand, damn it, I wanted to be paid like a proper Asian back-shed worker so I could use my ill-gotten gains to get a Babie doll, the poor man's version of Barbie. Babie looked like Barbie, but all her hair lifted up at the back so she had a severe undercut, as if she were auditioning to join a white supremacist gang, and when she sat down her legs splayed wide like the fingers of my hand showing Mum how much I was due to be paid, in a pathetic attempt to procure cash from her instead of an umbrella.

Mum used that umbrella when it rained and she had to deliver her wares. Mum did not deliver her wares to the shops in the inner city because the upmarket clientele of Collins Street was a completely foreign world. The Paris end of Melbourne, they called it, where women walked around with faces like Chanel ads. The kind of beauty that would leak down their necks if it rained. I don't even think Mum had been up there more than once in her life. She was more used to the markets of Phnom Penh and Saigon. Carrying the Spoony umbrella and the fake Gucci handbag (that my brother had brought her from China) into a Collins Street jewelry store would mean that the carefully coiffeured ladies would be speaking about her long after she had left. Although Mum's jewelry was entirely handmade, she transported it around wrapped in McDonald's napkins in her fifteen-dollar handbag, and she never wore makeup.

She delivered the hard, shining fruits of her labor to places along the small shopping strips of suburbs brimming with South-east Asians: the Vietnamese, the Cambodians, the ethnic Chinese. She would set her bag on their narrow glass counters below which was displayed bright red velvet dotted with coveted twenty-four-karat gold: pendants shaped like Mercedes-Benz signs, rings with dragons and Buddhas on them, blingy necklaces with chains as thick as my little finger.

My brother and I would sit on the chairs reserved for customers who needed their pieces adjusted on the spot—rings too large or bracelets too short. "When will you be done?" we would whine. "When will you be done, Mum?" We would walk toward the trays of gold behind the cabinets and breathe on the glass.

Mum was trying to do business, so this time she handed me four dollars and told me to go two stores down to buy pork bread rolls from the Vietnamese bakery. We came back with the food and sat back down. We peeled back the white paper bags and bit into the bread. "Aiyoh!" Mum yelled at us, "don't eat in other people's stores!" The store was tiny so all ears were alert. "Embarrassments to society, that's what you are!" We put the bread away, shut our mouths and learned to wait. We waited while the jewelry store owners pored over each ring.

"This one's a good one," Mum told the owner earnestly, "Kim Heng from the other store ordered seventeen of those." I looked at the little pendants with the massive faces of Jesus rendered in three-dimensional twenty-four-karat gold and wondered why I never saw anyone wear such a thing. Some of the rings even had tiny emerald or blue cubic zirconias in the eye sockets.

The store owner, a Vietnamese man, turned the pieces around in his hands. His fingers were gnarled like ginseng from his own outworking in the stuffy room near the back of the cramped shop. "How much?" he asked Mum.

"Four-fifty," she said. Four-fifty for her four and a half hours of labor.

"Four-fifty, sister?" he repeated.

My mother answered in the affirmative. "You know that was the price last time I was here."

"Four-fifty is too much," said the man.

"What do you mean, too much, brother?"

"Four-fifty is not what the new brother from Cambodia is charging."

"What new brother from Cambodia?"

"The one who used to be a goldsmith in Cambodia. He brought along some of his old tools. He's been doing it for only six years, but wah! is he good in his detail! Must be because he's so young."

Mum shifted her glasses. Mum never used to wear glasses until her eyesight became shot from too much close work attaching tiny clasps and polishing pendants of the Lord's face with care. Mum didn't know what to say. "Come on, I've been delivering to you for so long, brother," Mum cajoled.

It did not work, because the new man had better tools and more nimble fingers.

"The new brother only charges four dollars."

"But that's ridiculous!"

The small store owner did not say a thing, because there was no need to. He knew that new migrants were desperate to find work and they would settle with any work they could find at any cost. They were just so grateful. And Mum, having worked for over a decade, was not so replete with gratitude or the youthful fervor of ambition. She just wanted the money so we would not be snot-nosed sooks loitering the streets like she did when she was twelve and they closed down her Chinese school in Cambodia. She wanted to make sure we stayed in school, that we did not need to enter a factory as she did at thirteen.

"Okay. Four dollars then, brother."

By then, my brother and I had lost interest in the Jesus pendants and even the rings encrusted with red jewels as massive as minor melanomas. We wanted to bite back into our bread rolls. We wanted to leave the sticky seats and the red and gold decor of the store.

But we watched as the store owner measured out ounces of gold on scales, in payment, because he did not have cash on hand that day. Mum had come too early and they had made no sales. Mum watched to make sure that the scales were balanced exactly right, that they were not dodgily weighted in any way. Mum wrote down a few figures of what was owing to her on a small notebook she carried in her handbag. Then she wrapped up the remainder of her wares in the now slightly torn McDonald's napkin, and then the small facecloth.

"Come on you two, let's go."

And she led us out down the street to the next store, where the whole scene would repeat itself all over again. But we had learned to wait.

When I was eight, I hated being eight. I smelled like piss all the time—before my sister was born, my mum's fluorescent yellow pools on our tiles, because she could not control her bladder when she had babies pushing against her pelvic floor, and after my sister was born her pale yellow streams soaked through the sheets. They did not call us Southeast Asians "yellow" for nothing, I supposed. I lit incense in front of our Buddha shrine—not due to any particular child's faith or piety, but just to disguise the smell of pee from the carpet.

I hated being stuck between the four walls of the house. If I had been born in Cambodia, all my friends my age would have had their babies slung over their backs and we would have played together in the streets. But growing up in sordid suburbia, in a house behind the Invicta carpet factories, my friends came over carrying their cabbage patch dolls while I had my sister Alison in my arms. "Let's go outside and walk to the school and hang around on the monkey bars!" they would tell me, dumping down their dolls on the tiles.

I couldn't do that with Alison. Live babies hollered, and stuff came out of their nappies and stuff came out of their mouths. A baby was cute for half an hour. But to an eight year old, that was the limit—after one hour, it got a bit tedious, and after a whole day, they went home muttering how weird that I had this baby that I could not give back to my mum to look after. Slowly, after a few weeks, my mates petered out, and I knew the only times I would be seeing them was at school. Sometimes their parents would see me balancing a baby on my hip and once, Bianca's dad exclaimed, "What? Another one?" as if at twelve I was responsible for new progeny in the family.

Mum, like me, was just supposed to be at home watching babies: that was her childhood dream. She grew up in Cambodia, narrowly escaping the country's closing acts of the 1970s, when curtains of bombs rained down between the borders to keep out the North Vietnamese, the Vietcong. The Charlies, the Americans called them, and wanted to blast them all out of existence. They were so worried the Charlies were hiding in the jungles of the Vietnam-Cambodia border that they didn't care how many Cambodian villagers they would kill in their pursuit of democracy.

My father survived the Cambodian killing fields, emerging as a skin-and-bones man so thin that if he turned sideways he would almost disappear from view. He and my grandmother led the living remnants of his family—his little sister and his wife— through three different countries on foot, sleeping on the floors of jungles when darkness rose. My father calls that trek their three-month backpacker honeymoon, and when they reached the Thai refugee camp, they spent a long sleepy year waiting. My father liked to tell people that I was manufactured in Thailand but as-sembled in Australia, because I was conceived on a small mat in that camp.

When Mum arrived here, eight months' pregnant with me at twenty-two, not knowing a word of English, she began with making jewelry molds, a sedentary and silent task suitable for new daughters-in-law who've been blessedly deposited in de-mocracies. She made rings by first planting little waxen trees— sometimes sherbet pink, sometimes opal green, growing from waxen stalks that she grew on rubber bases. These waxen trees would be the basis of plaster molds, which would then be filled with melted gold. After the birth of my brother, she moved on to working with gold. While others saw what dirty work it was and how little ill-gotten gains were to be had, Mum persisted with planting these artificial trees and sawing off their real-gold branches.

When I was fourteen, I realized why we weren't allowed to tell a soul what Mum did, and why Dad had told me once that it was a little like stealing. "We don't pay taxes on this," my mother said, "the government will get us." The government would tax Mum on her two dollars fifty an hour? That did not make sense even to me. But to illiterate migrants like Mum who were paid cash in hand and asked no questions, it made perfect sense.

Even when the surgeon's scalpel stabbed Mum through the palm so deep that the handle had to be unscrewed to get the blade out, we were not to tell. I remember Mum coming into the house, one hand holding the other like a dead bird. "The knife stabbed through," she gasped to Dad. The rims of her eyes were not even red-wet with reflexive tears.

Mum was brave, but it was only later in life that I came to this realization. When I was young, I didn't care. She was never in the house and I had howling babies to watch over, when all I wanted to do was muck around with my nine-year-old mates. Two decades later, Mum finally stopped working. I had made it to university, and my three siblings were looking as if they would follow suit.

When Mum stopped working, she discovered she could not be still. Her hands ached to the bone. She had a hacking cough from the potassium cyanide. She had puckered skin on her forearms from third-degree burns of the welding torch and scars from the surgeon's scalpel. Her eyesight was shot, and she needed to wear glasses, which she kept losing, because she never used them to read. She did not read, she could not read.

Mum was locked from the language of the outside world. She had spent two decades in that shed, making those rings and pendants and bracelets. A bracelet would earn her twenty dollars, but it would take her a whole day. That worked out to be a couple of dollars an hour for an eight-hour day. Two dollars fifty does not even get someone a cup of coffee at Starbucks these days. So of course, all our coffee came in massive tins of International Roast from the local Coles supermarket. She would also have tins of sweetened condensed milk in the cupboard, and she mixed it with the coffee with boiling water and gulped cupfuls of that stuff down like there was no tomorrow, even though she knew there was and that it would be exactly the same as the previous day, and the one before that, and the one before that. She woke up each morning blinking at the ceiling of our new house wondering what she would do for the next three decades. Mum was forty, and her life was finally confined to supermarket shopping. That was all. The rest of her world had receded into unintelligible sounds and symbols.

"Your mother's been here twenty years, why doesn't she speak English?" people at the university asked me in bewilderment. There was a group that called themselves the Socialist Alternative and they once invited me to one of their meetings, when one of them in my Global Politics class discovered what my mother did. "Tell us about how bad it was for your mother," they urged.

I thought about my mum working for two decades, an active independent business contractor. Then I thought about her not working, lying in bed at home with limp creaking limbs and Zoloft in her bloodstream. "It wasn't that bad, really."

We were all seated in a large circle on the floor and there was a cardboard box of organic cooperative food in the middle. One of the Alternative Socialists picked up a roll. "What do you mean it *wasn't that bad*? Of course it must be effing awful. It must have been, like, the living manifestation of the Third World in the First World."

"No." I was resolute in my conviction: "My mother's work gave her a sense of purpose and dignity."

"Dignity?" They were so wide-mouthed incredulous that I could see the masticated remnants of their beansprout alfalfa wholemeal rolls. "What kind of dignity is that? That's exploitation!"

They wanted to see me as stoic, because they wanted to offer polite charges of bravery before charging on to their manifestos of destroying the capitalists. They needed a scapegoat, but I thought about my mother's "friends" in the jewelry stores—the small-business owners: the Kims, the Trans, the Quachs—small industrious people with terror in their eyes whenever they saw parking inspectors let alone policemen. The university socialists needed to see me as a suffering victim who would stick with saying the mass line of overthrowing the whole exploitative system of labor. Instead, I became an employment lawyer.

At work, I visited sheltered workshops, places where people

with severe disabilities were supported in the most simple of tasks: folding small paper boxes, sorting donated clothing, putting a certain number of screws in containers. Some of the employees had worked there for over four decades, doing the exact same thing day in and day out. The workshops were beautiful austere spaces, every corner cleaner and neater than our entire house in Braybrook, where I grew up. As I visited these places, Mum lay in bed without the disability pension because her physical disabilities weren't severe enough to warrant any compensation from anyone, and perhaps by the time they became severe enough she would have become too old to work anyway.

Now the shed no longer vibrates with its massive-machine heartbeat. Red dust no longer floats out from beneath the door. But we are still not to speak of what Mum did for those two working decades of her life.

The door to the shed is still locked.

"The Shed" is a work of nonfiction based on the experiences of the author.

ARTICLE 26

The Right to Education

Ishmael Beah

ABC ANTIDOTE

Four years had passed slowly since the talking of guns ended. The birds had resumed their singing and nature was no longer afraid to whisper the passing of time through the breeze that brought day and night. Foday and Abu now lived in the capital city, where they did menial jobs such as carrying heavy loads, selling cigarettes on the street and anything that was lucrative, to pay for their secondary school fees. They ate one meal a day to save money, to finish secondary school and start at the university. Sometimes that meal was only a dried loaf of bread that they soaked in water and added sugar to.

The day had arrived, the first day of university, and the young men wore their prized blue jackets, well-starched khaki pants, shirts and ties, black shoes polished consistently for three days and briefcases with notebooks, pens and pencils. When they stepped out of their tin-body one-bedroom rental, their clothes made them look as though they didn't live in this run-down and poor part of town. Mr. Jabati, their landlord, saw them and said he would increase their rent. They laughed and told him they had saved money for years for this day. On any other day, they would have walked to school but today they took a taxi up the hill to the university campus.

Abu and Foday were earlier than any of the other students and they barely spoke to each other as they waited, nervously, pacing back and forth from their seats to the door and windows to see if anyone else was coming. At 9 a.m. students began pour-

340

ing into the classroom and, soon enough, Abu and Foday were surrounded by young men and women eager to learn. Most were naive about the fragility of life and everything around them. The professor walked into the classroom and introduced himself as the "all-purpose teacher." He said he would be teaching mathematics, English, history and maybe one more subject until other professors were employed. He carefully set his books down and began the lesson.

"I thought it would be important for today's class that we talk about education." He looked around the classroom and ran his finger down the names on the sheet of paper he had in his hands. He placed the paper on the desk near his briefcase and raised his head.

"It will be a way for us to get to know each other." He paused and waited for the air of silence to take hold of the classroom. He asked, "What does education mean to you? What do you think it does for a society, for an individual, what is its purpose?" He smiled to indicate that this would be an interesting discussion.

Many of the students who had been in school consistently raised their hands. Their answers and arguments filled the room.

"It provides us with the knowledge and tools to think and use our minds well."

"It teaches us how to reason and to be civilized; it provides us with careers and changes our perspective."

"It provides us with knowledge to be leaders of tomorrow."

All the students in the classroom had responded except Abu and Foday. The professor noticed and called on them.

"Mr. Abu Kamara and Mr. Foday Sesay. Do you have any opinions, gentlemen?" he asked, eyeing their clothes and applauding them with a nod.

It was quiet in the classroom. Foday and Abu looked at each other a bit nervously, as they were uncertain whether any answer they gave would be as good as the other seemingly sophisticated students' ones.

"It is a right." A student interrupted the silence, trying to impress the professor.

"It is only a right if we live in a peaceful society," Foday mumbled.

"Speak up, Foday, if you want to be heard."

The fires were high; their flames licked the dark night and consumed the darkness so that it was brighter for about a mile down the potholed road.

"Move it, move it. We need all the benches, desks and anything that can feed this fire." The commander who called himself "Prophet" shouted at the boys who were running from one classroom to another, their guns behind their backs, picking up books, bound papers and anything that could burn. They made various heaps on either side of the road and lit up the piles that lined from the school compound, which the squad used as an encampment, to the river. Commander Prophet always ordered this sort of burning to "illuminate the darkness so that the enemy can be seen from far away," he would tell his troops, pointing his long fingers over their heads. By tomorrow, they would most likely burn the buildings before departing. They were in the town of Motinga, where most of the soldier boys had gone to school, the same secondary school they now occupied.

As the fires were eating the benches and papers, the soldiers walked up and down the road tending to them. Foday, a now sixteen-year-old boy, had bent down to pick up a pile of bound papers that had rolled down a heap of fire. He was about to throw them into the flames when his eyes caught the writing on them. He unrolled the pages and read the essay questions about *The Rise and Fall of the Roman Empire*. He had taken this test when he was in his first year of secondary school. An image of his teacher, Sir Tucker, struck lightning in his head. He had stood in front of the class reciting Roman history to them without a textbook. He had been fascinated and excited by this man, who could have been his uncle. He knew so much about places in which he had never set foot.

"My mind has traveled through words and books, to places where my feet will never touch the earth," Sir Tucker would always tell his students when he saw wonder on their faces. It had made Foday's heart happy to listen to his teacher. But such feelings were now only memories to him, memories that were not easily woken. However, as he looked at the papers, he felt nostalgic for those days as a student.

"Throw the papers in the fire, soldier. We are not here to read but to fight a war." Commander Prophet interrupted Foday's thoughts.

"Yes sir," he said and threw the papers into the fire.

The commander shook his head and spoke loudly for everyone to hear.

"You are now receiving another kind of education, which is to stay alive and kill those who want to destroy this country. You cannot do that by reading. You can only do that by listening to me. Understand."

"Yes sir." The thin voices of boys sharply filled the night.

"Some of you might remember when you were in school and were told that the pen is mightier than the sword. Well, we have guns so they were not talking about us. Fall back into your places."

"Yes sir." The boys ran to their guarding posts.

Foday was now consumed with longing for his school days, but he tried hard to ignore any thoughts by starting to smoke marijuana and partake of the other drugs that were available in abundance. Night would soon depart the sky and he hoped that it would take with it the thoughts that had become burdensome to him.

It was when the fires were dying with nothing left to give them life that gunshots erupted. Everyone followed Commander Prophet back to the school compound. They gathered near the chapel, which used to be the assembly hall.

"Most of us know the grounds very well and we attended this school. So deploy to your posts. We must finish the night here, and it is our school so let us defend it," Commander Prophet whispered to his band of fighters. The boys knew where to station themselves, so they collected ammunition from the chapel and ran to ready themselves. Foday was stationed with Kotiwa, another boy his age who had gone to the school as well.

"This is the chemistry hall. You remember, Foday?" Kotiwa cocked his gun and fumbled in the corner by the window to properly position himself.

"If you want to stay alive, stop thinking about chemistry and get ready to shoot." Foday settled opposite his former schoolmate. They were quiet for a while. Then the gunmen and boys started coming up the hill, running quickly behind mango and guava trees. Foday and Kotiwa knew that to reach the school compound they would have to cross the open spaces with no trees. So the two boys waited to open fire when that happened. The gunmen and boys too seemed to know that they had to cross the open space, so they waited behind the trees. The wind spoke hesitantly as it got heavier, gathering strength to drive the night away to where it was now needed. A rocket-propelled grenade was launched at one of the school buildings and the exchange of gunfire began. Kotiwa and Foday didn't allow anyone to pass the opening on their watch. The fighting didn't last long when the attackers retreated. They were followed to the river. None of them were allowed to cross. Only their bodies and blood touched the shores on the other side.

That morning, Commander Prophet gave everyone the day off to do whatever it was that they wanted, as long as it was done on the school campus. Most of the boys no longer knew how to be children so they just sat around idly, playing with their guns, recounting what had happened the previous night. Foday, on the other hand, was now thinking strongly about his school days. He wandered off to visit various classrooms he had sat in to learn. At first, he could not make himself go inside any of the classrooms as he was afraid of remembering and what that might do to him as a soldier who had to stay alive with no interruption from memories, especially ones that were good, ones from before the war. But somehow, his feet, with tremendous resistance from his mind and heart, took him inside one of the now empty halls.

Foday looked around and began to hear the echo of chalk

squeaking on the blackboard, the teacher's voice pronouncing the word he was writing, and the students following in unison after the teacher. "Chlo-ro-phyll," they shouted.

The teacher moved away from the board so that the pupils would read the rest of what he had written.

"It is a green pigment found in most plants. It gives leaves their green color and it is vital for pho-to-syn-thesis, which allows plants to obtain energy from light." The pupils read excitedly, thin voices mingling with deeper ones.

It seemed so long ago, but Foday hadn't forgotten those words or the feeling of sitting in the classroom, in his neat and well-ironed uniform, the joy on his mother's face as she cupped his cheeks in her hands right before he went running off to school with his friends. And on his way back from school, he skipped and recited the lessons from that day. When he passed adults on the road, they laughed and smiled. His mother waited for him at the entrance of their compound with a cold calabash of water.

Foday sat down against the wall of the classroom, and felt tears inside his mind, but they couldn't come out. He no longer knew how to cry. Everything has changed, he thought. Whenever his small boys' unit entered any town these days, they brought gunshots and chaos and people ran away from them. It wasn't as it had been when the sight of him as a schoolboy made people smile and laugh and offer him cucumbers, and call him to read their letters from children who lived in the cities. People had expectations of remarkable happenings and hope painted on their faces. Now, it was only fear and blank faces that Foday saw everywhere.

He wasn't sure how long he had been sitting in the empty classroom with his eyes closed and losing awareness of his surroundings. Foday felt someone else next to him. He gently reached for his gun which leaned on the wall to his right.

"No need for that, Foday." The voice of Kotiwa reached his ears.

Foday opened his eyes to see that three boys of his squad had their eyes glued on his face.

Kotiwa had a grin on his face, but Ernest and Abu seemed perplexed. He let go of his gun and pushed the three faces away from his.

"Wai tin happin?" Kotiwa asked what had happened.

The boys sat facing each other.

"You were sing, singing, with with your eye, eyes closed," Ernest stuttered.

"Yes, yes you were," Abu and Kotiwa agreed.

"What did I sing?" he asked, his face tightening with fear of what would have happened if he had done such a thing in the presence of Commander Prophet. He hated when the boys talked about school or any other time before the war. Some boys had been stabbed to death once because while guarding a post they had started singing their school song quietly, not knowing that Commander Prophet was standing behind them.

"Na John Bull u been dae sing." Abu answered that Foday had been singing "John Bull," and loudly. They all knew the song, which they had learned in primary school as part of an exercise to remember the alphabet.

John B . . . U . . . L . . . L
John Bull is my boy I sent him to school
To learn how to spell John Bull
J O H N John, John, and B U L L Bull, Bull
And that is the way to spell John Bull.

Ernest sang quickly and quietly before the others could place their hands over his mouth. He said he was just explaining to Kotiwa how Foday had sounded, but the boys knew he just wanted to sing the song.

"Co-Commander Pro-Prophet will kill you for this." Ernest stood and pointed his gun toward the doorless entrance.

"Only if he finds out." Abu stood up as well and tied his pants that were too big for him.

"We will not tell him, none of you will or I will shoot you myself." Abu who was older, seventeen, pointed his fingers at the others. He pulled Kotiwa and Foday up and explained to them that many of the other boys had been reciting school songs and things they had learned before the war when they closed their eyes to rest, even if for a second. He felt that it was because they were camping in the school grounds. The boys began walking back to the chapel to eat their share of whatever little food was available.

"Do you think this is only happening because we are at this school compound? We have burned down many schools, you know," Kotiwa whispered to his friends.

"Do you have another explanation?" Abu asked.

"Maybe it is because we have burned all those books or maybe because we no longer have room in our brain for bad things so we are going back to what had been," Kotiwa said, and none of the other boys responded. They had sighted Commander Prophet walking toward them. They saluted him as he walked by, glaring at their faces. He always reminded the boys that he was a prophet and therefore could see their thoughts. They were afraid of him, terribly. Commander Prophet was on his way to his quarters, as he called the house that had belonged to the principal of the school.

That night, Kotiwa, Foday, Abu and Ernest sat together as though it were the only way they could keep their secret and also protect one another. They sat on the steps of the chapel and as the night grew thicker they heard boys singing various school songs in their sleep. The boys who weren't sleeping became terrified that they would be complicit to this action if Commander Prophet found out. They woke up the boys who sang in their sleep and threatened to kill them. None of the boys knew why a fellow soldier wanted to kill them. They wanted an explanation and when they were told what each had said in his sleep, they promised not to do it again.

"It is because we are not fighting as much anymore, too much time on our hands," one boy said and fired a couple of rounds into the night and walked away.

Each night things got worse, as more boys would either say

something about remembering their time at the school or recount things in their sleep. Some of the boys talked about "chro-
mosomes," some recited the multiplication tables, others had
spelling contests, and to make things more complicated, in the
midst of this chaos they had to secretly discuss how to put an
end to the madness, to make sure that Commander Prophet
didn't know what was happening. In order to come up with a
solution, they had to talk about what had happened, which was
dangerous. The boys felt that Commander Prophet would hear
them even if they whispered to one another. Abu decided that
they must do something to make sure that the sharp ears of
Commander Prophet were filled with something else while
some of the boys discussed a solution. A good number of the
boys would march and sing their squad song:

> We fight for this country,
> We kill for this country and we die for this country.
> We are soldiers in the army for freedom.
> With the barrel of our guns we will seek the truth and free
> this country . . .

The first night the boys tested this method, it worked very
well. To their surprise, Commander Prophet and his lieutenants
glowed with pride and engaged in firing to celebrate what they
thought was an enthusiasm and complete control over the minds
of the young soldiers. While this was going on, the boys at the
main guarding post, which included Kotiwa, Foday, Abu, Ernest
and two others, decided that they would make sure that none of
the boys slept enough to dream. They would take turns observing
to make sure no one sat by himself and therefore was able to
sleep. As the boys quickly chatted, Abu realized that the solution
would not work and that he had just discovered another. He
smiled at his friends and said, "This is the solution," pointing at
the marching boys.

"What do you mean?" Foday asked.

"We will just sing this war song to cover whoever is dreaming or singing. This way the ears of Commander Prophet are always pleased and he cannot hear the school songs." Abu jumped up from the guarding post and started singing and marching toward the gathering. The solution worked every night until the war came to an end a few weeks later. It allowed the young boys to hold on to some of their past, at least in their dreams, when it was possible.

The professor was now walking toward the back of the classroom where Foday and Abu sat.

"Education, whether brief or just memories of it, creates the anchors that prevent us from losing our humanity completely, as a society and as individuals," Abu spoke. His deep voice and confidence shocked him and sent blood rushing through his veins, making his hands tremble. The professor stopped and looked around the classroom.

"So you are saying that this isn't only a right, but that it in fact saves the life source of a society and its people." The professor faced Abu directly. Abu looked toward Foday for help.

"Education is the most powerful medicine that cures violence. It strengthens the mind to resist violence, to transform the elements of violence, which are fear and loss of self. Of course, one has to have some basic understanding of reality. In general, education can reawaken the mind and spirit after it has been broken," Foday said, looking at the professor.

The professor stood in silence for a while, and said, "I have taught for many years but never heard such an interesting answer to this question. Are you sure you should be in this class?" The class laughed, some hesitantly, others missing the point.

"What gave you such understanding about education?" the professor asked as he walked to the front of the classroom. Foday and Abu weren't expecting such a question, not on the first day of class. They both looked away. A student hesitantly entered the classroom and gave the professor a note. He read it and shook his head, dismissing the young man.

"I must go for an emergency meeting. We will continue this

discussion tomorrow. Good day." The professor picked up his belongings and hurried out the door. The students burst into chatter as they hurried off to various parts of the campus. Abu and
Foday remained seated in the classroom; memories of the past
had consumed them.

Cultural Life

Alan Garner

GRAY WOLF, PRINCE JACK, AND THE FIREBIRD

Once, long ago, not near, not far, not high, not low, at the place where seven rivers meet, there lived a king. And he was the king of the Stone Castle. He had three sons, and the name of the youngest was Jack.

The king had a garden, too, and round it a wall. And in the garden stood a tree. Gold was its trunk, and gold were its branches, gold its twigs, gold its leaves, and golden its fruit of apples. And there was never a moment when the king of the Stone Castle did not keep guards about this wondrous tree.

One night, at deep midnight, there came a music into the garden.

It was music with wings,
Trampling things, tightened strings,
Warrior, heroes, ghosts on their feet,
Boguls and boggarts, bells and snow
That set in sound lasting sleep
The whole great world
With the sweetness of the calming tunes
That music did play.

The next morning, the king walked in his garden, and he saw that a golden apple had been taken from the tree.

"Who has stolen my apple of gold?" said the king of the Stone Castle.

"No one," said the guard captain. "We watched all night."

"You did not," said the king. And he made the guards prisoners and sent them to work salt forever.

"Now," said the king, "which of my beloved sons will watch my tree? I shall give half my kingdom now, and all of it when I die, to the son who will catch this thief."

"I shall watch, father," said the oldest son. And he sat in the garden, his back against the tree.

At deep midnight, at dark midnight, there came a music over the wall.

> It was music with wings,
> Trampling things, tightened strings,
> Warrior, heroes, ghosts on their feet,
> Boguls and boggarts, bells and snow
> That set in sound lasting sleep
> The whole great world
> With the sweetness of the calming tunes
> That music did play.

And the oldest son slept.

The next morning, the king walked in his garden, and he saw that another golden apple had been taken from the tree.

"Who has stolen my apple of gold?" said the king of the Stone Castle. "Who is the thief?"

"No one, father," said the oldest son. "I watched all night."

"Tonight I shall watch," said the second son. And he sat in the garden, his back against the tree.

At deep midnight, at dark midnight, at blue midnight, there came a music into the garden.

> It was music with wings,
> Trampling things, tightened strings,
> Warriors, heroes, ghosts on their feet,
> Boguls and boggarts, bells and snow
> That set in sound lasting sleep

The whole great world
With the sweetness of the calming tunes
That music did play.

And the second son slept.

The next morning, the king walked in his garden, and he saw that another apple had been taken from the tree.

"Who has stolen my golden apple?" said the king of the Stone Castle. "Who is the thief?"

"No one, father," said the second son. "I watched all night."

"I shall watch," said Prince Jack. And he sat in the garden, his back against the tree. But he took his dagger and put it between his leg and the earth, the point upward, and the leg on the point.

At deep midnight, at dark midnight, at blue midnight, at the midnight of all, a music came into the garden.

It was music with wings,
Trampling things, tightening strings,
Warriors, heroes, ghosts on their feet,
Boguls and boggarts, bells and snow
That set in sound lasting sleep
The whole great world
With the sweetness of the calming tunes
That music did play.

And Prince Jack pushed his leg on the dagger, and a drop of blood fell to the earth, but he did not sleep.

Then flew the Firebird, with eyes of crystal, over the wall, over the garden, to the tree.

And Prince Jack pushed his leg on the dagger, and a second drop of his blood fell to the earth, but he did not sleep.

The Firebird perched on the lowest branch of the tree and took an apple in her beak.

Prince Jack pulled the dagger from his leg, and a third drop of his blood fell to the earth. He jumped to seize the Firebird, but his wound made him weak, and he caught hold of a tail feather only, and the Firebird flew away.

Jack wrapped the feather in his neck cloth and sat down again beside the tree.

The next morning the king walked in his garden, and he saw that another apple had been taken from the tree.

"Who has stolen the apple?" said the king of the Stone Castle. "Who is the thief?"

"It is the Firebird, father," said Prince Jack. "I did not sleep. Here are three drops of my blood upon the earth. And here the feather for you to see." And he unwrapped his neck cloth, and the garden, even in that morning, was filled with a flame of light.

The king of the Stone Castle said, "It is the Firebird." And he said to his two oldest sons, "Go. I give you my blessing. Bring the Firebird to me; and what I promised before I shall give to the one who brings me that bird."

The sons took their father's blessing and rode away.

"Father, let me go, too," said Prince Jack.

"I cannot lose all my sons," said the king. And Prince Jack went to his room and he thought; and he ran to the stables, took his horse, muffled its hooves, and rode away.

He rode near and far, he rode high and low, by lanes and ways and woods and swamps, for a long time or a short time; and he came to a wide field, a green meadow, an open plain. And on the meadow stood a pillar of stone, with words graven in it.

> "Go straight, know cold and hunger.
>   Go right, keep life, lose horse.
>   Go left, keep horse, lose life."

"Dear horse," said Prince Jack; and he turned to the right.

He rode one day. He rode two days. He rode three days. Then, in a dark forest, he met a Gray Wolf.

"Did you not read the rock?" said the Gray Wolf. And he took the horse, ripped it to bits, ate it; then went.

Prince Jack walked one day. He walked two days. He walked

three days. He walked until he was so tired that it could not be told in story. And the Gray Wolf came to him again.

"You are brave enough," said the Gray Wolf. "So I shall help you. I have eaten your good horse, and I shall serve you a service as payment. Sit you up on me and say where I must take you. The roads are open to the wise, and they are not closed to the foolish."

So Prince Jack sat up on the Gray Wolf.

The Gray Wolf struck the damp earth and ran, higher than the trees, lower than the clouds, and each leap measured a mile, from his feet flint flew, springs spouted, lakes boiled and mixed with yellow sand, and forests bent to the ground. Prince Jack shouted a shout, whistled a whistle, snake and adder hissed, nightingales sang, and beasts on chains began to roar. And the Gray Wolf stopped at a wall.

"Now, Prince Jack," he said, "get down from me, the Gray Wolf, climb over the wall, into the garden. It is the garden of the king of the Copper Castle. In the garden stand three cages. In the first cage there is a crow. In the next cage there is a jackdaw. In the golden cage there is the Firebird. Take the Firebird, put her in your neck cloth and come back. But do not, do not, do not ever take the golden cage."

Prince Jack climbed over the wall, passed the first cage, passed the second cage, and put the Firebird in his neck cloth. But the golden cage was so beautiful. He picked it up, and there sounded throughout the garden and throughout that kingdom a great clang of bells and a twang of harps, and five hundred watchmen came and took him to the king of the Copper Castle.

"Why do you steal the Firebird?" said the king.

"The Firebird stole my father's golden apples," said Prince Jack. "And he is a king."

"If you had come to me first, I would have given you the Firebird with honor," said the king of the Copper Castle. "But you came as a thief. How will it be with you now when I send through all the kingdoms that your father's son brought shame within my land?"

"The shame is great," said Prince Jack. "There is no place of honor left for me."

"I shall give you one chance, since you have been honest with me," said the king. "If you will ride across thrice nine lands, beyond the Tenth Kingdom, and get for me the Horse of the Golden Mane, I shall give you back your honor and, with all joy, the Firebird, too."

The five hundred watchmen took Prince Jack to the bounds of the garden and threw him out. The Gray Wolf came to him.

"You did not, and you would not, as I told you," said the Gray Wolf. "But this is not trouble yet. The trouble is to come. I have only a trotter and a sheep's cheek, and they must do."

Prince Jack and the Gray Wolf ate the trotter and the sheep's cheek. Then Prince Jack sat up on the Gray Wolf, and the Gray Wolf struck the damp earth and ran, higher than the trees, lower than the clouds, and each leap measured a mile, from his feet flint flew, springs sprouted, lakes boiled and mixed with yellow sand, and forests bent to the ground. Prince Jack shouted a shout, whistled a whistle, snake and adder hissed, nightingales sang, and beasts on chains began to roar.

The Gray Wolf stopped at white-walled stables.

"Get down from me, the Gray Wolf," he said, "into the white-walled stables. They are the white-walled stables of the king of the Iron Castle. Take the Horse of the Golden Mane. But do not, do not, do not ever take the gold bridle."

Prince Jack went into the white-walled stables and took the Horse of the Golden Mane. But the gold bridle was too beautiful to leave. He picked it up, and thunder sounded through the stables and five hundred grooms came and brought him to the king of the Iron Castle.

"Why did you steal the Horse of the Golden Mane?" said the king.

"The Firebird stole my father's golden apples," said Prince Jack. "And he is a king. Then I stole the Firebird, but was caught, and I am now."

"If you had come to me first, I would have given you the Horse of the Golden Mane with honor," said the king of the Iron Castle. "But you came as a thief. How will it be with you when I send through all the kingdoms that your father's son brought shame within my land?"

"The shame is great," said Prince Jack. "There is no place of honor left for me."

"I shall give you one chance, since you have been honest with me," said the king. "If you will ride across thrice nine lands, beyond the Tenth Kingdom, and get for me the Princess Helen the Fair, whose skin is so clear that you see the marrow flow from bone to bone, I shall give you back your honor, and with all joy, the Horse of the Golden Mane."

The five hundred grooms took Prince Jack to the door of the white-walled stables and threw him out. The Gray Wolf came to him.

"You did not, and you would not, as I told you," said the Gray Wolf. "But this is not trouble yet. The trouble is to come. I have only a trotter and a sheep's cheek, and they must do."

Prince Jack and the Gray Wolf ate the trotter and the sheep's cheek. Then Prince Jack sat up on the Gray Wolf, and the Gray Wolf struck the damp earth and ran, higher than the trees, lower than the clouds, and each leap measured a mile, from his feet flint flew, springs spouted, lakes boiled and mixed with yellow sand, and forests bent to the ground. Prince Jack shouted a shout, whistled a whistle, snake and adder hissed, nightingales sang, and beasts on chains began to roar.

The Gray Wolf stopped at the golden fence of the garden of Princess Helen the Fair, whose marrow flowed from bone to bone.

"Get down from me, the Gray Wolf," he said. "Go back along the road by which we came, and wait for me in the field with a green oak tree." So Prince Jack did.

But the Gray Wolf, he stayed.

And, at evening, Princess Helen the Fair came into the garden, and her marrow flowed from bone to bone. The Gray Wolf jumped into the garden, seized her, and ran off. He ran to the field of the green oak, where Prince Jack waited. Princess Helen the Fair dried her eyes fast when she saw Prince Jack.

"Sit up on me," said the Gray Wolf, "and hold the Princess in your arms."

Prince Jack sat up on the Gray Wolf, and held Princess Helen the Fair in his arms, and the Gray Wolf ran as only a wolf runs in story, until they came to the white-walled stables of the king of the Iron Castle with the Horse of the Golden Mane. But by now Prince Jack loved Princess Helen the Fair, and she loved him, and the Gray Wolf saw.

"I have served you in much," said the Gray Wolf. "I shall serve you in this. I shall be Princess Helen the Fair, and you will take me to the king, and he will give you the Horse of the Golden Mane. Then mount you the horse and ride far. And when you think of me, the Gray Wolf, I shall come to you."

And the Gray Wolf struck the damp earth, and became a False Princess, and Prince Jack took him to the white-walled stables. While Princess Helen the Fair stayed outside.

When he saw the False Princess, the king of the Iron Castle was pleased, and he gave Prince Jack the Horse of the Golden Mane with joy, and the gold bridle, and gave him back his honor, too. Then Prince Jack rode out of the white-walled stables on the Horse of the Golden Mane and put Princess Helen the Fair before him, and rode away.

The False Princess, the Gray Wolf, stayed one day in the king's palace. He stayed two days. And he stayed three. Then he asked the king if he might walk in the garden. So the king ordered serving-women to walk with the False Princess. And, as they walked, Prince Jack, far away, riding, called, "Gray Wolf! Gray Wolf! I am thinking of you now!"

The False Princess, walking in the garden with the serving-women, sprang up as the Gray Wolf, over the garden wall and ran as only wolves do in story until he came to Prince Jack.

"Sit up on me, the Gray Wolf," he said, "and let Princess Helen the Fair ride the Horse of the Golden Mane."

And so they went on together.

At last, after a long time or a short time, they came to the palace of the king of the Copper Castle who kept the Firebird.

"Dear friend! Gray Wolf!" said Prince Jack. "You have served me many services. Serve me one more."

"I shall serve you one more," said the Gray Wolf. And he struck the damp earth and became a False Horse, and Prince Jack mounted him and rode into the palace.

When the king of the Copper Palace saw the False Horse he was pleased, and he gave the Firebird in its golden cage to Prince Jack, and gave him back his honor, too.

Prince Jack left the palace and went to where Princess Helen the Fair was waiting with the Horse of the Golden Mane, and they rode toward the palace of Prince Jack's father, the king of the Stone Castle. They came into a dark forest.

And Prince Jack remembered, and called, "Gray Wolf! Gray Wolf! I am thinking of you now!" And straight away the Gray Wolf appeared. But he said, "Well, Prince Jack, here is where we met. I, the Gray Wolf, have paid for your horse. I am no more your servant." And he jumped into a thicket and was gone.

Prince Jack wept, and rode the Horse of the Golden Mane, with the gold bridle, Princess Helen before him, and in her arms the Firebird and its golden cage.

They rode one day. They rode two days. They rode three days. But whether the day was long or short, they grew tired, and when they came to the graven stone in the green meadow they rested against it, and slept.

And as they slept, the two older brothers came back from their empty wanderings, and when they saw Prince Jack with the Firebird in its golden cage, and the Horse of the Golden Mane and its gold bridle, and Princess Helen the Fair, whose marrow flowed from bone to bone, they cut Prince Jack into four pieces, and threw the four pieces to the four winds, and took the Firebird and the Horse of the Golden Mane and Princess Helen the Fair with them back to their father's palace.

The king of the Stone Castle was glad to see his sons and

to hold the Firebird in its golden cage. And the two brothers drew lots, and the first won Princess Helen the Fair, and the second took the Horse of the Golden Mane, and a wedding was ordered.

But Prince Jack lay dead, by lanes and ways and woods and swamps, out on the green meadow, cut into four parts.

He lay one day. He lay two days. He lay three days. And in the forest the Gray Wolf smelled the flesh and knew that it was the flesh of Prince Jack. He went where the pieces lay. And there came a crow with a brazen beak and brazen claws, with her two children, to feed on the flesh. But the Gray Wolf jumped and seized one of her children.

"Gray Wolf, wolf's son," said the crow, "do not eat my child. Do not tear off its rash little head. Do not take it from the bright world."

"Black Crow, crow's daughter," said the Gray Wolf, "serve me a service and I shall not hurt your child. Fly for me over the Glass Mountains to the Well of the Water of Death and the Well of the Water of Life. Bring me back those waters, and I, the Gray Wolf, shall loose your child. But if not, I shall tear off its rash little head. I shall take it from the bright world."

"I shall do you this service," said the crow. And she flew beyond the end of the earth, over the Glass Mountains, and she came back with the Water of Death and the Water of Life.

The Gray Wolf tore the crow's child to bits. He sprinkled the Water of Death over it, and the bits grew together. He sprinkled the Water of Life over it, and the crow's child awoke, shook itself, and flew away.

The Gray Wolf sprinkled the pieces of the body of Prince Jack with the Water of Death. And the pieces were joined. He sprinkled the Water of Life. And Prince Jack stretched himself, yawned, and said, "How long have I been asleep?"

"Yes, Prince Jack, and you would have slept forever had it not been for me, the Gray Wolf. Long hair, short wit. Sit up on me, for your oldest brother is to wed Princess Helen the Fair this very day."

Prince Jack sat up on the Gray Wolf, and the Gray Wolf struck the damp earth and ran, higher than the trees, lower than the clouds, and each leap measured a mile, from his feet flint flew, springs spurted, lakes boiled and mixed with yellow sand, and forests bent to the ground. Prince Jack shouted a shout, whistled a whistle, snake and adder hissed, nightingales sang, beasts on chains began to roar, all the way to the palace of the king of the Stone Castle.

Prince Jack got down from the Gray Wolf in the middle of the wedding, and when she saw him alive, Princess Helen the Fair ran to him, and they told the king all that had happened.

The anger of the king was a river in storm, and he called halt to the wedding, made his eldest son a scullion, his second son a cowherd, and fed them all their days on cockroach milk. But Prince Jack and Princess Helen the Fair were married that same night. And on all sides those that weep were weeping, those that shout were shouting, and those that sing were singing.

Prince Jack said, "Gray Wolf! Gray Wolf! How can I repay you? Stay with me forever. You shall never want. Go now forever through my ground. No arrow will be let at you. No trap will be set for you. Take any beast to take with you. Go now through my ground forever."

"Keep your herds and your flocks to yourself," said the Gray Wolf. "There is many a one I can trouble with a trotter and a cheek as well as you. I, the Gray Wolf, shall get flesh without putting trouble here. The tale is spent. Live long, Prince Jack. Live happy. But me you shall never see more." And the Gray Wolf struck the damp earth and was gone.

Prince Jack and Princess Helen the Fair lived in friendship and they lived in peace, they lived happy and they lived long; and if they are not dead yet, they are living still, and they feed the hens with stars.

But the Gray Wolf they did not see; though you may. And, if you do, what then?

Liana Badr

MARCH OF THE DINOSAURS

Like an enormous hen clucking, or like the Cyclops with its single eye, and the roar as it drew breath, it was continuously approaching the wall of the house.

It was strange, actually, that I hadn't seen it in the neighborhood since last night.

It was a giant Merkava-type tank, and whoever was inside was doing all they could to turn it into a mobile terror parade. With this in mind, they were racing it down the narrow alleys and passageways, on the lookout for one of us breaking the curfew. The smoke never stopped rising from it, like a gigantic dragon expiring.

I tried to sit and rest in the moments that were uninterrupted by outbreaks of gunfire and falling shells, leafing through old newspapers under the leaves of a shrub grape tree that our relatives (the Hebronites) had been cultivating in front of the house for seven years. I was speckled by dots of green light reflected by the trailing leaves, consoling myself, in flight from the screens of the Arab satellite TV channels that were taking pleasure in our situation. I still enjoyed going through these old pages, with their happy news spelled out in little black letters, reaffirming that life was still going on in other places in the world—far from the return of the Occupation to our lives, with its armored vehicles, which were destroying our city over the long weeks.

In spite of the nonstop curfew, the unceasing threats, the continuous sound of explosions, the despair of prolonged imprisonment within four walls and the sheer misery of the situation from which we could not escape, our most basic fear was that we would get used to the incursion. Strong feelings pushed us to ignore this sudden disaster that had come to rule over every minute of our lives—as though defying the curfew, which forbade our movement outdoors, meant we had erased it from our consciousness. In spite of all our efforts to adapt, the space inside the house was shrinking, transforming us into mere creatures incarcerated in cages.

I complained, along with everyone else I knew, about the lack of movement possible inside the house, which the army prevented us from leaving—as though our telephoned grumblings would lighten the despair of the prison within its walls. But every word we uttered sharpened our desire for movement, like the saltwater of the sea sharpens thirst.

Whenever I looked out between the bars on the window, I was led to watch the armored vehicles going about the streets instead of the familiar civilian cars. I felt I had been transported into the world of the film *Jurassic Park,* where monsters take over a place in which they have no right to be.

I vowed not to accept the loss of my everyday life, and resolved to exercise daily so my body would not become feeble and weak. Exercises had to be the best way to obliterate the daily grind—like taking antidepressants to cure the feeling of confinement.

I chose a time in which we were not threatened by direct shelling, so I could use the whole area of the room near the window. I jumped up and down and ran on the spot, without the thought ever leaving my mind that I must avoid getting in range of their snipers, who tracked every movement behind the windows. I was still frightened after they had aimed at me back in the earliest days of their previous occupation of our city, two months ago.

That day, I had been standing in the garden contemplating the shrub grape tree, which had not yet put out leaves, testing the smoothness of the green color of the tiny growths marking the branches, thinking I ought to visit my neighbor, when I heard the sound of Apache helicopters hovering in the sky above, looking for human targets to strike. I went toward the front door and a salvo of bullets burst forth.

If I hadn't run, if I hadn't got back crawling and clinging to the walls, if I hadn't managed to open the door to the house while squatting down to prevent them aiming accurately, if . . .

If!

I said it often to myself after I had seen the holes where I had been standing made by the stream of bullets from their snipers perched on the roof of the building opposite.

The most important thing for me was that I started to make use of the cassette player and do exercises, each time initiated with a ritual curse on their presence outside.

Today, it's the fifteenth day of the occupation—or the fourteenth, or sixteenth, or whatever—of the city of Ramallah. The setting sun, which Um Kulthum sang about at length, looks like an inflamed orange behind the windowpane.

I reached across automatically to the machine, and turned the cassette over so it would play my favorite music straight away. There were birds floating over some coast, and waves raging around them in an unending dance. The sun was warm, and a smell of salt pervaded the place . . . and the dolphins were dancing in green, green waters.

I felt something stir inside me, and was surprised by an enormous joy coursing through me.

Previously, I had always succumbed to that fear which makes the Occupation so burdensome, rejecting any enjoyment of the music as though simply listening to it during an incursion were a crime. But now, I felt their cruel desire to impose themselves on our lives with their aggressive presence being suddenly erased from my mind to an astonishing degree.

The first tune from the music of the Mediterranean islands that carried the cries of seagulls had not yet come to an end when I felt the floor of the room shake with the rhythm of grating metallic tracks devouring the earth beneath them.

I approached the window. Those children fresh out of secondary school, which the occupying state had despatched to us in their military outfits, must still be cruising in their armored cars, trying to spread terror in our alleyways and streets. Our children sometimes refused to obey the curfew orders, carrying on playing ball games outside the houses as though nothing were going on.

A number of our neighbors' children went behind their mothers' backs to join the army of stone-throwers, especially when their armored vehicles passed. The children of the street assailed them with mocking songs, infuriating the drivers of the tank, who immediately began to shell our street with sonic bombs and tear gas.

My surprise was increased when the cavalcade came to a standstill right in front of our house! We did not have any children who might have broken the curfew.

I waited to see who was behind the perforated screen, to see what they meant by stopping directly in front of our walls, in front of the gate of our house!

Did they have a telepathic sense that told them I had succeeded in ignoring their presence, told them about the cassette that I had begun to enjoy, about my desire to do a few exercises in spite of the orders they gave us over the loudspeakers carried by their tanks? "No going out! We'll fire on anyone who disobeys . . ."

It was a procession of armored personnel carriers, headed by the huge Merkava tank I knew well from its occasional passings, with its lowing voice, the shuddering of its movements unleashing an earthquake in the house and street. Alongside, there was an armored personnel carrier that bellowed like a monster and, around that, a number of military jeeps.

In front was that tank whose engine rattled, then turned into a roar which suddenly stopped. The soldier atop it remained visible no more than two seconds before descending back into its belly, hidden behind its turret, and its domed metal cover was shut once more.

I didn't keep on staring out the window for long, because the soldier who had peered out of the Merkava's turret at the door of our house and along this side of our street had now disappeared completely inside it and nothing could any longer be seen of the tank apart from the barrel of its gun, which had begun to rotate in the direction of the window I was standing behind, until it was more or less directly sighting the trellis of grapes growing around the entrance to the door.

I didn't understand what was happening as the mouth of the big gun of the Merkava came to rest pointing in the direction of the back entrance to our house. It seemed as though it was trying to adjust its aim. I decided to go out into the passageway and look over the wall.

We were playing host to some foreign journalists who were sitting with the family in the exposed open courtyard trying to get some information, and they were visibly anxious. The mouth of the gun kept swinging up and down in front of the door and we were unable to explain the point of this military display taking place outside our house.

I could see the guests regarding what was happening with an astonishment coupled with a terror that was not easy to conceal. There was a university lecturer there, standing among them, who stared through the gaps in the plants climbing the walls, his blue eyes narrowed with the intensity of his fear.

Finally, he sought help over his mobile phone, trying to find out what was going on that might explain or have some sort of relation to this direct threat.

We stood with the guests, discussing what might be the motive behind this brazen attack on us. Gradually, we came to the conclusion that it must have something to do with the suspicions of the military observation posts with regard to the group of journalists, who had rolled up in their white car in the middle of a strict curfew.

It was true that they had permits to circulate, but their car, packed as it was, must have made the soldiers suspicious when it spent a prolonged period parked in front of our house. Perhaps they didn't like there to be press coverage of what they were doing in the field, so they wanted to spread fear among whoever dared to move about!

A few of us peeked out between the climbing ivy, and we saw a number of soldiers, armed to the teeth, surrounding the car outside, quizzing its foreign driver, who was replying in a few confused, hesitant expressions that we couldn't hear.

The mouth of the Merkava gun kept on aiming and swiveling continuously in half circles in the direction of our house.

Unease pervaded our guests.

I began to talk, seeking to calm them down with a few words. I turned to a journalist whose expression described fear itself:

Gentlemen! It's just like *Jurassic Park*—you know, march of the dinosaurs? Don't be scared.

I thought my joke would calm the situation.

But the man's face just looked more yellow. It didn't seem as though any of them were interested in what I'd said.

The agitation of our guests increased, and they worked their mobile phones feverishly.

This is a house, our house!

Why do they begrudge it to us, to sit imprisoned here?

From the holes in the wall, soldiers could be seen fanning out in front of the house. Their helmets erased any trace of the humanity a person might hope to see from their rock-like faces.

Never mind. They'll go away eventually, like the other ones went.

Like all the tanks that come to stop for a long time in the middle of the street, then turn and find themselves forced to go because they can't stand being among us overnight.

Stay? They can't.

They can't stay here. They can't even bear to stay long enough to hear one mocking song from the children in our street, so how can they stay forever?

If they stayed a day, they would go the next day.

If they stayed a year, they would be forced to withdraw the following year.

And so on . . .

I was on the point of telling the guests, whose twitching hands had had enough of taking the nuts from the wooden dish on the table:

Seeing all those tanks day after day has really poisoned things for us. We're more bored than scared of them.

Do you want us to go out and scatter almonds and peanuts in front of them? We might be able to feed them and tame them like circus creatures!

But I changed my mind.

It would be difficult for them to get my joke, even though it was meant to console them.

Terror had sunk deeper and deeper into the face of the man with the blue eyes, and he was carrying on his phone calls as though he couldn't hear me.

How depressing! It seems my irony hadn't succeeded in lightening the atmosphere . . . the oppression was just weighing more heavily.

I felt I was light, free of their fear.

Inside me drifted a wave of feelings of relaxation, and I repeated to myself:

March of the dinosaurs!

March of the dinosaurs!

I remembered then, perhaps my affection for those creatures stemmed from when my son had collected pictures of them.

For years, he had stuck them on his exercise books, after classifying them into species.

I didn't understand then how a boy no older than twelve could be interested in making a hobby of knowing the species and fossils of dinosaurs! What was interesting about that?

Perhaps it was a necessity!

I said to myself:

And now! Have I discovered the march of the dinosaurs

right in front of my own house? In front of my little garden, grown with rosemary and fiery-colored geranium flowers?

It's the march! Land of the dinosaurs! Tanks running down our alleys and our streets every night, every hour depriving us of our lives, with every minute taking our lives away from us.

Tanks have a hard surface.

Dinosaurs have a rough skin.

Tanks are khaki.

Dinosaurs are brown . . . perhaps a bit on the khaki side.

It was an animal from my childhood, in any case. I liked its big size in the books my father read to me. I asked him to take me to the zoo so I could ride it. I thought getting on its back would be like climbing up onto the summit of a mountain. So he told me they were no longer to be found in the world.

I was four at the time, and I felt sorry for the absence of dinosaurs.

I would never, in my life, feel sorry for the absence of tanks.

Can't we tame these crazy wild metal animals? Perhaps we could give them a signal during the curfew to make them stop for us and drive us where we want to go. We could give the driver a few coins, like they do on those famous British red buses.

Do we need a ladder to climb up on it? Why does it go through our streets howling so wildly, as though a bitter agony were contorting its joints?

The dinosaur was still standing in front of the door of the house.

I laughed again, but bitterly this time.

The journalists began to gather their papers and bags. It seemed a telephone call had reassured them that the matter would be cleared up soon and they could go.

Shall I tell the one about the dinosaurs?

Shall I tell the one about the tanks?

My father used to tell me the story of the oil jug when I was a child.

Shall I tell you a story?

Shall I tell the one about the oil jug?

* * *

They've gone!

The guests. And the dinosaurs too!

The house was empty at last, and I went back inside, back to the curfew. Those who had come to us had been chased away.

We were alone in it again, and those who had been with us had disappeared!

Again, I contemplated the horizon from my window. Its bleeding red color had intensified.

I began to urge myself into starting the exercises again, but I was cautious at the sound of my steps, as though a hidden impulse inspired me to go gently so the soldiers wouldn't hear.

I put the cassette on to play my favorite music again, and carried on jumping and running on the spot in front of the windows.

I didn't know why I couldn't hear the sound of the waves on the Mediterranean islands whose birds sang in joy, while their sun dived gently, unhurriedly to the ocean floor, and the dolphins who danced in its blue waters, which had begun to turn gray, scattering the perfume of salt, gushing between rocks.

There was nothing but an imprisoned melody gushing weakly from the recorder, because the dinosaurs had encircled it.

There was nothing but the beats of my heart, still thumping with the roaring of the huge metallic tanks, which had begun to recede from our street.

Translated by J. Steel

Duty to Others

Rohinton Mistry
THE SCREAM

The first time I heard the scream outside my window, I had just fallen asleep. It was many nights ago. The sound pierced the darkness like a needle. Behind it, it pulled an invisible thread of pain.

The night was suffocating, I remember. There was no sign of rain. The terrible cry disturbed the dry, dusty air, then died in silence. Bullies, torturers, executioners all prefer silence. Exceptions are made for the sounds of their instruments, their grunts of effort, their victims' agony. The rest is silence. No wisdom like silence. Silence is golden. I associated silence with virtuous people. Or at least harmless, inoffensive people. I was thinking of Trappist monks, of gurus and babas who take vows of silence. I was wrong. Even at my great age, there are things to learn.

The scream disturbed none in the flat. No one opened a window and poked out a curious head. The buildings across the road were hushed as well. The light of the street lamp grew dimmer. No witnesses?

Could I have dreamed it? But the scream was followed by shrieks: Bachaaav, bachaav! yelled the man, help me, please! I opened my eyes, and there were more screams. Frightened, I shut my eyes. It was utterly horripilating. I was afraid to rise and look out the window. He begged them to stop hitting, to please forgive: Mut maaro, maaf karo!

That was nights ago. But when it gets dark and the light is switched off, I can think of nothing else. If I do think of something else, sooner or later the scream returns. It comes like a disembodied hand to clutch my throat and choke my windpipe. Then it is difficult to fall asleep, especially at my age, with my many worries. Signs of trouble are everywhere. The seagulls keep screeching. The seedlings are wilting and ready to die. The fishermen's glistening nets emerge from the sea, emptier than yesterday. All day long there is shouting and fighting. Buses and lorries thunder past. Mediocre politicians make loud speeches, bureaucrats wag arrogant fingers, fanatics howl blood-curdling threats. And even at night there is no peace.

I sleep on a mattress on the floor, in the front room. In the front room the light is better. The dust lies thick on the furniture. The others use the back room. My place, too, used to be there, among them. All night long I would hear their orchestra of wind instruments, their philharmonia of dyspepsia, when, with the switching off of the lights, it was as if a conductor had raised his baton and given the downbeat, for it started immediately, the snoring, wheezing, sighing, coughing, belching and farting. Not that I was entirely silent myself. But at least my age gives me the right; pipes grown old do not remain soundless. In that caliginous back room, verging on the hypogean, with its dark nooks and corners, often the air would be inspissated before half the night was through. And yet, it was so much better than being alone, so comforting to lie amidst warm, albeit noisy, bodies when one's own grew less and less warm, day by day.

Horripilating. Caliginous. Hypogean. Inspissated. It pleases me that these words are not lost on you. Well may you wonder why I use them, when equivalents of the common or garden variety would do. Patience, I am no show-off. Though I will readily admit that if gems like these sit unused inside me for too long, they make me costive. A periodic purge is essential for an old man's well-being. At my age, well-being is a relative concept. So I repeat, I am no exhibitionist, this is not a manifestation of logorrhea or wanton sesquipedalianism. At my age, there is no future in showing off. There are good reasons. Patience.

All my life I have feared mice, starvation and loneliness. But now that loneliness has arrived, it's not so bad. What could I do, the others no longer wanted me among them, in the back room. I suppose I was a nuisance. Hence my mattress on the floor, in the front room, wedged between the sofa and the baby grand. I am in a tight spot. One wrong turn and I could bruise a knee or crack my forehead. The others were only too glad to see me go. They began laying out the stained and lumpy mattress for me each night. Once, I pointed to the servant and said to them, "Let him carry it."

"He is not a servant, he is our son," they said, "don't you recognise your own grandchild?"

Such liars. Such lies they tell me, to make me think I am losing my mind. And they carry my mattress, wearing their supererogatory airs, as if concerned about an old man's welfare. But I know the truth hidden in their hearts. They are poor actors. They think at my age I can no longer separate the genuine from the spurious, the real from the acted, so why bother with elaborate efforts to dissimulate. They will learn, when they are old like me, that untangling the enemy's skein of deceit becomes easier as time goes by.

With your permission, I will give you an example. Sometimes I find it difficult to rise from my chair. So I call the servant: "Chhokra, give me a hand." If his masters are not watching, he comes at once. If they are, he ignores me, naturally, not wanting to cross them. Taking a leaf from their book, he even mocks me. I wonder why they spoil him so much. Good servants are hard to find, yes. But to let him eat with them at table? Sleep in the same room, on a mahogany four-poster? And for me a mattress flung across the floor. What days have come. Kaliyug is indeed upon us. It's a world gone arsy-versy.

After moving to the front room, I could read till late in the night. In the back room they would switch off the lamp; they would say my old eyes were too weak to read past midnight, I must rest, I must not go blind, I must see my grandson grow and marry and have many children. But my eyes were quickly forgotten as they carried out my torn, stained, lumpy mattress. "Whatever pleases you," they said, "we are here on earth to serve our elders." Hah!

In the front room, sometimes I read, but more often, after switching off the light, I go to the window. It has a cement ledge, nice and deep. I like sitting on it. Never for more than a few minutes, though. The cement is hard on my bones, on my shriveled old arse of wrinkled-skin bags. Once, it was firm and smooth and bouncy. Once, it was a bum that both men and women enjoyed gazing after. Not so deep as a well, nor so wide as a church door—just the right size, and without blackheads or pimples. Firm and smooth and bouncy are the precisely operative words. Not bouncy like a Rubenesque young woman's, but enough, so that if you were to slap or squeeze it in a friendly fashion, both of us would feel good.

The cement is cool to the touch. You might think it a blessing in this hot climate. I don't. Not when I am craving warmth. Would you believe me if I told you the ones in the back room chill the ledge with slabs of ice, to harass me?

But the window is convenient for making water at night. The water closet is through the back room; if I stumble past after the others are asleep, cursing and screaming follow me all the way. The neighborhood dogs use the shrubs that grow outside my window. They do not mind me. My water is pure H_2O. Without smell, without color. Nothing much left inside me, neither impurity nor substance.

I used to keep a milk bottle. I'd labeled it Nocturnal Micturition Bottle, so no one might utilize it after me for an incompatible purpose. The ones in the back room said the spelling was wrong, that it should be a-t-i-o-n, not i-t-i-o-n. Their audacity is immedicable. When they were little (and I was young), they used to ask me for meanings, spellings, explanations. I inculcated the dictionary habit in them. Now they question my spelling.

Like you. Yes, don't deny it. I see you reaching for the OED. No need to be sneaky, do it with open pride, it is one of the finest acts. To know the word—its spelling, the very bowels of its meaning, the womb which gave it birth—this is one of the few things in life worth pursuing.

Something strange started to occur after I began keeping the milk bottle. The volume of water I passed increased night by night. One bottle was no longer enough. It would not surprise me if the others were slipping a diuretic into my food or medicine to torment me. Soon there were six milk bottles, duly labeled, standing in a row at the foot of my mattress each night. They were always full before the sun rose. At the crack of dawn, I emptied them down the toilet bowl. I felt a pang of loss. Was there no better use for it?

But one night, a bottle slipped through my fingers while micturating. Wet shards glinted murderously on the floor. For days together, the others went on about it. My hands keep shaking because of this disease that I have. They tell me there is no cure. Should I believe them? The doctor said the same thing, granted. But how long does it take to bribe a doctor, slip him a few rupees?

The first night of the scream, I was not reading or sitting on the window ledge or micturating. I was asleep. Then the scream rose again in the street, the man begged for mercy. There was no mercy. He pleaded with them to be careful with his arm, that it would break. It only goaded them to more cruelty. He screamed again. Still no one awoke. Or they pretended not to.

Why do I have to listen to this, I asked myself. If only I could fall asleep again. So difficult, at my age. Oh, so cruel, finding sleep after long searching, only to have it torn away. And afterward, my scourge of worries and troubles to keep me company. Trishul-brandishing sadhus agitating for a trade union. Vermilion-horned cows sulking, spurning the grass offerings of devotees. The snake charmer's flute enraging the cobra. Stubborn funeral pyres defying the kindling torch.

That night, I shivered and sweated, afraid to rise from between the sofa and the baby grand to look out the window. An upright would have made more sense than a baby grand in this tight space, I thought. Lying on the mattress, I could reach the pedals with my feet and lift my arms to tickle the ivories, joining distantly in the back-room orchestra of wind instruments.

Once upon a time, I took piano lessons. I practiced on this very baby grand. After the second lesson my right-hand fingers were caught in the doors of the piano teacher's lift. Made from a mighty oak, they closed on my hand. I did not scream. When I retrieved my fingers, they were a good bit flattened. I smiled embarrassedly at my fellow passengers in the lift. There was no pain. My first thought was to restore the proper shape. I squeezed and kneaded the crushed fingers, comparing them to the undamaged left hand, to make sure I was achieving the correct contours. I could hear faint crunches. Then I fainted.

If I listen hard, I can hear those crunches of my bone fragments even now when I flex my fingers. Flexed in time and rhythm, they resemble dim castanets—I can do the "Spanish Gypsy Dance" and "Malagueña." These days, the only person who plays the piano is the servant boy. A piano for a servant, denying my mattress the floor space.

The other night a mouse ran over my ankles as I lay on the mattress. That was not unusual; almost every night a mouse brushes my hands or feet. But my feeling comforted by its soft touch was most disconcerting. Happily, the usual disgust and revulsion followed the pleasant sensation. I hated mice as a young man. I prefer to keep hating them as an old one. And the world stays a safer place.

Did you know, mice can nibble human toes without causing pain or waking the sleeper? The saliva of mice induces local anaesthesia and promotes coagulation, curbing excessive bleeding. Their exhaled breath, blown with expert gentleness on the digits in question, is quite soothing till the morning comes.

I tell the ones in the back room about my fears of murine amputation. They don't care. No doubt, they would be pleased if I woke up missing a few fingers or toes. They laugh at me. For them, whatever I say is a laughing matter, worthless rubbish. I am worthless, my thoughts are worthless, my words are worthless.

One day I lost my temper. "Floccinaucinihilipilificators!" I shouted in their general direction. Not comprehending, they laughed again, assuming I had lapsed into the galimatias of senescence.

You seem very sensible, for not laughing. Doubtless, you have also run into a mouse or two. If the feeding habits of *Mus musculus* interest you, I could tell you more. We shall return to it presently.

The screams on the street gave way to groaning. There were muffled thuds, blows landing on unprotected parts. Diaphragm, kidneys, stomach. Groaning again, then violent retching. I trembled, I was sweating, I wished it would end. The air was parched. If only there were thunder and rain. If there was screaming, and also thunder and rain, it might be bearable, I thought.

The mice leave the piano alone. They never run over the keys or romp among the wires and hammers. Still, I keep hoping to hear plinks, plonks, and accidental arpeggios in the night. Expectations created long, long ago by children's stories, I suspect. They have turned out to be lies, like so much else.

Flying cockroaches, for instance. They are not half as terrifying as they were made out to be. The secret is to keep a cool head when the whirring approaches your face. First, arm yourself with a slipper and stand still instead of flailing; then, as its flight pattern becomes predictable, kill it on the wing. Simple. I am proud to do it so well at my age. Flying or nonflying, cockroaches hold no fear for me. No, it is the insidious mouse with its anesthetic saliva and soothing suspiration that I dread when darkness falls.

Another night—not the one of the scream or the soft and pleasing mouse—when, sleepless, I looked out my window, a chanavala was approaching from Chaupatty, from the beach, his neck-slung basket poised before him, ready to serve. I smelled quantities of gram and peanuts in the basket. A tin can with its mixture of chopped onions, coriander, chili powder, pepper and

salt, along with a slice of lemon, added its aroma to the dry, rain-
less air. My mouth was watering.

The ones in the back room have forbidden me all spices. They
say the masala causes a sore throat, tonsillitis, diarrhea; and the
burden of these sicknesses will fall on their heads, they say. So
they give me food insipid as my saliva. And it always has too
much salt or no salt at all. Deliberately. In the beginning it made
me a little cross; I would yell and throw the dinner about. Then I
realized this was what they wanted, to starve me to death. An
abrupt change of tactics was called for. Now, the worse the meal,
the more I praise it. Their disappointed faces, deprived of the
daily spectacle, are a sight. Of course they pretend to be glad that
I am enjoying myself.

And their tricks do not stop at food. Even my medicine they
deprive me of, ignoring the schedule prescribed by the doctor.
Then, when my hands and feet shake violently, they point to
them and say, "See how sick you are? Let us take care of you. Be
good, listen to what we say."

Oh, wickedness. Oh, the tyranny of it. But I will get the better
of them. One of these days they will forget to hide the key to my
wardrobe. Then I will be dressed and gone to my solicitor before
they can say floccinaucinihilipilification.

The silhouette of the chanavala and his neck-slung basket
made me yearn for something. I could not identify the object of
my yearning. He had a small wire-handled brazier to roast the
peanuts. Charcoal glowed in the brazier. I wished I could reach
through the window and feel the warmth of that ember.

The chanavala was accosted by three men. They jostled him
viciously, though at first they greeted him like a friend. They
grabbed handfuls of peanuts and sauntered off. When the chanavala walked under a street lamp, I saw his tears. It might have
been sweat. He lifted a hand to wipe his face. Once, my eyes were
strong. Clear was my vision, piercing my gaze. Never a chance of
confusing tears with sweat.

The men who sleep outside the tall building across the road
were awake, and witnessed the assault. But they did not intercede

on the poor chanavala's behalf. Most of them are very muscular fellows. They went about getting ready for sleep as if nothing were happening. They might have been right. It is hard, at my age, to know if anything is happening.

Watching the muscular fellows is my favorite pastime at the midnight hour. There is always laughing and joking as they un-roll their sleeping bundles, strip down to their underpants, and take turns to use the tap in the alley beside the building. Pinching and slapping, pushing and shoving, their playful preparation for bed continues. Some share bedding with a friend, cuddling under a threadbare cloth, hugging and comforting. I know what it is like, the yearning for comfort. Sometimes a woman appears. She spends a little time with each of them, then disappears.

Unlike the building I live in, the one across the road includes many amenities: private nursing home, accountant's office, horo-scope and astrology service, furniture store, restaurant, auto shop. Lorries with various gods and slogans painted on their sides ar-rive daily at the building. The muscular men load or unload fur-niture and auto parts during the day. They are always in high spirits as they work.

Sometimes the prime minister visits from the capital to consult the astrologer about a favorable time for introducing new legisla-tion, or an auspicious month for holding general elections. Then the police cordon off the area; no one passes in or out of the build-ing. There are long traffic jams. People who want to obtain their rations, take children to school, give birth, go to the hospital, or see the latest film have to wait till the prime minister has finished with the nation's business.

The men who own the lorries also beseech the astrologer for propitious hours. The muscular men do not quibble about this. On the contrary, they are grateful: when the business was owned by unbelievers who did not take necessary precautions, a huge crate slipped and killed one of their comrades.

If the stars forbid the loading of lorries, the muscular men sit and watch the traffic. Once, on just such an idle day, a beggar stole a bun from the restaurant's front counter display. The waiters gave chase, caught him, and slapped him around till the muscular men rescued him. Then a policeman ran up to deliver the obligatory law-enforcement blows. The sun was very bright and hot. I was not squeamish about watching. I am not frightened of physical pain inflicted on others. Especially if it is in moderation. And there was nothing excessive about this action. Not like the police in that very backward northeastern state, poking rusty bicycle spokes in suspected criminals' eyes, then adding a dash of sulfuric acid.

The waiters took back the mangled bun. The muscular men produced a coin. They insisted that the beggar return to the restaurant and purchase the comestible with dignity. With tender concern they stood round him to watch him eat it.

But the muscular men never go to the rescue of the screamer. I do not understand it. Nor do I understand, given my unsqueamish nature, why I cannot endure the screaming anymore, the cries that occur at intervals every night, after midnight. I am shivering, my sweat feels cold, my knees ache and my brow is feverish, I am running out of things like mice, cockroaches, chanavalas to occupy my mind, the scream and pain keep displacing them. The neighbor's dog begins to bark.

Brownie begins to bark. Brownie is the brother of a dog called Lucky, who died of rabies. In the back room they are fond of dogs, but blame me for their not being able to keep one. I would trip over the dog, they say, I would trip and fall and break my bones, and the burden of my broken bones would land squarely on their unprotected heads, they say.

Sometimes, they borrow Brownie from next door, to play with him and feed him the bones they save at mealtimes. Nowadays, they won't let me suck the marrowbones. They snatch them from my plate for Brownie. Even my marrow spoon has been hidden away. The reason? A tiny splinter might choke me, they say, their excuses ever ready for the eyes and ears of the world. They try to teach Brownie to shake hands. The crotch-sniffing cur is not interested. He sticks his snout in my groin and knocks my onions around, like a performing seal. Day by day, they hang lower and lower. Great care must be taken every time I sit. Oh, to have again a scrotum tight as a fresh fig. The indignities of old age. Shrinking cucumber, and enlarging onions. That's fate. That's the way the ball bounces.

What destiny. Everything is my fault, according to the ones in the back room. They are so brave when it comes to subjugating an old man. No more nonsense about the scream, they warn me, it is all my imagination. Every day they tell me I have lost my mind, my memory, my sense of reality.

But wait. You be the judge. You weigh the evidence and form your opinion. Listen carefully to my words. Regard the concinnity of my phrasing. Observe the narrative coherence and the precise depiction of my pathetic state. Does this sound like a crazy man's story? Does it?

I implore you, plead my case with the ones in the back room. It is no more and no less than your duty. Apathy is a sin. This great age did not come upon me without teaching me virtue and vice. I speak the truth, I keep my promises. I am kind to the young and helpless. The young, I find, are seldom helpless.

Apathy is a sin. And yet, not one of them goes to help the screamer. How they can bear to sleep through it, night after night, I don't know. But what heroes they were, that morning, when we found a harmless drunkard under the stairs. He was sleeping like a baby, clutching to his stomach a khaki cloth bag. There were three hubcaps in the bag. Stolen, everyone proclaimed at once. They shook him awake. Neighbors came to look. They asked him questions. He did not wish to answer. They kicked the desire into him. When he answered, they could not understand his thick-tongued mumbles. But they have seen too many movies, so they kicked him again. Blubbering, he explained he was a mechanic, and produced a screwdriver from his pocket as evidence. The murder weapon, they shouted, and snatched it from him. Someone suggested he might be dangerous. So one of them got some string. It was the flat kind, like a thin ribbon, with print on it: Asoomal Sweets, Made Fresh Daily, it read. They tied him with it, trussed him like a stuffed bird.

Oh, what heroes. Not one dares to go out and look. The screams keep coming. I weep, I pray, but the screams do not stop. I sleep with two pillows. One under my aching head, the other between my thighs. Some days I awake to an audience towering over my mattress and me. All the back-room heroes, standing there and laughing, pointing at the pillow between my withered thighs. I am silent then. I know the time will come when they, too, seek comfort in ways that seem laughable to others.

When the screams drive me over the edge of despair, when I am tired of weeping and praying, then I remove the pillow between my thighs and press it over my ears. Now the scream-ing stops.

In the morning I am neglected as usual while the back room comes to life. I open the curtain and look out. I scratch my pen-dent onions. Men go about their business. The sun is hot already. There is shame and fatigue on their faces. Lately, I have begun to see this shame and fatigue everywhere. The ones in the back room also wear it.

The dust is thicker today on the furniture. I glance in the cold, pitiless mirror. The reflection takes me by surprise: now I know with certainty—if, perchance, the others have not yet heard the scream, the time is not far off. Soon it will rob them of their rest. Their day will come. Their night will come. Poor creatures. My anger is melting. All will be forgiven.

The air is still dry, we wait for rain. The beggars have gone on strike. The fields are sere, the fishnets empty. The blackmarket-eers have begun to hoard. People are filling the temples. The flies are dropping like men.

Indestructibility of Rights

Olja Knezevic
THE CLASSROOM

It's been a long break for me. The last time I looked through the windows of my classroom, there was nothing there, outside. I could only see my face reflected in the windowpane, and when I did, a childish thought came over me that if I were a house pet, I'd be an old cat called Frosty. I decided to ask for sick leave until spring.

I teach English Language, Intensive Course II, at the Institute for Foreign Languages; these are the classes for adults, held in the rented classrooms on the ground floor of the Faculty of Economics building. I don't know why it is called Intensive Course II, why this II? I myself teach different levels here, not the beginners, I skip the beginners, I hand them to my colleagues and I take them when they are capable of communication. I like to communicate. And today I have Level 6—Conversation. Soon, I will meet my new students.

In the second half of last November, dampened down by the mean drizzle, my friends said we needed to find an indoor space to gather and complain.

"Life is hard, love is a thief, physical pain the king, fun times laced with guilt . . ." We'd gather and start like this, but we'd quickly move on, our spirits flickering like a candle flame. Sometimes, in the sapphire, slow-falling nights, we'd laugh so much that we had to lean onto the cars parked on the pavements and cross our legs to hold the urine in. The young people who also met at that corner to proceed toward the town center and *korzo*

would stare and cross themselves thrice, grateful they were not
our children. We must have appeared drunk or worse. But autumn came and we could not hang around the street corners any
longer, stand and smoke in front of the grilled entrance to the
Inpek bakery; we were middle-aged, veins swollen with the slow
blood, our bones already injured, bitten by too many power cuts,
hand-washed diapers, cement floors. At the bars, cafés, latter-day
taverns, we had to spend money and mingle with others, many of
whom we didn't want to meet there, our children included. At
home, our families lurked, ready to scorn every word, memory or
plan; they always had better plans for us in mind, but that fact
had settled as one of the quite acceptable aspects of life: we had
plans for them, too. Plans—such a sad, abstract noun.

So I suggested we could use my classroom. As I pointed out, I
like communication. That's why I didn't want my group of
friends to be defeated by the lack of indoor space in the grisly
months from November through March when Podgorica is either soaked up in rain or frozen dead by the north wind.

The very next evening, we met in front of my classroom and I
unlocked it. Mirna had brought along a Thermos filled with coffee, another one with tea, paper cups and napkins.

"Is it only coffee and tea, then?" Rade asked her. "You haven't
by any chance mixed in some fire drink or another?" Rade never
married and he could have had a harem. I, too, had been in love
with him, long ago. He didn't age as well as I'd expected him to,
having been a dark-haired, olive-skinned young athlete once.
Now, from under the woollen blazer that he always wore from
autumn till summer, I could conjure up a body of an old nag. I
don't know how he looked in summer. Every summer, I went to
my husband's village of origin, where I gazed at the stars wrapped
in a blanket, missing my friends from the bakery's corner.

"Oh no, I haven't. Only coffee and tea this time," Mirna
blushed while answering Rade's question, as if ashamed for not
having been different, a little crazy for us and not the same
mumsy type she was at home.

For the following meeting, alcohol was smuggled in. From

then on, it was sometimes poured into tea, sometimes packed in wine bottles, depending on who had brought it. Some of us couldn't openly turn into disobeying teenagers when preparing for these gatherings; at the least, we'd be used as a household joke. But for Mirna, it would even be risky; she'd be spied on, confronted, insulted. Maybe even hit, kicked, I don't know, but it would surely mean she could no longer join us.

When I was young I was beautiful, but weren't we all? I never made use of it though, and I'm sorry now of course, but what I want to say is that maybe the main reason why I never made any use of my sparkly eyes and my high-bowed lips was that Mirna was my best friend. Mirna was magnetic. Most of her life she looked as if she were dying of a broken heart and people were drawn to her only to melt in her presence. Her face had an imprecise color, as if it had constantly been sprayed on with pollen, but it attracted the sun rays and she used to tan easily. Everything about her was long and melancholic and so different from the hives of the energetic, ever-moving bee girls around her. Everywhere we went she had someone fall in love with her for eternity. How do you cope with a best friend like that? You learn to love the side of her which loathed herself.

We met once a week in my classroom, which quickly became our classroom. At the street corner, we used to see each other almost every evening. But this new meeting point was farther away from the quarters where we all lived and so we decided to gather indoors on Tuesdays and if we went out for a walk or to the grocery store that was open late and encountered each other in the street on other days, well then, more blessings! We grew up in those same quarters and went to the local elementary school together. About two decades of life had scattered us apart until one day we all felt we suddenly had more time for ourselves again and, also, that we hadn't changed much; the changes had only been skin-deep. The music we liked was still the same—Oh, Delilah! Oh, Carol! We still found the same odd things funny and we instinctively went to the Inpek bakery's corner and stood there, waiting for someone. And someone came, we all did, half a dozen of us, more or less.

We were warm in my classroom. Outside, through its windows, none of which were broken or badly installed because I was known as Mrs. Stalin, we could see the bare, skinny trees with branches askew under the wind and rain, as if in surrender to the weather. We would arrange four desks to form a square and we'd place chairs around it. We felt safe and started communicating differently. Indoors, things were more obvious. Some of us were the quiet drinkers, smokers and listeners; others were the speakers, patrons, teasers. At first, we simply laughed a lot and raised paper cups in toasts for freedom, friendship, survival. Then, we tackled politics. And then, Rade held Mirna's hand for two hours. I realized: it was she he had loved all those years.

Mirna's fingers were still long and musical but instead of the piano concerts, she had to warm them up to fight the bouts of arthritic pain. And if she still looked as though she were dying of a broken heart, well, after a certain age it ceases to be attractive.

But Rade had known her in the days of her glory, as I'd known him. For him, she remained the same unusual enchantress she once had been. There was no end to that. And she talked about her marriage, her mean husband and the grown-up children who blamed her for everything because their father had always been frightening while Mirna was forever changing, trying to adapt, to become better, less provocative, more understanding, everything, but it was never enough and the final perception, or verdict, was that she was unstable. I knew this and accommodated her many times when she tried to run away and start over. Rade had no idea and now he found out and his manhood was resurrected. Oh well, good luck.

"My sister wanted to join in," I informed my friends one day, "but I told her it would harm the balance of the group somehow, don't you think?"

"Which sister?" Mirna asked.

"Ana," I said, and then added, "Ten years my junior," for those who didn't know.

"Ah, she's too happy for this group. Always has been." Mirna smiled.

"That's what I thought," I said. "The youngest sibling. The lucky one."

"But it is the firstborn that's usually considered lucky," Petar observed, blushing as always when he spoke. "The leader, they say. Ask my brother. I wouldn't let him join in either."

"They are not lucky, the firstborns," Rade said. "They become strong through the hardships, most are fucked up by their parents. Those who survive learn to fight everyone else."

"Speaking from experience?" I asked even though I knew the answer; any answer on Rade, who was finally demystified down to his nucleus for me. He nodded.

Rade had escaped his grim household first to become a boxing champion in Yugoslavia and then farther away, to make it abroad, in the West. He had disappeared after high school and came back years later, followed by the rumors that, abroad, in Munich and Düsseldorf, he had been living with wealthy older women. When he came back, we watched him drive the latest model of Mercedes Cabriolet slowly up and down the one boulevard in town. Music was heard from his car and long, brown cigarettes were held in his hand, which forever hung down outside the car's door, and we all wondered what he was thinking about and how he regarded us now, were we boring and small and ignorant? We knew we were poor and he wasn't, not anymore. He cruised in that car for a year or so and then, as if he'd done his research mission, he opened the first Italian restaurant in town and all the girls started drinking innumerable espressos and cappuccinos in there, waiting for him to come in, which he did, in those silly hours of early afternoons, carrying his sunglasses and newspapers. Always alone.

It is my firm belief that the devil enters each one of us during

our lifetimes and sometimes the devil wins and stays and sometimes we manage to shake him off. One afternoon long ago, the
devil entered me and I stayed and drank more than an acceptable
dose of caffeine in Rade's restaurant until I saw everybody off
and Rade joined me and, after some compulsory politeness, drove
me to his place. There, he made me do everything he wanted and
I discovered that love had turned me into a horse performer: en-
durable and big-mouthed, showy and four-legged. I wore a slim
cross on my necklace. "A tiny cross for a tiny communist," he
said, playing with my necklace afterward, the only thing he ever
said that bore an immediate connection with me. Other than that,
he was so distant that I labeled him mysterious and kept on hoping for years. Late at nights, while my parents were sleeping, I'd
sneak out and walk to his building and throw pebbles at his lit-up
window or knock on his door and I would slide a love note—or,
rather, an availability note—through the thin rectangle of nothingness between the closed door and the concrete floor and I'd sit
for the longest time on his doormat, which said Willkommen to
someone, but never again to me, curled there in the streams of
stomachache.

On the verge of becoming a spinster, I froze my heart and got
married to a man I'd known since we started emptying the gar-
bage cans outside and into the newly arranged street containers,
when we would steal some time to stay around the block and
practice French kissing with the local boys. Every woman has her
underdog and mine likes drinking beer, and as long as there's
beer in the fridge, I shouldn't really sound bitter about my life.

But I knew now, because my contact in the State Security had
informed me, that Rade had been contacted as well while he
was abroad, and persuaded to work for the government of
Yugoslavia and blend himself among the ex-pat community in
Germany, report back on what they had been up to, whether
they'd been planning and financing an anti-government activity
while singing along to the Chetnik or Ustasha songs. Soon, it
became clear that Rade had not been the type to blend into
something involuntarily and spy on it. He'd cut the connections

and moved on, outside the safety net of the contacts from his compatriots, to make money the only way he could: fighting ageing boxers and seducing older women.

"What about us, the middle ones?" I went on. "We have the worst reputation. Unloved, neglected, rushed over . . ." I saw Mirna pour herself more drink.

"I hear you," Petar raised his cup. "Here's to the middle children!"

"Seems the best thing to be is an only child," I concluded and Rade bit at it.

"Like Mirna," he said, turning his eyes full of adoration to her. He tried to take her hand but she pulled it back to her lap and stared down at it. One tear fell on the back of her palm, freckled and blue with the cords of veins.

"Mirna?" Rade whispered. "What's wrong?"

"Subject change, subject change!" I twittered.

But then he remembered. In a second, his smile waned and he lowered his head.

My eyes welled up. I tear easily. I took two cigarettes from someone's box, lit them up and tried to place one between Mirna's fingers. She pushed my hand gently and shook her head. Tears sneaked off her. Dara, our quiet friend, responsible for the delicious bakes on our desks, snatched that cigarette from me and smoked half of it in one draw. We waited in silence and Rade spoke first. "I'm sorry, love," he said to Mirna. "It was so long ago. I forgot . . ."

Mirna had a brother once. He had been the firstborn. He took care of her, took her to school every day and soon my parents trusted him enough to put me under his care as well. Slaven, Mirna's brother, always crossed the street on the pedestrian crossings, holding Mirna's and my hands and carrying our snack money and our sandwiches wrapped in foil. He asked about my homework and checked my times tables on the way to school. He was five years older than we were; a perfect, responsible boy.

One day after school, Mirna and I were waiting for Slaven in
the school park, hula hoops spinning around our waists. Some
older boys approached us and said something like they could tell
by the swaying of Mirna's hips that she would be great for sex.
We immediately stopped playing and sat on a bench, intuitive
about the danger of the situation when the word "sex" was mentioned. I remember staring down at our two identical pairs of
small feet, neatly packed into the white socks and black, lac-
quered shoes, not quite touching the dry earth beneath the bench.
Suddenly, Mirna's feet were swooped up in the air; two boys had
lifted her up and carried her away while she was trying to wrig-
gle out. I screamed and ran. I ran to the nearest kiosk; it was
closed and I hid behind it. I peeked and saw the boys take Mirna's
knickers off and grab her crotch, pushing her around. I saw
Slaven running to them, shouting his head off in the stillness of
the late afternoon. The boys, there were four or five of them, let
go of Mirna and got into a fight with Slaven. Soon, they threw
him on the ground and hit him in the head with their feet and the
stones they'd picked up. I ran home. Mirna never found out I had
seen it all and later she told me that, after the boys had scattered,
Slaven said to her: "Don't tell Mum and Dad about this, let's go
buy some ice cream," and off they went. In a nearby shop, Slaven
had bought some ice cream for Mirna and asked for some ice for
his head. Two days later, he died of a brain hematoma. Mirna was
forced to tell her parents what had happened in the school park
and was later mercilessly interrogated in the police station. My
parents paced our flat and whispered a lot in those days and decided I was too young to testify and that I didn't remember anything. One of the gang boys was a son of a high-ranked
government official. Nothing ever happened to any of them.
Mirna was the only one left to carry the blame. I think that was
when I realized that the worst enemy and the best friend that one
could have was the State.

Rade pushed his chair back. It made an unpleasant, screeching
sound against the floor. He got up and went to the windows.

"Bastards," he hissed, looking out into the night. "Bastards, bastards. Some more equal than the others, huh? I know who it was. He's still a bastard." The rest of us looked in his direction and through the windows, letting Mirna cry into her chest.

Rade turned back. "Mirna!" he said in a loud voice that escaped from his throat and shuffled the air like an upset ghost. "Mirna!" he walked to her. "You must stop blaming yourself. Please, love," he knelt down by her chair. "It's not too late. We'll make the bastard pay. I'll do it. I know where he lives. I'll beat the shit out of him and make sure he knows why. I'll make him apologize!"

Mirna slowly raised her head and gave Rade a sideways look of resentment.

"What nonsense," she said in a voice so coarse that I pressed my palms onto my mouth in order not to gasp in terror. "Excuse me," she whispered, getting up and turning away from Rade, who was still kneeling, his hands clasped as in prayer. "I really have to go now. It's been a while . . ." and she left us wondering what had been a while, but now I suppose it had simply been a while for each of us since anything happened. It had been forever.

I called her every day and we talked on the phone, circling around the source of pain. We knitted on and on about the things that were "just fine" until the phone receivers burned at our earlobes. I knew she wasn't going to come to the classroom on the following Tuesday, she was too fragile, insecure. But another Tuesday came and Rade entered, his eyes ablaze, no hat on his crazy hair, no blazer, only a short leather jacket, unzipped over a shirt with its top buttons undone. The years he had incinerated in a week! The devil! He had almost tricked me once and now he was back, ready to ruin Mirna, with his promises made of dust if she just forgave herself and stopped punishing herself and left her husband and her home and—and—what? Ran away with him?!

"Hello, rebel," I smiled at him. The rest of us had already gone over Mirna needing some time away from us, our mouths now full of Dara's delicacies.

"You think so?" Rade asked. He just stood there, above me. Did he remember me? Did he remember how I had once humiliated myself?

"Do I think so—what?" I asked. "That you're a rebel? Of course you are, look at you. Without a cause."

"What does it take for you people to wake up?" he said. "What would be the cause? When would you stop pushing the truth away by turning it into another joke?"

"And do what?" I asked him from my chair. "Kick some ass and then what? Leave our country, look for another homeland and have some peace there, for peace comes dropping slow. As you had done and then came back, among us, to die here, an old rebel without a cause."

"I'll give you a cause," he bent down and spoke into my face.

I laughed. "I'm not your enemy," I said, wanting to kiss him like a serpent.

"One can never be sure about you," he straightened up. "People say . . ." he paused.

"Oh, don't stop now," I laughed. "I can take it. What do they say?"

"I guess I should keep you close to me," he replied, drew up a chair and sat down. "I like that 'peace comes dropping slow' line," he said. "But that's a . . . a metaphor, is that right, Mrs. Teacher? For that kind of peace one can surely achieve only in one's head, right? And have you any peace in there?" he asked me and knocked on my skull with his forefinger. I felt thirty years younger and not in a good way.

"Why are you asking?" I said. "You, who had spied on our people in Germany, then came back to play a restaurant owner."

"Precisely because of that," Rade replied. "Well, I'm sick of them, sick of the same stories repeating themselves."

I was quiet, determined to let somebody else start another topic.

"What do you intend to do?" Petar asked Rade. "I'll help you with your plan. I have nephews . . ."

"Oh, this is a one on one," Rade went on. "That bastard who violated Mirna is going to pay for the whole system of lies and spies," and he winked at me. He rubbed his palms together and, sure of the success of his plan, stuffed a whole square of Dara's gibanica into his mouth. So, he remembered our night together. He believed that he still held me under that spell.

Rade was so stupid. I hated myself for having loved him once. The men who don't marry . . . remain stuck in a tug-of-war; they never predict that the other side can suddenly decide it was so useless, time to drop the rope and then the old farts fall back, on their backsides. They need to fall deep to learn, if they ever learn.

It's almost 5 p.m. I hear the voices of students gathering at the top of the long hallway which leads to my classroom. Most of them will have another cigarette there and mock themselves for their late ambition to learn a foreign language. When they come into my classroom, I'll assure them this was the best thing they could do for themselves.

I take out a small mirror and a lipstick the color of raw calf's meat. Time to change the shade. I was never like Mirna, who could put some Vaseline on her lips and appear made-up for the night out. I am neutral-looking enough and can afford some pink or orange on my lips. It's not like I should punish myself and voluntarily wilt away. I clasp the rouge and mirror set shut and feel my chest rise.

If I hadn't been the one to warn the State Security about Rade losing his mind, they would have found out anyway; they had never stopped tapping his phone. He had been one of us and then defected. The worst kind. They would've found out and they would have connected the dots and realized that I'd been there, at the source of his conspiracy, and I hadn't informed them. Well, I had set my priorities straight long ago.

However, I must say that my stomach sank when I read the statement from his lawyer in the opposition newspapers. Rade had been arrested in his restaurant, the lawyer claimed, then taken, kept and tortured in *betonjerka,* the solitary, bare, cold and wet cement cell, for forty-eight hours. Our official newspaper claimed that, on the contrary, he had been kept in the investigation cell and treated with procedural fairness, but, due to his age and a previous health condition, he had developed pneumonia. Not true, the lawyer replied the next day; Rade hadn't developed pneumonia. Both his kidneys stopped functioning because of the repeated beatings and now he was dying. He wasn't dying, the official newspaper reacted, and provided the statement from Rade's brother that Rade was doing fine; the brother had visited him in the prison hospital. Rade even regretted the criminal activity against the prominent government members, the brother was quoted saying. The brother, as far as I knew, was an incurable alcoholic. After this, the oppositional newspaper ran the photograph of Rade, which had somehow leaked from the prison hospital. He lay broken, unconscious and unrecognizable. Yes, he was dying. He had to die.

Mirna called me and she talked openly about Rade in front of her husband. "He loved me," she cried on the phone. I could hear her husband insulting her, probably sitting on a sofa behind her, digesting his stuffed cabbage rolls, and she would tell him to shut up in a new, firm voice. I even felt I'd done something good for Mirna; she had finally stood up to her husband.

"Calm down, Mirna," I told her. "He had it coming to him for some time. He was always problematic. Why had he turned to boxing in the first place? All that aggression . . ."

"What aggression, what aggression?" Mirna shouted. "He was so sweet. So rare," and she broke into sobs. "He'll be a ruin if they ever let him out of that prison."

They didn't have to. While we were on the phone, Rade was already dead, but the press was kept well under control. Before the paragraph about his death was printed in the corner of the black chronicle section, the media sector of the government had prepared a parade of good, little news to enlighten the upcoming holidays: the new, much-needed roads connecting the mountain villages were just about to open; there was going to be no restriction of electricity until January 15—let the lights glare on the happy New Year . . .

The day before New Year's Eve, Mirna dropped her plastic bags full of groceries in the middle of the swinging bridge and jumped off it into the river, the river which is dangerous enough to swim in even during summer, with its unexpected rocks and whirls, and its cold, cold water. I cried for her alone in this classroom one whole night until dawn. Once again I had witnessed how arrogance could suppress wisdom and experience and I wept for the imperfection of the human race. Some people may be clever and great to have as friends but they will never learn, will they, that their State is their fate and no matter how much you try to lead them into the corner where they could peacefully organize their lives, they push you away and choose to see things from an angle as immature and unstable as sitting on the top branches of a birch tree when you're already middle-aged.

The classroom fills up to the last chair on the first day of the term. Every spring, when the evenings last long, until the sunrise, never quite turning into night, people have hopes and dreams again. They unexpectedly meet their old friends they thought were dead and say: "Let's do something together."

I let the students chat for a while. When I feel it's time, I say in English: "Hello and welcome to my favorite level—conversation. Before you all tell us something interesting about yourselves, let me warn you that you have come to my classroom to learn English, not to plot against the government."

I always warn them; I warn every group. It's useless; after a couple of lessons, they all begin to talk about politics and blame our government for everything. This time too, the wave of laughter shakes the room and I know there soon will be plenty of material for me to report on to the authorities. Through the open windows, their laughter spills outside like a flood, where it scares the birds who sit in the treetops and are very easily frightened. They fly away.

Henning Mankell
SOFIA

About fifteen years ago a little girl was sitting in a rusty wheelchair outside the central hospital of Maputo, the capital of Mozambique. The girl had no legs and she was perhaps ten years old. When I passed I stopped and exchanged a few words with her. I still do not know why. Although she almost whispered I understood that her name was Sofia.

Today, many years later, Sofia is one of my closest and dearest friends. No one has taught as much as she about the conditions of being human. Nor has anyone taught me more about poor people's unprecedented power of resistance. Those who are forced to survive at the bottom of society in a world we all share and inhabit; so unjust, brutal and unnecessary.

That last word is very important. The unnecessary. Thus, one of the hardest things about our day and age is that so much suffering is unnecessary. While writing this sentence yet another child dies unnecessarily of malaria. At the same time, millions of children will not be able to read this, for them these words will be nothing more than mysterious signs for which they simply do not have the knowledge to understand. Being a writer as I am, that is perhaps the biggest disgrace today; in the year 2008 millions and millions of children are forced to live a life where they are denied the fundamental human right to learn how to read and write.

However, back to the girl in the wheelchair.

What happened to Sofia was that she and her sister were running along a small road close to the village where she lived with her mother and her other siblings. It was early morning, the mist above the fields, the sun just rising above the horizon. Sofia knew very well that she and her sister should keep to the road. There was something she called "earth crocodiles" buried in the ground by the side of the road and they could snap at you.

The girls were running. And children play, as it is their given right. And they forget, which is also their given right.

Looking back, it is possible to reconstruct the events that followed in a very precise way.

With her right foot Sofia accidentally stepped by the side of the road. She put her foot on a land mine. However, the mine had been placed in the ground in such a manner that the major part of the explosion that followed was directed at her sister Maria, who died instantly. Sofia was brought to the hospital, drenched in her own blood.

I have since then spoken to the doctor who took care of Sofia when she arrived at the hospital.

He said:

I will now tell you something that no doctor ever should. Nevertheless, I will do it so you will fully comprehend the remarkable strength of this young girl.

He said:

Since she was so seriously damaged, we were hoping that Sofia would die along with her sister. Her legs torn apart, her chest blown to pieces, everything.

Yet Sofia survived. She had greater strength than the entire military industrial complex which tried to take her life, which continues to hold the poor hostage, the poor who cannot defend themselves on equal terms. Within her body and mind Sofia carried with her the strong will to resist of the poor people of the world.

And she overcame. She survived.

Today, Sofia has two children. She is a very good seamstress, she studies and she wants to become a teacher. But more than this she has become a symbol all around the world for the resistance against the usage of land mines. For many young people she has become a heroine.

And she is a heroine for me as well.

If I should mention one moment when I experienced profound happiness in my life, it was probably the time I saw Sofia walk with her new artificial legs. At that very moment I also claimed what would later be my, as well as Sofia's, motto in life:

"It is never too late! Everything is still possible!"

At the time of the accident, Sofia was illiterate. Now she is able to write down her own experiences, her understandings and her dreams. Furthermore, she can write down what she is against.

Her two children are well cared for, her thoughts about the future are filled with hope.

Nevertheless, there are moments when I see her turn away, leaning against her crutches. Moments when she does not want to be part of what is going on.

It is when people around her dance. To a European woman that might not be such a big a deal. But to an African woman? I completely understand.

Once her life was blown apart. But she resisted, she fought back. Nothing could defeat her.

What Sofia brings me is hope, hope for the future. Her indomitable spirit cannot be broken.

THE UNIVERSAL DECLARATION
OF HUMAN RIGHTS

ARTICLE 1

All human beings are born free and equal in dignity and rights. They are endowed with reason and conscience and should act toward one another in a spirit of brotherhood.

ARTICLE 2

Everyone is entitled to all the rights and freedoms set forth in this Declaration, without distinction of any kind, such as race, color, sex, language, religion, political or other opinion, national or social origin, property, birth or other status. Furthermore, no distinction shall be made on the basis of the political, jurisdictional or international status of the country or territory to which a person belongs, whether it be independent, trust, non-self-governing or under any other limitation of sovereignty.

ARTICLE 3

Everyone has the right to life, liberty and security of person.

ARTICLE 4

No one shall be held in slavery or servitude; slavery and the slave trade shall be prohibited in all their forms.

ARTICLE 5

No one shall be subjected to torture or to cruel, inhuman or degrading treatment or punishment.

ARTICLE 6

Everyone has the right to recognition everywhere as a person before the law.

ARTICLE 7

All are equal before the law and are entitled without any discrimination to equal protection of the law. All are entitled to equal protection against any discrimination in violation of this Declaration and against any incitement to such discrimination.

ARTICLE 8

Everyone has the right to an effective remedy by the competent national tribunals for acts violating the fundamental rights granted him by the constitution or by law.

ARTICLE 9

No one shall be subjected to arbitrary arrest, detention or exile.

ARTICLE 10

Everyone is entitled in full equality to a fair and public hearing by an independent and impartial tribunal, in the determination of his rights and obligations and of any criminal charge against him.

ARTICLE 11

(1) Everyone charged with a penal offense has the right to be presumed innocent until proved guilty according to law in a public trial at which he has had all the guarantees necessary for his defense.

(2) No one shall be held guilty of any penal offense on account of any act or omission which did not constitute a penal offense, under national or international law, at the time when it was committed. Nor shall a heavier penalty be imposed than the one that was applicable at the time the penal offense was committed.

ARTICLE 12

No one shall be subjected to arbitrary interference with his privacy, family, home or correspondence, nor to attacks upon his honor and reputation. Everyone has the right to the protection of the law against such interference or attacks.

ARTICLE 13

(1) Everyone has the right to freedom of movement and residence within the borders of each state.

(2) Everyone has the right to leave any country, including his own, and to return to his country.

ARTICLE 14

(1) Everyone has the right to seek and to enjoy in other countries asylum from persecution.

(2) This right may not be invoked in the case of prosecutions genuinely arising from non-political crimes or from acts contrary to the purposes and principles of the United Nations.

ARTICLE 15

(1) Everyone has the right to a nationality.

(2) No one shall be arbitrarily deprived of his nationality nor denied the right to change his nationality.

ARTICLE 16

(1) Men and women of full age, without any limitation due to race, nationality or religion, have the right to marry and to found a family. They are entitled to equal rights as to marriage, during marriage and at its dissolution.

(2) Marriage shall be entered into only with the free and full consent of the intending spouses.

(3) The family is the natural and fundamental group unit of society and is entitled to protection by society and the State.

ARTICLE 17

Everyone has the right to own property alone as well as in association with others; no one shall be arbitrarily deprived of his property.

ARTICLE 18

Everyone has the right to freedom of thought, conscience and religion; this right includes freedom to change his religion or belief, and freedom, either alone or in community with others and in public or private, to manifest his religion or belief in teaching, practice, worship and observance.

ARTICLE 19

Everyone has the right to freedom of opinion and expression; this right includes freedom to hold opinions without interference and to seek, receive and impart information and ideas through any media and regardless of frontiers.

ARTICLE 20

(1) Everyone has the right to freedom of peaceful assembly and association.

(2) No one may be compelled to belong to an association.

ARTICLE 21

(1) Everyone has the right to take part in the government of his country, directly or through freely chosen representatives.

(2) Everyone has the right of equal access to public service in his country.

(3) The will of the people shall be the basis of the authority of government; this will shall be expressed in periodic and genuine elections which shall be by universal and equal suffrage and shall be held by secret vote or by equivalent free voting procedures.

ARTICLE 22

Everyone, as a member of society, has the right to realize the economic, social and cultural rights indispensable to their dignity.

ARTICLE 23

(1) Everyone has the right to work, to free choice of employ-

ment, to just and favorable conditions of work and to protection against unemployment.

(2) Everyone, without any discrimination, has the right to equal pay for equal work.

(3) Everyone who works has the right to just and favorable remuneration ensuring for himself and his family an existence worthy of human dignity, and supplemented, if necessary, by other means of social protection.

(4) Everyone has the right to form and to join trade unions for the protection of his interests.

ARTICLE 24

Everyone has the right to rest and leisure, including reasonable limitation of working hours and periodic holidays with pay.

ARTICLE 25

(1) Everyone has the right to a standard of living adequate for the health and well-being of himself and of his family, including food, clothing, housing and medical care and necessary social services, and the right to security in the event of unemployment, sickness, disability, widowhood, old age or other lack of livelihood in circumstances beyond his control.

(2) Motherhood and childhood are entitled to special care and assistance. All children, whether born in or out of wedlock, shall enjoy the same social protection.

ARTICLE 26

(1) Everyone has the right to education. Education shall be free, at least in the elementary and fundamental stages. Elementary education shall be compulsory. Technical and professional education shall be made generally available and higher education shall be equally accessible to all on the basis of merit.

(2) Education shall be directed to the full development of the human personality and to the strengthening of respect for human rights and fundamental freedoms. It shall promote understanding, tolerance and friendship among all nations,

racial or religious groups, and shall further the activities of the United Nations for the maintenance of peace.

(3) Parents have a prior right to choose the kind of education that shall be given to their children.

ARTICLE 27

(1) Everyone has the right freely to participate in the cultural life of the community, to enjoy the arts and to share in scientific advancement and its benefits.

(2) Everyone has the right to the protection of the moral and material interests resulting from any scientific, literary or artistic production of which he is the author.

ARTICLE 28

Everyone is entitled to a social and international order in which the rights and freedoms set forth in this Declaration can be fully realized.

ARTICLE 29

(1) Everyone has duties to the community in which alone the free and full development of his personality is possible.

(2) In the exercise of his rights and freedoms, everyone shall be subject only to such limitations as are determined by law solely for the purpose of securing due recognition and respect for the rights and freedoms of others and of meeting the just requirements of morality, public order and the general welfare in a democratic society.

(3) These rights and freedoms may in no case be exercised contrary to the purposes and principles of the United Nations.

ARTICLE 30

Nothing in this Declaration may be interpreted as implying for any State, group or person any right to engage in any activity or to perform any act aimed at the destruction of any of the rights and freedoms set forth herein.

CONTRIBUTORS

Chimamanda Ngozi Adichie was born in Nigeria in 1977. Her first novel, *Purple Hibiscus,* won the Commonwealth Writers' Prize and was also shortlisted for the Orange Prize for Fiction. *Half of a Yellow Sun,* set before and during the Biafran War, won the Orange Prize in 2007. She received the O. Henry Prize in 2003, and divides her time between the United States and Nigeria.

Mohammed Naseehu Ali, a native of Ghana, is a writer and musician. He has published fiction and essays in *The New Yorker* and the *New York Times,* among many other journals. His first book, *The Prophet of Zongo Street,* was published in 2006. He lives in Brooklyn, New York.

Gabriella Ambrosio lives in Rome. A former journalist, her first novel, *Prima di lasciarsi (Before We Say Goodbye),* about a suicide bombing in Jerusalem, was published both in Arabic and Hebrew in 2008 and has since been adopted by schools, colleges and human rights organizations working in the region. The novel will be published in English in 2010.

Kate Atkinson was born in York and now lives in Edinburgh. Her first novel, *Behind the Scenes at the Museum,* won the Whitbread Book of the Year Award. She is the author of the critically acclaimed novels *Human Croquet, Emotionally Weird, Case Histories,* and *One Good Turn.* Her latest novel, *When Will There Be Good News?,* won the Richard & Judy Book Club Best Read of the Year in 2009.

Liana Badr was born in Jerusalem and was raised in Jericho, where her father worked as a doctor with Palestinian refugees. During the 1967 war, she stayed in Jordan and did not get permission to return to her homeland until 1994, as a result of the Oslo Agreement. Her work includes many novels, short story collections and novellas. In her writing, she focuses on the themes of women and war, and exile.

Ishmael Beah, born in 1980 in Sierra Leone, West Africa, is the *New York Times* bestselling author of *A Long Way Gone: Memoirs of a Boy Soldier*. His work has appeared in the *New York Times Magazine, Vespertine Press* and in *LIT* and *Parabola* magazines. He currently resides in Brooklyn, New York.

Héctor Aguilar Camín was born in 1946. A journalist, historian and storyteller, much of his writing is devoted to analyzing the political life of Mexico. In 1998, he received the Mazatlán Prize for Literature for *A Blow on the River*. His novels include *Las mujeres de Adriano* (2002) and *Mandatos del corazón* (2003).

Amit Chaudhuri was born in Calcutta, India. His novels include *A Strange and Sublime Address* (1991), *Afternoon Raag* (1993), both shortlisted for the *Guardian* Fiction Prize, and *Freedom Song* (1998). Published in a single omnibus volume, *Freedom Song: Three Novels* won the Los Angeles Times Book Award for Fiction 2000 and was one of the New York Public Library's 25 Books to Remember. His fourth novel, *A New World,* won the Sahitya Akademi award 2002, India's highest literary honor for a single book. His fifth novel, *The Immortals,* was published in 2009. He is a Fellow of the Royal Society of Literature, and an acclaimed musician.

Paulo Coelho was born in Rio de Janeiro. In 1987, he published *The Alchemist,* which went on to become one of the bestselling Brazilian books of all time. It has since sold 35 million copies and is the most translated book in the world, being published in sixty-seven languages. He is a Messenger of Peace for the UN and was the Ambassador of the European Union for Intercultural Dialogue in 2008.

David Constantine was born in 1944 in Salford, Lancashire. He has published several volumes of poetry (most recently in 2009, *Nine*

Fathom Deep); also a novel and two collections of short stories, *Back at the Spike* (1994) and *Under the Dam* (2005). He is an editor and translator of Hölderlin, Goethe, Kleist and Brecht. With his wife Helen, he edits *Modern Poetry in Translation*. A new book of short stories, *The Shieling,* will be published in 2009.

Ariel Dorfman, a Chilean-American writer and human-rights activist, is a distinguished professor at Duke University. His books in Spanish and English have been translated into more than forty languages and his plays staged in over a hundred countries, receiving numerous awards, including the Laurence Olivier (for "Death and the Maiden," later made into a feature film by Roman Polanski). His story "Gringos" won the O. Henry Prize for Best Short Story 2007. A documentary based on his memoir was recently released to critical acclaim.

Helen Dunmore is a novelist, poet, short-story and children's writer. Among other awards her work has received the Orange Prize for Fiction, the McKitterick Prize, the Signal Award for Poetry and the Nestlé Children's Book Prize Silver Medal. Her books have also been shortlisted for the Whitbread Fiction Prize and the T.S. Eliot Prize. She is a Fellow of the Royal Society of Literature and a former chair of the Society of Authors.

Jon Fosse, born in 1959 in Haugesund, grew up by the fjord in Hardanger. A poet, novelist and dramatist, he has published some fifty books and written over thirty plays, and his work has been translated into forty languages. He has received many prizes and was awarded a lifetime grant from the Norwegian state. Fosse is a chevalier of the French l'Ordre National du Mérite and is commander of the Norwegian Order of St. Olav. He lives in Bergen.

Petina Gappah is a Zimbabwean writer and lawyer. She lives in Geneva, where she works as counsel in an international organization that provides legal aid on international trade law to developing countries. *An Elegy for Easterly,* her story collection, was published in

April 2009 and she is currently completing *The Book of Memory,* her first novel.

Alan Garner was born in England in 1934. His fantasy stories *The Weirdstone of Brisingamen* and *The Owl Service* are acknowledged classics of children's literature. His works have won the Guardian Award, the Carnegie Medal and the Lewis Carroll Shelf Award, and he received the Chicago International Film Festival 1st Prize for his educational film *Images*. In 2001, he was awarded an OBE for his services to literature and in 2007 was elected a Fellow of the Society of Antiquaries of London for services to archaeology.

Nadine Gordimer is the author of fourteen novels. Her most recent work, *Collected Stories,* was published in 2009. Educated in South Africa, she has been made an honorary fellow at universities including Harvard, Yale and Leuven, and she was awarded an honorary degree from Oxford University in 1994. She has received numerous literary awards for her work, and was awarded the Nobel Prize for Literature in 1991. She is vice president of International PEN.

Juan Goytisolo (born in Barcelona in 1931) went to Paris in voluntary, permanent exile in 1956 as a writer opposed to the dictatorship of General Franco. He has become Spain's preeminent novelist and political essayist. His work includes his autobiography *Forbidden Territory* and *Realms of Strife,* and the trilogy *Marks of Identity, Count Julian* and *Juan the Landless*. His articles as war correspondent for *El País* are published in *Landscapes of War: From Sarajevo to Chechnya*.

Patricia Grace was born in Wellington, New Zealand, in 1937. She lives on the ancestral land of Ngati Toa, Ngati Raukawa and Te Ati Awa, in proximity to her home marae at Hongoeka Bay. Awards for her work include the Hubert Church Prose award for the Best First Book for *Waiariki,* a New Zealand Fiction award for *Potiki* and the Deutz Medal for fiction for the novel *Tu* at the Montana New Zealand Book Awards in 2005. *Dogside Story* (2001) was longlisted for the Booker Prize. She received the Prime Minister's Award for Literary Achievement in 2006.

Richard Griffiths runs a Web service for students learning English as a foreign language. He writes short stories in his spare time and is working on his first collection. He's won the Bridport Prize and has been published in *The Guardian* and the *London Magazine*.

Xiaolu Guo was born in 1973 in a fishing village in south China. She has published seven books, including the novels *A Concise Chinese-English Dictionary for Lovers* (nominated for the Orange Prize for Fiction), *Twenty Fragments of a Ravenous Youth,* and recently *UFO in Her Eyes,* which has been published in six languages. She also wrote and directed the feature films *She, A Chinese* and *How Is Your Fish Today?*

Milton Hatoum was born in 1952 in Manaus, Brazil. He was professor of literature at the University of Amazonas and a visiting professor of Latin-American literature at the University of California (Berkeley). He is the author of the novels *Tale of a Certain Orient, The Brothers* and *Ashes of the Amazon,* which have been published in several countries and all of which were awarded the Jabuti, Brazil's most prestigious prize for fiction. His latest novel, *Orphans of Eldorado,* will be published in 2010. He lives in São Paulo.

A. L. Kennedy was born in Dundee, Scotland. Since the early 1990s, she has produced collections of short stories, stage plays and television scripts. Her novels include *Night Geometry and the Garscadden Trains* (1990), winner of several awards, including the *Mail on Sunday*/John Llewellyn Rhys Prize and the Saltire Society Scottish First Book of the Year Award, *Looking for the Possible Dance* (1993) and *Everything You Need*. Her latest novel is *Day,* winner of the 2007 Costa Book of the Year Award.

Olja Knezevic was born in the area of the former Yugoslavia now known as Montenegro. In 2008, she completed her MA in creative writing at Birkbeck College. This is her second published story, written in English, her second language. She is currently working on a novel set in London and Montenegro. She now lives in London with her family.

Marina Lewycka was born of Ukrainian parents in a refugee camp in Kiel, Germany, at the end of the Second World War, and now lives in Sheffield, Yorkshire. Her first novel, *A Short History of Tractors in Ukrainian* (2005), went on to sell a million copies in more than thirty languages. It was shortlisted for the 2005 Orange Prize for Fiction and longlisted for the Man Booker Prize. Marina's second novel, *Two Caravans* (2007), was shortlisted for the George Orwell prize for political writing. Her third novel, *We Are All Made of Glue,* will be published in 2009.

Henning Mankell was born in Stockholm in 1948, raised in a village in northern Sweden and now divides his time between Sweden and Maputo, Mozambique, where he works as the director of Teatro Avenida. An internationally acclaimed author, he has written numerous crime novels featuring inspector Kurt Wallander. His books consistently top the bestseller lists in Europe.

Yann Martel was born in 1963 and lives in the Canadian prairie province of Saskatchewan. *Life of Pi,* his second novel, was published to international acclaim in over forty countries and won the 2002 Man Booker Prize. His next novel, on the Holocaust, was published in 2010.

James Meek has written two books of short stories and four novels, including *The People's Act of Love* and *We Are Now Beginning Our Descent.* He has lived in Scotland, Russia and Ukraine, and now lives in London. He has won a number of awards for writing and for reportage.

Rohinton Mistry is the author of a collection of short stories, *Tales from Firozsha Baag* (1987), and three novels that have all been shortlisted for the Booker Prize: *Such a Long Journey* (1991), *A Fine Balance* (1996) and *Family Matters* (2002). His fiction has won, among other awards, the Commonwealth Writers Prize for Best Book, The Giller Prize and the Royal Society of Literature's Winifred Holtby Award. In translation, his work has been published in over twenty-five languages. Born in Bombay, he has lived in Canada since 1975.

David Mitchell was born in Worcestershire, England, in 1969. His novel *Ghostwritten* won the John Llewellyn-Rhys Prize, *Number9dream* and *Cloud Atlas* were both shortlisted for the Man Booker Prize, and *Black Swan Green* was shortlisted for the Costa Prize. His work is published in over twenty languages. He lives in County Cork, Ireland, with his family.

Walter Mosley is the author of seventeen critically acclaimed books. He is most widely recognized for his crime fiction, featuring the detective Easy Rawlins. His short fiction has been published in *The New Yorker, GQ, Esquire* and the *Los Angeles Times Magazine.* He was an editor and contributor to the book *Black Genius* and was the guest editor for *The Best American Short Stories of 2003.*

Joyce Carol Oates is an American novelist, short-story writer and essayist. Her first novel, *With Shuddering Fall,* was published when she was twenty-eight. She received the National Book Award for *them.* Her other novels include *You Must Remember This; Because It Is Bitter, and Because It Is My Heart; Solstice;* and *Marya: A Life.* In 1996, she received the PEN/Malamud Award for "a lifetime of literary achievement."

Alice Pung is an Australian author and lawyer. Her first book, *Unpolished Gem,* won the Newcomer of the Year Award at the Australian Book Industry Awards and is studied in secondary and tertiary schools around Australia. Alice writes regularly for *The Monthly,* the *Age* newspaper and literary journals.

Mahmoud Saeed, who currently resides in Chicago, is an Iraqi novelist who has published twenty novels and short-story collections. As a dissident under Saddam Hussein, he was imprisoned six times between 1963 and 1980. The English translation of his novel *Saddam City* relates the story of one of these lengthy imprisonments. Scores of critics consider his book *Zanka Bin Baraka* one of the best Arabic novels of the twentieth century.

Ali Smith was born in Inverness, Scotland. Her novels have received many awards, including the Saltire Society Scottish First Book of the Year Award for *Free Love and Other Stories* (1995), the Encore Award and the inaugural Scottish Arts Council Book of the Year Award for *Hotel World* (2001), which was also shortlisted for both the Orange Prize for Fiction and the Booker Prize. Her 2005 novel *The Accidental* won the Whitbread Novel Award. She lives in Cambridge.

Alexis Wright is one of Australia's finest writers and a member of the Waanyi nation of the southern highlands of the Gulf of Carpentaria. Her books include the novel *Plains of Promise,* which was shortlisted for the Commonwealth Prize and the NSW Premier's Award. In 2007, her novel *Carpentaria* won the prestigious Miles Franklin Literary Award.

Banana Yoshimoto was born in Tokyo in 1964. She has won numerous prizes in her native Japan, including the Kaien Newcomer Writers' Prize and the Izumi Kyoka Literary Prize for her first book, *Kitchen*. Her novel *Tugumi* was awarded the Yamamoto Shugoro Literary Prize in 1989, and in 1995 she won the Murasaki Shikibu Prize for *Amurita*.

ABOUT AMNESTY INTERNATIONAL

Amnesty International is a global movement of ordinary people committed to an extraordinary mission: to mobilize millions of individuals around the world to protect the rights of all people to live free from violence and injustice. We are committed to building a world in which everyone can enjoy all the rights and freedoms set forth in the Universal Declaration of Human Rights. The movement began in 1961 when British lawyer Peter Benenson read about two Portuguese students who were jailed for raising their glasses in a toast to freedom. Outraged, he wrote a newspaper appeal calling for the release of anyone imprisoned for political or religious beliefs. That first appeal on behalf of "prisoners of conscience" was based on his belief that public pressure could challenge tyranny, and it inspired mass support for an international campaign to protect human rights. Amnesty International was born.

Today, Amnesty International unites the voices of more than 2.8 million people like you, from over 150 countries, to achieve our goals. More than 44,000 individuals have been freed from prison, saved from torture, or protected from death threats, following action by Amnesty International. Together, we have persuaded governments to change their laws and practices, stop torture, commute death sentences, and hold accountable those responsible for abuses. We campaigned successfully for the establishment of the International Criminal Court and the United Nations Convention Against Torture. We helped to achieve the abolition of the juvenile death penalty in the United States.

Our tenacious defense of human rights earned Amnesty International the 1977 Nobel Peace Prize.

We are all born free and equal in dignity and rights. Join Amnesty International and make a difference.

Amnesty International USA
5 Penn Plaza
New York, NY 10001
http://www.amnestyusa.org/join
(800) AMNESTY
aimember@aiusa.org